The
TROJAN
Dog

Thomas Dunne Books

St. Martin's Minotaur   New York

The
TROJAN
Dog

DOROTHY JOHNSTON

THOMAS DUNNE BOOKS.
An imprint of St. Martin's Press.

THE TROJAN DOG. Copyright © 2000 by Dorothy Johnston. All rights reserved. Printed in the United States of America. No part of this book may be used or reproduced in any manner whatsoever without written permission except in the case of brief quotations embodied in critical articles and reviews. For information, address St. Martin's Press, 175 Fifth Avenue, New York, N.Y. 10010.

ISBN 0-312-33247-5
EAN 978-0312-33247-1

First published by Wakefield Press, Kent Town, Australia, 2000
First published in the United States by Thomas Dunne Books,
St. Martin's Press

First U.S. Edition: March 2005

10   9   8   7   6   5   4   3   2   1

To Paul Malone

The

TROJAN

Dog

GIVE THE
LADY FLOWERS

HAT HAVE I KEPT of Rae Evans from the moment when she half stood behind her desk and held out her hand to shake mine? I think it is the impression of white—white face, white shirt between the two halves of a power dark suit. Hers were night colors, and though it was early in the morning, and she was my new boss, it seemed as though the business day had not quite caught up to us, and maybe never would.

I was conscious of feeling both grateful and nervous. Rae Evans had just given me a job. I'd been out of the work force for eight years, and for most of that time I'd been at home looking after my son, Peter. It was not that I considered myself poorly qualified, more that I was out of practice when it came to dealing professionally with people. I'd become overly introspective, passive, and shy. I was worried, not about my competence, but about making the wrong impression, and very much aware, now that my husband had gone to America for a year, of how much I needed an income.

Rae's voice was level, businesslike. Her handshake was firm. She was a senior public servant, head of the service industries branch of the Department of Labor Relations, in charge of advising the government and preparing policy papers on all the different service industries, from banking, to insurance, to the area I'd been hired to research—the growing number of women taking in clerical work to do at home.

I was the one holding the flowers, hugging them in fact, a potted cyclamen with pale pink blossoms. Rae glanced at it briefly, and did not quite smile.

We talked for a few minutes about the report it would be my task to complete. Rae hinted that there were a lot of ends that needed tying up, and that perhaps the people I'd be working with did not have the knots quite under control.

I waited for her to elaborate, or be more precise. I was interested in the problems faced by women who tried to make a living doing clerical work at home. They often combined it with caring for small children, frequently going into debt to buy the latest computer equipment while struggling to make ends meet. I'd written a small study myself, in the couple of years after Peter started school.

Rae looked at me and said, measuring her words, "Sandra? I don't know whether you're aware—I knew your mother, we used to meet at conferences. I liked her very much. How is she doing?"

I blushed, clutching my plant against my chest, and replied, "My mother died eight years ago."

There was a fractional pause before Rae, paler than ever, said, "I'm sorry to hear that."

I'd kept my mother's name when I married Derek. Perhaps Rae had recognized it when she read my job application. If so, she'd given no indication at the interview.

My knees shook, and sweat prickled the insides of my panty hose. I waited for Rae to say something more, or for words to come about my mother's illness, but they didn't.

Rae took me along a corridor to introduce me to Dianne and Bambi, the women with whom I was to share an office and finish the report. I felt disoriented. The corridor was gray—gray carpet, and the walls were painted a railway-station shade of it. I felt as though I was moving along inside a tube of paint, squishing about in an environment created by an artist with a limited budget and an even more limited imagination.

My new boss walked ahead of me, her walk as neat as the rest of her, legs long, feet straight and confident. I walked with my toes out, a fault I'd tried unsuccessfully to correct. Peter said "quack, quack" sometimes, when he saw me from behind.

Rae stopped at an open doorway. A glance at a clock told me it was three minutes past nine. Pale gray venetians lined the tops of the windows, and on the other side of them the fog was gray. I wondered why I had ever thought that I might hide behind a potted plant.

A woman who looked about fourteen was sitting at a desk next to the windows, dressed in a scarlet hooded cloak. She was introduced to me as Bambi. I shook her hand and smiled hello.

My plant slipped, and some soil fell out the bottom. With a murmured apology, I bent to pick it up.

I saw the man's toes first—black patent, lethal points. Gold toe caps winked against the carpet. My eyes traveled up dark trousers to a blue and green sweater with a design of a kingfisher diving into a river, then to a full black beard and curly hair, on which was perched a yellow and-brown striped beanie.

The man blinked, then smiled behind his beard, a shy smile for so loudly dressed a person.

"Ivan Semyonov," Rae Evans said, "this is Sandra Mahoney."

My name sounded strange spoken in Rae's cool voice, as if it didn't belong to me. I reached out my hand uncertainly toward the man, and felt my plant slipping again.

Rae looked straight at me out of clear, river-colored eyes. "Bambi will show you around, Sandra." She didn't smile, but I felt her concern for me, as well as a determination to pretend that everything was normal. Again, I thought it strange that she hadn't asked me any questions about my mother.

The room was very cold.

3

"Isn't the heater working?" I asked Bambi after Rae had gone.

Bambi was back behind her desk. She shook her head, silently watching me, composed in her red cloak. The man with the kingfisher sweater had disappeared.

I'd dressed up for my first day at work—in a dark blue suit, and shoes with higher heels than I'd worn in a long time. I felt uncomfortable, but I was glad to get out of the jeans and sneakers that had been my uniform for what seemed like a lifetime. I'd had my hair cut and styled as well. Dark blonde, the hairdresser called it. My unkinder girlfriends called it mousy.

The office was small. There was barely space enough for three desks, with a phone and a computer on each one. Old-fashioned steel filing cabinets separated two of the desks. Mine was wedged into a corner.

"Is that man in here, too?" I asked.

Bambi waved her hand in a bored way toward the office next door.

I opened the folder of material Rae Evans had given me to read, wondering when the owner of the third desk would show up. Bambi ignored me, and I didn't feel like asking her any more questions. She picked up the phone and began talking to it like a 1940s movie queen.

The folder contained sheets of wage statistics and copies of the major political parties' policies on outwork, or home-based work. The policies, if you could call them that, were very short. For the most part, as I already knew, political parties found regulating home-based work too difficult. This was one of the problems faced by anybody researching the area and hoping to assist in bringing about an improvement to the generally low wages. I was committed to working for such a change and considered this a debt, long overdue, to my upbringing.

After reading and making notes for an hour, I grabbed my bag and headed for the Ladies. At the back of the building, the corridors were lined with plywood room dividers that reminded me of the temporary classrooms at my primary school. The smell was the same, too. I poked my head through several doors, discovering offices basically the same as mine—desks and PCs close together—a library, and a tiny tea room and first-aid room.

I brought back a glass of water to give my plant a drink, though it didn't need it, but when I looked over from the doorway, my desk was empty.

"My cyclamen," I said. "It's gone."

Bambi stared at me with an expression of distaste and pulled her cape more closely round her shoulders.

I laid a finger on my desk. It was damp, and there was a speck of black potting mix to the left of my computer keyboard.

I said inanely, "My potted plant, where's it gone?"

Bambi stood up and bumped into the edge of her desk. Her phone rang and she sat down again to answer it, pursing her lips as though someone had offered her a lemon to suck.

Feeling ridiculous, I walked to the window and looked down on two backpackers heading away from the travel center. For one wild moment, I thought they might have taken my cyclamen. Did I see a delinquent petal, a furtive dark green leaf pressed against a shoulder, caught between two straps?

I heard laughter across the partition that divided my office from the next. I walked around and stood hesitantly in the doorway. A blond man and a young woman in a short black skirt and jacket were standing with their backs to me, studying something by the window. The man spoke softly. The woman turned around, and I was struck by the nerveless appearance of her face, her perfect makeup, her glance of appeal toward the man. I nodded hello. I couldn't bring myself to ask either of them if they knew what had happened to my plant.

I hadn't seen any sign of the hairy man in the beanie. I took a bottle of vitamin C tablets from my bag and chewed through five of them, then drank the glass of water.

PETER BEGAN AFTER-SCHOOL CARE that afternoon, a new routine for him, the routine of the child of a working mother.

He was waiting for me at the entrance to the after-school care building. His hands were blocks of ice. I took them between mine and rubbed them till the blood came to the surface.

"How was your day then?" I asked.

"Fine," he answered, without looking at me, and I resisted an impulse to push his floppy brown hair off his face.

At Dickson shops, where we called in to buy something for dinner, a street musician was singing outside the supermarket. His voice was broken stones one minute, sweet as fudge the next, carrying for miles in the freezing dusk. His teasing late-night song freed me from my day, and it was comforting to turn into Northbourne Avenue with bags of groceries on the seat beside me. The lights were already on, pink and gray parrots roosting on their long silver arms.

While we were preparing our food and eating it—Peter and I frequently picked and tasted as we went, so that what we eventually sat down to eat hot, from plates, was only a fraction of our dinner—I said, "Something weird happened to me today."

Peter turned to face me with a handful of grated cheese halfway to his mouth. I could see him remembering that it had been a special day for me.

"Someone pinched my plant. You know, the one I took to work?"

Peter began eating the cheese, then asked with his mouth full, "Did you report it to the police?"

"No."

"Mum?" He reached his hand toward the bowl again and, when I shook my head, resorted to licking his fingers. "I know! You could set a trap, and catch the thief pink-handed!"

We laughed. Not many other people laughed at our jokes. Peter's father, Derek, was scornful of them. But Derek was away for a year, and in his absence we indulged ourselves in all kinds of small ways.

MEMORIES CAN BE A sudden black-and-white still shot in the middle of a color movie.

That night, I recalled my mother coming home from one of her conferences. It was the end of a long Saturday afternoon. I'd switched the heater on and sat in front of it, yet I still felt cold.

I was twelve or thirteen. The still shot is photographed through thirteen-year-old eyes, the way a disgruntled teenager might store the faces of two middle-aged women, one of them her mother. I have a generalized memory of Mum carting me about with her to conferences and meetings, but I have no picture at all of what I'd been doing on this particular weekend when I'd elected—been allowed?—to stay at home. My mother frowned on the popular activities of girls my age, and when I indulged in them it had to be in secret, so maybe, earlier that day, I'd been trying out some mascara, or tinting my hair.

My mother came in unceremoniously, with no apologies for being late. She walked into the living room where I was sitting in the fading light. Behind her was a woman whom I'd never seen before. Mum introduced us, then left the room to hang up their coats.

It happened quite often that she brought someone back with her for a drink or a meal—someone she'd met at work, or through a work-related activity. If she hadn't had me, they would have gone to a pub or a cheap restaurant, but she was stuck with me, and so she brought them home.

The stranger and I stood and stared at one another. She was smartly dressed, about my mother's age. I knew immediately that she belonged to a different class. Was it then that the picture became fixed, the still shot I've added to as I've been writing about it here, a single image to which I've tried to give a before-and-after meaning? Myself, awkward in front of this unknown woman, annoyed with Mum, and probably tired and hungry as well, cross because it was becoming obvious, without anybody needing to say anything, that the evening would be theirs.

The woman had straight dark hair cut just below her ears, gray-blue-green eyes above high cheekbones, a thin straight nose. She was dressed in a suit, in contrast to my mother, who was wearing pants of some sort and a bulky sweater. She felt no need to make small talk, and neither did

7

I. We simply stood and looked at one another till my mother came back into the room. That woman, as I see her now, was Rae Evans.

NEXT MORNING, THE CYCLAMEN was sitting on my desk, with a note tied to it by a piece of blue ribbon. *Thanks for the loan*, the note said. *Hope I've returned it with interest.*

Bambi was on the phone to someone, tapping her pen on the edge of the desk. At the third desk was a young woman dressed in black, with tangled blonde hair. I knew she must be Dianne Trapani, who'd designed the statistical framework for the report, but who, for reasons I didn't understand, seemed unable or unwilling to continue with it.

The bearded man appeared in the doorway, dressed again in his kingfisher sweater. He bowed and clicked his heels, then dipped his head with a bird-like jerk, gesturing with a flourish toward my computer.

"Turn it on! Have a look!"

My monitor whirred and came to life. Filling the screen was an almost perfect reproduction of my cyclamen. It seemed to me that whoever had done it could have produced a flawless photographic image if he or she had wished—I wasn't sure if it was the bearded man or not—but had decided to tilt the image ever so slightly off the true. I leant closer, discovering leaves that were more rounded, petals flat. There were no shadows. There was no background at all. It was a pink still life statement of a flower, covering a pale gray screen.

The man, whose name I was trying to recall accurately, was staring at me with the expression of a hopeful puppy.

"Have lunch with me," he said. When I didn't reply, willing him to leave, he shouted, "Okay! You don't have to! You can tell me to get stuffed!"

"Get stuffed," I told him.

"Done!" he cried. "A deal! Twelve-thirty!"

And so, by thirty-three minutes past twelve, Ivan Semyonov and I were on our way out of the Jolimont building, Ivan leaping ahead, me hurrying to keep up.

He stopped abruptly by the lifts. "You're cursing your luck for having landed in an office next to mine, right? I look like a weirdo. I pinch your comfort toy! Cor, look at that! Looks about twenty-five! Beaut age for retirement!"

I swiveled to see the poster he was pointing to. A young woman with long pale hair was swinging in a hammock in front of what was probably a beach.

"Softening us up!" Ivan said in a penetrating stage whisper.

"What for?" I took a step back, wishing the lift would come.

"God!" Ivan startled a pair of dove gray suits who'd come quietly up behind us and were also waiting for the lift. "Let's not waste any more of our lunch-hour studying this crap!"

Outside, the air was what people called bracing when they didn't want to depress you with the thought that it might go on like this until November. Ivan walked with a bounce, with long, uneven, energetic strides, hesitating for a fraction of a second before placing each foot down with a surprising sideways twist, as though he'd just noticed that he was about to tread on a dollop of dog poo.

"Cor, look at that will you?" he cried, and I turned to look obediently, wondering if this was his favorite expression.

Four men in dark suits were walking abreast along the street, their jackets flapping in the wind. Three of them were talking into mobile phones while the fourth looked around uncertainly, as though he'd just lost a friend.

"Do you always walk like this?" I asked him.

"Like what?" Ivan shouted.

"You shouldn't have done that with my cyclamen, you know."

"Why not? I made you laugh! You don't laugh enough."

"How the hell would you know? And I didn't."

We found a vacant bench in Glebe Park and I opened my packet of sandwiches. The toes of my new shoes were pinching. I eased my feet out of them surreptitiously.

Ivan grinned at me. "You are a woman who mistrusts loud voices and strong emotions, Sandra. Am I right?"

I shrugged, then blushed, wishing I did not feel so self-conscious.

Ivan pulled a folded magazine from his jacket pocket. "Listen! Bet this is just up your street! Ready?" He lifted his lion's head and raised an eyebrow to make sure he had my full attention, then began to read. "'*Comico* editor Andrea Schultz says her company is taking a deliberate chance by targeting the graphic novel to women. The comic book market tends to be dominated by fifteen-year-old boys with power fantasies.'" Ivan's mouth worked excitedly, and his broad flask of a body moved from side to side. "'Comics have in general ignored women.' There you are! A new field!"

"I think you must be mad," I told him.

"Maybe it's something you could get into, comics." Ivan saw my expression and said kindly, "Well, Sandra, there's not much future where you are now. I mean, that poster is a case in point."

"Oh, I don't know." I tried to keep my tone light. "I might just be at the start of a long and flourishing career."

"Our lady of the white face and gracious condescension might look after you?"

I glanced sharply at Ivan, then said, "Rae Evans and I have history. Of a kind."

When Ivan said nothing, I asked him, "What do you think of her?"

He made a face and said, "When you've got the next Prime Minister threatening to abolish your department, and you don't want to spend the rest of your life in a hammock—let's just say that over the next few months everybody's going to be looking for somewhere moderately soft to land."

His voice was inflexible, but then he smiled again, no longer challenging me, daring me to reject him for his crude behavior and opinions, his deliberate awkwardness that was like an extra layer of clothes when he already wore too many. It was the shy smile of the day before. Hello, it said, nice to have you aboard.

A few minutes before the hour was up, Ivan got to his feet, brushing bits of parsley and Lebanese bread from his lap, and muttered something about needing to buy a toothbrush.

I nodded and leant back against the green wooden seat, murmuring, "See you upstairs, then."

Someone had thrown a T-shirt into a tree. At least I say thrown, because it was hanging from such thin branches—twigs really, so thin that a kitten could hardly have climbed out on them. Yet the T-shirt was hanging there as though someone had arranged it deliberately and with artistry—arms out, neck open, ready to slip over sun-warmed skin—the pencil twigs conveniently acting as a clothes hanger. Had the wind played a clever trick? For whom exactly was it waiting?

It wasn't until I stood up to go that I noticed the graphics magazine lying on the seat. I picked it up and began flicking through it. Where was the article on comics for women? Funny. I went back to the beginning, looked more carefully, scanned the index. There was no such piece, no Andrea Schultz. Had Ivan made it up, or read about it somewhere else?

He wasn't there when I got back to the office. I replaced the magazine on his overcrowded desk.

LOOKED AT NOW, BALDLY set out like that, the beginning of my friendship with Ivan seems composed of negatives. My other impressions of him have sunk beneath the theft of my cyclamen and the business with the magazine. It occurs to me that we, or our memories, are never so selective as when reconstructing the beginning of a friendship.

And something else, maybe peculiar to me. People who at first meeting make me anxious or cross—a mixture of the two, but there's always an element of fear—will go on to become important in my life.

With Rae, that first meeting, if it was the first, happened when I was still a child. Then at the job interview there was nothing, or only the ordinary reactions of a person being judged. But early in the morning on my first day at work, when she dropped that question about my mother, that's when it began.

JOLLY
JOLIMONT

I HAD TO PINCH myself some mornings to remind myself that I'd really done it, joined the workforce in the last years of the 1990s, on a slippery slide to the end of the millennium, in a department soon to be abolished if our next Prime Minister had his way. I was on the move. It seemed that everyone around me was on the move as well.

My department squatted on top of a travel center like a frog on a restless lily pad. Every time I went in and out of the building, I met people going places. Greyhound had their terminal there, long gray concrete bays for the buses backing onto Moore Street. Next to them was the red Canberra Explorer, leaving regularly on a tourist drive around the city. There was CountryLink, where you could plan and book your train journey. The Tourist Commission filled the windows along Northbourne Avenue with a medley of local attractions, from Parliament House to the snowfields less than three hours away.

There were two takeaway food places, the larger being the Jolimont Bistro, which had a sit-down menu as well. The music from the bistro blasted out onto the footpath and was regularly interrupted by passenger calls.

"Your attention ladies and gentlemen, this is the first and final call for passengers traveling on Pioneer Service 112 to Orange," would be shouted over the top of "Jumping Jack Flash." I wondered how many passengers had missed their calls because of the Mick Jagger nostalgia of whoever was choosing the music.

The bistro reminded me of that Telecom ad with Clive James in an American food hall—Clive James plump-faced and deadpan as a koala, trying to decide what to have for breakfast. The other place specialized in muffins big as shrunken heads. You could get every flavor from chocolate to feta cheese and olives.

Most of the coach passengers sat on dark blue chairs set in rows, watching a TV fixed to the ceiling. The loudspeakers were loudest in the toilets, which contained shower cubicles, though I never saw anybody using them.

Every morning on the way to the lifts, I picked my way between women with bags and rugs, and excited or fretful children. Young couples who'd arrived on the overnight service from Adelaide or Melbourne slept leaning against each other. None of the people looked well-off, and I wondered what they were doing in Canberra. How long would they stay? What did they hope to find here?

Whatever their hopes, the ugly, barn-like building bustled at the bottom with constant movement, the nervous sweat of travel, the confusion of arrival and departure, the faces of men, women, and children who would see other horizons, other skylines before the sun went down.

RAE EVANS WORE THE uniform of the successful female executive as though she'd been born in it. The branch she was in charge of contained half-a-dozen sections, but she took a special interest in clerical work, and told me she had always done so. I was still curious to know why she'd picked me for the job.

If Bambi and Dianne Trapani had been more friendly, I would have asked them about Rae, and Ivan Semyonov, and the blond man and the woman who shared the office next to ours. We would have had a good gossip and then got down to work. But they weren't friendly. They made it clear that they didn't want me there at all.

Bambi was constantly moving the furniture around in her corner of the office. She seemed to be in a state of warfare with the objects around her and was always bumping into things. She often wore the red cloak that I'd first seen her in, and there was a gray-and-green outfit with overlapping pieces that she also liked a lot. She called it "winter water." All Bambi's clothes belonged to the categories of earth, air, fire, and water, and she alternated them depending on her reading of the astrological charts and her mood of the day.

If you wanted to have a sane conversation with Di Trapani, you had to go downstairs to the travel center with her so she could smoke while she talked. One lunchtime, about a week after I arrived, I saw her in the bistro and decided to take a seat at her table.

I started off trying to make general conversation, determined to improve relations between us if I could.

Dianne replied to my first couple of questions in monosyllables, and then not at all. I looked across at a boy asleep with the hood of his parka pulled right over his face. The color had gone in the TV, and the sound was no more than a whisper, but people were still lined up watching it with apparent interest. Behind us, a woman was talking on an orange pay phone with the receiver tucked into her neck and both hands over her ears, as though she was in pain.

"Don't you care what happens to the report?" I asked. "Don't you want it to be finished before the elections?"

Dianne took a last pull on her cigarette, then bent over and squashed the butt under a sharp black patent heel.

She looked at me and spread her hands, then exercised her fingers by pulling them one by one. "Who cares?" she demanded.

Was she saying no one cared whether I did the work I'd been hired to do? No one cared if the report was ever finished, or if a new government decided that it was a waste of money collecting information on home-based work, because nothing would ever be done with it?

"I don't understand," I said. "The framework you've designed is great. The report seemed to go well in its initial stages. Another few months, if you and I were to put our heads together over it, I'm sure we could get it done—and Bambi, well, Bambi could be given things to do."

Dianne smiled suddenly, in a way that made her look much younger. "She's smarter than she looks, our Bambi."

"Well then, why is she being allowed to get away with swanning round the office and having long dim-witted conversations on the phone?"

Dianne shrugged. "You'd have to ask Madam about that."

"What have you got against Rae Evans?"

She shrugged again, and turned her attention to removing the cellophane from a packet of Longbeach. Instead of dropping the cellophane, or crushing it, she flattened it carefully on the table in front of her, pointedly ignoring me.

Murmuring that I'd see her later, I made my way across the travel center, past a woman with a bright purple-headed mop. I bought a muffin that tasted of straight bicarbonate of soda, and dumped most of it in a trash bin next to the lifts.

BLACK WAS THE FAVORITE color of the young. Dianne's was rust black, pre-loved, pre-knocked about a fair bit. She wore grumpy black dresses dating from a time when people still gave each other ashtrays as presents. The young. Why did I distance her in my mind like that? She was probably four or five years younger than I was, but in my more hopeful moments I still thought of myself as young.

It was because Dianne had said she didn't want to have children. I knew that the office wasn't an appropriate place for getting out baby photos. There'd be precious little mother-talk. I didn't mind. I'd had eight years of that, and I was ready for a change.

Dianne had a stop-go kind of voice, breaking up her sentences in odd places and leaving you wondering about their meaning. She'd let her breath out hard when she said "who cares," back there in the travel center, and I'd waited for her to cough. Her voice didn't have a smoker's harshness, but there was a small cough that followed many of her sentences. I suspected she'd stopped hearing it.

After our talk, even though we seemed to have reached no sensible conclusion, Dianne seemed less hostile to me, willing to work with me on some basic level at least. Though I was at a loss to understand her reasoning, I felt pleased, and resolved to make the most of it in case she changed her mind.

MY TIME WITH RAE Evans, at the start of that winter, brought back memories that were like vertical lines running up and down through my childhood, pointing black noses up into the present. I felt excited in her company, and proud and privileged that she sought me out, but I was uneasy, too. I didn't want to be reminded of the 1970s, those days of big changes when the landmark equal pay decisions had been made. I didn't want to be played back in a time warp that made me think too much about my mother.

Maybe for Rae—it had been like this for my mother in the months before she died—reliving the past was like ritually descending some steps that led to a place that was dark and warm. But the past Rae liked to recall wasn't one my mother had shared. It was one she'd yearned to share.

Though I did not doubt my memory of the day Mum had brought Rae home with her, I found it difficult to picture the two of them together. Rae belonged to a higher class. My mother, who'd never had much formal education, had been in awe of women like her. Mum had her pride and, though she would never have admitted this, she was frightened of people who were clearly several rungs above her on the social ladder.

My mother's attitudes had confused and frustrated me when I was growing up. I have a clear recollection of the time when Prime Minister Gough Whitlam appointed Mary Gaudron government advocate for the equal pay hearing in 1972, and the historic national wage decision that followed, with its new definition of equal pay for work of equal value. What this meant, my mother had explained to me, was that women would be able to insist on receiving the same wages as men, instead of half, or less than half, as they were getting then. I was at an age when I hated being lectured at by my mother, and I dismissed these reverent pronouncements with a sneer.

Mary Gaudron was the first female judge ever to be appointed to the High Court. I remembered coming across my mother sitting at the dining-room table with a fuzzy newspaper photograph of her. Mum was sitting quite still, with an expression I'd only ever seen before in religious pictures. I'd wanted to hug her and shake her and screw up the newspaper, all at once.

What did Rae see in me? A daughter carrying the torch? Or a kind of innocence that set me apart from my colleagues, even those who were younger than I was? I'd seen so much through my mother's eyes, even if reluctantly. And now much of what her generation had gained seemed likely to disappear.

Under our conversations, running like a tidal drift, was the knowledge that all types of outwork—textile, shoemaking, clerical—had been growing outside the government's wage-fixing system, and had never been adequately monitored, let alone controlled. When we speculated about the future, we agreed that off-site workers were going to find it harder and harder to obtain fair wages and conditions.

It had happened to me before—that an experience gained a recognizable shape only when I relinquished it, understood that it was finished. There was a moment when knowing became knowing you could not go back. I'd grown up in the years between those campaigns and the present. It was like seeing the earth from a distance. I tried to say this to Rae, but it came out wrong. She looked at me steadily, without replying, for a few moments, then she said that the earth from a distance was very beautiful.

My mother's name was Lilian. She married Simon Mahoney and kept his surname, though he left us when I was barely a year old. She worked as a shorthand typist at the Trades Hall in Lygon Street. At the time she started taking me with her, to meetings and demonstrations, two unions were sharing her. One was the meatworkers, and I can't remember the other one. My mother didn't dislike her job. She said it gave her opportunities she would never have in an ordinary office. But she was basically a servant. I used to wonder what she would have done if she'd had the opportunity of staying home—that is, if my father hadn't run off and left her to bring me up. She never seemed to show any interest in remarrying.

Rae and I had lunch at Café Moore, off Pilgrim Place, practically across the road from the department. Rae never took more than half an hour for lunch, so going somewhere close was crucial.

It wasn't really cold in the café. Most of the patrons had taken off their coats and scarves. Only one or two were still rugged up. Rae's nose had turned pink in the short walk across Moore Street. Her hair was silver in the light, her silk shirt ivory.

She smiled and said, "I knew you were your mother's daughter the minute I set eyes on you."

I blushed and thought, you couldn't possibly have known anything of the kind.

Our vegetarian filos came with salad. I didn't feel like eating in front of Rae, but I made myself. Her claim on me caused splinters of doubt under my skin. But I wonder now if perhaps I'm exaggerating that, if all the things that happened since have made me more conscious of my doubts than I was at the time. I was proud of my mother, and I told Rae so.

"Why did you hire Bambi and Dianne for the project?" I asked, taking the opportunity to voice a question that had been on my mind since my first day in the office.

"I would hope," Rae answered carefully, "that if I needed it, someone would give me a second chance."

She must mean Bambi, I thought, waiting for an explanation.

When it didn't come, I asked, "And Di Trapani?"

"Dianne has a first-class degree in statistics."

"What went wrong?"

"We had a—a disagreement."

"What about?"

"I don't think I can tell you that."

19

I blushed again, realizing I had gone too far. Rae seemed to invite familiarity, even intimacy, then, at the crucial moment, she drew back.

"You're new to public service, Sandra." She smiled her patrician smile. "Besides, I'm sure Dianne will come round."

Come round from where? I wanted to ask, but didn't.

"The project was running over time," Rae continued. "I knew how important it was to get it finished before the elections. I managed to scrape together the money to hire you." She looked across at me carefully, studiously. "I sometimes wonder if the sole purpose of being promoted is to get yourself into a position where you can no longer do anything worthwhile. I spend my days in meetings, dealing with administrative problems which God knows I have no interest in, drowning under seas of paper. I can't recall when I last got my teeth into a project that mattered to me."

"The home-based work?" I ventured.

Rae smiled again and said, "I want you to do it well. I'm sure you will."

IN THE MIDDLE OF the night, when the frost was thick and Peter had been asleep for hours, I let myself out the back door of my house. Concrete steps led down to a small square of grass, a clothesline, and a swing that Peter had grown out of years ago. The 3 A.M. cold seeped through the thin soles of my slippers.

The smells of cooling toast and untouched tea, and my mother with that photo of Mary Gaudron at the kitchen table. My mother bringing Rae Evans home with her late on a winter afternoon. The two of us staring at one another. Black-and-white still shots these were, and physical, visceral memories, too, that stopped my heart and made me take in great gulps of freezing air. Memories I did not want had pulled me in, and down, since Rae Evans chose me, gave me her ambiguous blessing. When I found myself falling, it took hours to claw my way back.

Two absolutes—being and non-being. I hadn't been able to get past that. My mother had taken years to die. Why had I been so ill-prepared for her death when it finally came? Why had I, in that part of myself where love was lodged, never been able to accept it?

I'd pretended for too long that my mother was still with me when she wasn't. I yelled at the trees along the fence, the winter night that held its secrets close between white breasts. Grief was a hot ball inside my chest, a volcano in Antarctica.

MY FIRST BATCH OF completed questionnaires arrived, and I began the work of compiling and assessing them. The outworkers' responses were of great interest to me, and while my news for the most part wasn't good, in that they seemed to be getting royally ripped off, there was a pleasure in the routine of work that I hadn't anticipated.

One lunchtime, Ivan Semyonov and I took a roundabout route to the park. We'd fallen into the habit of having lunch at Glebe Park once a week or so.

"We need a cross section of their rates of pay," I said, lengthening my stride to keep up with his, something I now did automatically. "Whether or not they *are* substantially lower."

The sun was out, but there was a knife-bite in the wind. We passed the discount clothing shops and Clint's Crazy Bargains, who'd moved all their goods out onto the walkway as though they needed sun.

Ivan muttered, "Are they?"

"There's a huge range, but so far, yes."

"What does that prove?" he asked, sidestepping a woman with a pram. "If they charge more, they won't get the work. They know that, and you know it, too."

I rose to his bait. I couldn't help it "If other workers had accepted that," I said, "they'd still be on starvation wages."

Ivan waved and called "G'day" to a plump man in a blue jacket, who was taking plastic covers off his tables in preparation for the lunchtime crowd. He always met people he knew on our walk to the park. We skirted the merry-go-round, still and silent in its metal cage.

"Sandushka." He smiled at me condescendingly. "You would have got on well with my mother. You would have understood one another very well."

I stared at him, then asked, "What did your mother believe in?"

"Us," he said. "Her children."

"And your father?"

"Not in the movie."

"Your father was dead?"

"No, just AWOL. In his head at least. In another country."

We passed a man dressed from head to toe in orange plastic cleaning a fountain with a fast funnel of water from a high-pressure hose.

The double row of casuarinas in front of the Boulevard Cinema looked half-dead as usual, but I knew that soon the male trees would be covered in long, dull orange flowers, modest strings of flame dry as a hennaed wig.

The park, when we reached it, was a kind of gasp, a breath of different air. As we headed for our usual bench, I realized that my stomach was clenched tight.

It had always seemed the coldest part of Glebe Park to me, the green metal seats Ivan favored, near the barbecues and playground. In my previous life, I'd eked out long windy afternoons there, with Peter threatening to fall from the cage at the top of the climbing net. I was always torn between wanting him to come down and knowing that he'd complain if I made him—the selfish part of me wanting him to be occupied, even if riskily; wanting to be left alone to read my book.

If I described those afternoons to Ivan, would he have any idea what I was talking about?

Because it was so cold, we had the whole space of green and brown to ourselves, empty flower beds curving round us like fat sleeping fingers.

"I want to show that women aren't computer-illiterate or shy," I said. "No more than men. They've just been learning as they go along."

I watched Ivan unwrap his falafel roll. As usual, the chili sauce had run and everything was pink. "Do *you* find any difference," I asked him, "dealing with men and women?"

Ivan glared at me suspiciously. "Is that an on-the-record question? You're putting me in your survey?"

"You've had more experience than most."

"Well shit, there's your two, Black & Decker. Couple of computer jocks if ever I saw one. Or should I say jockettes?"

I laughed. "Dianne's got a huge chip on her shoulder, and Bambi's— well, you know."

"So what's the big deal?" Ivan growled. "Voice activation's just around the corner. No more boring keystrokes. Anyway," he went on nastily, "you won't get it finished. When your section gets the chop, this report you're so proud of will be just another draft for the shredder."

"But I want to do it anyway. It matters to me, and you shouldn't be rude about it. Whatever happens in the future, it's—it's sort of in honor of my mother."

"Where's your mother now?"

"She's dead. She died while I was pregnant with Peter."

Ivan looked at me. I felt as though he was looking at me properly for the first time.

"I'm sorry," he said.

OVER THE WEEKS, I noticed how Ivan helped us when we got a glitch in our machines—me in particular, because I didn't yet understand how our local network operated, or how to connect with other networks. He found files that had been given up as lost.

Ivan was thankful that he didn't have to wear a suit. He said it was the main reason he never went for promotion. No one bothered to call IT if Ivan was there. IT was short for Information Technology, but I soon found out that the letters also referred to a man called Felix, who was director of the section. When something went wrong and you called IT, the call had to be written up and paid for, whereas Ivan was just there. There was no record of your having stuffed up, and it didn't cost the section money. It was like having a home handyman, as opposed to calling in the plumber.

I wondered why he hadn't set up his own computer business, and it occurred to me that, under his ideas and his puzzling, often contradictory personality, he lacked confidence. It wasn't just a question of not having enough money.

Another lunchtime in the park I asked him, "Are you married?"

"Was."

"Strictly past tense?"

Ivan held up three fingers in a Cub Scout salute, and clicked his heels. "And you?" he asked.

"I'm a wife on pause," I told him.

FRAMED PICTURES
ON A GRAY SCREEN

M Y OFFICE PHONE RANG late one afternoon.

"Sandy. Hi." It was an old Melbourne University friend, Gail Trembath, now working at the *Canberra Times*.

"Got something strange here," Gail said in her rough contralto voice. "Hoping you can throw some light on it. This story turned up on my computer. Hour or so ago. About someone called Rae Evans."

"Yes?"

"It just appeared," Gail said. "Actually, it's weird."

She began to tell me the gist of the story, which was that Rae had been siphoning off our department's funds in the guise of a grant to an organization called Access Computing. "Some dinky self-help women's outfit." Gail sounded as though she was quoting from her screen. "I should ask your accountant if he's missing nine hundred thousand bucks."

"Who sent it?"

"Didn't leave his calling card. Or hers. Any ideas?"

"No."

"It's quite long. Three pages printed out. There's even a copy of the payment notification."

"How can a story just turn up?"

"Like I said, it's weird."

"I'll get back to you. Rae Evans is out of town at a conference. Don't do anything till I call back."

"Normally I mistrust anonymous tips, you know? Like, we get them all the time."

I remembered Gail's habit of simply not hearing questions or statements she did not wish to reply to. "Spooky," she said. "The way it lit itself up on my screen. I almost expected it to talk."

For a few years—studying, looking for our first jobs—Gail and I had been friends. We'd lost touch, met up again in Canberra. But Gail had been on the fast track for young female reporters, while I stayed at home with Peter, writing articles and research papers, struggling to keep my hand in.

When I went looking for Rae, her personal assistant, Deirdre, said primly that she wasn't expected back that day. For a second, I thought my spur-of-the-moment lie to Gail about the conference might turn out to be correct.

Deirdre would not tell me where Rae was. She looked like her boss, in the way young women used to look like Princess Diana, getting the resemblance almost right. In Deirdre's case, she'd got Rae's straight gray hair, her tailored skirts and jackets, without the dignity or class.

Deirdre was flushed. She hadn't had time to refresh her makeup.

The phone rang and she said, "Excuse me."

Gail wasn't answering when I rang her back from my office. I shuffled papers into my briefcase, and made an excuse to Di and Bambi, who looked at me with identical expressions of mistrust.

I had Rae's home number, but before I picked up the phone to dial it, I knew that there would be no answer. I had half a mind to go round to her flat. But what good would I do, sitting on her doorstep?

Every half-hour or so that night, between serving dinner and helping Peter with his homework, I tried Gail, and Ivan, who hadn't been at work that day, and Rae as well. I left messages on Gail's answering machine, but it was clear that she had no intention of getting back to me.

Next morning's *Canberra Times* story carried Gail's byline, and the news editor's as well.

SANITIZED CORRUPTION

Fraud, or sleight of hand?

Access Computing, a computer group for women, based in Brisbane, was recently awarded a $100,000 grant by the Department of Labor Relations. Information received by the Canberra Times *suggests that the group was instead paid $1 million. Two directors are named on the grant application, Ms. Isobel Merewether and Ms. Angela Carlishaw. Ms. Merewether claims to know nothing about her organization's gift from the government. Perhaps $900,000 was sent to Access Computing's bank account by magic, or a generous fairy godmother?*

When asked to explain Ms. Carlishaw's absence from Australia, Ms. Merewether said she was currently on leave in a remote part of Scotland. Who is Angela Carlishaw? And who is really behind Access Computing?

I SAID TO IVAN, "there's got to be someone who can contact this place in Scotland. No phone, nothing—what sort of an outfit are they? How do they do business?"

"Maybe by carrier pitheon." Ivan's cheeks were swollen. His voice was oddly slurred, his pronunciation clumsy.

I stared at him and asked, "Where were you yesterday?"

"Denthisth's," Ivan mumbled.

"Till eleven at night? I kept trying to ring you."

Ivan opened his big mouth wide. At the back of his lower jaw were two red clammy holes.

"Took two Mogadon at eighth. Knocked me outh. Must've schlep right through the phone."

I felt cross, as though Ivan had deliberately misled me. "What are you doing at work then? I thought it took at least a week to get over having your wisdom teeth out."

Ivan tried to smile. His bruised, hairy cheeks squished in and out. "I'm a'right," he muttered through them, "s'long's I don't eath or laugh or swallow anything."

I looked out the window. A man was walking along Northbourne Avenue with his head hunched forward, neck and shoulders bent. He wore a green felt hat, and a baggy coat with long sagging pockets that came down past his knees. He looked like a caricature of an aging criminal, a man who'd had something to hide for so long it had become irrelevant.

I turned to Ivan and said, "For Christ's sake, why don't you just go home?"

Then I felt contrite. There was a lonely awkwardness in Ivan. That day I was feeling lonely myself, anxious about Rae, and disappointed that she hadn't tried to contact me.

I put out my hand to Ivan, hesitating, conscious of a raw feeling—the lack of an adult person to go home to, an empty space ahead of and below me like an elevator shaft yawning in a twenty-story building.

"Whatever it is Rae Evans is supposed to have done," I said, "she didn't do it."

That statement was a leap of faith, as great as any I had taken in my life so far. But I was not aware of its importance then. I liked Rae, and I cared what happened to her. She might confuse me, but that morning I simply felt that she had, for some reason, been falsely accused. There had been a mistake. I wanted to tell her this and to offer her my support.

Rae was expected on a midmorning flight, but no, Deirdre said with the expression of a flustered princess, I would not be able to see her.

If Rae did show up at work that day, she didn't come anywhere near me. I caught no sight of her, though I prowled the first floor corridors and pestered Deirdre. I felt that Rae had moved far away from me. I longed suddenly to be back at Café Moore with her, just the two of us, even if she did bring disturbing memories to the surface. The time seemed precious, and already lost. I thought how, when you broke a thermometer, the mercury balled, rolled along the tilted surface of a table, then dropped to the floor, a jewel in a bed of broken glass.

On that night's news, Isobel Merewether repeated her assertions that Access Computing had done nothing wrong. It wasn't their fault that they'd been paid a million dollars, instead of a hundred thousand, as they should have been. Isobel was a name that stuck in my throat along with Angela—Angela Carlishaw, whom the press had still not been able to track down. The television reporter tried to trip Isobel up, and clever cutting made her look deceitful. Physically, she seemed a ruffled, slightly darker version of Claire Disraeli, the young woman who shared an office with Ivan and Guy Harmer—a little shorter than Claire maybe, a little less classically correct.

I changed channels.

"So you don't believe Angela Carlishaw exists?" a smirking interviewer asked the leader of the Opposition.

"Whoever invented her should have invented a more plausible-sounding name," the Opposition leader replied, trading pompous smirks with the reporter.

"What's up, Mum?" asked Peter.

"It looks like a friend of mine's in trouble."

"Has he been stealing gold watches?"

I glanced across at my son and smiled. "No way."

"Has he been arrested?"

"She," I said. "I hope it's not that bad."

"Mum? When Dad comes home we might get a dog."

"You know Dad doesn't like dogs."

Peter nodded, unconvinced.

"You see," I said a few minutes later, "I don't think my friend has done anything wrong."

Peter frowned, wanting to change the subject—well, he'd tried doing that.

He started making what he called a thunderbird with his LEGOS, waiting for the news to finish, his hands moving now calmly, deliberately; now in a fidgety, impatient way.

I turned back to the television. Was it libelous to say of a person that you did not believe in them, that to you they were a figment of someone else's criminal imagination? Maybe when Angela Carlishaw appeared she'd sue the tits off that smart reporter. On the other hand, the politicians and the journalists were only making use of a goldplate opportunity.

I tried to comfort myself with the thought that there were a thousand ways of forcing people to behave as though they were guilty, but relatively few ways of proving it. It was all so vague. No one had produced any hard evidence implicating Rae. The *Times*'s anonymous tipster had accused her, but that could be a lie.

Rae was saying nothing, and neither was anybody else in the department. Reputations might be dented, but they could be repaired.

Peter asked, "Mum? Can I watch a video?"

"Maybe," I answered him. "When the news is over."

I held my mother and Rae Evans together in my mind. The thought of my mother made me still inside. There was a flat, full space that had to be kept steady, or else it would suck me under.

My mother, Lilian Mahoney, dead at forty-four from breast cancer, was loyal to the people and the causes she believed in. She assumed I would be, too—in the way, I realized, looking at Peter, parents assume some characteristics will just automatically be passed on, with the simplicity of drinking water, breathing air.

WINTER
DISCONTENT

N A MORNING OF seventeen degrees, I walked with Peter across a crackling oval to the primary school, then to the bus stop. My car battery had died in the night. Rubbish from the high school was frozen and frosted into crazy shapes. A milk container, tossed aside half-full, had grown frozen lips of brownish yellow. A boy was bashing iced-up leaves and plastic bottles with a long black stick.

There was a morning interview with the Opposition leader on 2CN. I borrowed the tea lady's radio, and listened hunched over while he talked about public service wastage and corruption. After the first five minutes I'd had enough, but I couldn't bring myself to switch it off.

Our Deputy Secretary made a brief appearance to tell us that all press inquiries were to be referred to him.

"Wonderful facility for repetition," Ivan commented with a grimace. "What does he think we've been doing for the last twenty-four hours?"

Jim Wilcox, Rae Evans's division head, gathered all of his division into the large conference room on the first floor. It was like a school assembly when something unthinkable has been done, meriting instant expulsion for the culprit, who is surely within an inch of being caught. In the mean time everyone, from the most senior student to the youngest, feels the tingle of guilt by association, rats' feet up and down the spine.

I dawdled in Ivan's office doorway after Wilcox had lectured then dismissed us, putting off having to face the smirk on Di Trapani's face, her birch-blonde hair a dry, upstanding accusation. Or Bambi breathing on the telephone, nestling in her thick, blood-colored cloak. They were pleased Rae was in trouble, and they wanted me to see it. Nor could I face writing the introduction to my report. I'd been looking forward to it, but that morning the words felt like shell-grit on my tongue.

Guy Harmer and Claire Disraeli watched me—Claire with a small smile, Guy with an expression of concern. Ivan fidgeted behind them, his thick lips clamped together. His cheeks were still a bit swollen, but he looked much better.

I felt as though I was trapped in a small, enclosed, high space, a bubble with a fatally limited air supply. No one was speaking up for Rae, or expressing any doubt that she had stolen the money.

FELIX WENBORN, (ALIAS IT), and I sat facing one another, both staring at a large booklet on his desk with the single word **SECURITY** printed in large black letters on the cover. For one ridiculous moment, I thought Felix was going to ask me to place my right hand on the book and swear an oath. His eyes kept returning to it, and I wondered whether he'd hastily memorized the rules inside and was reminding himself of them. I wished I could say "Go ahead and look something up if you want to," but I knew he'd take offense.

Felix's blond hair curled against his collar, framing a smooth, round, dimpled face. At last he looked up at me and asked, "What did you say to that reporter?"

"Which reporter?"

"The one you were talking to on the phone. From the *Canberra Times*."

Bambi and Di had both been in the office when Gail Trembath rang me. I was sure I hadn't said her name. But I'd referred to Rae by name on the phone, and it wouldn't have been hard to work out what the call was about.

I folded my hands in front of me, and said quietly, "I didn't tell her anything."

Felix was several grades above me in the hierarchy. That day, he was wearing a fawn button-up cardigan over a white shirt and dark-patterned tie. He dressed like a 1950s paterfamilias, except when he went running. Then he dressed in a red T-shirt and shorts, with a red sweatband holding his blond curls off his face.

He touched his soft upper lip with his right forefinger and said, "Perhaps you'd like to tell me where *you* think the money is."

Rae hadn't been formally accused of anything, much less proven guilty. The story in the *Times* did not have to be true. Everyone was so edgy in the lead-up to a federal election that any bit of bad publicity was enough to send them off. And Rae was unpopular. I'd been in the department long enough to know that, if not to understand the reasons for it.

Felix was waiting for an answer. I realized it would take very little, a whisper of breath on the wrong side of his face, for him to convince himself that I was guilty of more than speaking to the press.

I told him, "I have no idea."

Back in my office, I switched on my computer. Instead of the usual invitation to log in, colored lines like worms wriggled energetically across my screen.

I sat perfectly still, watching them. It was like suddenly finding myself in an aquarium. The worms traveled behind the glass, balling together rhythmically, then separating.

"Bambi? Can you come here a minute?"

Bambi stared at my monitor and said, "Wasn't me, cherie."

"What are they?" I asked.

But my unhelpful colleague had turned around, and I found myself speaking to her back.

Ivan was out on a job, and Di Trapani interviewing. I switched my computer off, then on again, but all I got were rainbow-colored worms.

I pressed my nose flat against the screen, and it was for all the world like a large sheet of glass, the front of an aquarium. Behind it ran a mass of moving, treacherous water, hiding who knew what submerged ravines, what icebergs far from home.

When Ivan got back, he made a sign saying QUARANTINE STATION and stuck it on my door.

He hunched over my computer, his big back and hairy head offering a barricade I had no wish to pass.

He and Felix worked on the worm together, while I fidgeted behind them, wishing I could disappear.

Felix stood up, gave me a cold blue stare, and said, "Even in a small department such as ours, we seem to have more than our share of willing ostriches. They believe they're smart as all get-out, but they don't want to know about computers. You should have had more sense."

He stared at me with what seemed unmovable dislike, the whites of his eyes luminous and somehow sickly-looking.

I had no reply, because I did not know what I'd done.

I waited for Ivan to take a break, but it was halfway through the afternoon before he talked to me.

"Viruses can hibernate until the part of the program that contains them is executed."

"Speak English," I told him.

"My guess, Sandy, is your little worms hid themselves in a part of a program that you haven't been using."

"But how did they get there?"

"I don't know."

"Will they spread to other computers?"

"That's why we've quarantined everyone you've been connected to." Ivan smiled like a Cheshire cat. "Relax. No one's putting you to bed without any supper."

It wasn't the first time the computers in our section had been attacked by a virus. Once, when I'd been in Rae Evans's office, bringing her up to date on my progress with the report, we'd watched a low wall of gray stones build itself up, block by hewn block, until it covered her computer screen entirely. Across the top in loud black letters, a laughing rough voice cried, "Stone wall, ha, ha, you're stoned!"

"Damn," Rae had said. With a stoic annoyance, she'd reached for the phone, pushed Felix's extension and said, "Send someone to fix it."

Ivan's beard looked thicker, as though the virus hunt had given it a growth spurt. I asked him why he thought Felix was so certain the virus was my fault.

Instead of answering me, he said, "A cup of coffee and a walk around the block. Come on. We both need a break."

Our corridor felt narrower, the gray more oppressive, as Ivan galloped along it to the lifts. The plywood office dividers seemed closer together, as though people had been secretly cribbing space on either side, leaving the walkway smaller.

"Some nerd makes up a virus," Ivan said, "it gets copied, passed along. If you can trace it back to its source you're a bloody magician."

I began to feel a bit less of a pariah, but I was suspicious, too.

"Maybe it's more than that," I said. "Maybe something more is going on."

As Ivan leant forward to press the button, the lift doors opened. Rae and Felix Wenborn emerged shoulder to shoulder, staring straight ahead.

I don't think Rae was aware of me as more than a blur of flesh and clothing. She was completely absorbed in the anger between herself and Felix, anger given form, as though there was another person darting between them.

Ivan looked from Felix to Rae and back again, with an expression of delighted concentration, as if they were a couple of good stand-up comics, or Wimbledon tennis finalists.

Safely in the lift, I said, "Poor Felix. Looks like he's had to miss his run two days in a row."

"Don't be catty."

"He hates Rae, doesn't he? What is he, some sort of new-age misogynist?"

Ivan threw back his head and laughed immoderately. He lost his footing as the lift bumped to a halt at the ground floor.

"I know that what I say is usually hilarious," I told him.

Ivan rubbed his head where he'd knocked it. Outside, he took the lead.

"Felix is sure Rae stole that money." I was thinking aloud. "It's like he's been waiting for something like this. For an excuse."

"Sandy, I'm fresh from the wars, okay? This was meant to be a break. Maybe Evans reminds him of his mother. Now that *is* a thought."

Café Moore looked as though it had been refurbished since I'd last been there with Rae. I couldn't put my finger on exactly what was different. There was a hint of fresh paint, though it was hard to be sure under the smells of coffee, chocolate, and the ubiquitous muffins. The muffins looked like pouter pigeons after a meal of soda bicarb.

The same Matthew Perceval prints of the Kimberleys were in the section by the windows where I'd sat with Rae, and they still matched the gray-blue of the walls and tabletops. In a corner, a man spoke urgently into a mobile phone, rubbing his nose to emphasize a point.

Patrons pulled their coats tight, lowered their necks into thick sweaters, made their hot drinks last.

After we had ordered, Ivan leant back, stretching his arms and then his fingers.

"You know those digital images I do—like your cyclamen?" he said. "I want them to be a window on the world. No one here thinks of computers like that. Number-crunchers, data processors—how many people think of their potential for art?"

He made his eyes big, daring me to answer. It seemed to me that he was wrong, that not a week went by when there wasn't some TV program on computer graphics, art, or animation.

"The perspective's all *this* way." Ivan made an inverted V with his hands, fingers barely touching.

For all his thick beard and long hair, Ivan's hands were surprisingly smooth, as though whoever modeled him had had their fun by the time they'd made his head. I loved to watch Ivan's hands move over his computer keyboard like a professional musician's. But I'd never watched a pianist close up, improvising, the way I watched Ivan. He had a gentle, precise touch. Mostly, it wasn't sound he was producing, but pictures and words on a screen, and the relationship between his fingers and what they created was a hidden one. I wondered whether, if I ever came to understand each keystroke as he executed it, watching him would lose its fascination.

The waitress put our coffees down, along with a croissant for Ivan. I reached for the sugar, and my hand brushed his.

"I want to change all that," he said quietly, but with an underlying hardness I had come to recognize. "I want to teach people that computers can help them look out there. The opposite of what these guys are after."

"Who?" I asked. "What *are* they after?"

"They want people to build walls around their computers so that *they*, the hackers, can bust them. Otherwise there'd be no challenge for them, you see."

"Who does?" I insisted.

Ivan took a huge bite of croissant. Jam and melted butter spurted out the end. "Some smart-aleck kid would be my bet," he said.

Outside our window was a smokers' corner, with blue slatted seats facing one another, and white bins the size of horse troughs where small bushes, geraniums, and ferns survived shoulder-to-shoulder through the winter. Smokers stood around chatting to each other. Some wore gloves. I wondered if Dianne ever joined them. She didn't seem to stray further than the travel center.

"Like a bloody reformed smoker," Ivan said.

I started, wondering if he'd read my mind.

"Felix. Born-again security freak. He'd never be this bad if he wasn't feeling guilty."

"Guilty?" I repeated.

"The buck stops with Felix. You screw up, he cops it. Evans screws up, the same."

"You mean he's taking the blame for the missing money? You think that's what they'd been arguing about back there?"

Ivan spooned the froth off his cappuccino. He seemed to have forgotten my question.

"I want to use computers to expand human perception," he declared. "You never thought of what's on a computer screen as a way of looking out, have you? I bet you haven't. A way of connecting with what's out there? I bet you never thought of that."

He smiled condescendingly. I wished he would shut up. He didn't give a damn what my answer was. His question was directed past me, maybe toward Felix, who was making life uncomfortable for everyone. But then I had a sudden, optimistic vision of each of us packing away our defenses, the way you'd pack away some cards you'd made a brittle house from. Sitting down together with good will, presenting a united front. I smiled and nodded, and bit back the sarcasm waiting on my tongue.

I thought of Rae again, and wondered when I'd get to speak to her. Emotions can fill up a scene, becoming all a person is able to perceive, while normally solid objects lose their outlines. When I went to pay, I noticed that the white paint on the counter was still scratched. Lined brown wood showed through. Surely anybody giving the café a facelift would have repainted that.

"Felix needs a girlfriend," I said, as we passed the church—a modern one, with huge square blocks of glass. "What about Bambi?"

"Bloody hell," said Ivan.

"Why not? They both like wearing red."

"He's married, donkey," Ivan said.

The corner of the travel center came into view. The national airline boasted four nights at Kuta for $967. Better than a Greyhound to Orange or Cooma, if you had escape in mind.

I told Ivan I needed to buy stamps, and we separated at the post office.

Recalling Rae's furious expression as she came out of the lift, I was struck by a similarity between her appearance and Felix's. Both were blue-eyed, roughly the same height. Felix had a boy's round face and dimpled chin. Rae's face was more angular. Her nose was higher and thinner, and her cheekbones more pronounced. She could have been born into an upper-class English or Scots family, and when she was angry her air of looking down her nose at everyone was obvious.

But reined-in anger had made Felix's baby face older and stronger, while it had made Rae's childish, in spite of her Julius Caesar haircut and patrician disdain.

IVAN RELAXED FOR THE rest of the afternoon by playing with some smart new software. When I went into his office for a chat before going home, there was a huge, hairy face filling his computer screen.

A mouth opened in the middle of the face. A mushroom cloud rose from the bottom of the screen, white flecked through with yellow. As the focus shifted and definition sharpened, the cloud became a meat pie with potato and cheese topping. The mouth opened wide to swallow mottled bits of meat and gravy. In a sequence that was at once grotesque and natural, the mouth attached itself to throat, stomach, intestines, each internal organ appearing as you might see your own insides in a nightmare.

The sticky mouth opened one last time, letting out a giant burp.

Ivan turned to me and winked, handing me a brochure.

"Relax Sandy, it's just a demo. Compic strutting their stuff."

"Who?"

"Local talent."

Guy Harmer was standing behind Ivan, watching the animation over his shoulder, cool as ever, but obviously enjoying himself.

BYOP. 256 colors. The information across the top of the screen seemed an optional extra, like tomato sauce.

"What's that mean?" I asked.

"Build your own pie."

More words appeared, this time rainbow-colored, in a fancy script: *In the beginning there was Compic, and the world of computer art was born.*

"Who wrote this garbage?" I complained. "It's even blasphemous."

39

"What do you care?" Ivan said. "You're an atheist. It's *advertising*."

"Where did it come from?"

"Felix gave it to us."

All I was producing was a humble report on clerical outwork. A colored cover would stretch our project's budget to the limit. If the department was planning on buying sexy new graphics software, it obviously wasn't to make my work more alluring.

I mumbled something to this effect, and left Guy and Ivan chuckling like a pair of off-course punters who both had dreams of winning.

AS I WAS LEAVING the building, I looked up and saw Rae Evans at the other end of the corridor, heading toward the fire stairs. She was carrying what looked like a stuffed briefcase and wearing her overcoat and scarf.

I called her name. Without replying, or glancing in my direction, Rae quickened her pace. She was opening the heavy fire doors when I caught up to her.

"Rae!" I called again.

She turned toward me, her eyes as gray and flat as the lake under fog.

"Where are you going?"

She shook her head and almost smiled. "I'm not allowed to answer questions, Sandra. Not even yours."

Her voice was low, controlled. I stared at her neat fringe, wings of hair at the sides immobile in their silver clasps, her skin the color of an expensive envelope. It seemed that if I put out my hand to touch her arm, or any part of her, the edges of the envelope would shrivel, browning into sepia.

I couldn't believe she was giving up, not even putting up the semblance of a fight.

I said, "But surely you can—"

She interrupted me. "I gave Access Computing a grant. They deserved it. Their application was by far the best. I signed for the money. That's all there was to it."

"I believe you."

Rae bit her lip and turned away. There was nothing I could do to stop her.

Bodies lower their guards, I thought, after I'd watched her walk slowly down the stairs, wondering whether she'd make good her escape before somebody else called her, asked unwelcome questions.

I spent the next day telling anyone who would listen that I was sure Rae had not stolen any money. I don't know what I achieved by it, beyond providing entertainment for people with nothing better to do than gossip about me and my discredited benefactor.

I could not get the picture of Rae disappearing down the stairs out of my mind. People do lower their guards, physically and psychologically. There is a kind of languor, a weary letting go, a lowering of invisible barriers. Then disease laughingly trips across the broken wall. Keats knew about it. And Sylvia Plath.

People say it's been a hard winter. They mean cold even for Canberra, frosts and bitter winds hanging on right through October, and the sun with barely strength enough to thaw a frozen bird.

And I say yes, it has been hard, because I remember those things, too. But I remember Rae leaving that day, and I mean something else. Senses can stay dormant, frozen, then thaw in the most unlikely ways.

CHEATING

PRACTICALLY BEFORE I'D PULLED up in our driveway, Peter was out of his seat belt and bolting across the front lawn to the letterbox. He'd seen the blue aerogram poking out. He was too excited even to try to read Derek's careful, rather squashy handwriting.

Usually it was hard to get Peter to write anything except "love, Peter" at the bottom of my letters, but last time he'd laboriously added a paragraph asking his father to send some pictures of cream cheese being made.

I scanned down the lines of the aerogram. Derek's sarcasm sliced across the Pacific Ocean. *Looks like you've collected another lame duck.* In my last letter I'd told him about Ivan.

I looked up at Peter. "It's just something for me, I think."

Peter turned away so that I wouldn't see his disappointment. Quickly, I checked the rest of the letter for something I could read aloud. My eyes blurred with anger at Derek—no photos, not even a mention of cream cheese.

"Maybe Dad's written to you separately," I said, hitching up my groceries, and handing Peter the front door key. "Your letter could be on its way right now."

As soon as he was inside, Peter turned the television on and flopped full length in front of it. I bent down and put my arm around him. He wriggled to shake me off. I knew he was trying not to cry.

I turned away to get our tea, chopping carrots so hard with my vegetable knife that a whole lot flew off the bench and jumped across the kitchen floor.

One of my earliest memories of Derek has him standing with his back to the King George statue outside the old Parliament House. I'm walking toward my future husband, and he's smiling. We don't know each other well. We've met maybe twice, maybe three times, through friends of friends. Derek calls my name and waves, leaning loosely back against the statue.

I can't remember what we said and it's not important. It's somehow like a scene from a silent movie, the crowd around us fading away, Derek's face in close-up.

Self-contained people have always attracted me, even when, as has sometimes been the case, I've found that their self-containment was a sham. It's their ability not to give themselves away immediately, as I have a habit of doing, that I find attractive. Reserved people make me consider my words and actions more carefully, at the same time building up a tension that is nearly always sexual. Good-looking reserved people can pretty well rely on getting me to eat out of their hands.

Derek was—is—a snob. He considered that there were bits of me missing, the way other kinds of snobs consider people without much formal education to be missing manners, or taste. Derek has definite ideas about how an intelligent person should behave. One of these, I soon learnt, was never to forget a face. But why, propping up King George on a windy Canberra afternoon, did he pick *my* face out of the crowd?

It became apparent, after we'd exchanged a dozen of those words that didn't matter, that we were going to spend the rest of the day, and possibly the night together. I was attracted to Derek partly because he was so certain of his judgments that he absolved me, at least temporarily, from making any. With Derek on permanent alert for the shortcomings of others, I was free for a more charitable response. This is what I believe now. I wouldn't have put it that way while I was getting to know him.

Derek considered me incomplete, but at the time he married me he trusted in his vision of the finished product. And now, from as far away as America, he was watching to see that I behaved correctly. But I'd changed in the few weeks since he left. Derek would have criticized me for impulsively defending Rae Evans. I didn't care. I was glad I'd spoken out.

NEXT MORNING, THE FROST was thicker on the ground than I'd ever seen it, covering the grass with a thoroughness, a deep-freeze coldness, that took my breath away. When Peter and I stepped out onto its crunchy surface, it looked like the snow I waited for each winter, but had seen only once.

We turned the corner, and noticed that the streetlights were still on. Something must have gone wrong with the time switch. They were huge and mustard-colored. High-school kids cracked open white grass with a soccer ball.

Peter complained about having to stay in the playground while I went to speak to his teacher, but there seemed no alternative. No one was allowed inside before nine, he told me crossly.

The interview was the teacher's idea, not mine, and as I approached Peter's classroom, my heels clattering on green lino tiles, I wondered what it was about.

The classroom was empty. I stood beside the teacher's desk and looked out the window. In the couple of minutes it had taken me to find the right room, the sun had come out. The windows glittered with it, their ledges lined with plants, paint tins, art and craft work in various stages of completion. I wanted to suck up into my spirit, hold and keep the picture of the sun on frosty grass.

There was a bowl of daphne on the teacher's desk. The bowl was round, dark blue, the winter flowers arranged neatly in a bed of dark green leaves. I leant over to smell them, heard a step in the corridor, and turned round.

"Mrs. Mahoney," Peter's teacher said. "Won't you take a seat?"

She held my hand briefly rather than shook it. She was well-groomed, well-fed, giving off the afterglow of croissants and hot coffee like an expensive scent. She made me conscious of the fact that I'd had no time for breakfast.

"Mrs. Mahoney," she repeated, and came straight to the point. "I'm sorry to have to tell you this. Peter is cheating."

"Cheating?" I repeated. "How do you mean cheating?"

The teacher sat down, careful not to crease her skirt, and handed two sheets of paper to me across the desk.

"Same mistakes as the boy sitting next to him," she rapped out. "Spelling mistakes the same."

"How do you know Peter is copying, and not the other boy?" I asked, skidding around in my mind for a halfway suitable approach, at the same time hating this woman, instantly and completely.

"I hoped moving your son might stop it, but it doesn't matter who he's sitting next to. Moving his desk right away from the other children is a bigger step, one they'll all notice, I'm afraid."

"Have you talked to Peter?"

"He just denies it. I understand his father is away?"

"That's right. He's gone to America for a year."

"And Peter misses him?"

"Look—I had no idea about any of this."

"There'll be teasing if I put Peter at a desk by himself."

I stared at the teacher in disbelief. "Can you wait? At least until I've spoken to him?"

At first she refused, but after arguing for a while, I got her to agree.

* * *

45

SIMPLY BY LOOKING AT me, Peter would be able to tell that something was wrong. I walked up to him and squeezed his hand, expecting him to pull away, knowing any public show of affection from me was an embarrassment. I whispered to him that I'd pick him up as early as I could.

"What was it, Mum?" Peter searched my face. "What did she want?"

"We'll talk about it tonight, okay?" I knew it wasn't, and Peter knew as well, but he nodded, mouth wary and down-turned. I hurried to my car, jangling my key in the ignition, twisting it fiercely when it happened to stick.

"YOU DON'T NEED TO copy from other kids," I told Peter that evening. "You'll never learn that way."

His eyes were fixed on *Captain Planet*. I walked over to the television set and knocked him off.

Peter leapt up to turn the TV back on, shouting, "That old bag! What would she know!"

I was ready for this and I blocked him, arms stretched out as if to catch a bird in flight.

A little while later, when we were calm enough to open our mouths without shouting, I said, "Do you want me to speak to the principal then, if you're sure Mrs. Correa has made a mistake?"

"No."

"Well then, how about we do some practice at home?"

No answer.

"We'll start in the morning."

No answer.

Though it was late, I gathered an armful of kindling, lit the fire, and watched the orange eyes of flame grow stronger. I poured myself a generous glass of wine, a treat that was usually postponed until I'd navigated the twin shoals of dinner and homework.

There was a louder-than-usual sound of tires skidding on the icy road outside. Peter's eyes flicked from the TV to the doorway. It was the way he'd waited for Derek since he was a baby, since before he could ask, "When's Dad coming home?"

When I came back with our meal already served on two plates, a bottle of tomato sauce under one arm, Peter lifted his chin toward me with the same silent, watchful reproach that had made his baby's face look older.

He walked to the table in a careful, adult way. I picked up my knife and fork and began eating, only realizing then how hungry I was, and how stupid I'd been to mention the cheating business before we'd had dinner. That night I experienced one of those sudden, unpleasant shifts of perception that occur to parents, when you notice a difference in your child that's been coming over a long time, and you're faced with it, and at the same time you're groping back to touch the child they were a minute before, while a somehow unaccountable, unpredictable person is watching you, waiting for you to catch up with them, contemptuous because you haven't.

I reached for my wine glass, realized I'd left it sitting on the kitchen bench, and said, "Damn," softly, to myself. It was such a simple thing, but just then I couldn't get up off my chair to fetch it.

Peter said, still with an odd expression that was part disdain, part stoic dignity, "I'm going to get the juice." He came back with my wine as well.

While we ate, we talked about everything but cheating. I finished my wine. Peter picked up the dirty plates without being asked and carried them out to the kitchen.

I washed our few dishes, and he dried them. We never ordinarily bothered to dry things, but picking up a tea towel and helping me in the kitchen was part of the change in my son that evening. I realized that we'd passed the point where I'd insist that he tell me the truth, but that in the morning he might be prepared to let me help him.

I MISSED DEREK THAT night. I longed to tell him about Rae and what had happened to her, even though I was sure what his response would be. I still had to calculate the time difference whenever I phoned Philadelphia.

Derek was in a meeting at some government office, I was told when I rang. No one knew when he was expected back.

I got ready for bed, knowing I'd have trouble sleeping.

Derek had been as surprised as I was when I got the job in Labor Relations. "Maybe it's like rats and a sinking ship," I'd said to him shortly before he left. "If everyone knows the ship's sinking, who cares if the odd stray rat climbs aboard?"

I'd laughed. Derek had looked dour and displeased, as he often did when I tried to joke about something that mattered to me. Of course I'd wondered why they'd picked me for the job. With unemployment nudging eleven percent—sinking ship or no sinking ship, they must have had plenty of applicants.

But then I thought about it. I'd published quite a bit on outwork. Off-site work. Home-based work. All its names were ugly. A few years ago, I'd done some research for the clothing union that had been quoted and used all over the place. I was pretty proud of that. More recently, I'd written a paper on outwork in white-collar industries. When I put together a list of publications, it didn't look so bad.

Some time after my conversation with Derek, when I thought he'd forgotten about it, he said, "We're assuming the election result's a foregone conclusion, but it mightn't be." He didn't sound very pleased about the prospect that I might have a job past the end of the year.

He'd been sorting through his papers, deciding what to take. I'd left him to it and escaped into the kitchen, whispering crossly to myself that maybe, just maybe, I'd been the best person for the job.

Now I lay in bed and thought about my shaky and confusing start in the department, and about Peter, going back over the interview with his teacher.

I recalled an evening when Peter was six, an age when print should be beginning to make sense.

I forced him to read to me. I thought it was the only way he'd learn. He came up with every excuse he could think of. He was tired. His stomach hurt. A boy had poked him in the eye at recess. I insisted that he read every evening. Of course I knew he was tired after a day at school, but I still insisted, sitting tense and determined on his bed, digging my thumbnail into my index finger as a reminder to encourage rather than criticize, to make some progress, however slight.

That night—it wasn't late, but felt it—after twenty minutes of stumbling and being corrected, Peter had stared blankly at a word, then muttered, "three." He was so anxious to get through the hated task that if the word looked like "there" or "three" or "they," what did it *matter*, his expression said.

"No, no," I'd told him.

He'd thrown the book at the wall, so that the spine broke, and loose, broken pages fluttered down.

"You stupid child!" I'd shouted.

Peter had shaken his head from side to side, faster and faster, his whole body a trembling pendulum. I left him like that, scared to stay in the room with him in case I hit him.

I sat in the living room, staring at the wall, wanting and yet fearing the moment when Derek walked in, dismayed with myself for losing my temper, for going backwards, for making next time harder.

John can run. Betty can jump. My first reader was pink, orange-pink. Who could fail to understand that run was run, and jump was jump, with Betty showing them, splay-legged over a puddle? Ever afterwards, these words had had their places, and there was no clammy hole to fall into, no gap of forgetting, no need to scramble back to that picture of Betty with her knickers showing that had first told me what the letters meant.

Try as I might, I simply could not understand why it was impossible for my son to do as I had.

Letters for Peter were little sightless birds that might as well go up the page as down, fly right to left, as badly, or as well. The night I shouted at him, he had made his stab and missed, in a low, murmuring voice, hoping I wouldn't notice. But I had noticed, and then he'd thrown the book, to break its spine, to kill it on the bedroom wall.

I wished I'd had someone to talk to back then. There had only been Derek, who'd blamed me for failing to teach Peter to read, who'd made our failure worse. Yet still, perversely, I felt desperate to talk to him. I rang America again, and was told that he was in another meeting.

BLOCK-IT

EXT MORNING, I SWITCHED on my PC with some trepidation, even though Ivan had assured me that everything was fine. The huge hairy face of a gorilla appeared. His mouth opened wide, and he said in an ingratiating voice, "Good morning, ladies. I'm squeaky clean! Virus-free, as you can see! Next time, don't forGET. Use disINFECT!"

I knew, without turning round, that Ivan was hovering in my doorway with a look of shy expectancy, like that other time when he'd pinched my cyclamen.

"Get rid of the ape, smart-arse," I said.

I glanced over my shoulder. Ivan was pouting, lips pressed together. "If you promise to do as the gentleman says," he told me.

He walked over and lowered his hand onto my shoulder, winked at me and said, "Computers can die of a virus, you know, Sandy. Just like people."

The sleeve of his sweater brushed against my cheek. It felt alive.

I glanced up. His eyes were on the screen. My skin felt tingly, strange.

I rubbed my cheek and said, "Thank you for the warning."

I discovered that Ivan had stayed back after work the night before to draw his own comment on our office situation. A caricature of Rae on a big black horse bent over and pointed a long, schoolmasterish lance at an innocent-looking Felix, who was staring up at the horse's shining withers, vulnerable in his red jogging gear. Representatives of the press, our Minister and Secretary, and a blonde, ethereal figure that I took to be Angela Carlishaw, made darting entries and exits in the background.

Ivan had a way of asking questions with his eyes and hands. He also, as I discovered that morning, had a way of taking on the demeanor of his latest creation. For a while after he'd shown me his cartoon of Rae and Felix as jousting medieval knights, he wore a hard down-the-nose look that was exactly Rae's. For a few minutes, his own burly nose became straight and thin, high-ridged and superior. Then his hair seemed to grow curiously fairer, his nose to shorten and turn up at the tip. His whole aspect grew healthier, his skin glowed as if he was just back from a run, and for a few unnerving moments he was Felix Wenborn.

I argued with Dianne and Bambi that morning—Bambi in the act of picking up the phone to make another mystery call, Di going through some questionnaires. They stared at me like fish waiting to be fed.

In a loud voice, I said I couldn't understand why they wouldn't even consider that Rae Evans might have been set up. They probably wouldn't have a job, I pointed out, if it hadn't been for her. Neither bothered to answer me. They looked superior, as though they knew something about Rae that I was too dumb to figure out.

Bambi raised her head.

I turned, following her line of sight, and there was Claire Disraeli standing in the doorway, one long smooth leg slightly in front of the other, as though she'd been about to come in, then had stopped when she heard my voice.

Claire smiled derisively.

"Did you want something?" I asked.

"Never mind Sandra," she said. "It can wait."

I INVITED IVAN HOME for tea. I did not want him to guess that I was lonely, though I'm sure he did. I felt very much alone that day, and tired, upset about Rae, and the fact that, though I'd left messages, Derek hadn't rung me back. I could not accept Bambi's and Dianne's hostility to Rae, and the cynicism of others around the department made me sick.

We stopped off at Video Ezy to rent a movie, something Peter had been nagging me to do for weeks.

"Couldn't you try and trace whoever sent the viruses?" I asked Ivan, at the same time holding a cassette out to Peter, who was crouched beside me, laboriously reading the titles on the bottom shelf.

"Here's *Milo and Otis*." I waved the picture of a dog and cat in front of him. "You'd like this one."

"Hey, Mum!" Peter gave a low crow of pleasure. "Batman Second!"

"No, you had a fighty one last time."

"Mum!"

"Defense have turned all their PCs into fortresses," Ivan growled at my elbow. "They've used Block-it. Just what the name suggests. Nothing to do with sunscreen."

"I can see their point of view," I said. "Three months ago I wouldn't have been able to, but now I can."

While I scanned the rows of garish covers for a compromise with Peter, Ivan made a box out of videos, oblivious to the curious stares of other customers and the young attendant eyeing him warily from behind the counter.

"Know what it costs, this Block-it?" he said loudly. "About four hundred dollars per PC. *Per PC.* Know what it's like running them? It's like buying a Ferrari and signing a pledge that you'll only ever drive it in first gear. Walls within walls." He gestured to the makeshift model with his foot, then knocked it over with a quick tap from the toe of his black shoe. "A clever hacker can get through as easily as that."

"If I get *Ilo and Motis*, can I have a Crunchie for dessert?" asked Peter.

Exhausted by the thought of further negotiating, I tried to will myself into good humor and failed, as I'd known I would. "Oh, all right!" I said.

"Yes!" Peter made fists of both hands in front of his chest, while Ivan replaced the jumble of cassettes on the shelf and said, "Why is he watching any of this crap? Just buy him a computer."

We stopped in at the supermarket.

I handed Ivan a loaf of white Tip Top, and he chucked it up and down in one hand, the grasp of his broad fingers pronouncing the bread mushy, overpriced and lightweight. He scratched his armpit under his parka and checked flannel shirt. A woman wearing leather fur-lined gloves, pushing a full trolley, turned to stare.

Peter scurried around the aisle with a tin of dog food. "Mum! If we get a dog!"

I told him to put it back. Ivan scowled at me and reached an arm around Peter's narrow shoulders. "You know, little dude," he said, "a lot of things happen at supermarkets. For instance, you should never sneeze in a supermarket."

"Why not?" Peter demanded.

"Because, dude, you might knock a whole pile of tins over with the force of your sneeze!"

We braved Peter's clamoring to have lunch at McDonald's.

"Like a hungry young starling, you are!" Ivan told him. "Parp, parp, parp, parp!"

Peter looked shocked for a moment, then he laughed.

"Who's that? Listen!"

I looked to where Ivan was pointing. It was my favorite street musician, singing for his supper.

I remembered how I'd felt the first night I'd heard him, how he'd made me believe I was sitting in a warm café and someone was stroking the inside of my arm with long, slow strokes.

I walked over and dropped a two dollar coin into his guitar case. We exchanged a private smile, the young man's hair rough red, his blunt face red and white and chapped.

In the car, Peter sang the theme to *Play School* with rude words. Normally, it didn't bother me.

"There was this case in Melbourne," Ivan said. "Four college students. No one could trace them. Caused hundreds of thousands of dollars worth of damage. Maybe you read about it?"

I shook my head. The gears grated as I tried to get out of reverse. Ivan winced, scrunched with no leg room in the seat beside me.

"They all had their favorite signatures, buzzwords." Ivan leant forward and drew a hieroglyphic in the dashboard dust. "Kids are like that. Be patient—in the end they'll give themselves away."

My eyes stuck on a square of icy road. "Felix told me he ran a secure ship," I said. "It was impossible to break in from outside."

"Until someone did! In that lump in his chest that passes for a heart, Felix knows that total security's impossible. And to be fair to him, people bring in dodgy software, pirate games for their kids, all the time. He's had more trouble than you can poke a stick at. And everyone treats it as his problem, not something *they* could have avoided."

"They were caught eventually," I asked, "those Melbourne kids?"

I pulled up too suddenly at the lights, throwing Ivan forward. "Remind me to walk next time," he complained. "Caught, but not convicted."

In the back seat, Peter improvised on the *Play School* theme. He was tone deaf, like his father.

Crossing Northbourne Avenue, I looked up and saw the smoke from hundreds of fireplaces, a gray-white wall on Lyneham Hill. Ahead were the trees I'd named my sentinels in the days when I'd walked toward them with Peter in his pram. There they were on their hill, looking down at us, clear outlines in the dusk, while the trees around them dissolved into one dark shape. It was as though they had some special reprieve from the night. I thought how knowledge is not fixed, so that once you've learnt something you'll always know it. You can know and then forget, or half-forget then know again, and when you do, it's like prodding an old bruise.

I thought of Peter learning to read, the way he conquered, retreated, one step forward and half-a-dozen back.

"I'LL TELL YOU A secret," I heard in a loud whisper from Peter's bedroom while I was putting away groceries, cheating by pouring myself a glass of wine before I'd started on the dinner. "I never learnt to read till I was ten years old."

"Why?" Peter's voice was petulant, tired, not wanting to be humored.

"Well," I heard Ivan say, "I think it was because my parents didn't settle in one place. My family first came to Australia when I was younger than you. My Dad worked for the government, you see. But Dad hated it here, so after a year or so we went back. But he hated it in Russia. And Mum did even more. After a few more years, he got another posting to Australia. But he didn't like that either. I went to good schools, but I kind of got mixed up."

I tiptoed to the hall doorway so that I could eavesdrop more effectively.

"Let's take a look at this guy," Ivan said. "Hos-pit-al. You think of the syllables as legs. This dude's got three. Can you sit on him? Okay, if they're big fat legs like this! If your Mum had a computer I could show you. Hey, how 'bout we talk her into it?"

In the kitchen, a little while later, while Ivan was taking ten minutes to peel an onion, Peter came running in from the TV, yelling, "Hey guys! I just had a great idea for a dog-proof garbage bin!"

He waved a large white sheet of paper at us, and Ivan staggered back, holding up his onion in defense. Peter took no notice. "This sort of clamp! D'y'see? D'y'get how it works? A dog's got no hands, so he can't undo it, see? It's the same basic garbage bin apart from that. I'll have to build a model if I'm going to patent it, won't I? Won't I, Ivan?"

"Sure dude," Ivan told him.

"He wants a dog," I said, when Peter had run off again. "What can I do?"

"Buy him one."

"And leave it shut up all day in this pissy little backyard? Take it for walks in the freezing dark?"

That evening, I watched Ivan offering Peter a friendship that was easy and masculine, yet with an edge to it—the way his friendship with me had an edge.

It seemed that Ivan spoke in someone else's voice when he talked about the old Soviet Union, a voice with an obvious accent.

"Did you ever go back?" I asked him later, after Peter was asleep and we were drinking hot chocolate in front of the combustion stove. "I mean, after you grew up?"

Each time they moved, Ivan told me, his father had been full of hope that life would be better now. But after a few months he became disillusioned again, and began renouncing the country he was in, and all it stood for.

"A traitor, you see, within the privacy of family. Of course, he couldn't say what he really thought outside it."

"So you're a diplomat's son."

Ivan winced. "Just glad that when they went back the second time I was old enough to stay. Enrolled myself at Queensland Uni. Far enough away to stop them pestering me."

"What happened to your parents?"

"Dad died of heart disease when he was forty-eight. That second time back was a death sentence, and my mother knew it."

"And your mother?"

"She died eighteen months later."

So neither of us had a family. "Will you go back?" I asked. "Now that things have changed?"

After the Soviet Union fell, he'd bought a plane ticket. "It was unreal. From the minute I walked into the travel center, it was like I'd left reality on the other side of the door. I couldn't renew my passport, couldn't phone anybody to tell them I was coming. I just physically could not do those things. So I cashed it in, the ticket. Bought myself a new computer."

"You were frightened."

"Of course."

I finished my hot chocolate and debated with myself whether I felt greedy enough to be bothered making more. There was a Friday-night feeling of not having to clean up, not having to worry that I'd run out of Peter's favorite breakfast cereal. I felt reassured by the house's neutrality.

As each week without Derek passed, I felt my house creaking and shifting, settling, getting used to holding two people not quite a family. Derek still hadn't rung, but that didn't hurt so much now. Perhaps nobody had passed on my messages.

I said, "Thanks for talking to Peter about reading."

"That's okay." Ivan tilted his head back, draining the last of the sweet liquid from the bottom of his mug.

"It would be great if you could—"

"Sure. It's cool." Ivan cut me off. "I'll help him if I can. I like him."

I murmured thanks again, but I was feeling that I should not have asked, that I should have waited till I had a clearer idea of what Ivan might expect in return. Then I felt contrite for not trusting his generosity.

Ivan was watching me, waiting for me to say the next thing. I stood up and began to collect mugs and empty plates onto a tray.

He followed me out to the kitchen.

There was no need to switch on a light in the short corridor between my living room and kitchen. I turned and looked at Ivan over my shoulder. The oblique light shining through the door caught his springy hair. It seemed to be growing while I watched it. I wanted to reach out my hand, to feel that movement and that growth. Almost too late, I remembered I was carrying a tray. I recovered and kept walking.

I turned on taps and blurted out, "What's going to happen to Rae Evans?"

Ivan frowned.

"You believe Rae had this coming to her, don't you? Why? Why doesn't anybody like her?"

Ivan walked over to the window. He opened the kitchen curtains a crack, and stared out through them. His pose struck me as oddly familiar, as though he often stood like that, alone in his own house, spying on the frost.

"You're a technical person," I said, annoyed that he didn't turn around, that I was speaking to his back. "You should know Rae couldn't have stolen that money. She didn't have the skills."

Since Ivan didn't seem to think this worth replying to, I continued, "Someone must have framed her."

"I'd stop saying that around the department, if I were you. Felix knows you've been shooting off your mouth defending Evans, and implying that he's somehow to blame."

"I haven't—"I began, but he interrupted.

"Forget it. Forget Evans, Sandy. She's dead meat."

I'd thought we were in tune with one another. I was so angry and upset that I couldn't speak.

AFTER IVAN LEFT, I went to bed thinking about the word "hacker." It didn't have the aura that surrounds obvious criminal labels like "thief" or "murderer." Even "forger" or "embezzler." And in the dictionary, you didn't find a hacker described as someone who breaks into computers. Not in the Oxford, anyway, which I got up to check.

"To hack" has many meanings, some of which surprised me. I found "to put to indiscriminate or promiscuous use; to make common by such treatment: a prostitute or bawd, 1730." A hack in 1681 was a miner's pick, so perhaps the first hacker wielded one. Later, "a common drudge, especially literary drudge; a poor writer, a mere scribbler, 1700."

"Hack into: to mangle by jagged cuts." Perhaps that definition came closest.

The new meaning is still raw around the edges. It took me a long time to grasp the importance of something obvious, and that is the anonymity of the crime. The computer criminal can be absent, even thousands of kilometres away—and there's no one on the spot doing the dirty work, either. Everything appears perfectly normal, while millions of dollars are busy disappearing, and no one's fingerprints are left behind.

Oh yes, and one more thing. Though the image the word "hacker" brings to mind is of a long-haired, thin young man with glasses, the label itself is, for better or for worse, androgynous.

IMPREGNATED
WITH A VIRUS

I HAD JUST OPENED an e-mail attachment when all the words in the last line of the document fell to the bottom of the screen.

I stared at them and thought, not again. More words began to fall from the next line up, then the next one and the next. My screen was filled with tumbling letters that huddled at the bottom. It was like a game on *Sesame Street*, played with letters that fell and lay side-on, and then grew arms and legs.

I wanted to crawl inside my monitor and push all those words back where they belonged. I caught my breath as they formed themselves into a message.

Rae Evans is a thief and a liar. If you know what's good for you, you'll stop defending her.

Surely whoever had sent this childish threat could be traced. It had to be somebody who knew me.

I showed Ivan, who clicked his tongue and said it looked like a job for Felix.

Felix was busy when I rang. He called me into his office later in the morning.

He was sitting at one of his computers when I knocked, dressed in a

Fair Isle sweater in shades of navy blue, damp hair clinging in yellow curls to his forehead and the back of his neck.

His office reminded me of the LEGO houses Peter sometimes made, the proportions perfect except for one Escher-like oddity: a row of steps starting halfway up a wall, a window in the floor. I couldn't spot what it was that had a skewed perspective, but I knew that if I looked long enough I'd find it. The personal touches were a photograph of an athletics team with Felix at the front, long hair held back by a sweat band, and another which I took to be of his wife, her arms around two small children.

Felix swiveled his chair around to face me, legs apart and shoulders back. The gray wool of his trousers stretched tight across his thighs.

He stared at me accusingly and said, "I understand the virus came in on your attachment."

Felix couldn't help lecturing people. I doubted if he was even aware that he was doing it. He held up his hand like a traffic cop and said, "In code, it looks like a perfectly ordinary piece of text. But it isn't."

He swung his chair close to a whiteboard on the wall opposite the window, picked up a red felt pen, and began sketching rapidly. He drew a red square with a whole lot of little squares going off it, like a sunburnt sow with piglets.

"Server." He pointed at the mother pig, then her offspring. "Evans, you, Trapani, Red Riding Hood. Tell me exactly what you did."

"I *was* checking my mail," I said uncertainly.

"It's like cars." Felix ground his teeth. "When your car breaks down, you want it fixed. But you don't want to be bored by long tedious explanations of what's under the hood."

I went red, recalling Ivan's warning.

Felix fixed me with his albumen eyes. "With computers, you have to start with the ABC, and believe me, even that's too sophisticated for some. But it doesn't stop them treating the Director of Information Technology like a car mechanic."

His first-floor office had a clear view of Northbourne Avenue, across to the duty-free shops on the other side and the glass-fronted tower rising above them. I stared out over the street at a reflection of our building—concrete and glass, but wavery, fluid, as though I was looking into water. The threatening message seemed to come at me from everywhere.

If you know what's good for you. . . .

"We haven't been able to determine—" Felix stood up and gave his chair a shove, so that it banged into his desk "—if the virus is programmed to destroy data, or just make pretty pictures. There may be a date. If there is, it's well hidden. It turns out our mail system has a loophole. Someone out there has written a program that's attached itself to an innocuous-looking document and then had itself executed as a command."

"Out there?" I repeated. "It's a personal threat. It was sent by somebody who knows me."

Felix glared at me without replying.

"Do you think whoever sent it also sent those worms?" I asked.

He waved his hand dismissively.

"What are you going to do about it? It must have come from inside this building."

"I'll inform the police."

"Thank you."

Felix's lip curled in a sneer, and I realized that he shared the sentiments of whoever had told me to stop defending Rae. He repeated his speech about there being a weakness in the mail system. Now he'd admitted this, I could see that it was niggling away at him. He was like a shopkeeper who every now and again has noticed five dollars missing from his till, but has let it go. And then suddenly he's missing a lot more than the odd five dollars.

"These viruses," I said, "the missing money—could they be linked? Could the same person be responsible?"

He stared at me for a long time with an odd, pouting expression, arms folded across his fancy sweater, as if my question could only be described as being in bad taste.

"It's a war of nerves," he said.

"I FOUND THE TIMER," Ivan told me over afternoon tea.

He explained that he'd spent a few hours decoding my virus into assembly language.

Between mouthfuls of buttered Sao biscuit and strong black tea, he said it had been timed to start at 10 A.M.

"You mean, kind of like a chain letter?"

"Letter bomb more like it. Replicating itself every thirty seconds. There's a small mistake that made it go much slower. You were lucky."

I stared at a heap of used tea bags on a saucer. They looked like dead mice with bits of cardboard tied to their tails.

"Lucky?" I repeated. "That message made me feel terrific. I wish I could be as lucky as this every day."

"Now Sandra." Ivan had on his hopeful puppy look; yet more knowing: a knowledge of what people might get up to. I recalled the picture of my cyclamen, and how he'd hoped for praise.

He wagged a finger at me. "I'm on your side." He moved his finger closer. "No biting, see?"

We walked back to his office. There was a stack of boxes on his desk, all bearing the Compic logo.

"More meat pies," I said.

Guy Harmer looked up from his corner and smiled.

I asked, "Why so many?"

Ivan shrugged. "Felix's idea. He thinks Compic's the best thing since sliced bread."

"But what are you going to do with them?"

"Persuade you guys to use them."

"You're kidding."

Ivan clasped his hands in prayer position. "Believe me Sandy, it's not just the publications people who need to make their work look good."

"You mean every section will be given one?"

"Why not?"

I picked up a box. The price—nearly three hundred dollars—was on the back.

"What a waste. Does Felix have to get approval when he buys heaps of junk like this?"

"It's not junk," Ivan said.

THE SECRETARY PUT OUT a statement. Rae Evans had been suspended pending an inquiry. It was clear that the Secretary, indeed the whole department, was cutting Rae off, unmooring her. She'd become a small dinghy with a faulty outboard motor. And in the way these things become apparent—I was too slow to see the patterns—it seemed that Rae had never had her anchor firmly fixed.

Bambi swathed herself in her capes and long gray-blue-green skirts. She bumped into desks and swore in a stage whisper, while Di Trapani's black eyes said I told you so.

You could have cut our small section off at the lifts, and we might have floated out over the city like one of those incredibly expensive balloons that tourists go for rides in. There we would have hung, hundreds of feet in the air, forced at last to cooperate or to begin tossing each other out. A balloon basket full of malcontents, pepper falling from a giant's pot.

There was one Finance busybody—it seemed to be the same guy all the time—as persistent as winter rain. And a staffer from the Minister's office, even though he didn't trust any of us to say "Have a nice day," seemed to think he had a perfect right to pester us all day long, us and Kerry Arnold from Admin., the certifier who'd signed for Access Computing's grant money, and was copping his share of brown stains from the fan.

I'd been hired to get Rae's pet project finished before the elections, and she'd singled me out for personal attention, which I'd been more than willing to accept. I'd made no secret of the fact that I believed she'd been unfairly accused of theft. I felt scared and helpless, but this time it made me so angry I could not keep still.

I hurried down the stairs and began circling the block so fast that I bumped into people—first Jim Wilcox carrying a bulging paper bag, then a woman pushing a shopping trolley. I was sick of innuendo, snide remarks, curled lips, and bitchiness in general. I'd been given a job to do, and I'd be damned if I was going to give up on it. Okay, Rae Evans had been sacked. Okay, nobody but me cared about a report on women working in sweatshop conditions and getting into debt. The point was, I cared.

In that dash around the block, I made some decisions that might have been foolhardy, but were actually incredibly easy to make just then. Since this was the first proper job I'd had in more than eight years, I would get on with it and finish it. And instead of backing off, or being frightened off, I *would* offer Rae Evans my support. I would find a way to meet her. I would not take no for an answer. I was sick of being passive. Passive was the old me. I looked over my shoulder as I turned a corner, and it was as clear as if I'd left another person, an old Sandra, behind.

As far as the viruses and the missing money were concerned, I had suspicions, hunches, but nothing to back them up. I would go with my hunches and see where they led.

KERRY ARNOLD WAS A slight man nearing fifty, or else he'd passed that milestone quietly and was holding his looks well. Brown eyes were set well back in a gray-gold, thinning cage of hair. He was neat and quick in all his movements. I wasn't surprised to learn that he played table tennis and I could imagine him, even now, holding his own against star Chinese opponents.

I learnt all I could from Ivan about our department's electronic payment system before making an excuse to go and see Kerry in his office.

Signing for grant money meant keying YES at the bottom of a page. So far as I understood the procedure, the certifier's fingers never touched a pen or paper.

"Do you think someone stole your password?" I asked him.

Kerry's dark brown eyes were troubled. "It was quiet that day," he said. "Phone didn't ring more than about ten times. I remember that, because I got through early. I was pleased. I was playing in a tournament that night."

He sighed. I smiled encouragingly, thinking maybe Kerry didn't mind my questions. Maybe it was a relief for him to talk to somebody who didn't matter.

"I feel like a pilot who's crashed a plane, and the bosses have gone through the black box again and again without finding anything."

"It must be awful."

"If that figure was changed before the authorization went to Finance," Kerry said, "it had to have been after I signed for it. If anyone tried to change *before* I signed, the computer would have refused authorization." His voice took on the hard, obsessive tone of someone going over the same few facts without eliciting anything new from them. "The computer would not have *let* me sign for a million dollars. If I told them that once, I must have told them twenty times."

"Was it somebody from our department who changed the figure?"

Kerry stared at me and said, "It was Rae Evans, wasn't it? The police seem pretty sure of that."

"Rae Evans doesn't know a lot about computers. How could she have done it?"

Kerry shook his head, as if suddenly realizing he shouldn't be telling me what he thought.

"I told the police what could be done and what couldn't, but they kept on asking the same questions, as though I'd change my mind if they asked me often enough. I could *not* have signed for a million for Access Computing. The computer wouldn't let me. It's got nothing to do with what I can remember, or whether I could have made a mistake." He ticked the steps off on his fingers. "I signed for the grants on the Thursday afternoon. The disk went to Finance on the Friday. Finance made the payment direct into Access Computing's bank account. But somewhere along the line the figure got changed. The figure on the disk that went to Finance is a million, and that's what Finance paid. If you ask me, can that happen, I'll tell you it's impossible. That's what I told the police, the big one and that grim young woman."

"So there was a twenty-four-hour period between when you signed for the money and when the disk went across to Finance. I don't suppose you thought to check back again, some time on the Friday?"

"Why should I?" Kerry glanced at me sharply, then told me he had work to do.

Whoever it was might have left a trace, I said to myself as I hurried along the corridor and up the fire stairs, not wanting to be seen. Not a trace of fingerprints, of course. But *something*.

AS A RESULT OF the viruses I got to know Guy Harmer a little better, and Claire Disraeli, his elegant blonde companion. They often arrived at work together, and though they were quiet and courteous, not loud and obvious like Ivan, I always knew when they were next door. I'd once remarked to Ivan that he and Harmer were IT support staff, Claire was a systems analyst so what were they doing sharing an office? Ivan had replied with one word—space. There was none of that to spare, I knew, but I also suspected that Claire might have arranged it so she could be with Guy. There were more IT people on the second floor, and Felix, as director, had an office to himself on the first.

Guy had short fair hair that caught and held the winter sun. He wore pure wool calf-length coats, a variety of hand-woven scarves, and fine gray suits with pastel shirts. He swam regularly and exercised in a gym. Claire was an even lighter blonde, with the pale eyebrows and skin that suggested her hair was natural. She wore it long and straight to her shoulders, or in a ponytail. She was tall and slim, with a careful, detached elegance I'd only ever seen in fashion magazines. People stopped and looked at Guy and Claire when they walked along the corridor together. They shared one of those old-fashioned coat and hat stands, and it, too, looked like something out of a weekend glossy. No one else ever hung their coats on it. I don't know whether Claire would have stopped them if they'd tried. The connection between her and Guy was so strong that when one of them was alone, I kept looking round for the other.

I was often in and out of their room, chatting to Ivan, or leaving him a message. I'd watched Claire, sitting within touching distance of Guy's shoulder, listen to the phone on his desk ring twice, then pick it up and say in her soft voice, "Guy Harmer's phone." And then, when Guy shook his head, she'd say with what sounded like genuine regret, "He's not here at the moment. Can I take a message?"

I wondered who would cover for me if I chose not to be there. I wondered if she loved him. Claire was so cool, so professional. She did not have the slightest air of being used.

"I'm sure neither of those viruses was your fault," Guy said kindly.

When I asked him who'd been saying they were, he smiled and told me to relax.

"I'm sure it was students. It's just the sort of malicious prank they love."

He smiled again, and said it was amazing what kids these days got up to. Had I read about hackers breaking into the telecommunications tower?

I shook my head, realizing I did not want to speculate in front of Guy.

It was Di Trapani who told me Guy was married with a couple of young kids. She said that every department had its Romeo, and he was ours. "But he's harmless, Sandy. Too narcissistic to even dirty his shirt cuffs."

* * *

I WAS FUMBLING WITH my umbrella at the automatic doors when I bumped into Felix in his brick red T-shirt and shorts, coming back from a run. His clothes were dripping wet and smelt strongly of new cotton. Water silvered off his blond hair and dimpled chin.

"A word of warning," Felix panted, chest heaving up and down, eyes cold beneath his red sweatband. "Not only does departmental policy forbid any of us from talking to the press, but the whole matter is now the subject of a suppression order. If you talk to anyone about it, you're breaking the law."

"What's a suppression order?" I asked, feeling as though I'd like to poke his red butt with my umbrella.

"Just relax and do as you're told, Sandra, and you'll be all right."

Baby-faced men age in special ways, I thought, as I headed to the bank through the downpour. Their snub noses don't change, or their round, dimpled chins. Felix would one day grow drooping, purple pouches under his blue eyes. He was blond, compact, his head was small, and his features were what I thought of as cherubic—baby-faced, though I've never yet seen a baby who looks like him, and I hope I never do.

I DECIDED IT WOULD help to research the legal situation; find out what Rae Evans was up against, at least.

The definition of hacking was a tricky one, especially in the Australian Capital Territory, as I found out in the university's law library on Saturday afternoon, while Ivan was taking Peter to lunch, and then to a computer shop. When I'd said goodbye to Peter, he'd had the half-smug, half-worried look he wore when he'd talked me into something. I'd squeezed Ivan's hand as a thank-you in advance, at the same time reminding him how little money I had to play around with.

It was raining again. I've always loved libraries on rainy days. The feeling of being surrounded by books is more comforting when the trees and grass outside are foreshortened by a wet gray curtain. You can smell it through the glass.

For a couple of hours, I sat reading casebooks, trying to pin the misuse of electronic equipment under one or another of our criminal codes.

The extraction of confidential information from a computer system was not theft, one book told me. "Theft is a concept that can only be applied to property, and intangible information is not classified as property for the purposes of the criminal law."

Next, I tried fraud. "There have been several cases in recent years . . ."

I began to skim down paragraphs rather than read each one carefully.

"It is illogical to talk of deceiving a machine." Fair enough, too. But not of a machine deceiving a person. That happens all the time.

It seemed the law had not yet made up its mind on fraud.

Malicious damage sounded more promising. Yet, here again, in most cases that had been brought to trial, the defense lawyers had argued their way out.

The new offense of "dishonest use of computers" had recently been introduced in Canberra. I photocopied the relevant sections of the Crimes Act and took them home to study.

THE
INFORMATION
GAME

HEN THE *CANBERRA TIMES* building was in the centre of the city, there used to be a dozen places round about to go for a cup of coffee or a drink with a journalist. But since their offices had moved to Fyshwick, one of Canberra's light industrial zones, meetings needed to be formally arranged.

Gail Trembath and I agreed to meet at a café at the Fyshwick markets. I hoped the shopping crowds would give us cover. I was beginning to like the idea of becoming an amateur investigator. I was too embarrassed to admit this to Gail, though I definitely needed to find out more about the story she'd written that had started all the fuss. Most of all, I needed to talk to Rae. I didn't care about the suppression order, but Rae did, and despite my best efforts was refusing to meet me.

I sat at a scratched white plastic table drinking bitter cappuccino while I waited for Gail to turn up. I thought I'd chosen a seat out of the wind, but it found me easily enough, full and confident, on a downhill run from the Snowy Mountains.

I wrapped my new coat more tightly around me. It was an expensive coat, pure wool, dark cherry red. I loved it. It was still a novelty for me to have money of my own to spend. Spending a lot at once gave me a delicious sense of breaking rules, though the rules of economy were my own, as was the conclusion that I ought to be saving while I had the chance.

Jonquils from the flower shop climbed above my head in terraced wooden boxes. At another stall, weak sunlight shone through rows of orange juice; squeezed and bottled on the spot, the sign said. Jars of local honey were stacked in a pyramid—huge plastic buckets at the bottom, tiny breakfast pots at the top. Bulk honey, juice—you could come here to shop once every six months. Maybe there were people who did that, who hated shopping and owned freezers the size of small warehouses.

In spite of the casual coming and going of shoppers minding their own business and a small girl shouting constantly for ice cream, I felt conspicuous, and told myself not to be an idiot. No one cared where I was. Nobody was watching me.

Fifteen minutes each way from the Jolimont Center to Fyshwick didn't leave much of my lunch hour for talking, and it didn't help that Gail was late. Just when I'd decided she wasn't going to show, she appeared in a swish of dark blue coat and flying red hair.

I said hello and then, "You know, I shouldn't be here."

"Neither should I." Gail grinned. "Relax."

Why did people keep saying that? It wasn't working.

The screaming child was silenced by a Bubble-O-Bill ice cream. Peter had sampled one once, and pronounced it gross. I had a sudden urge to complain to Gail about Rae Evans, tell her what a frustrating person Rae was. I bit my tongue.

Gail was looking at me shrewdly. "If we're caught," she said, "we can bum out on the dole together. Oh, I forgot, you're married."

"While you're used to taking risks."

Gail wasn't put off by my sarcasm. She studied me with amused hazel eyes. She'd been dissatisfied with her looks as a student, hair ginger rather than auburn, skin too pale and freckled. I'd known her for two years before I saw her without makeup. Now she seemed to have grown into her looks, grown along with them. She'd lost her habit of glancing sideways at me when she spoke.

"What are you having?"

I held up a polystyrene cup. "Something to keep me warm while I was waiting. I wouldn't recommend it. Tastes like the scrapings off those bird cages down there."

Ignoring my warning, Gail walked over to the counter and came back with a lidded cup, gray murk bubbling out of the hole in the center of the lid.

"The only thing I'm allowed to say is I'm not allowed to say anything," she said, waving a bent spoon at me before heaping in the sugar.

"An interesting story."

"It would be if I could write it."

"I thought you had already."

Something had shifted in the few moments it had taken Gail to get her coffee and come back.

"Could this whole thing be political?" I asked.

"A few months before a federal election? What did you say you had for breakfast, Sandy?"

"Farex. With just a touch of milk."

"Cheers." Gail lifted her cup a fraction from the table.

"On the question of style," I said, "I didn't much like your mixed metaphors. Should have picked one and stuck to it. Your very own lead, or did you have a literary adviser?"

"If you'd suggested the *correct* metaphor?" Gail swallowed a mouthful, and grimaced. "That day I phoned? Put me on track, so to speak?"

"I asked you to wait. Had you been talking to anyone else, or did you call me first?"

Gail's mobile rang, as though on cue. She fished for it in the folds of her coat.

Her conversation consisted of three noes and a yes. "Who tipped you off?" I asked when she'd finished.

She raised an eyebrow. Okay, I said to myself, I didn't really think you'd tell me. I was already sick of pushing words back and forth like bad coffee. I looked around. The gourmet butchers offered free-range chickens, pheasant, quail, guinea fowl, kangaroo, water buffalo, and game berries, whatever they were. The budgies at the pet shop chattered without pause. Would budgies be next on the menu?

Gail started speaking quickly. "Loony rings me up, offers to sell me a tape of the Prime Minister fucking his grandmother. Two thousand bucks? Two-and-a-half? Happens all the time." She took another gulp of coffee, and I fancied I saw the muddy path it made down her throat. "Any rate, more often than you'd think, 'specially when there's an election looming. If you go ahead and buy it you've got a vested interest in believing what it says. I still haven't managed to figure that one out. Your guy gave us his loot for free."

"So it was a man?" I asked.

She ignored my question. In summary, she said, this had been the chain of events. After her phone call to me, she'd decided to sit on the story for a while, chew it over while she worked on something else. But then the chief of staff had done the rounds with his usual question, "What have you got?" and she'd blurted it out.

The chief had been tickled pink. "We'll get the techies on to tracing it right away!"

He rang his contact in the Minister's office, and before long half the resources of the paper had been turned toward Gail's story.

"Everyone put in their two bob's worth. I've never been in the middle of anything like it before. Even the cartoonist."

"Maybe they had advance warning of the suppression order," I said dryly.

Gail pulled out a cigarette. Something in her voice dismayed me. Her account had been so easy. She didn't care what happened to Rae Evans. In fact, Rae the person scarcely figured in her version at all.

"Who was it?" I asked. "You must have some idea."

If she did know who'd sent her the story, now was the time to trot out the chestnut about journalists protecting their sources. Gail—at least the Gail I'd known in Melbourne—didn't like admitting ignorance. What she'd said rang true to me. If she'd chosen to lie, it would have been in a way that showed her in a better light.

"Listen," I said. "The story needs balance—"

"You know that's a breakfast cereal? I tried it, it's foul."

"The concept, dear heart. Access Computing has been given the once-over. They handled it badly. I suppose it's possible this Angela Carlishaw has taken off with the dough. But no one's proved that Rae Evans had anything to do with it. She wouldn't steal. She's honest. What's more, I don't believe she *could* have. She barely knows one end of a computer from the other."

Gail took a drag on her cigarette and said, "You always were a tight-arsed little moralist, Sandy."

I opened my mouth to tell her about the viruses and the nasty message I'd been sent, then shut it again. It would be just like Gail to mock me, and dismiss the threat as some sort of children's game. Indeed, it had an element of that, with all those falling letters. Anonymous letters and messages *were* childish, but that did not make them benign.

Though a part of me wanted to get up and walk away, annoyed by Gail's refusal, or inability, to take Rae's predicament seriously, I needed her help. I wanted her to use her position as a journalist to help me to information I would find much harder to gather on my own.

My eye caught a long bottle of homemade vinegar on the shelf next to the orange juice. Sprigs of dill or sage floated upright in it, curving over themselves like spiky seahorses preserved in formalin.

"I want you to do something for me," I said. "A story on clerical out-workers. Single mums who've mortgaged their underwear to buy computers. Trying to work from home with screaming babies in the next room. No need to mention any of the legal players."

"I don't think so."

"Just a whack of good old bleeding hearts, Gail. It's the story of the moment, and no one's bothering to write it."

"Don't think the boss will buy it."

"Don't tell him till you've written it," I said. "If it's a good read, he'll print it. I'll give you some names and help you with the metaphors."

Gail smiled. I held my breath, realizing that, in two seconds, without giving it any thought, I'd offered Gail names from the list of women who'd taken part in my department's survey. She'd picked this up immediately.

She shook her head and said, "Too much of a hassle."

"But you'll do it," I told her, "for old times' sake."

A guinea pig bit a small boy's finger, and he yelled blue murder. I thought it might be time to leave.

THE NEW GLASS-FRONTED BUILDINGS in Northbourne Avenue formed a guard of honor, regular, in uniform, standing to attention, their chests polished as dress swords. They bore their logos with a military bearing—Unisys, Sun Microsystems, IBM—the names of giants.

And the little ones, the small fry, were growing unnoticed, like mammals in the age of dinosaurs. Y and Z Technology included Chinese characters alongside the English, and an amateur sign in block capitals offering TUTORIAL OF SOFTWARE. I looked up computer companies in the phone book. There were pages of them now.

FINGERPRINTING

HE POLICE TURNED UP in our section early the next morning.

At first glance, the detectives looked like two well-cut suits joined together at the shoulders, Siamese twins who had miraculously grown to adulthood. Then they separated into a policeman and woman conferring soberly together.

Detective Constable Gleeson was cool, unsmiling. Her expression never seemed to change. I watched her face while she grasped my hand by the wrist to bring it right over the ink pad. Holding the base of my thumb, she firmly pressed my thumb pad down.

I wondered how many times she had taken fingerprints, smelling the nervous sweat of suspects while a line of people filed past, polite, affronted, or guilty-looking in spite of themselves. I guessed she wouldn't speak or interfere, unless it was to tell the person that it hadn't worked, to try again. No twitch of facial muscles, no smile of reassurance would escape her.

What if the police found my prints on Rae's computer keyboard? Was it possible, and, if so, would they think it unusual? Had they been told about the public files we all used? Our working arrangements seemed open to a number of interpretations.

Before she left, Constable Gleeson went through Rae's desk and rubbish bin. Ivan told me about it. The constable had left Rae's door open a crack, and he'd peeked through it and seen her.

"Where was Deirdre?" I asked.

Ivan didn't know. He laughed, flicked a fingernail against my PC, and said, "Don't they know the clues are all in here?"

DETECTIVE SERGEANT HALL INTERVIEWED me. He wore a perfectly fitting dark blue suit that smelt strongly of dry-cleaning fluid. The cut and obvious expense of his clothes indicated a man conscious of his appearance. At the same time, he looked and sounded bored. It was only when he asked me about my relationship with Rae Evans that his voice deepened into something like curiosity or interest.

Hall had chosen, or been offered, a small room off the reception area on the first floor to conduct his interviews. There was nothing in it but a table holding a tape recorder, a computer that wasn't plugged in, and two black swivel chairs. As soon as the detective had shaken my hand, leaning across the table to do so, he sat down in one chair, and pulled the other one close, indicating it to me. I felt too nervous and unsure of myself to move it back.

When he asked a question, he held his face right up next to mine, the way some children do when they want to tell you something. It was extraordinarily disconcerting. I hoped that, by not reacting at all, by staying calm, I'd make him drop the tactic, switch to something else.

He kept his voice low, so that if I wanted to hear every word I had to listen carefully, couldn't pull back too far. I licked my lips, and passed my hand across my forehead.

"Does Ms. Evans have any enemies that you're aware of?" he asked, making *Ms.* sound like an insult.

"Felix Wenborn," I said, then added, "Dianne Trapani has shown a degree of personal dislike."

The detective looked at me and waited. He would already have spoken to Felix, Jim Wilcox the division head, the deputy secretary, and the secretary, too, for all I knew, starting at the top and working his way down. He would have gathered people's opinions of Rae, and would know she was unpopular. He might have been told that she'd singled me out for special attention.

"How would you describe your working relationships. Mrs. Mahoney?"

"I'd say they were cordial."

"You were happy to get the job here?"

"Very happy."

Hall was clean-shaven, with a face that I could imagine sculptors being drawn to, chunky without being fat, bones squared off at the jaw and temples, eyes wide-spaced with flawless whites, as though their clarity in close-up could bore a confession out. His hair was dark brown with a flickering of gray.

"That message you got—"

I interrupted him to ask, "Have you traced it?"

He gave his head the slightest possible shake. "It came in with a virus."

"I know that."

"Do you have any idea who sent it?"

"The first virus—" I looked at him inquiringly, to make sure he knew about this. "I thought it could have been anyone. Students perhaps. The second, and that message, had to be from someone who knows me."

"Why would you be warned to stop defending Ms. Evans?"

"Because I have been."

"How?"

"By talking to people, telling them what I think."

"Which is?"

"That she didn't steal that money, firstly because I believe that she's an honest person, and secondly because she wouldn't have known how."

The detective leant closer again. I realized that my fingers were clenched tight. Deliberately, giving the action all my attention, I unclenched them, and moved my chair back a fraction.

His eyes flicked to my chair's new position on the floor. "Was Ms. Evans worried about what might happen after the elections? Possibility of having her budget cut to ribbons?"

"No more than anybody else in the department. The thief had to be someone who was able to override the electronic payment system," I went on, "or dismantle it. Have any of you asked Ms. Evans how she was able to do that? Give her a basic computer test. She hardly knows anything about them."

Hall ignored both my question and my sarcasm. Instead he asked, "What's your opinion of Access Computing?"

"I'm not sure what you mean."

"Is it a bona fide organization?"

"I've no reason to doubt that it is."

"Have you had anything to do with them?"

"No."

"This Angela Carlishaw, you reckon she's for real?"

I knew it was a mistake, but I couldn't help myself. In a loud voice I said, "If I was planning to make a bogus grant to an organization, the very *least* I'd do would be to make it payable to a real person."

HEART RACING, I STOMPED back to my office.

Ivan patted me on the shoulder and made a sympathetic face.

He had his own theory about the police search. "Knew they couldn't find anything, but they had to put up some sort of show. Did you watch their faces? They were just as pissed off being here as *we* were with *them*."

I noticed with surprise that Ivan was not wearing his beanie, or his sweater with the kingfisher design. I looked down. It seemed he'd even pressed his trousers, or attempted to. Perhaps he'd decided he'd get on better with the police if he looked relatively normal.

When his turn came to be interviewed, he seemed to get through it without any problem.

He grinned and said, in his old teasing way, that he'd suggested to Constable Gleeson a more efficient way of putting their fingerprint files on computer.

"How did she take that?"

"Philosophically."

I GUESSED THAT THE man in the crumpled blue suit talking to Detective Sergeant Hall in the corridor was another policeman. He was much shorter than Hall, and shorter than Detective Constable Gleeson as well. The two men stood conferring together in a shallow alcove by the lifts, Hall stooping a little, and the shorter, stockier man shifting his weight around and moving his arms, his face half-hidden under a wide-brimmed Akubra hat. He managed to look unyielding and vulnerable at the same time.

It was what happened next that made me remember the smaller man. In mid-sentence, he stumbled against Hall, knocking his arm and throwing him off balance. Hall moved quickly and gently to steady him and help him upright. Nobody had pushed him, and there'd been nothing for him to stumble over, but I had the feeling that neither man was surprised, that whatever it was had happened before.

AFTER DI TRAPANI'S INTERVIEW with the police, she disappeared into the warm arms of the travel center, either recovering from hard questions or catching up on smokes. When she came back upstairs, she looked more withdrawn and miserable than I'd ever seen her.

The atmosphere in our small office was thickly quiet. The words of the introduction I was trying to write blurred and wriggled in front of my eyes. I glanced up through the window at the trees in Northbourne Avenue. There will be a point, I thought, when the questions will cease. The police will have found out all they can. The inquiry will be over. Maybe it will be next week, or the week after. Maybe I won't know until the questions stop, but I will know it's happened. Like a sponge layer cake that collapses so slowly you don't notice until it has gone flat.

I felt very much alone just then, too frightened of incriminating myself to try and talk to Di, or Bambi, or even Ivan. My belief in Rae Evans's innocence began to seem slippery, dodgy, unsustainable.

Outside, a strong wind, growing stronger, tormented the trees. People hurried, many of them half-crouching, along the footpaths and across the street.

I began to think that maybe the approach the police had used wasn't so silly after all. Taking fingerprints gave them a chance to watch us together, and separately, to note whether we cooperated or objected, whether we were inclined to laugh at the proceedings. If this was a tactic, rather than a way of gaining information valuable in itself, it must be because they suspected one of us.

THERE WAS A PHONE message waiting for me when I returned to my office after a late lunch. Peter was in the sick bay at school with a sore throat and earache. I had to bring him back to work.

I found a spare chair, and sat Peter down beside me while I rang for an appointment at the doctor's.

"G'day there." I heard Guy Harmer's voice as I was putting down the phone. "Ladies got you working, have they?"

I turned to see Peter hesitate for a second, then give Guy a speculative grin. "Nah," he said. "I've got tonsil—tonsil . . ."

"Tonsillitis?"

Peter nodded, taking Guy in from the top of his smooth head to his buffed Italian shoes.

I introduced them. Guy said, "Tonsillitis hurts, doesn't it?"

"A bit," Peter admitted.

"Would you like a butter menthol?" Guy reached into a pocket of his coat and brought out an orange-and-blue packet. He handed the packet to Peter, saying, "Vanessa loves them."

"Who's Vanessa?" Peter asked, taking one of the sweets and beginning to suck on it experimentally.

"My daughter."

"Oh," said Peter. "Has she got a sore throat?"

"She did have," Guy said, taking back the packet. He glanced at me. "Well, I best be making tracks."

"Thanks," said Peter with his mouth full.

I felt grateful to Guy for taking the trouble to notice Peter and say a few kind words to him. Neither Di nor Bambi had bothered. Ivan was out on a job. No other passerby had stopped to say hello.

A public-service office was no place for an eight-year-old. But I couldn't believe that it had never happened before, that I was the first mother ever to bring a sick child into work with her. Because of Guy's friendliness, the department was suddenly a nicer place to be.

I had a meeting at three-thirty. When Ivan came back, I asked him if he'd keep an eye on Peter for an hour or so.

When my meeting finished, I found my son engrossed in a computer game, and Ivan on the phone.

A credible outline of a dog appeared on the screen, a black dog with a big head. Peter labored over the teeth and ears, but the smaller the features the harder he found it. The creature ended up with great long fangs, and ears that might have suited a giant rabbit. But Peter was so pleased with himself he could hardly stay still long enough to finish it. He leapt about in front of the printer, calling excitedly as he watched the thick lines taking shape on the paper.

"Here he is! Here he is! I'll call him Deefa! Like Paul Jennings' story!"

Ivan finished his conversation, and walked across to stand beside me. "A bit like MacDraw," he said shyly, "with a tad more Oz content."

"You wrote it?"

"Yep."

He put an arm round Peter's shoulders while he shut the program down.

"Relax," he told me. "You're a prickly little woman, Sandy. You know that? An echidna woman."

"I wish people would stop saying that."

Ivan looked much nicer without his garish clothes. I wondered if perhaps they were a hangover from some past gesture, or rebellious mood, and that, now he'd discarded them, he'd realized he didn't need to make the statement any longer.

I knew better than to mention it, or compliment him on the change. I thought how defiance can form the core of a person's character, so that you don't know when, if ever, they will get beyond it. And then they can confound you by changing from one minute to the next.

I have to take in new experiences a little at a time. I get confused when a lot is happening at once. I do best when I am able to absorb information slowly, resisting, not always successfully, the impulse to run away and hide behind what I already know.

That evening, when Peter was getting ready for Cubs, I became aware of an odd resemblance between him and Ivan. When Peter pulled his cap down hard on his head, his hair stuck out under it, and to the sides, the way Ivan's used to, under his striped beanie.

"I wonder what Dad's doing right now," Peter said, avoiding looking at me by fidgeting with his blue-and-yellow scarf.

"I guess he's at work. He might be having lunch."

I expected Peter to laugh, as he had before, tickled by the time difference. I wanted him to laugh.

Instead, he looked straight at me and asked, "When's Dad coming home?"

I told him, though I'd told him a dozen times already. He started chattering, telling me a story about a trip he and Derek had made to the Shoalhaven last summer, pretending to forget how often he'd already told me, or perhaps he did forget. But I had the feeling, listening, watching my son, that he was buying time, occupying my attention while he worked out just what questions he could ask and expect a truthful answer.

Ivan didn't present himself as a figure of success to Peter, someone to be admired. Sure, he knew a lot of things, and some he was passionate about, but there was no demand to follow in his footsteps. I don't think anything I'd ever said to Peter impressed him as much as Ivan's story of travel and confusion, and failing to learn to read. It wasn't told as a cautionary tale—simply, that was the boy I was.

Ivan's face reminded me of a landscape with mountains and volcanoes. But it's his mixture of awkwardness and defiance that has stayed with me, as though those two qualities formed one necessary edge. As though he couldn't, or wouldn't, decide which personality suited him best. He had to dare people to pigeon-hole him. And then he had to dare himself to live up, or down, to their expectations.

Life, for Ivan, wasn't what it is for most of us—the tension of relationships, the pull and counter-pull and drift of love. It was his own personality that held him in thrall. His persona, his character, was a piece of elastic, to be pulled and then let snap.

He had his own special greeting for me in the mornings:

When I went into Peter's room that night to clear away roll-up wrappers and empty fruit boxes, our new computer screen was a huge kaleidoscopic eye, noting my every move.

Ivan had brought Peter a christening present, a spelling program he'd designed himself. Cartoon characters sprouted words from the tops of their heads. The common words Peter had trouble with grew legs and arms, made farting noises. Peter had pronounced it awesome.

Gail Trembath phoned while I was brushing my teeth.

"I rang some of those women," she said. "Like you asked me to, you know?"

I apologized for having a mouthful of toothpaste, then began to thank her. She cut me off.

"Was quizzing one about her jobs, her kids, sticking to the brief you gave me. She told me her name and address had found its way onto a mailing list for a software company. Scads of junk mail, brochures for stuff she couldn't possibly afford. Phone calls at night. She told them to stop, but the message was rather slow in getting through."

"What's the name of the company?"

"Compic."

"Had you heard of them before?"

"Looked them up in the book. Local outfit."

"And?"

"I checked to see if we've got any of their stuff at work."

"Have you?"

"A CD. Some crap about meat pies."

I laughed, remembering the cloud of potato.

"That's interesting," I said. "Our IT director bought a heap of their software. Is that CD a demonstration one, or has your office bought the package, too?"

"Dunno," Gail said.

"Can you check?"

"Does it matter?"

"Maybe not," I said. "But if the package is popular enough to be turning up everywhere, I'd like to find out why."

BREAKING
RULES

E'RE INVISIBLE," I SAID to Rae. "We're definitely
not here."

There was just enough light left for me to catch
her smile. I thought how strange it was that while
I'd been shy during our lunches, holding some-
thing back, then rebuffed in my attempts to contact her since her suspen-
sion from the department, now that Rae was to be tried in the Supreme
Court and we were meeting in secret, I felt relaxed in her company, ready
for anything.

I could feel her breath in the near dark, and was glad of the clouds
that had brought an early sunset to the lake by Black Mountain Penin-
sula. I hoped the twilight might make her more inclined to confide in me.
I was aware that at any moment she might change her mind, tell me she
couldn't talk to me after all, jump into her car and disappear.

We began walking slowly along a gravel path a few meters from the
water's edge. Some trees seemed to catch the wind a lot more than others,
as though the wind was being deliberately selective. Rae's coat blew open,
and her white blouse seemed to reach out to the coming night.

"Who did this to you?" I asked. "You must have some idea."

"I didn't know anyone disliked me quite that much," she said.

I had the feeling that, through some added sense, the borrowing of some nocturnal animal's large eyes, Rae could see me better than I could see her. The last of the purple light seemed to come off the water, rather than the sky. A flock of ducks passed overhead, a darker shadow against the lake.

"They're up late," I said.

I'd never taken Peter for a swim in the lake. Something about the water bothered me, and now my unease seemed justified, closer to its source. When I'd pulled up in the parking lot, I'd noticed pelicans on the roundabout—three, maybe one more lying down. They were sharply angled, reminding me of those metal construction sets that had been replaced by LEGO.

"What were you and Felix Wenborn arguing about that day in the lift?"

At first I thought Rae wasn't going to answer, then she said, "I was asked to deal with a complaint about a contract. Not by Felix. Jim Wilcox asked me. Felix had given a development contract to this company, a local company actually, and there was a complaint about collusive tendering. Wilcox asked me to look into it."

"I don't understand. What's collusive tendering?"

"It's when favorable treatment is given to a company. Departments have big budgets, and there's an awful lot of people out there competing for a share." Rae laughed unhappily, no doubt thinking of Access Computing, and the bonus share of money they'd received. "What's supposed to happen," she went on, "—and this applies to everything from small printing jobs to big software engineering contracts—is that firms bid for them, send in quotes, and so on. That's called tendering. And collusive tendering is when the official in charge doesn't follow the proper procedure, but shows favoritism."

After this long speech, Rae sighed, and I felt the tickle of her breath against my cheek.

"What was the name of the company?"

"Compic."

"Had you heard of them before?"

"No."

The coincidence made me feel light-headed. I'd asked Gail exactly the same questions only the night before. I did not feel that I could tell Rae about my conversation with Gail. She'd want to know how a reporter had got hold of contact details for my outworkers. If I told her the truth, she might refuse to talk to me anymore. It had been hard enough getting her to agree to this meeting.

"Who filed the complaint?" I asked.

"A man named Bernard Whitelaw. His company's called Phoenix Enterprises. I don't know anything about them. I had to leave before I could find out."

"Were you arguing with Felix because he didn't think you should be checking up on him?"

"You could put it like that."

"Did you suspect that he'd been playing favorites?"

"I was just doing what Wilcox told me to do. I was surprised he'd picked me, but he was my boss. I couldn't say no. And then, of course, when the money went missing—Felix was furious about that."

The wind strengthened, and I pulled my jacket tighter.

"How far did you get with the complaint?"

Rae was silent.

"What happened?"

"I was threatened," she said softly.

"How? Who by?"

"E-mails," Rae said. "I asked Felix to trace them. He couldn't. He said he couldn't, anyhow."

"What did they say?"

"To back off." Rae paused. Now I wished the light was strong enough for me to be able to see her expression clearly. When she spoke again, her voice was still soft, but full of contempt. "I was to write back and tell Mr. Whitelaw that all the correct procedures had been followed."

"The e-mails told you to ignore the complaint?"

"That's right."

89

"How many?"

"Five altogether."

"From the same address?"

"No. Different ones."

"Do you have copies?"

"So far as I know, they're still on my computer. I made hard copies, too."

"What did you do about the warning?"

"Apart from informing Felix? I ignored it."

I told Rae about my virus then, and the message that had come with it, adding that I thought it had to be someone from our building.

"Sandra," Rae said when I'd finished. Her voice was unnaturally calm. "It's worse than you think. There was a deposit in my bank account. A big one. Twenty thousand."

"Your cut of the million dollars?"

"Obviously meant to look like it.' Rae was silent for a moment, then went on, "Do you know—the police took my electric toaster. It's funny isn't it? I don't even have a home computer."

"It must have been horrible."

"It was unbelievable."

"I guess they were searching for bank records."

"I always keep my bank statements in the toaster," Rae said coldly. "I find it does them to a turn."

"Could it be somebody from Compic?"

"I did a bit of background checking before they threw me out. Compic's been very successful with their graphics, and now they're expanding. I don't know if they have the expertise to do what they claim to be able to. There's only one director, a young woman." Rae gave another short, unhappy laugh. "Though I, of all people, shouldn't consider *that* a drawback. Why shouldn't a young woman be capable of heading up a successful company?"

"What's her name?"

"Allison something. Edgecliff—Edgeware—that's it. I don't know why Felix gave her firm the contract. He was furious with me, and I found it impossible to talk to him about it. But it seems to me there were questions that needed to be asked, and that Mr. Whitelaw might have had a case."

"What's the contract for?"

"To develop a program for something the department needs, or would need, if it stays afloat. A user-friendly way of organizing our regulations on-line, the ones we're always being asked about, that affect so many businesses and workers."

"But that's a massive job."

"Well, Compic got it."

"By manipulating the system from the inside?"

"There's no evidence of that, Sandra," Rae said, looking directly at me, "I've told you all this because you've been good enough to say you believe in me. I didn't steal that money, but you should stay out of it. It really isn't any of your business."

"I can't *stay* out. I'm already in."

"Why do you want to help me, anyway?"

"Let's just put it down to old loyalties."

After another short silence, I asked, "Does Access Computing have any sister outfits?"

"If you mean similar self-help organizations for women, then I'm not aware of any."

"What about other organizations who applied for that grant and weren't successful?"

Rae swung round and began walking back the way we'd come. It seemed I'd said something to offend her.

"Angela Carlishaw is on a retreat,' she said. 'If Angela was a priest in a cassock, would people believe her? It's a beautiful place apparently, a spiritual place. An old Scottish nunnery."

"You've talked to Angela Carlishaw yourself?"

"No. I spoke to the other one, Isobel. On the phone. She told me Angela was in Scotland. There isn't any phone."

"And you believed this Isobel person?"

"Why shouldn't I? You know—" Rae turned to stare behind her at the water. "Ages ago, when they were flooding the lake, I came down here to watch. Slow brown water just edging toward me. And the earth underneath it was brown, too. Silky. I used to think how easy it would be."

"Don't," said. The palms of my hands began to sweat. I repeated my assurance that I'd help her if I could.

Rae thanked me with a catch in her voice, then asked, "Remember our lunch that day?"

I wondered which one she meant.

"You asked me why I hadn't fired Dianne for not doing the work. You know, I don't believe in omens. But the truth is I'd given up on Di and Bambi. What was one more report when the whole department was going to be trashed? But there was just enough money to hire an extra person for six months. And then I saw your name on the list of applicants. I wanted one good thing to come out of the mess."

"I'll make sure our report gets out on time. I'm not sure I understand. What was the omen?"

When Rae didn't answer, I asked, "You'd got one of those e-mails?"

"That morning."

"Why didn't you tell anyone?"

"I told Felix."

I'd meant, of course, why hadn't she told me.

"Sandra?'

"Yes?"

"Don't tell anyone you've been talking to me, will you?"

I promised that I wouldn't.

DRIVING HOME, I COULDN'T help thinking how differently my mother would have reacted. My mother would have shouted, run about, hired three lawyers, sacked them, hired half-a-dozen more, until she found one with the guts and spirit to give the case her best.

I'd left the parking lot feeling that Rae was now, somehow, depending on me. A set of headlights stayed roughly the same distance behind me, turning left when I did onto Barry Drive, and then Northbourne Avenue. I supposed there was nothing unusual in that. I felt clumsy and disoriented. A cyclist wearing black, and with only a dim headlight, veered in front of me, and I almost hit him. I was glad Peter was having dinner at Ivan's. I wasn't thinking clearly. The idea that Access Computing might have rivals niggled away at the back of my mind. On the whole, I decided I'd rather look up the information on their grants myself. Jim Wilcox, who was Felix's boss as well as Rae's and mine, had deliberately put Rae in the position of having to check up on Felix. Why?

Rae had let the press have a field day, chasing the retreating Angela, making fun of her. It occurred to me that she might be protecting someone. But why should that someone be worth her own career?

IVAN BROUGHT PETER HOME hours late, red-faced, flushed with triumph. They'd found a fault in one of the machines in the video arcade, and had been playing it for free all evening.

"What happened to dinner?" I hustled Peter through the door and glared at Ivan. "Don't you know what time it is?"

"Mum!" cried Peter. "The guy was such a dork! He didn't even see!"

Peter's skin was glassy, his forehead hot. He was asleep practically before I'd turned the light out.

Ivan put on the saucepan for hot chocolate.

His frown said he could see that I was angry, but no harm had been done. The cold of the winter night came off him in small waves, and he looked very Russian.

We sat at the kitchen table with our drinks between us.

"There's these parent-teacher interviews," I said. "Next week. She hasn't isolated Peter like she threatened to, but that doesn't mean she won't."

Ivan gave me a straight look. "Why don't I come with you?"

"You?"

He jutted his chin out, twisting his mouth in a parody of eager help-fulness. "Why not?"

"You're not Peter's father."

"Full marks for that one, Sandy."

I'd hurt him, and I'd meant to, and there was an awful, shameful pleasure in it. I couldn't tell him I'd been talking to Rae Evans. I couldn't tell him he'd chosen the worst possible night to keep my son out late.

"I told you what that teacher's like. She implied that Peter's trouble in class was caused by his father going to America. And then you turn up."

"Are you sure you're not exaggerating?" Ivan's voice was calm now, his face closed. He'd retreated into himself. That was usually my tactic.

"I might be," I said. "But it's not worth the risk."

Ivan stood up and took his mug over to the sink. The sound of run-ning water as he rinsed it grated on my nerves.

He turned and looked at me, hesitating, then took a step toward the door. I knew he was waiting for me to speak again, end our conversation on a friendlier note.

I could not think what to say that would be conciliatory, yet truthful; for the truth was, just then I did not want Ivan in my house at all.

My meeting with Rae, and everything she'd told me, weighed darkly on my mind. My promise not speak of the meeting had come easily and naturally when I'd made it, but now I realized what it meant. I could talk to no one, share my feelings and ideas with no one. I couldn't break that promise, but I wished I hadn't made it. In spite of Ivan's evident dislike for Rae, in spite of my irritation with him for keeping Peter out late, I longed to sit him back down again, tell him how I'd spent the evening, where I'd been.

My fear that I would do this made me say, brusquely and coldly, "Goodnight."

"Goodnight," Ivan repeated. "Don't get up. I'll let myself out."

* * *

AS SOON AS I got to work the next morning, I asked Deirdre if I could have a look at the grant applications. I wasn't sure what I was hoping to find—a rival company with a grudge against Access Computing that stuck out a mile? An individual, or set of individuals with a golden motive, not to mention opportunity, for stealing the money and pinning the theft on Rae?

Deirdre looked at me from under her flat gray fringe and asked, "What for?"

"Well, we're doing a section on current government assistance for the report," I told her, biting my tongue with the lameness of my reason. "I need to have a look at what kinds of groups put in applications."

"The police went through them all."

I was aware of Deirdre's uncertainty, and how it mustn't be much fun sitting in her small office adjoining Rae's empty one, day after day, copping endless questions and insinuations.

"That big detective sergeant's a pain, isn't he?" I smiled, hoping Deirdre would smile back.

She didn't, but she stood up and moved over to the filing cabinet.

I took the grant applications back to my office and read them over lunch, while things were quiet. I didn't want Ivan, or anybody else, breathing down my neck.

There were twenty-six, but it didn't take me long to go through them. Applicants had to answer questions about the origins of their group or company, how long they'd been in business, their philosophy, and their commitment to fostering computer literacy and awareness in the community. There were several retail stores claiming to provide special services to customers, and seven or eight small businesses whose sole purpose seemed to be to provide technical support. The rest were software companies. Compic, I noted, was not among them. On the face of it, Access Computing seemed a clear winner. Their application stood out like a parrot in a bedraggled flock of starlings.

Ivan propped in the doorway and told me I was working too hard.

I wanted to apologize for the night before, but I couldn't find the right words.

I asked him if he knew that Rae Evans had been asked to deal with a complaint about a contract.

He nodded, and told me that Felix had made a fuss about it, outraged that anyone would dare to question his integrity.

"Why was Rae Evans asked to deal with it?"

"Search me. She managed to get Felix's back up even further, that I do know."

I turned away, annoyed again with Ivan for using the opportunity to say something critical about Rae. I didn't invite him over that night, and he said nothing about his after-work arrangements.

I took the applications back to Deirdre and thanked her for letting me see them.

IN THE MIDDLE OF the night, my bedroom door opened.

"Mum?" Peter's voice was husky with fear.

"What is it?"

"Mummy?" He stood still, just inside the doorway. "I had a bad dream," he said in a small child's voice.

As a toddler, Peter had come hurtling to Derek and me in the night, howling and flinging himself on our bed, as if only the speed of reaching us could push the nightmare back.

I reached up and switched on my bed light. Still, Peter didn't move.

I held out my arms. "Come and have a cuddle."

He slid into bed beside me. I kissed the top of his head, then his forehead at the hairline, where the hair grew fluffy.

He snuggled up to me as he hadn't done for ages, to whisper in my ear, "When's Dad coming home?"

"At Christmas."

"Why won't Dad be here for my birthday?"

"Because it's too expensive."

"I want to stay with Dad for the school holidays."

A dagger of cold air passed between us. I could tell by Peter's voice that he'd thought of this plan some time ago.

I took him back to his room and tucked him in. He told me that he was old enough to go to America on his own, and Dad would take him to a cheese factory to make up for forgetting to send those pictures.

PETER AND
THE WOLF

IANNE TRAPANI PULLED OUT another cigarette. Her brother, Tony, gave her a sideways glance, his full lips set in an expression of discomfort.

I'd been going to spend my lunch hour doing messages when Di had waved me over.

"What's up?" I'd asked. It was obvious that something was bugging her more than usual.

Now fifteen minutes had passed, and I'd given up my shopping plans. I munched a leaky salad roll while Dianne told me the story of her brother's troubles at the university.

The head of the computing department was convinced that Tony and his friends had been pinching time on his Internet account.

"Have you?" I asked, looking straight at Tony.

He shook his head, moving the froth around on the top of his cappuccino. He had his sister's blue-black eyebrows, and the hair to go with them.

Di blew a smoke ring, exchanged another glance with her brother, and said, "If Mum and Dad find out, they'll stop supporting him. Poor old Tone will be out on his ear." She coughed and picked at a spot on her black dress with long purple fingernails. Her dress looked worn and dusty, her dyed and carefully mussed-up hair more like a wig than ever.

"What happened?" I asked Tony.

"One of our assignments." Tony's voice was soft and shy. "A question had a mistake in it. Like two, actually. I pointed them out to Prof. Bailey, and he argued with me. He left the question as it was, so no one got it right. Some of the guys complained, and he took it out on me."

"But someone's been using the professor's account? Is that correct?"

"Yeah, but that's not to say we did. It could be anyone."

Tony glanced at Dianne from under thick black eyelashes. The connection between them was momentarily so strong it was like a fourth person sitting at the table. I finished my roll. I still felt hungry, but I didn't want to waste time in a queue of bus travelers.

It may have been the lighting, and her purple nails and lipstick, but the whole of Dianne's face looked flat. I tried and failed to imagine what it would be like to have her for a sister.

"What school does your son go to, Sandra?" she asked me.

"Lyneham Primary," I said, thinking she already knew this.

"Bailey lives in your area doesn't he? Close to the university. Does he have any children at your son's school?"

"His youngest daughter. I've seen him with her at school functions. Once or twice. I don't go to them often."

Suddenly, I saw a way, or thought I did, to improve relations between Dianne and myself, perhaps even make her obligated to me.

"There's a fund-raising event coming up," I said. "Would you like me to try and talk to Bailey, if he's there? I might be able to find out a bit more about what's going on."

"That would be great," Dianne said, narrowing her eyes at her brother, who nodded and smiled at me encouragingly.

"I'll see what I can do," I told them.

That evening, as I drove across the lake to pick Peter up from his new friend's house, I decided that if I was going to speak to Bailey on Tony's behalf, I needed to speak to Tony again first.

I recalled Dianne's look of satisfaction when I'd offered to try and help her brother. I was beginning to wish I'd kept my mouth shut. It wasn't as though Bailey was a pal. I'd only met him at a school concert, and a bush dance where he'd mashed my feet in Split the Willow.

I'd plunged back into full-time work, into a project I cared about that a new government would axe, and that, with Rae Evans gone, had no one in charge of it, no one to steer it through. I was a single parent for a year. Surely that was enough. But I was determined to defend Rae somehow, and defend myself against that nasty message. Though Di had shown no sign of support for Rae, I needed all the allies and potential allies I could get.

I looked up and saw the Parliament House flag hanging motionless on its giant mast, steam from the boilers rising underneath it. It's wrong to say that evergreen trees have no seasons. From June onward, the wattle is getting ready to flower, from a distance a dull yellow haze against the leaves. Blossoms slowly swell under the green skin of acacias.

COMING BACK FROM A lightning trip to the mall next day, I saw Tony Trapani at a corner table of the bistro, sharing a coffee with a boy about his own age. The boy was smoking, and scowling into what looked like an empty cup. I noticed that his black leather jacket had two perfectly round holes on the left side, as though someone had shot at him or, perhaps, a former owner of the jacket.

"Hi," I said, walking toward them.

Both looked up, Tony surprised. The other boy's scowl barely shifted.

"Have you seen my sister?" Tony asked. "She was supposed to meet us down here."

"She was upstairs when I left."

I held my hand out to the boy in black, introduced myself, then sat down.

"I was going to phone you," I said to Tony, "before I try talking to Professor Bailey."

Tony blushed, glancing mutely at his friend.

"Bailey sucks," the boy in black said.

"Tell me about it." I found it hard to keep my eyes from the lethal holes in his leather jacket.

"Mad bomber. Opens fire for no reason."

"You mean in lectures?"

"All to do with quotas. He told us at the start he was gonna fail a third of us. The whole system sucks."

"Nobody likes him." Tony's voice was gentler, but his condemnation in a way was more severe.

"Know what some of the guys did once?" the boy in black went on. "Had all calls to his office switched to Rosie's. That's, like, a brothel out in Fyshwick."

"That was you two, was it?"

"No way."

"It was just a joke," Tony explained.

His friend rubbed the rim of the cup as though more coffee might magically appear, and said, "Bailey's dishonest, he's sloppy and he hates students. He's the best argument for getting rid of tenure that I know."

When it came to understanding male adolescents, I had it all ahead of me, but I saw Peter in Tony Trapani, in his look of slyness when he was trying not to smile, when his lips just wouldn't hang a straight line, and in the swing of his fine black hair, darker than Peter's, and much longer, his skin soft as the first morning without frost.

"Do you have any other brothers or sisters?" I asked him, when his friend got up to buy more coffee.

"No, just Di and me."

"How did your sister get a job in Labor Relations?"

Tony looked surprised, then said, 'Di knows heaps about statistical modeling, all that stuff." After a moment he added, "Evans wanted my sister, so she had to take that whats-her-name as well."

"Bambi, you mean? You know her?"

"Nah." He blushed. "Well, I've, like, seen her in the park. Ateeq's incredible, you know. His folks are from Pakistan. He never had a Christmas present till I gave him one."

Ateeq came back with a single cup of coffee. Following a routine that was clearly well established, he sugared the coffee, swallowed a large mouthful, and handed it across to Tony.

That morning, I'd asked Dianne why she thought Bailey suspected her brother. She'd explained that Tony and a few of his friends had been spending their nights logged on to various computer clubs. The main point seemed to be that the entertainment they were into was expensive.

"Why don't you go to one of your other teachers?" I asked Tony. "Or the student counselor?"

"No one'll go against Bailey. They're all, like, really scared of him."

I turned to Ateeq, and asked bluntly, "Who pays *your* bills?"

"Teeq's parents own Akewa Hi-Fi," Tony answered for him.

"So your parents pay?"

Ateeq nodded with a bored expression.

"Do you keep the bills?"

"Of course."

"Then why don't you present Professor Bailey with them? Explain that money's no problem. You don't need to use his account."

"He ripped the bills up. Said they were a fake." Tony spoke so softly he was almost whispering, then ran his tongue around his teeth.

Ateeq looked at his watch and nodded, and the two young men got up to go. Tony said goodbye politely. Ateeq barely glanced at me.

I WAS IRRITATED THAT I'd been roped into the costume party. Peter had insisted. He'd come home from school yabbering about it. But now I had a motive for going.

It was Ivan, of course it was Ivan, who gave us the idea for our costumes. When I told him about the party, and said I didn't think I could get out of it, Ivan smiled as though just such an opportunity was bound to have come up. He had it all worked out.

"We shall be three wise guys from *Peter and the Wolf*. Peter as himself, naturally, myself as Ivan the Cat, and you, my dear Sandy as—the hunter!"

Half-protesting, I said, "It's just an idea the social committee's dreamed up. Are you sure you can be bothered?"

"Only problem's finding a cat skin," Ivan growled. "Have to go bush and skin me a feral cat!"

"Yuk!" cried Peter. "Can I come?"

Peter's costume was easy. He could wear his own gum boots with tracksuit pants and a red cloth cap that Ivan produced from his collection, and carry a coil of rope and a popgun.

Ivan seemed to have sources from which he could produce practically anything at short notice. I hadn't seen a popgun like it since I was a kid. It was the traditional tin rifle, with a cork on a string. The cork and the string were both new, but the gun itself looked old.

Peter had his own plans. He intended going to the party as Croc Dundee, and got as far as borrowing a neighbor's scout hat and stock-whip.

He writhed around the living room making huge snapping movements with his jaws, then, switching roles in the flash of an eye, cracked his whip and chased an imaginary crocodile across the tropical river of our carpet, yelling like a demon.

I was all for letting Peter do what he wanted. What did it matter? It was just a dumb old school fund-raiser. But Ivan was determined that we should do this his way. Peter and the Wolf it was going to be.

I spent an hour riffling through costumes in a theater supply and-hire place, looking for something to wear, while Peter spent a fortune in the video arcade next door.

Through the thin dividing wall, I could hear the guns and high nasal whirr of fighter planes. When Peter appeared in the doorway asking for more money, I still hadn't made up my mind. In the end he helped me choose, and I paid the sales assistant, who sat on a high stool in a corner with her knitting and her radio, and glared at me like the public lavatory attendants used to when he was a toddler. She bunged my costume into a plastic bag and warned me against tearing or staining it.

"Do you want the gun?"

"Pardon?"

"There's a gun that goes with the costume. Do you wish to take it as well?"

"Go on Mum!" cried Peter.

"Well, okay," I said. "I guess. If it's no extra."

Walking into the street after the tense stuffiness of the shop was like entering a giant refrigerator, feeling a knife blade slice underneath my sinuses, filling spaces I did not know I had with freezing air.

IVAN HAD A CLARINET, and surprisingly, or not surprisingly, he could play a few notes on it. On the night of the party, he entered our hosts' living room to a reedy rendition of Prokofiev's triumph, Peter marching in step beside him, alternately speechless with self-importance, and overcome with giggles.

We paused for effect in the doorway, or rather Ivan did. I got stuck behind him. Peter ducked under our elbows with a cry of "Yo, Ian!"

Within fifteen minutes, my son had shed the lot—gun and rope, hat and boots—borrowed a samurai sword, and was alternately stuffing his mouth with chips, and chopping great slices out of his classmates.

"Bambi should be here," I murmured. "With her flair for dressing up."

Ivan was cross because no one took much notice of us. I watched from a corner of the living room as new arrivals entered the spotlight, expecting the audience in front of them to applaud in some way, to laugh at the humor of their costumes, or to clap. Disappointment was cold on their faces when they saw more imaginative or funnier characters than they had dreamed up, or, their moment of entry having come and gone, they stood looking deflated, as laughter and clapping greeted the next arrival, rival in their eyes.

I felt embarrassed for Ivan, and annoyed with him, for competing with these people and for showing it.

I recognized a couple of Lyneham parents under their masks and makeup, but my lack of participation in school functions was obvious to me and, I was afraid, to everybody else. I was one of those mothers who never did canteen, or any other kind of school duty, and here I was attempting to make up for it. I'd forked out thirty bucks at the door, because I suddenly couldn't bear the thought of Ivan paying for himself.

A large man with a bottle of claret approached Ivan demanding loudly, "Cheshire or Garfield?"

Ivan shoved his cat's head off his face with the back of his hand and ignored the offered wine, replying rudely, "Nothing so boring, *mate*."

He spotted a pride of lions in a corner by the fireplace, handling a champagne bottle with great care. The big cats, some with manes, greeted him with raised paws.

A little later, I heard him declaiming to a bald man, "VR systems eat MIPs for breakfast." The man looked puzzled, but nodded his head with the shiny regularity of a metronome.

Another man was vaguely familiar to me behind a Roman centurion's helmet that hid most of his face. He held out his hand to shake mine, tipping his visor back with his other hand. I recognised Professor Bailey.

Plunging in, I told him I'd met Tony Trapani, that he seemed a likeable sort of kid, and I wondered what the trouble was.

"I know that girl," Bailey said with a scowl, his visor slipping back over his eyes. "Trapani's sister. Smart kid. They both are. Pity."

I hadn't bargained on having to talk to Bailey without being able to see his face. I took a deep breath and said, "I'm sure it can be sorted out."

Bailey hissed through his visor, "There is a *ring*. A student racket. Don't know if Trapani's at the center of it, but he's definitely involved."

"What exactly did they do?"

"Believe me, there's no doubt of it. I'm not responsible for the messes these kids get themselves into, and I thank God for that!"

"But what's Tony done?" I persisted.

"Computer security's non-existent on campus!" Bailey shouted. I realized too late that he was drunk. "Police don't want to know! Even if they did, they haven't got the skills or the resources! Trapani's a miserable little fish who happened to get himself sucked in!"

I was conscious of people staring at us, my grasp on the situation slipping right away.

"I'll tell you what I have got!" Bailey yelled. "I've got over four hundred students, most of whom have the sense to stay out of trouble! This time I've caught the ringleaders, and I'm giving them the mother of all frights!"

He swung around, performing a complicated maneuver with his spear, and called out, "Ivan Dimitrich! Silicon jockey of the old school! How are you, you mangy feline!"

Ivan hadn't been anywhere near me when I'd started talking to Bailey. Now he was just behind us.

Startled, I said, "I didn't realize you two knew each other."

Peter came running up, wanting to know where the toilet was.

Ivan offered to take him, while Bailey clasped my hand and pulled me closer. He pushed his helmet back again, and shoved his red face right up next to mine, shouting, "Caught the little turds red-handed!"

"Excuse me." I moved back, wrenching my hand from his grip.

"Goners! Hoist by their own petards!"

I resisted the impulse to take out my handkerchief and wipe my face.

Bailey thumped his spear on the floor. I noticed that it was made out of an old broom handle. He clearly loved the chance to dress up and bang things on the floor.

Defeated, I backed away, saying, "I think I'd better check up on my son."

I found Ivan in the kitchen. A woman in a long white dress had pushed him up against the fridge and was lecturing him in a hissing voice.

"I hate computers. Horrible soulless things."

"Ivan," I said, pulling him by the arm.

"Just a minute, Sandy. Your washing machine and your stove, do you hate them, too?" Ivan asked the woman in a voice that was dangerously polite. "Your fridge?" He reached behind him and calmly patted the one that was holding him up, or preventing his escape.

A small girl in a fairy costume asked if I could pour her a glass of water.

"That's different," I heard the woman in white say. "People glorify computers."

When I turned around again, Ivan had his cat skin pushed right to the back of his head. "I'll tell you one thing computers are better at than humans," he said, his politeness turning acid. "It's a small thing, but it's important. Once you tell a computer something, it never forgets."

With a look of disgust, the woman turned her back on him, emptying the remains of a bottle of Jim Beam into her wine glass.

I moved Ivan out of the kitchen to a corridor, where we were alone except for a man in a crisp new trench coat, felt hat, and dark glasses, waiting with apparent nonchalance outside the bathroom door.

"Did you know Di Trapani's brother and his friends are going to be called before a university tribunal?"

Ivan shook his head.

"Go back in there and talk to Bailey. Find out what's really going on. How could you let me front up to him like that without telling me you knew him?"

"I can explain that."

I pushed Ivan in the middle of the back. "Just go!"

His cat's head gave a lurch. I watched him walk up to Bailey and begin talking. Bailey did some more spear thumping, then pointedly turned his back.

The party was spoilt for me. I went into the bedroom to get my coat. As I bent to pick it up from underneath the pile, I heard a loud rip. Cold air flashed across my backside. I clasped my hand over torn taffeta. My underwear was gaping through a hole in my costume.

I stood in the doorway, looking round for Peter. He was talking excitedly in a circle of his friends. They were getting ready to announce the prizes. I couldn't see Bailey anywhere. Maybe he'd passed out, or maybe the woman in the white dress had got him. Ivan was on his own behind a group of children. I could edge my way toward him. Probably no one would notice the rip in my pants. Most of the kids were squashed together on the floor, their costumes blending together, too, Cinderella into Batman, a clutch of Ninja Turtles.

I caught Ivan's attention and waved him over to me.

In the hallway, Peter giggled at the sight of me and cried, "Mum! Y'll havta mend it!"

AS A REWARD FOR not complaining about missing out on supper, I gave Peter four chocolate biscuits as soon as we got home. He shoved them into his mouth two at a time while I helped him with his boots.

When he was finally in bed, I asked Ivan what he'd managed to get out of Bailey.

"It's no big deal," Ivan said.

"Well he obviously wants to expel them, so it is for them. And he was talking about some sort of student racket. What did he tell you about that?"

"He was too drunk to make sense."

"How well do you know him?"

"Well enough to keep my distance."

Ivan's cat skin was draped over the back of the sofa. Away from the party lights, it looked mangy and moth-eaten. Actually, it had looked pretty mangy at the party, too. Its tabby grays and browns were dull, and the fur had thinned in spots to nothing but dry skin. Once Ivan had shed it, along with his coat and boots, he paid no attention to it.

"I keep thinking of Peter needing help and not knowing how to ask for it," I said.

"You can't be everybody's fairy godmother, Sandra."

Hurt, I turned away.

Ivan followed me. "Bailey should have locked Tony and his mates out, and left it at that. They're *kids* for Christ's sake! Instead of which he dances round like Nellie Melba with ants in her knickers. He was like that when I worked for him."

"You used to work for him?"

Ivan nodded, and said he'd worked in Bailey's department the first year he'd come back to Canberra. They'd disliked each other intensely from day one, and Bailey had had Ivan replaced as soon as he could.

"You should have told me all of this before."

"I know. It was dumb. I'm sorry."

Stories were somehow skewed, off-center, in the way Ivan told them, passed them on. And the stories he became part of had a habit of turning on their sides. After that party, the original version of *Peter and the Wolf*, the one I'd known as a child, came back to surprise me, a small nervous hiatus between one heartbeat and the next. It reminded me how far the three of us—Ivan, Peter, and myself—had come, and what, on the night of the party, marked a turning point.

THE GIFT
HORSE

LYING NAKED IN FRONT of a combustion stove is not at all the same as lying naked in front of an open fire. My combustion stove was a relatively small one, black, on four squat legs. I opened the doors and tried to fluff up the coals, while Ivan fussed in the kitchen. You had to sit up to see the fire. You couldn't lie down, or lean on one elbow, and watch it at the same time, and there was no way it was going to warm the whole length of you. I pulled floor cushions closer to the hearth tiles. The living-room light was off, but the light from the kitchen, shining through open doors, was enough to see our hot chocolate by. We sipped it, and then, because there was nothing left to do, we got undressed.

Ivan stood in front of the stove, blocking the square of light it gave. The fine black hair covering his chest seemed to take the shape of a kite, decorated with letters in an unknown alphabet. At the same time, through some strange displacement, the light he blocked looked as though it was shining out of him, from his skin and bright black thatch of hair.

"Why me?" I asked softly, half not wanting him to hear me.

"Your look of desperation, Sandy," Ivan whispered back. "That first day. The way you hid behind that dinky plant of yours."

"Dinky? I'll admit to nervous."

"Me, too," he said. "I get nervous, too."

Our lovemaking was so quiet and unassuming that I was fooled into believing I'd stepped over no fiery line, no burning branch of mine or anybody else's planting.

That night, I dreamed of Rae Evans standing in a courtroom. The magistrate and everybody else, including me, wore gowns of rusty black, while Rae's white face was huge, expressionless, a mask without an actor. White was for brides, shining; also for surrenders.

I woke Ivan in the middle of the night to ask, "What did your mother die of?"

He said, "A broken heart, I think."

I made him get out of bed and leave before dawn, well before I heard the first stirrings of the new day from Peter's room.

I puttered about the house all morning, while Peter played computer games. In the afternoon, we went over to Ivan's place.

His garden was a mess, which did not surprise me. He had never struck me as a man who'd spend hours mowing lawns. Of course, you didn't need to mow your lawn in winter, but last summer's long dead whispering grass brushed against the fences and veranda posts, making a faint woosha in the wind, overlaid and accompanied by an irregular tlunking sound. I looked around to see what it was—a loose bit of tin on the carport roof.

Peter said it was like the enchanted wood. He had sore ears again, and I'd made him wear a woolen hat and scarf. At Ivan's front door he ripped them off, calling, "Ivan! Hiya! We're here!" There was no bell, or door knocker, but a sleeping giant would have heard him.

Grass and weeds grew thickly round the carport, and through cracks in the concrete.

Peter was dancing from one foot to the other, shouting, "Mum! Try round the back!" when Ivan opened his front door.

"Welcome to my devil's kitchen." He winked and made a face, arms held out for Peter to run into them.

Peter ran straight past, while I looked around, keeping an eye out for a photograph, the residue of a woman's touch, blushing because I couldn't imagine Ivan's ex-wife in any but a *Penthouse* kind of way.

For a moment I was back there, in the ease and quietness of the night before, with the feeling that what had happened was some small and scarcely counted further step that both of us might ignore if we chose.

"Biggest computer museum in the southern hemisphere," Ivan boasted, leading us to the door of his workroom, standing aside for us to admire.

This time Peter didn't let him down. "Wow!" he cried, running from one piece of equipment to another, trying out whatever he could get his hands on.

I didn't want to touch anything. I didn't even want to step inside.

The light in the room was silver, filtered through grevillea juniperina, the same spiky dark green bush that Derek had planted in front of our house because it grew so fast. I cut it back each year to stop it strangling the daphne.

Thick nests of cables filled the shadows, while the walls of Ivan's museum, as he called it, were painted black and white, like an enormous checkerboard. On one wall hung a row of framed certificates with red seals at the bottom. Bachelor of Computer Science—I read the nearest one—University of Queensland.

Peter skittered from screen to screen. He skimmed and landed, giving each machine a pollen-dusting of attention.

A large map covered the wall closest to the door. Moving closer, I saw that it was of the Moscow underground, patched in several places with clear sticky tape.

A row of hats sat along the top of a bookshelf filled with CDs, boxes of floppy disks, and manuals. On the bottom shelf, a large orange Garfield was arranged in the act of pouncing on a mouse.

"Who's that?" I pointed to a black-and-white photograph of a man with a long silver beard cut square above a flowered cravat. White hair, standing up at the top and out to the sides, matched lowering white eyebrows and a thick moustache. From what I could see of the man's mouth, it looked as though he might be in the middle of an argument with the photographer. He wore a black suit, and the entire background to the photograph was black, so that his face, hair, and beard stood out remarkably. He looked like Ivan might in thirty, thirty-five years time.

"You don't know? That's Alexander Graham Bell."

On the opposite wall was what looked like an entire telephone exchange suitable for a small town. Red and green lights flashed along the bottom. There was a drawing of Wilhelm Leibniz showing his Stepped Reckoner to the Royal Society in 1694, and a much larger drawing of Charles Babbage's Analytical Engine. And, beneath them, what Ivan later explained to me was a scale model of the Harvard Mark I, completed in 1944. The original was fifteen meters long and two-and-a-half meters high.

He turned away from my bewilderment to answer Peter's questions. Listening to the two of them, I had another disconcerting, kaleidoscopic memory. Peter was six months old. I was lifting him out of the bath when, without warning, he twisted in my hands, wriggling furiously, all four limbs going at once, uttering a long low hoot of excitement and delight. I tightened my grip. He howled with rage as he felt my hands close around him. Another time—a temper tantrum. Peter was three. He flung himself across the floor, hitting his head on a cupboard. I picked him up and held him tightly, afraid he would hurt himself. He turned, twisted, bit my hand as hard as he could. I cried out with surprise and pain.

I'd seen virtual reality on television—not what Ivan promised us that afternoon, but programs about it, how it could be used to train pilots, and as a tool for architects and surgeons. I expected Ivan to have some glorified computer game to show us, something with lots of shooting, only instead of aiming a mouse at a moving colored target, you aimed a joystick.

He told Peter with a grin, "We'll let your mum go first, to show her that it's harmless."

I stepped onto a round platform of shiny silver metal. Around me was a padded leather cage, a kind of corral. I felt a prickle of nervousness inside my clothes. The helmet, too, was made of metal and soft padded leather. The eyepieces were round; bright blue incandescent eyes, spaced as they would be on a human head.

"Man! This is excellent!" cried Peter, when Ivan lifted up the helmet.

It felt like having to carry a load of bricks on my head, and I hadn't got the balance right.

"How much did this thing cost?" I was relieved to hear my voice sounding almost normal.

Ivan said proudly, "You don't want to know."

I swayed a little sideways, and he steadied me with one arm around my waist.

There was a picture of a flower-pot upside down. "Is this right? I feel as though I'm standing on my head."

"It's for the focus. Just tell me if the outline's clear."

He pressed the eyepieces right up against my eyes, like swimming goggles, and tightened the helmet a notch or two so that it fitted snugly on my head.

"Now, see the stick in front of you? It should be right underneath the flowerpot. Take it with both hands."

I saw a hand come up in front of my eyes—a simulated hand, not mine, but moving exactly as my hand did. I took hold of the joystick and the fake hand mimicked mine. Of course, I couldn't see my real hand— all I could see was the black space in front of my eyes, the flowerpot, the stick, and the fake hand.

"Now feel the button on the top. That's it. Press it and you should begin to move."

"It's still all black," I said after a moment. "It's like I'm in a dark room and I can't find the light switch."

"Relax. You'll soon see where you are."

At first I thought it was meant to be the inside of an early settler's bark hut, with the door shut, the light dim through regular gaps or cracks in wood, not the gray or silver-gray of night, or the pure black background to the flowerpot.

114

I noticed that the walls didn't join at right angles. Now I thought I might be inside a boat, or, since whatever it was had a roof that curved in the same way—long, curved, overlapping planks of wood—an oval-shaped coffin? The unlikely wooden belly of a submarine? I heard voices whispering in a foreign language.

Suddenly I understood. It was the horse. The ancient sting. Ivan had built it, not *out there*, to touch and climb on and drag innocently through the gates of Troy. He had built the experience of being inside the Trojan Horse.

There were the barbed ends of spears as we were jostled one against the other. Sweating and afraid, I saw another soldier's hairy leg and foot, in its dusty leather sandal, shuffle next to mine. Metal against metal, wood against wood, the clat and brush of bodies flung together. The sound of children singing through a wooden wall.

I moved the joystick forward. The horse moved, with me inside it. I turned it sideways until I reached what felt like my spot against the clinkered wall, the spot in which to sink down, and wait and watch, a voyeuristic traveler from the future.

So many. No mercy shown to children. Those sweet voices just outside.

My head and sinuses ached, and there was this feeling of being sucked along. My throat felt as if it was being pulled from the back, somewhere near my tonsils.

I realized that I was crouching against the hoop. I wasn't aware of getting myself into this position, only of the need to find my special spot inside the horse. The leather gave under my fingers, molded itself to my cheek.

Everything was upside down. The blue leather was barbed and splintered, new-felled wood that no carpenter had had time to smooth. Solid substances were changing places quicker than an adult human sense could follow. A boy might slip between the cracks. A bearded Peter Pan.

I took the helmet off, knowing that I could never walk into Ivan's room and see that stationary silver disk, the cage really nothing more than two parallel hoops of expensive leather, joined by vertical struts—I knew I could never again look at them and see them as simple objects. And they were just the props.

I felt a need to understand the program Ivan must have written, the nuts and bolts of it, to unravel and comprehend it in a practical, mechanical way, and set this against my fear.

"It's not finished yet," he told me.

"Let me try! It's my go!" Peter shouted.

I said, "I didn't want to be there."

"It's just a game, Sandra. Don't go all huffy on me now."

Ivan turned away from me to help Peter with the helmet. I watched him move the joystick to and fro.

My hands were cold. I rubbed them, feeling once again surrounded by the rumbling, dim, hot insides of the statue. My eye caught the glint of a companion's spear next to my bare thigh, when we were thrown from one side to the other. My ears heard that terrible, unknowing song as the Trojans hauled on their ropes and pulled us through the city gates.

In Ivan's kitchen, I found bread, cheese, margarine. I made a sandwich and put the kettle on, waiting till I felt calm enough to tell him it had been too much for me.

"Got a great idea for what to do next!" Ivan called out through the open door.

I found some biscuits that were almost fresh. I felt I had to eat, though I wasn't ordinarily hungry, but heart-empty, hollowed out, and dizzy.

Ivan stood in the doorway with his arms crossed, frowning at the sight of me scavenging in his kitchen.

"Peter doesn't need an ancient battle foisted on him as a form of entertainment," I said stiffly, as I cleared a space at the table and sat down.

"Anything you do the first time can be a bit of a shock," Ivan said. As though the risk, the shock, were necessary.

"How can the insides of a wooden horse help anybody look *out there?*"

"It's a journey. Not all of it needs to make the kind of sense you're after."

116

Peter called from the other room for someone to help him off with the helmet, and Ivan said, "Be back in a minute," as though I was about to run away.

"What's it about?" yelled Peter, running in.

"Here." I handed him half a sandwich, and he began to eat.

Ivan told Peter the story. "They were just so sick of the siege, of hanging in there," he said, watching Peter munch his sandwich. He took nothing for himself, but sat with his hands flat on the table.

"I mean, being walled up in a town with enemies all round. The Greeks weren't having a picnic either. Between a rock and a hard place. The Trojans—food's short, but at least they're at home. You know, sometimes the best ideas come when you've reached the end of your tether—"

Peter chewed, considering this.

"You're just about to give up, and some joker says, 'Hey, man, why don't we . . .' And at first you think—nah—the sun's got to this dude. Fried his brains." Peter giggled. "But then you think about it, and you can't *stop* thinking about it, because, jeez man, there's nothing to do *but* think!"

Peter glanced at me, seeing that I disapproved of what Ivan had done, and perhaps what he was saying, too. But he wanted to hear the end of it.

"And then you say to yourself after a while—why not? Hell, man, *why not?* Fried brains."

Ivan grinned, and touched Peter lightly on the arm, as though he felt that this small contact was all he could allow himself.

Peter wriggled. "But who *won?*"

"The Greeks, of course."

After a long moment, Peter said, "I'd rather have a dog." He jumped up, and ran back to the museum.

"Why go to all that trouble? I still don't understand."

Ivan stared at me, trying to work out whether my question was an open one, or whether I planned to squash his answer as soon as he'd offered it.

"Just grabs me, that's all," he said quietly. "I've loved the story ever since I was a kid."

I wanted to leave, but I knew that if I walked out then, took Peter home, I'd never go back to Ivan's house again.

He said that learning anything requires an act of faith. And with the technology we were talking about, maybe more faith was required, not less. I called him a magician, thinking it would make him angry, but he said there might be something in that.

"You have to get the incantation of the spell exactly right, and it's all illusion anyway."

"How do you mean?"

"If you make even a titchy mistake in the program, the illusion's spoiled."

"So you're like that wizard."

"Who?"

"I've forgotten his name. In *The Wizard of Oz*."

"I see what you mean. Kind of, yes."

Ivan was right. An act of faith was required, an imaginative leap that he seemed to have no trouble making, a leap taken in trust and joy, without seat belts or life insurance. I felt inadequate and dull. Yet I would have found it easier to believe that there were spirits nattering in the blond grass outside his windows than to toss myself in faith, just then, through Ivan's window of the mind.

WHEN I HANDED PETER his dinner that night, he looked at me indulgently. Don't grow up too quickly, I thought, with a sudden stab of panic.

"Ivan's nice," he said.

"I think so," I answered carefully.

"Kinda weird, too, but—" Peter grinned the fey, childish grin that I was afraid he might soon abandon. "Y'know, y'get Ivan talking, and he forgets we're s'posed to be practicing my reading."

We washed up our dishes together, companionable and calm.

Peter had a bath, put on clean pajamas, and sat up in bed to read to me.

For the first time, I saw the words as he'd been seeing them, only with this difference: that he was beginning to come out of it, the way a baby comes out of crawling, only much more deliberately, with conscious courage, because he had already faced the black cliff-edge of failure.

I saw each letter of the words he was required—condemned—to read, not as clear curves and straight black lines, but as nervous flutters, raw fragile moth-ends, a soft filigree stretching into grayness, and a stab at meaning, the way he had grabbed hold of a stick when he was younger and speared a live moth that had been blown into the house.

"You're going well," I whispered. "Great."

Peter looked at me with clear eyes, and continued reading aloud in a sing-song voice quite unlike his own, running a finger under the lines, not jabbing at the words the way he used to, but with a smooth continuous movement.

"Who suggested that you read like that?" I asked, after he'd finished the page and I'd said, "Well done!"

"Ivan."

Peter got to the end of the story without making a mistake, though the meaning his gamelan voice gave to some of the sentences was very odd.

"Do you read like that at school?" I asked.

"No," he answered carefully, flicking the last page with his finger. He wasn't mocking me, but I stood corrected.

Then he looked at me as though I'd asked for a sweet from his hoarded bagful, grinned again, and said, "G'night Mum."

I picked up the book and switched off his bed light. I bent to kiss him goodnight, and he let me. The last thing I saw was the courage in my son's eyes, and faith in this new method that he and Ivan had concocted between them, a peculiar knowing and adult gallantry.

STEALING
PASSWORDS

ELIX WENBORN SUMMONED ME to his office first thing Monday morning.

I knocked and walked in. He looked up at me and barked, "Why wasn't I informed that you were working this weekend?"

"Someone's been using my computer?" I tried for a light tone. I was beginning to get used to Felix.

"And eaten it all up. Ha ha," he said. "Very funny."

His golden curls were a helmet, his anger another skin pressing on my own.

Someone had logged on to my computer on Saturday night, he told me, using my password. The log-in was there, as clear as a fingerprint to a police detective.

My hands began to shake. I pressed them together in anticipation of another threatening message, and said, "It couldn't have been me. I haven't got a modem at home. As a matter of fact I've only just bought a computer. What did they do?"

"That's what I'm trying to find out."

"What's this?" I pointed to two sets of numbers, separated by a colon, in the top right-hand corner of the monitor.

"The date."

"And this?"

"Time of log-in."

"21:38," I read, then turned to face Felix, breathing deeply with relief. "I was kicking up my heels at a costume party on Saturday night, and I've got about a hundred witnesses to prove it."

I'd only been using my current password for three weeks. Felix thought I was sloppy, but I hadn't written it down, and no one else knew it.

On the way back to my office, I thought of the interviews I'd written up, my interviewers' contact details, and records of my payments to them. It was a source of pride to me that all the women who'd taken part in the survey had been well paid.

Glad I'd kept a paper copy of every single thing, I unlocked my filing cabinet and took out my printed records. I opened the relevant computer file, found the list, and compared it with them. After about ten minutes, I came across a difference.

I could scarcely believe it when I saw it. I felt as though I'd gone to sleep and woken up a bad actor in a worse movie. There was a new address and record of payment on the computer, but not on my hard copy. I read it half-a-dozen times before convincing myself that it was really there. I kept staring at the screen, expecting it to disappear.

That morning I'd planned to transfer the file to Admin. The procedure was that Admin. sent a disk to Finance, who then authorized and paid the checks.

After looking for Ivan, and being told he had not come in to work yet, I went back to Felix and explained to him what I thought had happened. Felix was skeptical, and I despaired of ever getting through to him. But at last, after going over and over the same few facts I was certain of, he seemed to come around. It was a Melbourne address. We checked the street name. It did not exist.

I was leaving Felix's office when he called me back. "Sandra?" he said in a different voice, "I think I'm getting somewhere, then—"

Felix's usually pink cheeks looked grayish white, and there were premature dark pouches underneath his eyes.

"Can't you—" I began, but he interrupted, "I'd never thought about it. No, that's not right. You *have* to think about it. You have principles, procedures, mechanisms. But not this. I'd never thought about what happens when the whole damn thing goes haywire."

"Isn't there someone who can advise you? Someone you can go to?"

Felix gave me a pitying look. "The Director of Information Technology is also the head of Internal Security." He laughed. "It's not even in small print."

I glanced up through the window. A storm was ripping the last dead leaves off the oak trees on Northbourne Avenue. I hadn't even noticed it was raining.

"You know," Felix said. "I envy them. Semyonov. Harmer. Harmer collects his pay packet every fortnight, does just what he's required to do, and not one whit more."

This didn't strike me as an accurate description of Guy, though in his technical capacity it might well be true. Surely Felix recognized, as I did, that Guy was ambitious, that he was looking far beyond his present job. More than once I'd come upon him telling Ivan that they both needed to get out of the department before it collapsed around their ears.

I WAS STARTLED, WHEN I walked into my office, to find Ivan sitting in front of my computer.

"What are you doing?" I asked him.

He glanced at me with a grim expression, and said, "When you typed in your password, this little filly nabbed it."

"What filly?" I asked. "Grabbed what?"

Ivan had found a program in my computer that copied my name and password into a file, and told me INCORRECT LOG-IN. TRY AGAIN. Then it disappeared. Thinking I'd mistyped my password, I'd had another try. But in the process my password had been stolen.

"I don't remember being told my password was incorrect," I said.

"Don't worry, Sandy. It's a common trick."

"Great," I said. "That makes me feel terrific."

Ivan said the program was called a Trojan horse. I could see he expected me to share the pleasure of coincidence. It occurred to me, as it had before, that Ivan was a little mad.

He told me about a case in the United States, where a group of feminist hackers had used a Trojan horse to steal confidential military data, using cheesecake pictures as a lure. While the men ogled, a hidden program was busy copying files.

"What happened to them?"

"Still in jail, so far as I know." His big hands tied an imaginary knot, and pulled it. "One thing about the Yanks, they get convictions."

He smiled up at me.

I brushed the back of my hand along the sleeve of his brown sweater, recalling the first time I had done this.

Ivan smiled again, mischievously this time.

I'D FORGOTTEN ABOUT TONY Trapani, but I remembered later that morning when I ran into Dianne, smoking in the corridor.

"Puffing Billy," I said. "You'll set off the alarm."

Di took a last drag on her cigarette, squashed the butt, and aimed it inaccurately at a bin.

"I didn't have any luck with Bailey," I told her. "He's a real pig. Why didn't you tell me Tony had actually been caught?"

"I'm sure you did your best." Dianne narrowed her eyes and started walking quickly toward the lifts.

I followed her. "Why didn't you tell me Tony has to appear before a university tribunal?"

Dianne pressed the lift button hard with a long, purple nail.

I persisted. "What else has he done?"

"What the hell is wrong with this lift?"

"Maybe it broke down."

"Stuff it," Dianne said. "I'm walking."

She hurried to the fire stairs, but her spiked heels made it easy for me to keep up with her.

"Talking to Bailey was a waste of time," I said.

"Well, you offered, Sandra." Dianne looked at me and smiled, as though reminding herself that I had, after all, tried to do her favor. "It was nice of you to offer."

"Thanks. It was your idea, wasn't it? You found out Bailey's daughter was at Peter's school. You called me over that day in the bistro. You and your brother were waiting for me."

Dianne didn't deny it. "My parents have been giving Tone a seriously hard time. I did know he'd been caught, but I thought you might still be able to help. It makes no difference whose idea it was, since it didn't bloody work."

She pushed open the heavy door and began her descent, but after she'd gone about a dozen steps, she stopped and turned around.

"What did you tell Felix Wenborn about me?"

"Nothing," I said.

"Then why has the little shit put me through the wringer?"

"You're not the only one."

In the dim closeness of the stairwell, Dianne's stove-black dress looked menacing.

"Felix was downstairs talking to that reporter from the *Canberra Times*," she said.

"Which reporter?"

"The one with the red hair. I was behind the big drinks fridge, waiting for my cappuccino. You know what it's like when you run into someone. You say hi and chat for a couple of seconds and keep going. These two weren't like that."

"Did you hear what they were saying?"

"No. Felix had his jogging gear on." Dianne took out her cigarettes and lit one.

"And?"

"The weasel wasn't jogging, he was standing still. Sandra, let's just front him with it, and see what he says. We've been told not to talk to the press. That includes him."

"How do you know it was a reporter?"

Dianne inhaled a lungful of smoke, and turned her head self-consciously to blow it out. "That woman who broke the story about Evans—I saw her picture in the paper. Felix is the only one with total access. He often works late. He's here on his own. Well? Are you game to front the little prick or not?"

I thought for a moment, then I said, "Let's wait a while and watch him. We might see him talking to the redhead again."

I SPENT MY LUNCH hour in the library, comparing statistics on clerical outwork. At five to two, I grabbed a mushy tuna sandwich from the bistro. I was beginning to hate the atmosphere in the travel center, the hard, shadowless red and blue vinyl, the constant background noise of TV and loudspeakers, the restless, somehow purposeless milling and jostling of travelers.

And there was something else now, an undertow of anxiety, such as those weary or bland-faced passengers might feel about a bus overturning, a plane falling out of the sky. I didn't know whom to trust. In spite of trying to sound confident when talking to Dianne, I didn't have the stomach to pester anybody else with questions. I didn't have a plan.

There was a message on my desk telling me Jim Wilcox, our division head, wanted to see me.

Wilcox was one of our department's six first assistant secretaries. I'd never spoken to him personally, but I remembered the lecture he'd given us after the story about Access Computing first appeared.

Wilcox showed me in and asked me to sit down, his plump white face opening in greeting like a fresh bread roll. He said he understood I'd been having some problems with my computer files, and I told him what had happened.

He warned me to be careful. "We can't afford any more damaging publicity. And I mean *absolutely cannot*. Is that clear?"

I said it was.

Wilcox carried his weight precisely, envelopes of white flesh neatly contained by shirt collar and cuffs. One day I'd seen him in the corridor staring uncomprehendingly after Felix, togged up in his jolly red shorts and T-shirt, on his way out for a run.

As if to soften his warning a little, Wilcox asked me a few questions about the outwork report.

"We'll get it finished on time," I told him.

"How close are you?" His eyes flickered to his watch and back.

"Writing-up stage. All we need is the go-ahead to finish on our own."

"That shouldn't be a problem. I can sign off."

The phone rang and Wilcox turned to it, one hand raised to dismiss me.

I took the stairs to give me time to think. I'd been worried Wilcox was going to tell me they were scrapping my report. I recalled my promise to Rae. I was damned if I was going to let some crook set me up and get away with it.

INVISIBLE
CONNECTIONS

THE FIRST AID ROOM on our floor of the building was almost wide enough for a double bed, though there wasn't one—just a brown leather couch that I decided to rest on for ten minutes, till my headache went away.

I'd seldom seen the room being used by a sick person, though earlier that day I'd seen Bambi going in, and wondered if she had a headache, too. The leather was wrinkled, patched by a lay upholsterer's hand in one place, but the couch was made to last. I took two Panadol from a bottle in a cupboard, and swallowed them with water, then, on impulse, turned the key in the lock, lay back down on the couch and, without meaning to, of course, I fell asleep.

I was woken by the sound of Claire Disraeli's voice just outside the door.

"Only half an hour ago," she said.

A man's voice replied, too low for me to recognize the words, or who it was.

I sat up, careful not to make a noise, and looked around. On the far end of a bench was a plain, buff colored folder. I hadn't noticed it when I came in. I opened it. Inside was a floppy disk with nothing written on it, no label at all.

There was silence outside. Claire and her companion might have moved away. On the other hand, they might have tried the door, and be waiting for whoever they thought was in there to come out.

I sat still for a few more minutes, then decided that I couldn't wait forever.

When I opened the door, Claire stared at me and said angrily, "You look like the cat that ate the fish fingers."

I took the disk to Felix, then went back to my office, expecting him to call me and talk to me about it. When it was almost five and he still hadn't, I knocked on his door.

"Surely you can find out who it was," I said. "Maybe someone saw them."

Felix crossed and re-crossed his arms over his chest. He looked smaller. Worry was making him more compact by the day.

"What's on the disk?" I asked, taking a step toward the windows, careful to keep my voice neutral, feeling a brush of warm air from the air-conditioning ducts.

"It's simply a matter of knowing where to draw the line," he said. "If you lose your handbag, you don't expect twenty police officers to work day and night until they find it. Unless you're Prince Charles. But even he'd be pushing it—"

I wondered what on earth he was talking about.

"Someone left a floppy disk inside a manila folder in the first-aid room. I saw Bambi go in there earlier today. Can you please tell me what's on the disk?"

"At the moment, no. I'm afraid I can't do that."

Felix spread both hands in front of him, palms outward, an odd gesture, like a nervous preacher about to begin a sermon. "Sandra," he said. "Just watch—and *listen*."

"Listen for what?"

"For the unexpected."

"Do you really think Rae Evans stole that money?"

The thing is, for a few seconds I believed Felix was going to answer me, tell me what he did believe. There was one of those gaps of time that are impossible to measure, because they have been chilled by memory, and are recalled as the original sensation, as though preserved in ice.

"All I want is to get the matter dealt with internally," he said, "without any more harm being done."

"Getting Rae Evans charged with fraud and computer theft? That's your idea of internally?"

"The police did that, Sandra."

Why ask me to spy for him? As soon as I got away from Felix, I felt like shouting it. Why ask the one person he knew was on Rae's side? I could watch people sitting at their workstations. I could listen to what they said to each other. But they could be stealing passwords and changing files for all they were worth, and I wouldn't be able to tell. It was like trying to investigate a jewel robbery by standing outside the shop window and admiring its shelves.

Maybe Felix had asked others. Maybe his idea was to get half the department spying on the other half, and vice versa, the whole building looking up each other's skirts. Maybe that was his idea of solving the matter internally.

THAT NIGHT, I COULDN'T wait for Peter to go to bed, so I could talk to Ivan about Felix and the disk. I swallowed my wariness with Ivan where Rae was concerned. I wasn't going to break my promise and tell him I'd met her, but I was bursting to talk over all the rest.

I didn't want to burden Peter with my office troubles. I tried not to allow myself to be preoccupied with them during the few hours out of the twenty-four I spent with my son. The three of us ate dinner together, and laughed over silly things I can't remember now. Peter did his homework, Ivan alternately helping him and distracting him with further silliness. He asked if he could watch TV for half an hour and, though I wanted to pack him off to bed, I said he could.

As soon as he'd gone, I told Ivan the story of the first aid room, beginning with falling asleep in there, hearing voices, and finding a disk in a manila folder. Ivan raised an eyebrow at the falling asleep part, but he didn't interrupt. I said I'd seen Bambi going into the room earlier that day.

"The thing is, I've never been able to figure Bambi out. She acts mad and she looks mad, but maybe she's not at all. Maybe she's a good actress."

"I don't know, Sandy," Ivan said.

I waited for more.

"It's true. I really don't know. There's a lot of patronage and nepotism goes on. If you'd been around a bit longer, you'd understand."

"I'd accept it as normal?"

"More or less." Ivan gave me a straight look, and I knew he was thinking of the reasons Rae had hired me.

"It would be okay if Bambi would just make an effort," I said. "Instead of preening all day, and talking on the phone."

"It's not as though it's for much longer," Ivan reminded me. "She's only got a short-term contract." He didn't need to add, like you.

I recalled our early conversation in the park, when Ivan had warned me that the project I was supposed to be working on with Di and Bambi was destined to be "just another draft for the shredder." Though Ivan's words, and their meaning, could be interpreted as harsh, he'd moved across to sit next to me while we were talking, and put his arm around me.

"It's not necessarily a *bad* thing," I said, "to give someone like that a job."

I leant on his shoulder experimentally.

"Not at all. Just think, if Evans wasn't into patronage, I might never have met you."

"Oh," I said, wondering how much weight I was supposed to give this. Ivan wasn't inclined to amorous pronouncements, the opposite in fact, but he stayed sitting close to me, and I felt comforted in the circle of his arm.

Later on, in bed, I parted his beard, pretending to look for hidden treasure.

"It's just that I've never had a lover with so much hair before," I said.

Ivan sat up and made the face of a demented ogre.

I giggled, then remembered Peter. "Shh," I said.

Ivan was trying to keep up his ogre face, and not laugh at the same time. Like the first night, in front of my combustion stove, his big, broad body seemed both to block out light, and generate it. Sleeping with Ivan, being with him, guarded me against darker thoughts, more troubling considerations, but in a modest way, so that it was tempting to pretend nothing significant was taking place between us.

His silly face, and what it conjured up, made me think once again of Bambi. I was sure there was more to Bambi than a crazy lady for whom Rae Evans had once done a favor.

NEXT DAY, I TOOK time off to attend Rae's committal hearing.

The magistrate's court had an extra floor, a mezzanine, with the stuck-on look mezzanine floors have, like a child's afterthought when making a playhouse. I blinked and shook my head. That Rae might end up in jail had not been quite real to me until the moment I stepped inside the courtroom.

It was square and self-enclosed, with no windows to the outside. Though I was early, it was already crowded. Lawyers and detectives stood around in suits. A few uniformed police angled themselves against the wall to accommodate their guns and mobile phones. The defendants were a mixed bunch, some in jeans and sweatshirts, some in suits as good as, or better than the lawyers'. My eyes searched everywhere for a proud gray head, back of military straightness. Rae wasn't there.

The walls, carpet, and furniture were a dark plum color. I spotted an empty chair by the far wall, and hurried across to claim it. The furniture and people using it seemed suddenly like blow-ups, made to look lifelike by the obsessive attention to detail of a bored and lonely child. A woman whom I felt I ought to know, but didn't, leant out over the railing of the mezzanine. I dropped my bag and bent to pick it up.

Rae must have entered the courtroom in those few seconds while my head was lowered. I turned, and there she was. It was as though a candle glowed through her pale blouse, paler skin, shining from within each thread of silk. I tried to catch her eye, but she was walking with her head down, staring at the floor.

At the table where she took her place, lawyers sat so close together, leaning forward, that they appeared to be chewing on the microphones. More policemen and women were bowing in the doorway, taking up lumpy positions against the wall. The detective sergeant who'd interviewed me was in the front row. I caught him looking round in my direction, but, like Rae, he did not meet my eye.

The woman in the black gown was surely too young to be a magistrate. Long silver earrings swayed when she moved her head, and she pushed her black wavy hair back from her forehead with a ringless left hand. I understood that the custody cases were all heard first, those who'd been held in custody the night before. The magistrate spoke naturally, and I thought kindly, to each of the accused. But every case was called up only to be adjourned. No one was even listing charges, and I began to think that nothing would be dealt with that day at all.

It was more than an hour before Rae was summoned to the microphone. Detective Sergeant Hall read out the charges. I was glad he had his back to me, so I didn't have to look at his square jaw moving up and down.

I'd had no idea there were so many things you could do with a computer that were against the law. Rae didn't speak. When she was asked to enter a plea, her barrister said "not guilty" in a clear, judicious voice.

I LEANT AGAINST THE gray, cold metal folds of a statue outside the courtroom, hoping for a glimpse of Rae on her way out. The statue was long and finely curved. In midsummer, it would be too hot to touch. I looked for the name of the sculptor, remembering another statue with an upright bearing, in another life it seemed, and the man who was to become my husband waiting underneath.

Suddenly, Rae was there in front of me, walking beside her lawyer, with no time for me to compose my features into an appropriate expression.

"Hello Sandra." She smiled calmly, showing no surprise at seeing me. I reached out and took her hand, at a loss for words. It seemed to me that Rae was acting on automatic, going through the motions. Her eyes looked clear because her mind was somewhere else. I turned to her lawyer, feeling an irrational stab of dislike for him, as though her detachment was his fault. Before I could collect myself to say anything, he'd moved her on, one hand underneath her elbow.

When I arrived back at the Jolimont Center, I spotted Felix coming out. He wasn't wearing his jogging gear. Maybe I could follow him. I sidled behind three girls in calf-high logging boots and tight black jeans.

I kept Felix in sight, but stayed well behind him till he stopped at the Tie Rack in the middle of the mall. Meter-length silk scarves were knotted at one end to resemble ties. Felix held one and examined it, while I moved in behind two women holding babies at PixiFoto. I smiled encouragingly at their chubby cheeks and rosy fists. A large black leather umbrella was part of the photographer's equipment. Maybe she used it for outdoor assignments when the weather was unsettled. She glanced at me, and I could see her wondering if there was any chance that I might be a customer. Then she busied herself posing the first baby on a sheepskin arranged attractively over a pale blue blanket. A brochure underneath the umbrella advertised Bonus Pose. If you got your baby to do the right thing, you won a free photo opportunity.

Felix was certainly taking his time to choose a tie.

The baby squirmed on the sheepskin and began to yell. The photographer flapped a fluffy yellow duck at it, with spirit, but with hope diminishing. I was afraid the noise would make Felix turn around, but I couldn't see a better place to wait. Opposite PixiFoto, Australian Choice offered quilted oven holders decorated with kangaroos and wattle.

At last Felix moved. I followed him about thirty meters back. Down the escalator, in the food hall, I felt more secure, in familiar territory. I'd brought Peter there sometimes in the winter, let him cover himself with bolognaise sauce, and felt good because I wouldn't have to clean the table.

Felix chose a roll from the health bar. No gloppy spaghetti for him.

I was hungry, but I didn't dare queue up for anything myself. I squatted down behind a plastic fern, and kept him covered for about fifteen minutes. His fussy, careful way of eating infuriated me. I gave up.

On my way out of the mall, I paused at the window of the Teddy Bear Shop, where meter-high teddy bears posed, guaranteed to terrify children with their midnight shadows. But maybe it was only Peter who was subject to those fits of terror, face to face in the darkness with his beloved daytime toys.

The trees in Northbourne Avenue were urging themselves toward a gap, a breach in the months of winter, but I felt tired and depressed. I could sneak around after Felix for days, but where would it get me? I was no Le Carré hood.

It was Rae I should have been following, not Felix. Felix would never lead me further than a contemplation of his healthy lifestyle. I should have followed Rae, to see where she went after that careful, hand-under-the-elbow barrister left her to her own devices.

Was that why Rae always wore ivory shirts, or creamy white, I asked myself, to make this light when she walked, to carry it with her? Silently, in that courtroom, between chairs and carpet the color of used blood, she had proclaimed her innocence.

When I went back far enough, I came to a confluence of women. How important had my mother been to Rae? Would I ever get to talk to her again, in private, just the two of us? Would we ever be sufficiently relaxed and honest with each other to share our memories of the woman who had been my mother, and her friend? I wondered if that had been what Rae had wanted when she'd given me a job. What happened when she remembered her own childhood? Were there any black-and-white still shots in her colored movie?

On my way back to the office, I mulled over what I had managed to discover so far, and admitted that it was depressingly little. Rae had been accused of stealing nine hundred thousand dollars, twenty thousand of which had been deposited in her bank account. She might have stolen it herself, or helped someone from Access Computing to steal it, but I did not believe this, so I put the possibility aside. Rae did not have a single supporter in the department, except me. Dianne and Bambi were hostile to her, for reasons I didn't understand. Felix Wenborn showed an intense dislike for her, which may have included a large dose of guilt, because Rae—again for reasons I didn't understand—had been asked to investigate a charge against him of collusive tendering.

The company involved, Compic, had sold a large quantity of software to Felix, and to the *Canberra Times*. I could try and find out who else had bought their packages. Ivan might help me do that. When I thought of Ivan and Rae together, I remembered Ivan standing at my window, looking out at the frost and calling Rae dead meat. Running under my relationship with him, like a rip tide pulling the wrong way—sometimes strong, and sometimes barely noticeable—was his contempt for Rae, an attitude he would not, or could not explain. I reminded myself once more that I'd promised Rae I wouldn't tell anyone I'd spoken to her, and resolved to keep that promise.

My thoughts returned to Bambi, and a way to tackle her. Surely tackling Bambi should be within my grasp.

A HIDDEN
MICROPHONE

OME ON," GAIL TREMBATH told me. "I'd better wire you up before we get too pissed."

Hardly likely, since we'd only had one glass of wine. I agreed, though the closer I came to putting my plan into action, the more my feet felt like blocks of ice.

"Won't you be missed at work?" Gail asked.

"Won't you?" I replied.

"Twit," she said. "Reporters are meant to hunt around for stories."

Gail's flat smelt of absence, the absence of a single professional only home on weekends, and not for much of them. Her living room looked like a newspaper recycling depot. Stacks that had started in the corners were steadily moving inward, a slow-motion guerrilla attack on her furniture and carpet.

"Where do you entertain?" I asked.

Gail flung an arm through the bedroom door. Her bedroom looked only slightly less covered in paper than the living room. She went to fetch some sticking plaster. I thought she was taking a long time, then heard her yell, "Gotcha!"

She opened the packet, and we examined its contents together. This turned out to be a three-meter-long strip of heavy-duty Elastoplast, more suited to patching up an accident with a kitchen knife than securing a microphone onto my sensitive skin.

Gail ordered me to strip, and tried out the microphone against my throat, just above my breast-bone, beneath and between my breasts, holding it in place and clicking her tongue until she found a position that satisfied her.

"Hold it there," she said, while she peeled the wrapper from the length of adhesive.

The wire ran down to my waist and around to the small of my back. Gail quickly secured it with strips of plaster, one beneath the other.

"Ow," I said. "Go easy."

"Don't fidget or scratch," she told me. "You'll be able to move quite normally."

Gail had a certain glow. I didn't think it was the excitement of fixing me up with a hidden microphone. "Are you seeing anyone special?" I asked her.

"I wouldn't say *special*."

"We should go out one night," I said. "For old times' sake."

Gail went on working with her tongue out, obviously determined to use up the whole packet.

"Seriously. I can borrow a truck. We can go to the tip together. Have you ever been to the tip? It's one of Canberra's more interesting weekend venues. They take newspapers. You'd be doing a community service."

"Sandra, if I didn't know you better I'd say you were drunk."

"You know —" I squirmed "—sex and propaganda, it's not a healthy combination. You should just give it up."

"*Still*, I said."

Gail stood back and studied me with her hands on her hips, like a dressmaker pleased with a fitting. I half-expected her to raise my hem and begin pinning it.

"What time did you say you're meeting this Bambi person?"

"Not meeting. She works with me."

"Have you ever asked her to have lunch with you before? Don't you think she'll smell a rat?"

"Bambi is a rat."

My head felt surprisingly clear, as though the simple physical act of subterfuge I was about to undertake had gotten rid of the confusion.

"You'll have to wear something that won't show bumps. Not a T-shirt."

"I've got a denim shirt with pockets. Where does the recorder go?"

"Small of your back. What will you wear on the bottom half?"

"My suit skirt."

"Well, make sure the shirt's fluffed out above the waist band. I've covered you with so much tape the mike will stay put even if half of it comes unstuck. Now this is how you turn it on. This button. Can you reach it?"

Gail guided my hand to a button and I pressed it down, hearing a small click.

"The light's on, it should be recording. I'll walk across the room and talk to you from there. You'll need to know its range, and try and stay within it. It's not spectacularly powerful, but it should be fine for what you want."

We experimented for the next few minutes. When Gail was more than three meters away, her voice was faint, but closer than that I could hear every word. I practiced turning the tape on and off a few times.

"You'll have to find a loo on the way, and switch it on in there. If you do it too soon, the tape might run out."

"What about afterwards? Can you unhook me?"

"I have to go back to work. If you can't manage, you'll have to leave it till tonight."

She caught the look on my face. "Don't get spooked now, Sandra. It's only a microphone." She glanced at her watch. "Better be off. You've still got to change. Don't go jigging round. Just change your clothes."

"Gail?" I put out my hand to keep her there a moment. "Two things. Remember I asked you to check up on those Compic packages?"

"Oh yeah," Gail said, moving toward the door, "We did buy heaps of them. I found them sitting in a cupboard by the subs desk."

"You mean they're not being used?"

She shrugged impatiently. "Maybe by the layout people. Not by me, that's for sure."

"Who bought them?"

"Sandy, I'm already late."

"Please find out. And I have to ask you one last question. What were you doing talking to Felix Wenborn in the travel center bistro?"

"What travel center? What bistro?"

"On the ground floor of the Jolimont Center."

"Haven't been there for years. Didn't even know they had a bistro."

"Someone saw you talking to Felix Wenborn. He's head of IT and in charge of security."

"Well, they made a mistake," Gail flung over her shoulder as she disappeared. "It wasn't me."

"WHERE DID YOU GET the disk?" I asked Bambi later that day, sitting in the bistro with an untouched salad roll in front of me. "The one you left in the first aid room."

Bambi giggled and hid behind her swatch of hair like an old-fashioned movie queen.

"Are you all right, Sandra? You look uncomfortable."

"I'm fine. I saw you going into the first aid room. You were carrying a floppy disk, weren't you? Did someone ask you to leave it in there?"

"What first aid room?"

My sticking plaster itched. I felt like Huck Finn, itching in eleven different places.

"The one on our floor," I said patiently. "I saw you going in there."

Practicing with Gail, I'd twisted one way then another, turned my back and walked away from her, to check whether her voice could still be heard. Now, opposite Bambi, with only a bit of table between us, every move I made seemed horribly exaggerated, as though I'd swallowed some gesture-enhancing pill. Even crossing my legs seemed so large and inappropriate a movement that it caused a wave of damp air to pass between them.

"You thought the disk would be safe there?" I persisted. "You were planning to serve it up with the Panadol?"

Bambi looked hurt. She twisted her long hair round and round one finger. "No one ever sees me," she whispered. "I have to do things to make people see me."

"What? What do you have to do?"

Bambi answered with a pout, "I don't like you, Sandra. You're always looking down on me."

I groaned under my breath. "Rae Evans found a job for you, didn't she? Now someone's out to wreck her career. I'm going to find that person, but I need your help."

Testing the recorder in Gail's flat, I'd observed that I ummed and ahed a lot, sometimes masking what she said. I tried not to do this now, keeping my lips shut while I waited for Bambi to reply, digging my thumbnail into the flesh of my index finger as a reminder.

"Who told you Evans looked after me?" Bambi whispered at last, looking at me with the air of a puppy with a bindi thorn in its paw.

"She gave you a job."

Bambi shook her head, then clammed up and wouldn't say a word. A few minutes later, she got up to go. I didn't try and stop her. I felt hot, and exhausted. I'd never make a real detective. When it came to the crunch, I couldn't twist anybody's arm.

I hadn't said anything to Ivan about the microphone. I'd been too embarrassed, and now I was glad. I'd had a kind of crazy fantasy about playing him the tape with Bambi's confession, sewing up the whole case single-handed.

On my way to the toilets on the ground floor, I ran into Felix hurrying out of the lift.

I took a deep, painful breath and asked, "Have you met Allison Edgeware, Compic's young director?"

Felix turned away from me, heading for the automatic doors. Plastered up as I was, running after him wasn't so smart.

I grabbed him by the arm. "You must have met to discuss that contract."

Felix pulled away. I chased him. "And what about all those software packages you bought?"

He pushed through the doors, making good his escape.

"Bastard," I said under my breath.

My Elastoplast was beginning to itch unbearably. I made my second attempt to reach the Ladies, determined that this time nothing was going to stop me.

FOR THE REST OF the day, Bambi played the injured party to perfection, looking up at me sorrowfully from under black penciled eyebrows whenever I got up from my computer, or spoke to anybody on the phone.

She wrapped her cloak tightly round herself like a cocoon, fondled her hair, and glowered at me. The kohl around her eyes had run, and she'd smudged it further with a tissue.

Was all this a cover for another, cleverer, much less innocent bit of playacting? And, if my suspicions were correct, had she written the part herself, or had someone else prepared it for her? Bambi's wide brown eyes, with their injured expression, her habit of bumping into things, as though they were constantly moving around her and she was never sure of their place—if these were part of some kind of double bluff, a play within a play, then she was a much better actor than I would ever be. And, considering the number of bruises she must take home, a much more dedicated one. I'd been close enough when she acquired some of them to be sure that, if nothing else, those bruises were the real McCoy.

That night, after I'd spent half an hour rubbing cream into my raw and burning skin, I longed to have Derek beside me in our double bed, to hear his clear mind with its no-nonsense edges impose an order, pick out what was important from the mass of information and misinformation I was carrying around with me.

But Derek wasn't there, and I knew now that I couldn't say what I needed to on an international phone call. I could write a letter, but I knew how crazy it would look to him.

Instead, I rang Tony Trapani to ask him if he'd heard of Compic. I began by complaining that he hadn't told me the truth about Bailey and the Internet account.

When I mentioned Compic's director, Tony laughed nervously and said, "Like, everybody knows who *she* is."

I asked him if he'd arrange for me to meet her. He hesitated, then said he didn't know how he could do that do.

I ignored this. "It might be better if you're having coffee with Ms. Edgeware, and I turn up accidentally."

"But why would Allison have coffee with me?"

Tony sounded very young. I remembered the trouble I'd gone to on his behalf, and said, "Come on. Think of something."

Next, I phoned Gail Trembath and told her about my failure to get Bambi to confess. We laughed, and the episode didn't seem quite so humiliating.

"About that Compic stuff," she said. "It was the office manager."

"What's his name?"

"Graham Arnold."

"Has he ever done anything like that before?"

"Like what?"

"Buy heaps of software packages that there doesn't seem to be a use for."

"You know, I asked the subs. Useless is just about right. And no, in answer to your question. Not that I recall."

THE PHONE RANG AT seven-thirty in the morning. Peter got to it first. The joy in his face and voice stopped me in my tracks. Then his expression froze. I forced him to hand over the phone.

"What the hell do you think you're doing?" Derek demanded. "What's Peter going to do on his own all day while I'm at work? Why did you let him send that letter? How dare you set me up like that?"

"What letter?" I asked, gulping in great mouthfuls of cold air.

Eventually we got it sorted out, at least to the point where Derek stopped saying it was out of the question. Peter might be able to come for the school holidays. He'd look into taking a couple of weeks' leave, but he couldn't promise, and I'd better not spring anything like this on him again.

I hung up the phone and said to Peter, "I know how much you want to see your father, but don't you ever, *ever* go behind my back like that again."

OVER THE NEXT COUPLE days, Tony sent me cryptic e-mails about Compic and Allison Edgeware. They contained his own personal spellings and abbreviations. Allison was C/l, which I figured was short for cool. He'd persuaded her to have coffee with him in the Glebe Park café at eleven on Thursday.

I realized I had to get hold of the letter of complaint about the contract and, if possible, arrange to see Bernard Whitelaw. Then there were the threatening e-mails. Rae had said she'd kept hers. I wondered what excuse I could give for looking them up. I couldn't understand why Rae had been asked to deal with the complaint. The only reason I could think of was that Jim Wilcox wanted to cause trouble between her and Felix.

ON THURSDAY, I LOOKED across from the doorway of the café, and saw Tony Trapani and his friend Ateeq sitting at a table with a stunningly beautiful young woman.

Ateeq, dressed once again in his black leather jacket, was laughing and tapping an unlit cigarette against a saucer.

"Hi," I said, walking over.

"Oh, Sandra." Tony blushed.

Allison Edgeware looked up at me and smiled. Ateeq introduced us. Her auburn hair made Gail's ginger curls seem drab by comparison. Her eyes were dark brown, her skin a perfect light honey.

I shook her hand and said hello, then sat down without being invited to. The three of them went on talking about computer courses at the university.

Allison was dressed carefully and conventionally in a cream silk shirt and soft brown waistcoat with matching pants. A classy suede coat hung on the back of her chair. She reached behind her and felt toward a pocket, then apparently changed her mind.

She turned to me and asked, "Where do you work Sandra?"

"In Labor Relations," I said, feeling that she already knew this. "And you?"

Ateeq narrowed his eyes and said, "Allison heads up the fastest growing software company in town."

I congratulated her.

"Have you tried our new graphics package?" she asked.

I shook my head and said that graphics weren't my line.

Allison smiled and said that was probably because I'd never used a really good package. I'd be amazed what it could do.

"The competition for new government contracts must be pretty fierce."

"It certainly is," Allison agreed. "But having a top-drawer product definitely helps."

Ateeq began talking then, entertaining us with his plans to make his first million, and relieving us from our exchange of clichés. Tony barely said a word.

Allison reached into her coat pocket for a second time, pulled out a packet of Players, and caught Ateeq's eye. Her lips narrowed into a rigid line as she pulled off the cellophane. I thought she might be annoyed with something Ateeq had said. Then it occurred to me that she was nervous.

For a moment, she looked very young indeed, younger even than Ateeq, because she lacked his veneer of confident disdain.

Instead of lighting her cigarette, she stood up and said she had to go. I told her I'd been pleased to meet her and we said good-bye.

I RANG RAE FROM a phone box round the corner, and told her that I'd just met Allison from Compic. I asked Rae what she could remember about her, if there was anything Felix, or anyone else had said.

Rae told me she'd think about it. She sounded cool and distant. I wondered how she was occupying herself, at home in the middle of the day.

"Those e-mails you were sent. Where are they?"

"I copied them to the file dealing with the complaint."

"Tell me your user ID and password."

"Why do you want to know?"

"So I can check the file myself."

"How will you do that?"

"I might be able to get into your office."

"How?" Rae repeated.

"I'll stay back late. I'll figure something out. So if I could just have your password."

Rae told me, then said, "Felix might have disabled it."

"I'll take my chance with that."

I explained about the disk I'd found in the first aid room, and Felix's refusal to tell me what was on it. Rae listened without comment. Then I told her about the false address that had been added to my list of outworkers. She warned me to be careful. I asked her for her lawyer's phone number. She recited two numbers, then said she had to go.

I hung up the receiver, glad I'd decided to phone her from a public box.

Allison. Angela. They were names that sounded the same to me, reminded me of china dolls. Angela. Allison. The press reports had named

145

Angela Carlishaw as a director of Access Computing. The second director, Isobel Merewether, had been unable to produce her.

Was the similarity coincidental? For a crazy moment, I wondered if they were the same person. Maybe the journalist who'd queried Angela Carlishaw's existence was spot on. But Allison was real enough. For the rest of that day, I fancied I saw her around every corner, her beauty multiplied on reflecting surfaces, from the glass-fronted airline companies in Northbourne Avenue, to the small pool and fountain in Glebe Park.

In these imagined reflections of mine, Allison was laughing at me, yet I didn't mind. I liked my pictures of her, and hoped that, in time, they would disclose their secrets. Reflections could be skewed, off true, yet more revealing than a clear and proper likeness.

I wondered if Allison and Felix *had* met to talk about the contract that had so fortunately gone Compic's way. I didn't think it meant much that Felix had refused to answer when I'd asked him. Perhaps Di Trapani had seen Allison with Felix in the bistro. But why would they meet there? Surely, if they'd met in person, it would have been upstairs, in Felix's office.

Of course, it was always possible that there'd been no redhead in the travel center, that Dianne had been lying through her teeth.

LIAR, LIAR,
PANTS ON FIRE

E WERE TOLD TO keep calm. No one was to panic, but this was not a drill. Real fire trucks were at that moment beating through the traffic on Northbourne Avenue. Real firemen were hauling their extension ladders to the white face of the Jolimont Center.

The wardens for our floor got us out onto the fire stairs quickly. They kept everyone in line, their white helmets shiny in the smoke-filled air. Doors kept opening above and below us, and the stairs were flush with evacuees from other floors. Di, Bambi, and I stuck together, moving quickly in the shush of skirts and woolen suits, the press of unfamiliar shoulders, the rasp of feet on concrete.

A jowly purple face gaped at me from the landing below, dribble hanging from the corner of a wide, slack mouth. With a shock, I recognized Jim Wilcox. He looked as though he was about to faint.

The travel center had never looked so bright and various, colors rich, polished plastic undulating like silk held up to dry. Safe, silly with relief, I grinned and waved to Kerry Arnold, who was wearing a red chief warden's hat a good three sizes too big for him.

Muffin vendors and espresso attendants stood outside on the footpath, cheek by steamy cheek. In my jacket pocket, I fingered the disks containing backups of the outwork report. I'd snatched them before dashing for the stairs. Ivan was carrying a box full of disks and CDs. He must have worked fast collecting them, because he was outside before I was, holding forth to a queue of bus passengers, waving his free arm above his head like a propeller.

A crowd watched the fire trucks from a respectful distance, the tops of ladders resting against broken fourth-floor windows. Charcoal gray and black smoke moved in slow motion along Northbourne Avenue. With no wind to disperse it, it rose slowly, a viscous, greasy cloud.

I spotted the Secretary talking to the Dep. Sec. Tall men in expensive suits, they were joined by one of our senior executives, a woman who'd spoken to me kindly in the lift one morning when Peter had been sick.

Jim Wilcox walked up to them, waving pudgy hands. He appeared to have recovered from his fright on the stairs. I remembered the warning Wilcox had given me about damaging publicity. I'd spoken to him in the lift as well, one lunchtime when he'd been carrying a huge bagful of chocolate muffins, with a naughty, half-defiant expression, as if he planned to eat them all at one sitting.

It wasn't long before we were told the fire was out. Only a small section of the building had been damaged.

A couple of hours later, we were allowed back inside. The smell of smoke was everywhere, but the smoke itself had cleared. The carpets in our corridor and office were drenched with water. Though none of the furniture seemed to have been burnt, a film of soot hung over everything.

I opened my filing cabinet and stopped, unable to believe my eyes. When the fire alarm had sounded, I'd grabbed my bag and coat, and then the back-up disks. I'd run for the fire stairs like everybody else, not thinking to stay for a few more minutes and clear out my cabinet.

My records were gone. My hard copies had disappeared, those copies I'd been so glad to have when I'd discovered that someone had been tampering with my computer.

Stomach lurching, I pulled my chair toward me and sat down. I had to compose myself before Di and Bambi arrived to collect their things, not to mention the trio from next door. I would ask no questions. I would give none of them the satisfaction of seeing how upset I was.

The thief was in the building. He or she was someone working close to me, maybe on my floor, definitely under the same roof. Maybe I knew her scent. Maybe he shared the lift with me twice or three times a day.

In the general confusion, I borrowed a set of keys from Deirdre's desk, and raced downstairs to get them copied. I urgently needed to check Rae's filing cabinet and computer, but I was afraid I was too late.

I didn't dare to try and stay late that night. The security people were keen to get everybody out.

THE FOLLOWING NIGHT WAS a Wednesday, Peter's Cubs night. He went home from school with one of his friends from Cubs, and I arranged to pick him up at nine o'clock.

At six o'clock, I walked along the corridor to Rae's office, trying to look as though I had every right to be there. I'd followed Deirdre downstairs at ten past five, relieved that she was leaving on time, then gone back to my own office to wait.

If anyone caught me, I'd say Friday was my deadline for the report, and there was some information that I had to check. It was a thin excuse, but it might work. I figured that it looked less suspicious if I was found in Rae's office while it was relatively early

I closed the door behind me, but didn't lock it, reasoning that if somebody came past and saw the light on, then tried the door and found it locked, they might raise the alarm.

The computer seemed to take forever to boot up. I typed in Rae's username and password, and began looking for the file on the complaint.

I raised my head at the sound of a step in the corridor. Someone was coming. I flicked across to an innocuous document.

The door opened.

"Goodness me, the smell is bad in here." It was Rahoul from transport industries. I'd said maybe ten words to him in my time at the department.

"You're working late."

I leant back so he could see the screen and said, "No choice, I'm afraid."

"Want some coffee? I'm just on my way to make some."

"Thanks, no." I forced a smile. "Just got about twenty minutes left here, then I'm done." I cursed myself as soon as I'd said this. I'd have to stay in Rae's office now for another twenty minutes, no matter what I found, or failed to find.

Rahoul smiled in what seemed a sly and knowing way, and said, "Everything is such a mess." I nodded agreement, willing him to leave.

As soon as he clicked the door shut, I went back to my search for the file on the complaint. It wasn't there.

I fitted a key into the top drawer of the filing cabinet, twiddling it for what seemed like a year before I got it to turn. I didn't know what heading the correspondence concerning the complaint would be under. There was nothing labelled Compic, Tenders, or Complaints, but Correspondence took up the whole of the second drawer.

With a glance at my watch, I began to go through it one folder at a time. Two doors down, I could hear the sound of the electric jug, a faint rattle of cups, a fridge door shutting with a small flat clap. My twenty minutes was used up, plus an extra ten, when I finally admitted to myself that my search had got me nowhere. There was no file containing the correspondence about the contract that had gone to Compic, or the complaint about it, in any of the four drawers of the cabinet, in Rae's or Deirdre's desks, or on the bookshelves. I'd looked everywhere I could think of. If there was a file, and I had no reason to doubt Rae's word that there had been, someone had removed it. Had they used the fire to do this, or had the information disappeared long before?

On my way out, I mulled over what might have happened if I hadn't kept all my original copies of my interviews' details. And what might happen to me now that they'd been stolen.

It wasn't nearly time to pick Peter up, but I didn't feel like going home. I got myself a meal in a Chinese restaurant, but was too preoccupied to enjoy it.

I wondered if the basic plot had been the same, in my case and in Rae's, if it was only luck and timing that had made the outcome different. The thief could have pinched my password, made a single alteration, then counted on letting the electronic payment system do the rest. The next step might have been to leak a story to the *Canberra Times* about our department sending money to a false address. Of course, the amount was negligible. Of course, I was a tiny fish to bait and catch. But then, Rae wasn't that big a fish herself. If the design had been to discredit our department in the lead-up to the elections, then perhaps whoever had conceived it intended incremental damage, allegations of theft and corruption that accumulated, one on top of the other. He, or she, or they—I found it difficult to imagine one person carrying through such a plan—were relying on the pre-election paranoia that the Opposition was creating. But didn't this theory leave out Access Computing, and the questionable way they operated, with one of their directors holed up in a Scottish nunnery? It also left out the complaint against Compic.

I knew that our Admin. computer's operating system could not be accessed through my PC. My password would not let a hacker in. Neither would Rae's, or Ivan's, or Guy Harmer's. A hacker, whether male or female, whether from inside the building, or somewhere far away, needed Kerry Arnold's password, or that of someone with the authority to override him—the system manager, or someone masquerading as the system manager. I was sure Kerry had been telling the truth when he said the amount for Access Computing's grant must have been changed from $100,000 to $1 million *after* he had signed for it. But wasn't it possible that someone with authority over Kerry had been able to make whatever changes to the system he or she had wished?

I left the restaurant, walked to my car, and drove slowly over the bridge. A pair of headlights stayed the same distance behind me. When I pulled to one side to check the address of Peter's friend, the car went past, but later, as I negotiated unfamiliar streets, I noticed another car sitting twenty meters back and staying there, turning when I turned.

Mirrors within mirrors surrounded me, leads that weren't leads, but forever doubled back on themselves. The thief hadn't reckoned on my keeping those hard copies of my interviewers' names and addresses. Did this mean it had to be someone who didn't know me all that well, who couldn't have predicted that I was the sort of person who kept everything? And who then took the opportunity provided by the fire, or created it, to clear out my filing cabinet?

We never did find out how the fire started. My guess was that it was meant to be a big one, a proper conflagration, but for some reason the plan hadn't quite worked out. How convenient it would have been for the department to be gutted, all our records burnt.

There was no quick move to clean things up, and this, in a way, was more worrying than the fire itself. The regular cleaners did the best they could, but no new furniture was bought to replace items that had been damaged by the smoke and soot. People brought rugs and covers from home to protect their clothes, and the more industrious got busy with upholstery shampoo.

STRAY DOG

O N THE SATURDAY AFTER the fire, I talked Ivan into taking Peter to the movies, so I could visit Rae.

I followed her out to the kitchen with the bottle of wine I'd brought, and watched her open it and pour two glasses. Her kitchen was inhumanly clean, and though she hadn't forbidden me to visit her, it seemed clear, from the first moment, that she didn't want me there.

We sat opposite each other across a low glass table in the living room, and talked about the fire and the stolen records. Rae seemed helpless in the face of what had happened. She had no practical suggestions to make. Her skin looked dry as parchment, as if no amount of face cream would ever be enough to moisten it. Her once-shiny silver hair was dull and dry. I realized that the first time I'd seen her—well, maybe not when I was a child—but since that morning I'd stood in her office clutching a potted cyclamen, she'd had these brittle edges. She'd had them well before the story broke about the missing money.

"How did that money get into your account?" I asked. "Who sent it?"

"Access Computing." Rae sounded surprised, but she hadn't told me this before.

"I don't believe Allison Edgeware can be running Compic on her own," I said.

Rae slowly twirled her wine glass by its stem. "She must hire programmers. That's how a lot of these new firms operate, so I believe. They hire, on short term contracts, whoever is best for a particular job."

"That doesn't explain how Allison managed to land a big contract with Labor Relations."

"No it doesn't. But Sandra, I can't believe that anyone would actually start a fire in order to destroy records. People might have been hurt, or even burnt to death."

"You were hurt," I reminded her, "in ways that aren't so obvious, but effective none the less. Maybe a fire *is* over the top. It means that whoever lit it is very determined."

"Do you have a family, Sandra? I mean brothers and sisters, uncles, aunts?"

I stared at Rae, wondering where this question had come from, trying to remember what I'd already told her.

"My mother lost contact with her family," I said.

Rae's eyes were dark gray. All the depth and moisture that had gone from her face seemed to soak down into them.

"Did your mother mention me?" she asked. "Did she talk about me?"

"Not that I recall."

"I guess I hoped that somewhere along the line my name might have come up, Lilian might have talked to you about me."

"My mother was ill for years before she died. How come you didn't know?"

I'd hesitated before asking this question. It was one I'd often thought about. In my moment of hesitation, I saw that Rae was stuck—not in the way my mother had been stuck, from lack of education, and the need to fill my mouth and hers, but stuck because of a gap, something missing from her personality.

She licked dry lips and said, "Lilian told me she didn't want to see me again. I didn't accept that. I mean, I tried—pestered her I suppose—and then I gave up, because I couldn't see that there was anything else for me to do."

Okay, I thought. But Mum's been dead for eight long years.

Rae sat hunched over, shoulders rounded. In a bulky tracksuit top, crinkled at armpits and neck, she looked lumpy, overweight.

"Did you give me a job as a way of getting to my mother?"

I expected Rae to be angry, but her voice was calm. "When I met you at the interview, I liked you straight away. I knew that you could do the work, and do it well. I had no trouble convincing the rest of the panel."

"You were counting on the fact that I'd tell Mum about my new job, tell her about *you*. Mum would be up here some time visiting me. There'd be a way for you to meet."

Rae said in a cold voice, "If that was true, I would have paid no more attention to you once I found out she was dead."

I'd had enough. I stood up

"My mother was nothing like you," I said. "I don't want to discuss her."

I headed for the door. Rae didn't try to stop me. She said good-bye to my departing back.

As I drove home, her dark face by the lake, the face I hadn't been able to see clearly, kept coming back to me. My mother and Rae Evans. I waited for it, the sick, empty feeling. It didn't come. There was dullness, apathy, where I expected raw chafing and a plunge into the dark.

Once again, I thought it was possible that I was being followed. I pulled over, and the car that had been sitting right behind me passed. I cursed myself for not being quick enough to read the registration number.

A picture came to me, of myself outside a house with my hand raised, about to knock. Then the door, the house, everything disappeared. I thought of Allison again, how beautiful she was. I thought of the fire, and how lucky it was that no one had been burnt.

PEOPLE WHO WRITE ABOUT investigations must surely all have this problem—they know the result before they start. They can beat up the whole story, make it appear more dramatic than it was, cramming incidents together that were isolated in time, and that no one at the time believed were connected, squeezing from them a tension altogether different from the anxiety and confusion they felt. Or they can go too far in the other direction, playing down events and the connections between them, out of some misplaced sense of tact. The conduct of an investigation is inevitably colored by its conclusion—or lack of conclusion—and memory, unreliable memory, grasshoppers backwards more or less where it will.

In spite of the fact that Rae was never far from my thoughts, most of my energy over the next few days was taken up with rescuing a dog.

ON MONDAY, I WALKED around the corner to pick Peter up from after-school care, and disturbed a puppy licking up a line of worms that rippled down a slope of wet asphalt bordering the playground.

I squatted and held out my hand. The dog took off across the oval, so thin it seemed to carry a dark cave inside it, huge hollow shadows between each rib, a face all bones and ears. I felt guilty for making it waste what little energy it had in running.

Peter complained of earache as soon as we got home. My stomach dropped and I thought, not again. We were out of Panadol, so I sat him in front of *The Simpsons* with a drink, and told him I'd be back in a few minutes.

At the chemist's, I saw the dog again, a flash of brown, four leg bones curved like a miniature wrecked ship, darting through the automatic doors.

The doors closed behind me with a click, and I heard a loud voice say, "It's the third time that animal's been in here. I should call the pound."

It was the combination of callousness and inaction in the pharmacist's grim voice that made me say, hoping to forestall her, "Dogs shouldn't be allowed to run round loose. *I'll* phone the pound when I get home."

The pharmacist stared at me, then asked, "Did you want something?"

"Oh," I said, feeling the clean indifference of commercial carpet through the soles of my shoes. "Yes, please. Liquid Panadol."

Peter knew he was supposed to stay inside, but as I parked the car I heard him nattering over the fence to the Chinese boy whose family had just moved in next door. I left him there and went straight to the phone.

The woman at the RSPCA sounded young, harassed.

"It must have been abandoned," I said. "It's got no collar and it's obviously starving."

Peter came running in. "What's starving?"

"You," I said, hanging up the phone.

"Who were you talking to?"

"Just someone."

Peter had dashed in, flushed and grinning, his hair flopping in his eyes. He pushed it back with four fingers together, held stiff as a plank. At my evasion, his shoulders rounded, shrinking yet defiant. I wondered how old he'd be before he accused me of lying, instead of just looking at me like that. I poured the analgesic into a green plastic crocodile with measurements along the side, and handed it to him without meeting his eyes.

"IN THE MORNING WE'LL go," I said. "In the morning, I promise we'll go and look for him."

It was a few hours later. Peter was sitting up in bed, reading to me in the voice he knew I liked best, pausing at full stops and commas.

I hadn't intended telling him about the dog. It just came out.

"Mum!" Peter leapt out of bed, book flying, feet tangling in the sheet. "What if he's still there!"

I had to stop him from running out the front door.

"First thing in the morning," I assured him.

* * *

WE FOUND THE DOG drinking at a long puddle on the edge of the play-ground. Again, it reminded me of a small wrecked ship that you might find on a beach after many winters, washed and scoured by sand.

Peter ran, and it took off toward the road, but not very fast. It was limping. Peter threw himself, arching his body over the skinny, miserable creature, and brought him to the ground.

"Careful!" I called out.

Peter was groaning and laughing and crying. "Got him! Mum! I did it! I've got him!"

I rang work, and told the woman on the switchboard I was sick. I said nothing to Peter about missing school. My next call was to the RSPCA.

"Do you want us to collect the dog?"

"We can keep him. But I wanted to check, I rang yesterday. Has any-one reported a puppy of that description missing?"

The receptionist took a long time to look it up, so long that I began to worry, though I was sure the dog was a stray. She came back on the line and told me no.

Within hours, he had put on weight. Peter would have fed him till he burst. The smell of flea soap hung around our back step, as though Lyne-ham had some special local air inversion just to keep it there.

He was christened Fred. Peter said that Fred was the right name for a dog who'd had to survive on worms. We took him to the vet. Close to him, I'd noticed a sweet, faintly rotting smell that reminded me of a time when I'd tried to cook sweet and sour pork and put in too much brown sugar. The vet said the smell was caused by ear mites, and gave us a bottle of stuff to wash his ears out with.

Peter was very solemn throughout the examination, each of his move-ments slow and careful, even so small an action as unclipping the new leash was a ceremony.

When it came to filling out his card, we guessed the dog's age, and the vet surprised us by saying that he was at least a year old, maybe more.

"But why isn't—why didn't—?" Peter stammered.

"He may have been living with a family," the vet said. "They may have moved, or maybe this fella left them."

"But we've called the PCA!" cried Peter. I moved to put my arm around him, but he shook me off, clutching the puppy by his brittle forepaws.

"If no one's reported the little fella missing, then I think you're pretty safe."

It was Peter who insisted on the flea wash, extra vitamins. If he forgot the ear-drops, he acted as though something terrible would happen, and I had to stop him pouring in a double, or a triple dose, to make up for the one he'd missed.

Ivan dropped by after work, and said that no self-respecting flea would dream of hitching a ride on such a heap of bones. Peter laughed, but there was no way Ivan could compete with Fred for his attention.

Peter wrote to Derek describing every detail of Fred's life, reading the sentences aloud as he composed them. I worried about Derek's response, but Peter was so happy that I couldn't bring myself to stop him. He made a toy out of a two-liter plastic bottle and a bit of rope. He called it dead bird, swung it round his head and yelled like a barbarian. Fred hid under the sofa, and wouldn't come out for a dog biscuit.

Peter went back to school next day with a note, but refused to go to after-school care. No threats or inducements made the slightest difference. I walked into the house at five-thirty to find him and Fred curled up in front of the TV, with various plates and cups licked clean and strewn around them on the floor.

HACKING

I WAS THINKING OF subscribing to Access Computing, so I could gain entry to the members' section of their Web site. It bothered me that I knew so little about the organization. Rae didn't seem to know a whole lot more. She'd spoken to Isobel Merewether on the phone and, so far as I knew, had no reason to doubt the woman's integrity. Angela Carlishaw's disappearance had not made Rae suspicious, though everybody else seemed to treat her whereabouts, indeed her existence, as a joke. Access Computing had made a very poor showing in the media, but, I reminded myself yet again, that did not prove them, or anybody connected to them, guilty of theft. Rae had claimed their grant application was the best, and I'd confirmed that much for myself at least.

I was curious to know just who their members were, what kinds of women used their services, and what *they* thought of the allegations and the rumors.

When I told Ivan my idea, he grinned mischievously and said, "You might have to pretend to be an *old* member, Sandy."

"Why?"

"Have you visited their site recently? It's closed to new subscribers."

I didn't ask why Ivan had taken the trouble to check. Instead, I asked him if he'd help me.

                              *   *   *

COMMUNICATING ILLEGALLY IN THE dark has a special, full-bodied feel
to it. Yet the whole point of hacking is that you can't see, or hear, or get a
whiff of your target's shape, let alone their gender. The point is that
you're invisible.

I have no precise recollection of Ivan's face the night we cheated our
way into Access Computing, but the conflicting emotions I felt are as
clear as though I am experiencing them now.

Ivan's room was dark. My vision was intently focused on a narrow
screen, yet I was so excited I could not keep still. I was crossing the
boundary between quarry and hunter, as though I'd known all along that
all I had to do was change my costume. Yet wasn't this what I was so critical of others for doing? Wasn't I about to commit a crime?

Ivan smiled, his head inclined a little to one side.

"You've done this kind of thing before," I said.

He was using a program he said he just happened to have lying
around, which tried out thousands of commonly used passwords. If we
were lucky, one of them would match a password chosen by an Access
Computing subscriber.

Much sooner than I'd dared to hope, he announced with satisfaction,
"Bingo!"

There were three new messages in the members' section of the site.
One was signed Anna D. My eyes jumped down the screen. Anna D's in-
dignation seemed to roll off it in waves.

> Has anyone received a CD from a company called
> Compic? The day after mine arrived, this woman
> from the company phoned and tried to talk me into
> buying a $600 package. She more or less told me
> that I had to have it! She phoned back the next day
> even though I'd told her no. Has anything like this
> happened to anybody else? I want to know how

they got my address and most of all, how they
knew I've recently gone freelance!

"Jesus," I said. "How did Compic get hold of Access Computing's list
of subscribers?"

Ivan scrolled rapidly forwards then backwards. "No one seems to
have replied to Anna D," he said.

"Can you get contact details for her?"

"I can try."

After the first couple of commands, I stopped being able to follow
what Ivan was doing. A list appeared. There were two Annas whose surname began with the letter D—Anna Dubowska and Anna Dunlop.

Ivan saved and printed out the list.

"Try this one first." He pointed to Anna Dubowska. "That's a good
solid Polish name."

My eyes were beginning to cross from staring at the screen. I looked
up. Alexander Graham Bell was frowning at me.

I turned back to Ivan. "Look for Angela Carlishaw."

Ivan searched backwards, forwards and sideways, but found no mention of her.

"Don't you think that's odd?"

"She's an embarrassment to them."

"Why don't they close the site down?"

Ivan gave his lion's head a scratch, and muttered that he didn't know.
Then he grinned and said, "You know, I haven't been sneaky like this in
years."

"Oh—when was the last time?"

"Jesus, Sandy, I don't know. Before I joined the public service?"

He punched me on the arm, and I pretended to fall over. My chair
scraped, and I remembered Peter, curled up asleep on the couch in Ivan's
living room, with Fred asleep beside him.

"We'd better go," I said.

"Just two more things."

Ivan installed a copy of the Trojan horse. He'd made one when it turned up on my machine at work. Now, he said, even if messages were deleted soon after they were posted, we should be able to retrieve them. He pointed out that the only three up there were ones that had been written that day, so it looked as though someone was getting rid of them pretty quickly.

I thanked him for his help. From now on, if I wanted information, I'd try sneaking in through a computer. I'd play dirty. It seemed the decision had been growing, like wattle buds, for weeks.

"What's the other thing?" I asked.

"Come with me."

"Oh," I said. "What about Peter?"

"Dead to the world. Let's live a little dangerously."

I'd never been into Ivan's bedroom before, and was overcome by the preparations he had made. The room was clean. He'd vacuumed it. I'd never seen any sign of a vacuum cleaner in Ivan's house. The sheets were freshly washed, and the doona cover, too. A small lamp stood on a table by the bed.

Because of what we'd just been doing, I sniffed and caught an unmistakable whiff of illegality in the air. It was the excitement of my first successful hack. Ivan understood. He watched me with a shy, but confident expression. He'd known how hacking would affect me. I felt a sharp surprise at realizing this, and what it meant—that in some ways Ivan knew me better than I knew myself. I remembered my journey inside the Trojan Horse, my reluctance and my fear, in the room that we'd just left behind. I thought how far I'd traveled since that Sunday afternoon.

Yes, Ivan knew things about me, saw them, and responded to them. I was more than ever conscious of the fullness of the air, the sweet smells of concealment.

He let me take the lead. I pulled off his old brown sweater, then his crumpled shirt. His large body, that, when I'd first met him, seemed to shriek out against his surroundings, fitted the whole of that neat room. I felt myself filled up with nerves, with the seductive pleasures of trespassing and make-believe. My spine prickled in anticipation of the touch of winter skin.

I made love to Ivan, and he lay quietly under me. I drew him along. I cried out. He pulled my head down. "Sh, sh," he whispered in my ear. But Peter and his dog, innocent in the next room, might have been a thousand miles away.

I did not want to leave, but I made myself get up, drive home, help my son into bed. Then, perversely but completely awake, I phoned Gail Trembath, with the list of subscribers sitting next to me. It was late, but I knew Gail kept late hours. I asked her if she'd ring some of the women on the list for the piece on home-based work she had promised me.

Gail groaned, and said she didn't know if she had the time.

"See if you can bring the conversation round to Compic. It seems they're into some pretty dodgy marketing. It's not just your office manager who's been persuaded to dish out big bucks."

"You know I asked him about that," Gail said. "He got really shitty and said it wasn't any of my business."

I didn't want to mention Access Computing by name just then. I knew Gail was convinced they were a bogus organization, and that Rae was hand in glove with them. I didn't want to give her more evidence for thinking so, not, at least, until I'd found out more about Access Computing and Compic myself.

"Something will blow," I said, "and when it does, you might just be the one who's standing underneath."

Gail laughed. We said goodnight.

WHEN IVAN AND I next logged on to Access Computing, the Trojan horse had done its job. While Peter played a game with Fred, we saved a list of e-mail addresses and passwords. Then we bundled a sleepy boy and dog into the car, drove back to my house, had a quick supper, and went to bed. If Peter was suspicious of Ivan's continuing nightly presence, then he gave no sign.

I woke when gray light was just beginning to stain the bottom of my curtains. I shook Ivan awake and he groaned and got up, while I lay listening for rain. I'd woken twice during the night to the sound of it.

"Hurry up," I whispered.

Ivan yawned, reaching for his clothes. Then he turned to face me, his T-shirt dangling from one hand and said, "So when are you telling the Derrick?"

Taken aback, I said, "I don't know."

Ivan scratched the skin under his beard. "Write your husband a letter, or ring him up. I don't care which."

I was fully awake, and shivering by then. I'd had no idea that Ivan cared whether or not Derek knew about us.

"And say what?"

"The truth."

"If I knew what that was, I wouldn't need to ask."

"Tell him, Sandra," Ivan said. "He might hate knowing, but at least he'll know."

GAIL RANG ME LATE that afternoon with some news. She'd done what I asked. The third woman she spoke to had raised the subject of Compic without her having to say anything.

"Out of the blue," Gail said excitedly. "Compic's been e-mailing the eyeballs off her, offering her all kinds of fabulous deals. She's not in a position to buy their stuff, or she hasn't been, but she's just landed a contract with this building company, the sort of crowd that might well fork out for smart-looking graphics. Here's the interesting bit. The lady claims Compic knew all this."

I was holding my breath. "Go on," I said.

"She saw that message on the Web site, the one you told me about. She tried to reply to it and got cut off."

I thanked Gail, who said she had a rush deadline and would talk to me later.

I wondered how Compic had stolen, bought, or perhaps been given, a list of Access Computing subscribers. Allison Edgeware might be clever and ambitious, as well as incredibly attractive, but that did not make her superwoman. Nor did she seem, from the little I had seen of her, to be the sort of person who would single-handedly plan and execute an aggressive marketing campaign.

I made a list of what I'd learnt about Compic so far, from the sale of their software to our department, and the *Canberra Times*, to the company's success in winning a development contract. Then there were the lists of home-based workers and Access Computing subscribers, which Compic had acquired, perhaps dishonestly, and were using to force their product onto unwilling buyers.

HATE MAIL

WHAT DO YOU THINK our Felix is doing right now?" I asked Ivan.

"Jogging," Ivan grunted.

It was Saturday afternoon, and Ivan and I were searching Felix Wenborn's office. Ivan had the computers, and I was going through boxes of disks and filing cabinets. The first thing to look for was a file dealing with the contract Compic had been awarded. I wasn't expecting to find it, and I didn't. If there was an irregularity in the way Felix had handled the contract, and he'd removed the files from Rae's office as part of covering this up, then he wouldn't leave evidence sitting in broad daylight in his own.

Provided no one interrupted us, we were in for a long afternoon. Peter was at a birthday party. Ivan had planted a small bug in the main operating system late on Friday afternoon. Then he'd volunteered to come in and work on it over the weekend. If we were challenged, I would say I was keeping him company. A thin excuse, but I was feeling confident that day.

"The beauty of this little bug, Sandushka," Ivan said, "is that to chase it I have to open all the system programs."

I laughed and hugged him. We were companions in crime. Ivan moved to another computer and began keying in commands. "Adding that zero to the grant money was a one-step job," he muttered to himself. "In and out. Quicker than a ten-dollar fuck. There's no trace. Don't know why I thought there would be."

He was grumbling that there was no way he could trace the viruses either, when I grabbed him by the arm.

"Ivan. Look."

"What?" He glanced at me and frowned.

I pushed a box of floppy disks toward him. "E-mail backups."

"So?"

The disks had been filed by individual PC. I searched through Rae's, looking for the threatening messages. Once again, I could find no trace of them. Disheartened, I pushed the box aside, and started on Jim Wilcox's.

"Jesus," I said a few minutes later, unable to believe the words staring at me from the screen.

Wilcox had sent heaps of abusive messages, calling Rae Evans everything from a "tight-arsed bitch" to "female chauvinist sow" to "that frigid blue-rinse femocrat." There was no doubt that they referred to Rae. She was named in nearly every one of them.

They were all to the same address. Someone had told me that e-mail fitted somewhere between a phone conversation and a written memo. Going through those informal, one-sided conversations, seeing a side of Jim Wilcox I'd never dreamed existed, was the most voyeuristic thing I'd ever done.

At least I knew now why he'd set Rae on a collision course with Felix. Though I didn't know *why* he hated her, I had doubt that he did. Anger was slowly beginning to take hold of me by the hair roots.

The e-mails had been sent to someone called Charles Craven. We looked him up, and found that he worked in the accounts section of the Department of Finance.

I said to Ivan, "Maybe it was *Craven* who changed the figure from a hundred grand to a million, not anyone from our department. I don't understand why the police haven't followed this up, or why Wilcox was stupid enough to send all those e-mails."

"Maybe the police don't know."

"Here's a scenario," I said. "Felix knows what's on these disks and he's blackmailing Wilcox, threatening to hand them over to the cops. Felix has his own copies, so it doesn't matter if Wilcox gets rid of this lot. He's left them in his office to make Wilcox sweat."

Ivan groaned. "Don't give me that cat's-bum smile, Sandy. You like Evans, so you're sure she's innocent. You don't like Felix, and if you find anything that sticks to him you'll be happier than a pig in mud."

"Felix is like the pig who's built his house of bricks, only it turns out, to his amazement, that the bricks are made of straw."

Ivan groaned again.

I thought over it. It seemed to me that Felix could well be guilty of stealing the money and framing Rae, either on his own, or with Jim Wilcox and Charles Craven.

While we were packing up—I took care to replace the boxes in exactly the right order—I said, "Thanks for helping me."

Ivan drew himself up to his full height and pretended to look down his nose.

"It's a matter of public service pride, Sandy. I know we're for the chop next year, but I'm buggered if I'll go down with a mess like this still on my hands. It'll just prove everything the politicians say about our inefficiency."

"And if the criminal turns out to be one of us?"

"Ah—but if I find her, or him, toss the bad apple out, then I'm exonerated, aren't I?"

"So you're doing it for your own professional advancement."

"Aren't you?"

I was stung. I hadn't thought about it this way, but perhaps Ivan was partly right.

"If I find that Evans is guilty, I'm prepared to accept it," Ivan said. "That's the difference between us."

"Because I'm not?"

"No, Sandy. You aren't."

I was silent, thinking about this, then remembered something that had slipped my mind.

"That Compic software," I said.

"What about it?"

"Did you find out how much other departments have bought?"

Ivan nodded. "I asked Harmer. He said lots. It's popular."

"Oh," I said. I hadn't meant for Ivan to ask Guy, or anybody for that matter, directly. It wasn't Ivan's fault. I hadn't told him I wanted him to make inquiries without letting on that he was making them. I'd thought he would simply understand the need for discretion.

"Popular," I repeated. "Why do you think it's popular?"

Ivan shrugged. "It's cute. You saw the demo."

"How many of our sections have you talked into using it?"

Ivan shrugged again.

"Could it be because of Allison, their beautiful director?"

"Maybe. Don't worry, Sandy. Girls like that aren't my type."

I did not know how to reply to this. "What about Felix?" I asked after a few moments. "Is Allison his type, do you think?"

"No. Felix is your old-fashioned married man. Don't be fooled by the red shorts."

"He bought all that software from her, and he could well have shown favoritism when it came to the development contract."

"That's not like Felix either."

"It may not be *like* him, but there was a complaint. Have you ever seen Allison and Felix together?"

"No," Ivan repeated.

Before I could quiz him further, he asked, "What about Derek? Have you written to him?"

"I—" I began, then bit my lip. "I have to pinch myself sometimes to remember that I'm married to him." This was true, but it wasn't the whole truth. At other times, I wanted to be with Derek, wanted him to be with me. I'd never tried to explain these contradictory feelings to Ivan, and despaired of doing so just then.

"I don't know what to tell him."

"Figure it out," Ivan said.

We argued over what to tell the police about the e-mails.

In the end, I insisted on doing it my way. After being asked to wait for a few minutes, I was put through to Hall, the detective who'd interviewed me and read the charges against Rae at her committal hearing. Glad to find him working on a Saturday, I told him what we'd found. He asked a few questions and said he'd arrange to have someone go through the disks as soon as possible.

My next call was to Rae's lawyer. She'd given me his home, as well as his office number. I told him everything I knew—about the e-mails, Charles Craven in Finance, how easy it would have been for Craven and Wilcox to plot the theft together and pin it on Rae.

The lawyer didn't interrupt. I hoped he was making notes. He didn't ask me any questions. As soon as I'd finished, he thanked me and rang off.

I asked Ivan back to my place, but he said that he had things to do. I didn't try and change his mind. I didn't want to quarrel—over Derek, or Felix, or the e-mails. I had kept too many of my thoughts from Ivan, I realized just then, for any relationship with him to be open and straightforward. Telling Derek we were sleeping together was the least of it.

Saying goodbye, which we did with a kiss, and a quick, half apologetic hug, I pictured the spatial element of words and numbers, my bits of clues that might not be clues at all, singing out through wires, through space, more solitary than a humpback's song.

What becomes wicked is only an extension of the ordinary along a certain plane. No one has to pass through a needle's eye to get there. The ordinary can extend into a vast, unfitting shape, or else contract into a needle's eye.

ON MONDAY AFTERNOON, I met Felix in the travel center on his way back from a run.

"What were you and Rae Evans arguing about that day in the lift?" I asked.

"Never give up, do you?" Felix stared at me, chest pumping. "Listening at keyholes. That's just about your level."

"You asked me to listen, remember? Why was Rae Evans asked to deal with a complaint about the contract that you gave to Compic?"

"She volunteered."

"I've got another idea," I said. "Jim Wilcox ordered her to do it. He knew it would mean trouble between the two of you, and he hates her guts."

Felix turned away from me without bothering to comment. I watched him go, admiring his supple, athletic stride. I felt strongly connected to him, as though we were bound together by some soft skin that would hurt if I pulled on it. My eyes fixed on the disappearing back of his neck. Maybe Felix had had his hair cut, or the low neck of his T-shirt made it look different. The skin was very pale there. Seen from behind, his head looked thinner, older, without the snub features that gave his face its boyish expression.

Walking up the stairs—I seemed to have developed an aversion to the lift—I mulled over how much strife between people could be traced back to first impressions. The more Felix claimed to be in control, the less he really was. He knew that. He'd as much as admitted it to me. Felix had to be thinking of the future. Where would he go when outsourcing made his job redundant, or when the department collapsed beneath him? Who would take him on? Of course, once Rae was found guilty and sentenced, Felix began to look a whole lot better. A man who knew his job and did it.

That afternoon, I got the go-ahead to finish the outwork report, and used my tea break to ring Rae from a public box, glad to have some good news to share.

Rae sounded tired, but pleased to hear from me. I said I was sorry I'd walked out of her flat like that.

She apologized as well. "I didn't mean to upset you, Sandra."

Her voice had an undercurrent that I didn't like, but I was delighted that we were talking again, so I didn't pay attention to it.

"Want me to come round? I could come this evening."

Rae hesitated, then said, "No. You'd better not."

"I rang your lawyer. Did he tell you?"

"Yes."

Quickly, I filled her in on the abusive e-mails, reflecting that I'd rung to share good news, and was hardly doing that. I'd said I'd spoken to Detective Sergeant Hall as well.

Rae said nothing in response to this. Instead she said, "I'd better go now. I can hear the doorbell."

I debated going round there, even though she'd told me not to. She'd sounded weak and lonely. It was bad for her to be sitting in her flat with nobody to talk to. But I felt a kind of lethargy soaking through my clothes, my skin, like the smoke from the fire that had soaked into everything. I went upstairs, and concentrated on my report for the next two hours. After that, I felt exhausted. I took the fire stairs back to the ground floor, and hunched my shoulders over coffee that tasted of damp soot.

I pictured Rae in the corridor, on her way out of the building after she had been suspended, telling me she couldn't talk, then outside the magistrate's court where I'd waited for her, leaning against a statue. That day, Rae had been remote, removed, as though she'd retreated to some place where nothing could touch her.

I rang Detective Sergeant Hall to see what progress had been made with the e-mails, and was told he was unavailable. I left a message.

LOVE IN THE
(SUB) TROPICS

O NE SUNDAY, SHORTLY BEFORE Peter left for Philadelphia to spend the school holidays with his father, we took Fred for a walk up Mount Majura.

I'd often seen the mountain from the oval, or from a parallel height on O'Connor Ridge, but never, in all my years in Canberra, climbed it for itself. That Sunday morning, it seemed the mountain had been waiting to spread us out along its palomino flanks. Or it may have been the light, sun with the first assured warmth in it, which in Canberra has the quality of new-blown glass. Outdoors for the first time without coats, susceptible to such breaking light, high-stepping, could anything have stopped us?

Ivan was some way ahead. Fred ran backwards, forward, and sideways, never in a straight line. He smelt something, barked once, and took off underneath a fence. I had to give Peter a leg up over it, so he could chase his dog and bring him back to the path.

I caught up with Ivan, and we began to talk about a computer show that was coming up in Brisbane. He'd been preparing a virtual reality display for it with Guy Harmer.

"Why don't I come, too?" I suggested. "I've never been to Brisbane. A long weekend in the tropics—we could kill two birds with one stone."

Ivan frowned. Then he grinned and said, "Well, I suppose so, Sandy. If you enjoy killing birds with stones."

THE DAY BEFORE IVAN and I left for Brisbane, two things happened. I said goodbye to Peter, and I ran into Allison Edgeware in Garema Place.

At the last minute, when Peter was packing his rucksack, he said he couldn't go to America because Fred would miss him too much.

"I'll be looking after Fred for you," I said.

"But you won't know what to feed him!"

"Fred and I will get along fine."

"But you're going to Brisbane!"

I sighed and pressed my thumbnail into the tip of my left index finger. "Only for three days. And the lady at the kennels is nice. You said so yourself."

For a few seconds, Peter swayed on the edge of a stubborn and complete refusal. He threw himself down on his bed, and I decided to leave him there. Whose idea had it been for him to visit his father anyway? But I knew Peter wouldn't have written that letter to Derek after we found Fred.

A while later, I heard the back door open, and Peter's love-murmurings and assurances that his dog would survive the weeks without him.

At the airport, my son looked small, round-shouldered, amazingly grown-up. I told him to take care, and he reminded me that Fred had to have milk in the mornings for his bones. I watched the back of his head bob up and down level with the air hostess's armpit, then disappear into the belly of the bird that would take him half a world away.

ON MY WAY BACK from the airport, I stopped off at the bank. It didn't seem real that tomorrow I'd be setting out myself, a bona fide traveler with a suitcase. How much cash do you need for a long weekend in Brisbane? I was hurrying out through the bank's automatic doors when I spotted Allison in Bunda Street.

She was looking straight ahead and walking purposefully, but I had only to keep going straight myself, and our paths would cross. Somehow, I couldn't believe that this was accidental.

"Hi," I said.

"Oh. Hello." Allison stopped a couple of meters away from me, and smiled. I thought she was pretending to be surprised to see me.

"How long have you been with Compic?" I asked her.

She looked offended. "It's my company," she said. "I own it."

"Then you'd know exactly how your company came to be in possession of Access Computing's list of subscribers."

"Access Computing? Isn't that the women's group that was in the news? I think they might have bought one of our graphics packages. It's very popular. It's doing even better than we hoped."

She glanced at her watch and murmured, "Look, I'm really sorry, it was lovely to see you, but I've got to run."

I returned the compliment. On reflection, I decided it was too far-fetched to suppose that Allison had deliberately bumped into me.

Allison. Angela. Isobel. Allison was in Canberra. Angela had disappeared into the strong arms of a Scottish nunnery. If my plan worked, I might soon be meeting Isobel.

All good detectives, in the novels I nightly took to bed with me, possessed an ability that I most clearly lacked. When I let my mind wander, hoping it would yield up significant facts and the logical connections between them, it came up, instead, with images of women whose mascara never ran. I filled my late-night hours picturing Angelas and Allisons, crooked ladies who never broke a nail, whose hair would never be presented to the world as gray.

I felt them all around me, smooth women, polished like expensive furniture, heads inclined gracefully over matching keyboards.

Are hackers, I asked myself, for the most part pranksters, mischief-makers? Or voyeurs, snoopers, invaders of privacy? Agents of espionage, or industrial spies? What about trespassers? I thought of my one attempt so far, aided and abetted by Ivan. We'd invaded the privacy of others, seen what had not been meant for our eyes. Was it dishonest of me to claim, in my own mind at least, that it had been in a good cause? I did not feel guilty. Given the chance, I would do the same again.

I'd got nowhere with Detective Sergeant Hall. I felt alone again, dependent on my own devices. Perhaps, I decided, hacking was best described as impersonation.

I'D NEVER FLOWN FROM a cold part of the country to a warm one, never on that magic carpet, lifting off from Canberra airport at seven in the morning, when the temperature was minus two degrees. Nor had I ever really felt the urge to.

It had been one of the shadows before Derek left—that I obstinately refused to appreciate the pleasures of travel. To Derek, it was as though I was refusing to live, preferring a job in a stuffy, uninteresting office, in a soulless city.

I hugged myself with delight, walking down the aluminum steps at Brisbane airport. The warm air was like a kiss. It was incredibly corny in a way, and commonplace to Ivan, who had circumnavigated the globe more times than he cared to remember, and for whom Canberra to Brisbane was as close to going home as he seemed likely to get. Even Peter, by bunny-hopping to the States, had already traveled further than I had, and perhaps ever would.

"Smell it!" I said. "Ivan!"

I led him through the arrival gate. "Love in the tropics," I said, teasing myself with it.

Our hotel room smelt of air freshener. I spent ten minutes trying to get the window open, then gave up. The green-and-white curtains were made of muslin, or some other thin stuff, but that was all they needed to be, because there was no freezing 2 A.M. air waiting to walk through them. I'm not normally a person who complains about the weather, but all through that first day I kept thinking, how can we go back? What will we be going back to? Strolling down a hill to find somewhere to eat, through a park smelling of frangipani, I held my breath, not wanting to let go of the sweetness.

While Ivan went to set up his display—Guy Harmer was arriving on a mid-afternoon flight—I took a bus along Brisbane's winding, hilly streets to an address I'd memorized.

I was still trying to decide whether to be myself, or a woman working from home wanting information. As the bus wound up the hill, I closed my eyes and let the swaying fill my head. I was sitting at the back, near a clutch of schoolgirls in kelp-colored uniforms. A couple were swinging in their seats, exaggerating the labored movements of the bus and giggling. I felt again as I had when I stepped off the plane, that this northern space, this movement, was a gift.

The girls got out. The bus kept clanking and winding upward until I was the last person on it. Was Access Computing's office in a suburban shopping center, then? Would we come to it in a minute, round a bend?

At the last stop, the sliding doors closed after me with a hiss and a thud, and I turned to see the driver check his watch and pull a packet of cigarettes from his shirt pocket.

The stop was a yellow post in the ground. There was no bus shelter, and nobody about. Most of the houses were set back, with high fences or hedges.

The footpath sloped upward under my feet. Ahead of me were some shabby old cement-rendered flats with outside wooden staircases. I'd thought the tops of hills were usually reserved for the rich.

When I stopped outside number six, I was even more surprised. It seemed that the building might well have been one of the first in the area. It had double red-brick chimneys, and a peculiar domed tower at one end. I imagined it hanging above the city until at last the suburbs rose to meet it, feeling their way with paved roads and curved gutters, and a sun-colored stick for a bus stop.

I looked over the mailboxes until I spotted thirteen. Half the boxes had mail in them. I took a step closer, flicked the envelope in thirteen so that I could see the name on the front, and, as pleased with myself as if I'd solved one of life's larger mysteries, made my way into the building.

I rang a doorbell. The door was opened by a woman with black hair, dressed for a winter's day in Canberra.

She peered at me and said, "It's the office you want, dearie? It's on the next floor, right above our heads."

I opened my mouth to ask, isn't this number thirteen? But the woman was quicker. "Are you from the police?"

"Just visiting."

"They've had a lot of visitors." A smile of amusement and complicity creased the woman's lips. "Would you like something to drink, dear? You look hot. Been walking up the hill?"

"Thank you," I said. "That would be very nice."

I was startled by my eagerness to pry. Finding Access Computing's office had been an adventure, part of the adventure of being away from home. I hadn't planned exactly what I would do when I got there.

The woman's name was Mrs. Styvcek. We introduced ourselves while she led me down a narrow hallway. Her flat was full of indoor plants with a look of piracy about them. She motioned me to sit in a bower between polished leaves larger than dinner plates, pinched from the Daintree maybe, or some other northern rainforest. Her skin was deeply lined around the eyes and mouth, her hair dyed a flat shade and pulled back in a bun, giving prominence to her clever eyes. I knew she'd already taken in as much of me as she could from first impressions, from my wedding ring to southern style of dress.

Mrs. Styvcek brought me lemon cordial with ice cubes, peering at me round her outsize plants.

I thanked her, then asked, "How many people use the office upstairs? Do you see much of them?"

"We've had the police here, dear. The *Federal* Police." Mrs. Styvcek's high cheekbones shone with recognition of a kindred snooper. "The police asked me lots of questions." She leant forward confidentially. "*They* asked me how often there was someone in the office, whether there was someone there all the time. I had to say I didn't know."

"Do you know who's there right now?"

Her eyes widened, a twinkle at the back of them. "Well, I don't know whether there's *always* someone there, now do I dear? The walls are thick in these old flats. I do hear the phone ringing quite a lot, I will say that. They asked me what the rent was," she continued. "Why didn't they ask her that, if they wanted to know?"

"Her? Would that be Isobel Merewether?"

Mrs. Styvcek nodded, then pressed her lips together.

"What about this Angela person?" I asked.

"I've never set eyes on her."

I smiled, then we both began to laugh.

I finished my drink, took a deep breath of pampered indoor garden, and said, "I was wondering, would you do me a small favor? I'm going up there now. Do you think you could—after I've been inside for five minutes—could you knock on the door and ask to speak to—"

"Isobel? You want me to speak to Isobel, dear? What about?"

"Anything," I answered. "Talk about the weather. No, wait. Tell Isobel you've just had a call from the police. You're not sure what to tell them."

"Well, dear, she knows the police have interviewed everybody in the block."

"Say the police have asked you to inform them when she leaves and at what time."

Mrs. Styvcek gave a deep, sly chuckle. "And my conscience is pricking at me. Why would it do that?"

"Nothing illegal or sinister," I assured her. "I just need a couple of minutes in there on my own."

* * *

CLIMBING THE STAIRS, I could hear the weary, determined cry of a child who would just as soon stop, but wasn't going to give in while its mother was in earshot.

I came to a white door with a sign in dark blue that said ACCESS COMPUTING.

I knocked. A young woman opened the door and frowned at me. I recognized her as Isobel Merewether from her television interviews.

"Is this Access Computing?" I asked as politely as I could.

"I'm afraid we're closed at present." When Isobel spoke, her mouth scarcely moved.

"Oh," I said. "Will you be open later today?"

"We're closed indefinitely. What did you want?" Isobel spread the fingers of her left hand and smoothed back her hair. Her nails were long, with fresh, peach-colored varnish, and she wore no rings.

On TV, Isobel had reminded me of Claire Disraeli, Guy Harmer's girlfriend. In person, her hair and skin were darker, her eyes brown, not blue. But the resemblance was there, in long slim legs and general polish.

I took another deep breath, and explained that I was from Lismore. I was trying to set myself up to do word processing and other kinds of contract work from home. I'd heard about Access Computing, and since I'd had to come to Brisbane for a few days, I thought it would be the perfect opportunity to find out more about them.

Isobel listened to all of this, making no attempt to hide her impatience.

"I'm sorry, but I can't help you," she said as soon as I'd finished.

"If you're busy, perhaps I could see your other director, Angela Carlishaw?"

"Angela's away."

"Well, could I at least have a glass of water, please? I've had rather a long walk to get here."

Isobel's eyes darkened from Italian leather brown to almost black.

"Excuse me for a minute."

She disappeared down a corridor, turning left, while I stepped through an open doorway to my right.

Cream curtains had been pulled right back, and sunlight filled the room. Two blank-faced computers were placed side by side. A bowl of dead fuchsias sat on a window ledge. The office had a feeling of lightness, almost of dizziness, a combination of height and the penetrating sun. I wondered what it would be like in a storm. A cardboard box held a printer, a couple of modems, a mouse, and other sundries. Clearly, Isobel was packing up.

A quick tug at the drawers convinced me that the filing cabinet was locked. I flicked through some brochures lying on a low glass table, and popped one in my bag, while I looked for a handwritten note, a phone number, anything.

Mrs. Styvcek was right on cue. Her knock was loud, peremptory. It startled me, even though I was expecting it. Isobel glared at me, glass of water in one hand. I smiled reassuringly, and she turned toward the door.

"Oh, Mrs. Styvcek,' I heard her say. "I'm busy, I'm afraid. I have someone with me."

I opened the door of a built-in cupboard. Boxes with Compic's name and logo were stacked in three tall piles. I picked one up. It felt light. I flicked it over. There was no price on the back.

I heard Isobel's step behind me, and turned round with another smile.

Isobel was hanging on to her manners by a fingernail. "I told you we're not open. Now I really *must* ask you to leave."

I insisted on the glass of water, and took my time to drink it, pretending indifference to the hostility coming in waves off Isobel's designer T-shirt.

I was walking down the stairs when Mrs. Styvcek appeared, her small malicious face reminding me of a neighbor's cat that liked to hiss at Fred.

She beckoned me over, and said in a stage whisper, "You are from the police, aren't you?"

"No, really. I'm not."

"A private investigator?"

"Unfortunately, no."

I would have liked to quiz Mrs. Styvcek further, but I was already imagining everything I'd said being relayed back to Isobel.

"Did you get what you want, dearie?"

"Yes, thank you," I said. "Thank you very much."

Mrs. Styvcek's black eyes followed me as I walked away, resolutely not looking back.

I felt as though I'd eaten something rotten. Isobel was so slimy you could slip on her and break both legs. I pictured Access Computing's office stripped and empty. Impossibly distant from the city, from clients and potential clients, suspended over that hillside—who was the show for?

I returned to the bus stop, wishing I'd been sensible enough to bring a hat. There was a bus waiting, and I ran toward it.

Safe inside, I looked back along the street. Already the block of flats seemed like a mirage. I stared at its fading image, splay-legged on the rim of the hill, both decrepit and cocksure.

I wondered if Rae had tried to be all things to all women. Femocrat. I hated that word. She had never struck me as a woman who liked having power over others. Too remote, too proud. Women who enjoyed using power showed it. It came off them like a scent. Favoritism, yes. She was capable of that. After all, she'd shown it to me.

For a moment, I imagined standing in Rae's shoes. I felt the customary slide of silk against my throat, as I dressed for the working day. I felt what it must be like to spend years building a career, and then have that career ripped out from underneath me.

Perhaps Isobel Merewether and her organization had done nothing wrong, but after meeting her, and seeing the office, I was no longer inclined to give her the benefit of the doubt. Compic might have stolen Access Computing's list of subscribers, but it seemed to me that this explanation relied on an unlikely coincidence. If Isobel and her group were innocent of any wrongdoing, then surely they would have supported their subscribers' complaints, and this support would have been apparent to any members who logged on to their site. If a million dollars had simply appeared in their account, if twenty thousand had been transferred to Rae by some mysterious third party, Isobel would have reacted very differently when questioned by the press. I realized that I had never believed Angela Carlishaw was real. She'd struck me, from the first time I heard her name, as make-believe.

Then there were those Compic boxes in the cupboard, back there in the office. I wished I'd been able to open one, or steal it. If they'd been smaller, I'd have tried. I wished I'd thought to wear a coat.

Rae should have found out more about Access Computing before she awarded them the grant. Would *I* have found out more, if I'd been in her position? The old Sandra might have done exactly as Rae had done, taken their grant application at face value, mistaking appearances for the substance underneath. I flattered myself that the new Sandra, the Sandra I hoped I was becoming, would have asked more questions, dug a little deeper. And that complaint about the contract Felix gave to Compic—it should have been clear to Rae, from the minute she was asked to deal with the complaint, that it was a trap.

There was something unworldly, otherworldly, about Rae. People interpreted her manner as cold and disdainful, and it was true, she could be both these things. At the lake, when she'd made that remark about watching the water rise, she had struck me as frighteningly vulnerable. One minute she'd seemed to push away my offers of assistance, and the next to acknowledge that she needed them.

I wondered again about the paper records that had disappeared, and who knew that files relating to the Compic contract had gone missing. Every government department has a multitude of checks and cross-references, people whose job it is to look over other people's shoulders. But a determined shadow had stolen between them.

A new thought came to me. What if Access Computing had never existed as a separate entity? It might explain that office in the middle of nowhere, Isobel and the fictitious Angela. Access Computing *had* designed courses for women, and given advice, run a Web site, and successfully applied for a grant. But what if their main purpose was altogether different?

I saw Allison Edgeware, at that moment, as a beautiful but deadly spider. And Isobel Merewether. Another china-doll name for another deceitful female, spinning silk webs with false, gracious smiles. Could it be, was it possible, that Access Computing was Allison's creation?

I COULD SEE PEOPLE dancing there—it was obviously a floor made for dancing on—maybe next weekend, when the computer show had packed up and gone home. I felt dwarfed by the flat glossy spaces of the convention center, the smells of floor polish and expensive electronics. Looking around for stand E 59, I heard a voice over-primed with alcohol complaining about recycled hash from Expo.

All the stands were full. Young women dressed for a night out brushed against students in black baseball caps and Michael Jordan sweatshirts. Most carried plastic bags full of advertising brochures. The kids moved quickly from exhibit to exhibit, trying out the demonstrations, confidently logging on.

The big guns were there—IBM, Canon, Microsoft. I passed their stands, barely registering the familiar names and logos. The hall was air-conditioned, and I began to shiver.

Security men in black nylon jackets looked as interested as anybody, each one carrying a mobile phone. There were plenty of them, but it was hard to see how any of the gear could be ripped off. Each stand had three or four minders, sometimes half-a-dozen.

I spotted Guy Harmer operating Ivan's virtual reality equipment. I smiled hello. He nodded, preoccupied with a circle of young women waiting for a turn. Guy never missed a trick. I told myself that in a second I would turn round, and there would be Ivan.

Guy adjusted the headset on a woman wearing a shiny black suit. She moved slowly inside the harness, turning from right to left and back again, grasping the joystick as if it was some sort of lifeline.

"Guy?" I said. "Where's Ivan?"

He hesitated, as if about to tell me that he didn't know, then gestured with his free arm, while he helped the woman in black to regain her balance. I looked to where he pointed, and saw Ivan leaning against a concrete column, drinking from a plastic cup. I'd seen the woman, his companion, before—that is, he'd once shown me a photo of her. It was Lauren, his ex-wife.

GUY OFFERED TO BUY me dinner.

"Thanks," I said, "but I think I'll just go back to the hotel."

"Not the best idea you've ever had, Sandy." Guy put his arm around my shoulders, smiling kindly. "Help me pack this stuff up, and then we'll grab a bite."

"But don't you have a—" I was going to say date.

Guy smiled again, and shook his head, parodying a small boy accused of doing something wrong. He was as neat and smooth and cool as though he'd just had his suit pressed, not spent hours answering questions and helping people on and off a platform. I began to wrap the headset carefully in bubble plastic, not looking toward the fake Greek column from which Ivan had disappeared with Lauren.

An hour or so later, I was watching Guy order in a seafood restaurant he said he'd tried on a previous trip—"wasn't too bad then." I bit my tongue and didn't tell him that places with starched, fluted serviettes, and a wine list as long as your arm were definitely not my style. I let him order for me. When the wine came, I drank my first glass quickly.

"Ivan never talked about her," I said. Was my voice really cracking? I wasn't going to cry in the middle of a classy restaurant. I took another gulp of wine.

"Half of Brisbane was there. She probably just turned up. I bet there's nothing in it."

There was no sarcasm or amusement in Guy's voice, or his clear gray eyes. At the same time, it was like him to pretend that any event he was associated with must be hugely popular.

"Have you ever met her?"

"I've worked with Ivan for about five years. I knew he'd been married, but that's all."

"You know, I met this fairy-tale person today," I said, to change the subject. "A kind of Rapunzel."

"Rapunzel, Rapunzel, let down your hair?"

I nodded. "But a wicked one."

"Wicked?" A smile fanned Guy's smooth cheeks.

"Way up at the top of a block of flats," I said.

"Are all good girls wicked underneath?"

"I wouldn't know."

"Did Rapunzel seem like my type?" Guy continued. "This is interesting."

"Blonde. Tall. Immaculate. I guess so, yes."

Guy laughed. "Perhaps you know something about me I don't know myself."

I laughed with him. I glimpsed how he would look in middle age if things went according to plan—perfectly groomed, wealthy, dining in expensive restaurants with women half his age.

Our food arrived, and I bent my head to it gratefully while the waiter refilled my glass.

"Is she Evans's type?" Guy persisted. "This fairy-story character of yours?"

"Why do you ask that?"

"Can you see the two of them together?"

"No,' I said. 'I can't."

Guy lowered his eyes and concentrated on his barramundi. The fish looked delicious. We didn't speak for a few moments. I was more than ever conscious that he didn't belong in the public service, and also that this judgment was unfair. Why should public servants all be of one type? The ones I'd met certainly weren't. Still, I knew that if I'd reminded Guy just then that he worked for a government department, he would have stared at me as though my comment was in the worst possible taste.

"You know," he said, "I'm surprised none of the reporters asked

Evans whether she'd been to Brisbane recently. Or better still, did their homework and found out for themselves."

"Why would Rae Evans come to Brisbane?"

"Protecting her investment."

I helped myself to salad. "Why do you dislike Rae? What's she done to you?"

Instead of answering, Guy looked at me with frank sexual appraisal. I resisted an impulse to run my fingers through my hair.

He smiled again. "I wouldn't worry too much about our Russki friend."

"Ivan left you in the lurch tonight as well." I tried for a lighter tone, filing away the information that Guy hadn't answered my question about Rae. Like Di Trapani and Ivan, he evaded the question of what he had against her.

Guy smiled without rancor, letting me know that he didn't consider Ivan a rival, either personally or professionally. He was in Brisbane for reasons of his own, maybe something as simple as picking up a new girl.

"How did you know about us?" I asked. "About Ivan and me."

He raised a perfect eyebrow. "You two would hardly win first prize for discretion. But I'm sure this will sort itself out. Semyonov will be feeling guilty as hell."

"Ivan looked as though—" I began. But I couldn't think how he had looked. Drunk. But he wasn't. Ivan didn't drink, part of his reaction against his father and his father's habits.

Guy picked up his glass, studying the pale green-gold wine, or perhaps his reflection.

"Poor bastard was in *shock*," he said.

"SANDRA."

Ivan heaved himself up onto his elbows and peered at the digital clock. "Where the hell have you been?"

"Walking," I said. "And—with Guy. Where's Lauren?"

188

"I took her to dinner in the revolving restaurant. Should be called revolting restaurant."

Ivan's anger and frustration filled the room.

"Why didn't you tell me?" I asked him. "Why let me walk into it like that?"

"Lauren read my name in a flier. Does it matter? Christ! I didn't invite her. Would I have done it like that? Humiliation gets so damn boring after a while. I get so damn bored. Christ!"

I began to undress, feeling cold and cheated. It was like a broken promise that the city had made me, to stand there shivering with cold.

"I never wanted to get married,' Ivan said accusingly. "It was tempting fate. Tempting? Hey, look down here, you fates! Here's a guy just asking for it!"

I thought about getting another room, but I was practically undressed and too tired to be bothered.

"When Lauren left, a part of me thought, well, it had to happen!"

Now Ivan had begun, he might go on all night.

"A body *has* to lie low! Lauren never understood that. Why should she? Adultery has to be paid for! You're a coward, Sandra! Too scared to write to that yuppie husband of yours and tell him you're having an affair. What do you think he's going to do? Fly home and shoot us both? Othello with a ponytail?'

Inside my head I was screaming, *but there's Peter*.

I WOKE UP EARLY, feeling terribly thirsty. On my way to the basin to get a glass of water, I walked through a great wad of sunlight that the thin curtains seemed to invite into the room.

Ivan didn't move. I thought of Lauren and the things he'd said about her, holding his words in front of me like a curtain of some fine material Desire and belonging and knowledge all were there, but when I clutched at them, there was nothing for me to get a grip on. I tried to see the pattern for what it was, at the same time afraid that it was beyond me.

Still thirsty, I poured myself a second glass of water. Outside, the weather began to change. I smelt it through the curtains. When I finally managed to open the window, the wind was cool and damp.

I turned round. Ivan was awake and looking at me. "At least put some knickers on," he said. "If you're going to parade in front of the window."

"It's what people do in the tropics," I told him, "when they haven't got a ceiling fan."

"For the hundred and fifty-fifth time, Brisbane is not the fucking tropics."

I splashed cold water on my face, for a few seconds hearing no other sound than the wind outside, rushing to fill a vacuum.

I'd tucked the brochure I'd taken from Access Computing at the bottom of my bag. Two numbers were listed. I tried them while Ivan was in the shower. The first was an answering machine, Isobel's recorded voice. I let the second ring until I heard the shower turned off.

"Will we just take it back, the hire car?" I asked Ivan while he was getting dressed.

"No, we'll go to the beach. Why not?"

"Are you seeing her tonight?"

"Lauren is a bitch."

I let the words sink in, then said, "I didn't realize that you still loved her." I wanted simply to set it out between us as a piece of information.

IVAN LAY IN THE sun, reading. Every now and then, he lifted his head and stared at the sea through his sunglasses. Tanned people were scattered along the beach. We were conspicuous, pale winter slugs with northern hedonists all round us.

I was longing to tell him about Access Computing, but I didn't. I was building up a store of secrets I was keeping from Ivan. I wondered how many secrets you had to have from someone, and for how long, before they became top-heavy, before you reached a point where you simply had to tell them, or passed that point and knew you never would.

190

I let my mind be taken by the tide. The water was pale green, disconcertingly warm when I stepped into it. I swam out through the shore break to where I could no longer stand, trod water, then turned back to the shore. The swell was no more than a mild nudge. It would become a rush, but not for hours yet.

If this was Ivan's way of loving, I thought, this mixture of bitterness, anger, and resignation, did I want it?

While I was rubbing myself down with a sandy towel, he said, "This sunblock stuff only lasts for fifty minutes."

I leant over and touched him gently on the shoulder. He looked up, but past me, his glasses hiding his expression. I was frightened then, the way people become afraid of some sideways thing. I thought of Peter and the way he'd set limits, the way he still did, from a distance. The sky was the colors of bruises, old and new. The sea turned gray and sticky, shot with yellow. For a while the sun fought back. Rising wind turned our arms and legs to sandpaper.

"Come on!" Ivan jumped to his feet, crisply decisive, impersonal as I'd never seen him. "We'll get soaked to the bone!"

He drove the hire car too fast. I was hungry, and my insides felt hollowed out from the unrelieved promise of sex, and the anxiety of not knowing where we were going. Blood was thick in my ears, and when we started to climb a hill, it was as though I was behind the car, pushing it along.

We bought hot chips at a takeaway and sat down to eat them on white plastic chairs. The rain came down in a perfect silver curtain. We burnt our tongues on the hot, soft potato, and watched people run to shelter.

A man bumped into our table, glasses fogged over, blinded by the rain. A fair-haired elf ran past, a blond, diminutive Felix in a red wetsuit that looked like a second skin.

"That sunny dome," I said, blowing on a chip. "Those caves of ice."

Ivan frowned, but I continued the poem, because the lines were marvelous, drugs or no drugs, person from Porlock or no. The air was steamy with cooking oil and hot breath and wet bodies. "Honeydew," I whispered to myself, and then, "the milk of paradise."

191

SEEING IS
BELIEVING

RANG RAE FROM a phone box near the city bus terminal, waiting my turn behind two young men in Indian cotton with dreadlocks dyed the color of Di Trapani's dresses.

"I'm not talking to you," I said. "This conversation has never taken place."

Rae laughed. Immediately, I felt better.

"How well do you know Isobel from Access Computing?" I asked her.

"I told you, Sandra. I only ever spoke to her once on the phone."

I took a deep breath and said, "Isobel. Angela. They're fake."

Rae was quick to take offense. "Access Computing runs very useful courses for women. I've seen their prospectus."

"I know they do. And I know they put in a good grant application. But I've been there. Isobel's got fake written all over her. And Angela never existed. Isobel, or someone, made her up."

"Why would they do that?"

To get money under false pretenses was one reason. Rae surely must have thought of that. "I'm going to find out," I said. "The office is closing down, and there's a cupboard full of Compic boxes."

Rae said nothing.

"Who are you protecting?"

She gave a small dry laugh. "I can't even protect myself."

I asked her again what she knew about Allison Edgeware, if there was anything she'd forgotten to tell me. Surely Allison and Felix must have met to discuss the Compic contract. Had Rae ever seen her around the department?

She said softly, "I've told you everything I know Sandra. I can't think of anything more."

"How are you bearing up?"

"Okay."

"Look after yourself," I said "Take care."

I did not want to burden Rae further buy telling her about Ivan and Lauren, yet I longed to talk to her properly, and after that somehow start again. Twin pictures of Isobel and Lauren snaked in front of my eyes, Angela Carlishaw hovering over them like an angel on a Christmas card.

I thought of the solitary life I'd lived since Peter's birth. Loss pushes you out toward things, so often blindly. I did not want to go blindly. I wanted to understand what I did and why, even if afterwards I was proved to have been wrong.

IN MY MAILBOX, THERE was a note from Gail Trembath, asking me to phone her.

"How about Manuka this time?" I asked when I got through, again using a public phone. It was a precaution I wasn't sure I needed, but it made me feel better to take it, just in case.

The line was bad and I had to shout. "It's not much further for you! At least we'll get a decent cup of coffee!"

"Okay." Gail sounded as though she was talking with her mouth crammed full.

Derek rang that night. He sounded happy, fatherly. He'd taken Peter to a cheese factory. The thought that within two weeks I'd be seeing Peter again, holding his boy's body in my arms, was a live warmth, fire in my bones.

* * *

I WAS STANDING AT the counter at Pellegrini's in Manuka when a voice behind me said, "I'll take another look at you."

I swung round. It wasn't a voice I recognized, and neither was the face it belonged to, a rather heavy one framed in curly hair dyed a brooding red.

"Hi," I said, pleased that it was my turn to be served, so I could give my order and pay for it while I tried to remember who the hell this woman was.

She smiled and said, "Would you like to join me?"

My skin began to prickle. "Sorry," I apologised, "but I'm meeting a friend." I cursed Gail under my breath for being late again.

Pellegrini's tables were made of some sort of polished black wood. I couldn't tell if it was veneer, or the real thing. Behind me, a woman was talking to a baby in the strained conversational voice of someone who has no one else to talk to from one day to the next. The baby was grizzling and refusing his bottle. "You just want to sit up, don't you," the woman said, falsely bright, "and see what's going on." I winced, thinking of the things I'd done to keep Peter entertained when he was that age. The café seemed full of women at loose ends. Or was that my paranoia?

Each table had a single daffodil in a thin white vase. The curtains were black-and-white, with a touch of green here and there to match the daffodil stems. There were floor-length mirrors along one wall. I certainly didn't want to see a double of myself, or the redhead spying on me. I tossed up whether or not to wait outside. Thankfully, the woman who claimed to know me left the café, with an uncertain smile in my direction.

Pellegrini's in Melbourne was one of the first cafés I could remember going to on my own, without my mother, the first time I sat on a bar stool in a narrow, noisy un-Australian place. The coffee had been too strong and rich to drink, the small fingers of pastry unbelievably crumbly and sweet.

I stared out the window of the Canberra café, so edgy by then that it

194

was all I could do to stop myself from running away. It was too early for the lunchtime crowd from Parliament House and the departments that hugged its base—Finance and Treasury, Foreign Affairs, and Trade. Small groups of well-dressed people decorated the footpath. I wondered why they looked so different from me. Was it the classier setting? If our department happened to be located on the south side of the lake, would Ivan with his leaking falafel sandwiches have blended in okay?

Rae's uniform went anywhere, but it hadn't saved her.

GAIL SURROUNDED HERSELF WITH platefuls of goodies, stuck out her lower lip, and with an obscene tongue licked up butter, croissant crumbs, chocolate cream.

Her gluttony was startling. "Haven't you eaten for a week?" I asked her.

"Gave up cigarettes two weeks ago. Fifteen days, to be precise."

"Sorry," I said. "Well done."

She glanced up. Her eyes misted over and she said, "Look at those two women smoking. Isn't that just the loveliest thing?"

"Your method seems to be working."

She threw me a look that said, what would you know? She was right. In the days when Gail had started getting herself hooked on nicotine, I'd chucked my heart out one night in the ladies' toilets at Watson's wine bar, from a combination of raw red wine and cigarettes. I'd never been able to look at either since. I wondered if Gail remembered that night as well as I did.

"Why are you always late?" I asked her.

Paying no attention to my question, Gail brushed crumbs from her jacket lapels with a busy hand and asked, "How was Queensland?"

"Surprising."

She made a large inquiring gesture, fingers dripping butter but I was saved from having to explain. A man with long gray hair tied back in a ponytail was looming over us.

Gail half-stood to shake his hand, then thought better of it.

He smiled and said, "Great news about Phil."

"Magnificent!" Gail wiped her fingers vigorously on a paper napkin. "Mind you, I've had the weepers and wailers on to me already."

I listened to them talking, sipped my coffee and tried to breathe evenly and slowly. After the man had moved on, Gail explained that there'd been a row over the Press Council elections.

"I hope he doesn't know who I am."

"Macca? If you had a mane and tail he might. Only interested in racehorses. Actually"—her face registered alarm and then bewilderment—"it is Wednesday, isn't it? I have never, *ever*, seen Macca in town on a midweek race day before."

"How does someone like that make a living as a journalist?"

"Are you kidding?"

Gail waved and grinned. I turned to look. Macca was talking to a woman in a miniskirt. She blew Gail a kiss.

"You know too many people here," I said.

She shrugged. "You know, Sandra, chappy rang me while you were away."

"What sort of chappy?"

"Anonymous. Cheery. Mr. Good News. Like his footy team had just won."

"What did he sound like? How old?"

"Youngish, oldish, couldn't tell."

"But youngish?"

"Yeah, I'd say youngish. Coming on. You know the kind of voice. All balls. Said he sent the story about your boss. Said she had it coming to her."

I stared at Gail. "You don't sound like you believed him."

"Mr. Anonymous? Why believe a guy who's got nothing to say except, 'Hey, man! It was me!'"

I could think of lots of reasons, and I was sure she could, too.

Gail made a face. "Thought he might be a Kiwi. You know how New

Zealanders swallow their i's? B'g t'ts? Sounded like it over the phone. I'd just been reading a piece on regional accents. That's what made me think of it."

"He offered to sell you something, didn't he? And you said no. Why?"

"Hang on. One step at a time, or you'll give me indigestion."

"For Christ's sake! How much did he want?"

"Five thousand up front," Gail said, licking her fingers one last time. "I put it to Brian and he said sorry, no money in the kitty. I told him if he was going to be so miserly, at least come up with a good excuse."

"How did that go down?"

Gail rolled her eyes. "As you might expect." She stretched back, satisfied, and said, "Here's what I think. Your blue-eyed boss was squirreling away some nuts for the winter. Face it. She knew she'd be looking for a job next year. She pinched the dough, or else helped that Access crowd to pinch it."

"And your Mr. Anonymous found out and blew the whistle on her?"

Gail nodded slowly, then gave me a long stare. I stared back, looking for the moral line, as if looking hard enough would make it visible, catgut or nylon down a reporter's forehead, balancing one side of her face against the other.

"What about Compic?" I asked.

"What about them?"

"Your theory leaves them out altogether."

"I don't think there's much of a mystery there," Gail said. "They're gung-ho. They push their product for all they're worth. There're plenty like them. This town's awash with software companies. It's dog eat dog out there."

"What about your office manager? Did you get any more out of him?"

"Nope."

Gail picked up the wooden spatula she'd been using to stir her coffee, broke it deftly in two, then looked up at me and grinned.

"Goldilocks might run home through the woods," she said.

"What? Who? Angela, you mean?"

"The other one. Blondie who was interviewed on TV. Might give herself a well-earned holiday in Scotland."

"Isobel?"

Gail nodded.

I was startled. I hadn't told Gail about my visit to Access Computing. I wondered if she'd been following her own line of investigation, if she'd spoken to Isobel and knew the office was closed down.

She was watching me shrewdly, waiting for me to comment.

When I didn't, she said, "Tell me Sandy, why is it that the idea of a health farm in Scotland beggars credibility?"

She answered her own question. "Too bloody cold. Golf, yes. Running round in a bikini, yichk!"

I laughed and said, "Where did you get health farm? I thought it was supposed to be a nunnery."

BETRAYAL

T WAS OUR FOURTH day back, and still Ivan had not shown up at work. I hated the idea that he was avoiding me.

"Don't mope in here, Sandy," Guy said. "Come shopping with me. Its Joshua's birthday on Saturday."

"What are you getting him?" I asked, absurdly pleased that Guy was bothering to cheer me up.

"Wants a Game Boy. Has Peter got one?"

"No," I said. "Not yet."

Guy buttoned his brown leather jacket with one hand, smiled his crinkle-cut smile, then said, "Miranda doesn't like them."

"Who's Miranda?" I asked.

"My wife," Guy said with mild surprise, as though I should have known this.

I murmured something about having taken an early lunch break, and wished him luck with his present-buying.

At first I'd thought Guy's children must be pre-schoolers because he looked so young, but he had a son a few weeks older than Peter as well as Vanessa, his daughter. It was pleasant to talk about our kids.

When I called by Ivan's house that evening to see if he was all right, I expected him to be wary, distant, even to tell me he didn't want to see me. But Ivan was excited, full of the task he'd set himself, putting the finishing touches to a program that would record and print out every log-in to our department and its source, whether it came from another computer in the building, or via a modem from outside.

He'd borrowed a computer and a printer, which he was setting up to be permanently on guard.

Confused, I asked him, "Isn't Felix already doing that?"

Ivan had opened the door to me with a small, distracted nod, just barely distinguishing me from the Avon lady or a Mormon. He'd walked straight back down the corridor to his workroom. From behind, his gait was that of a nervous horseman whose mount might bolt at any moment.

"We're going about this bastard the wrong way, Sandushka!" he'd called over his shoulder. "Need to think about it as a technical problem with a technical solution!"

He sat down at his keyboard. I stared past him at a screen of symbols that meant nothing to me.

"Felix's log is useless!" he shouted as though I was a block away. "Doesn't tell you whether the call is internal, or coming from outside. My little baby does just that!"

His moustache jutted over lips pursed in concentration. He explained how it had come to him on the plane. "While you were fast asleep."

I'd only been pretending to sleep, so we wouldn't have to talk. But Ivan seemed to have forgotten everything that had happened in Brisbane. Setting up a foolproof watching system was the answer. He was certain of it. Out of need or greed, the thieves would return and trap themselves.

"Won't they see you?" I asked, unconvinced.

"If my program's working properly, no one will."

"Won't it cost a fortune?"

Ivan grinned. "Have to cut down on the caviar! Now for a little test run. Here's what I want you to do. Tomorrow morning, try and access a file of mine from your PC. You won't be able to, because you don't know my password. But I should be able to see you trying."

My mind began to whirr like overworked machinery. "So will Felix," I said.

Ivan ignored this. "Do it first thing, then phone me here. No, hang on, don't phone me from your desk, nip downstairs and use the bistro phone. Can you do that?"

I felt I had to get out of Ivan's workroom, though I'd only just arrived. I wondered if this was a pattern for him, plunging himself into some new scheme to take his mind off whatever had gone wrong with his personal life. Had he been in touch with Lauren since he got back to Canberra?

I found a Lipton's tea bag in a jar on the kitchen bench. It was discolored with age, but I didn't think it had been used. While the water was boiling, I tried not to notice the egg and bacon dishes in the sink, the rubbish bin that looked as though it hadn't been emptied since before we left for Brisbane.

I sat at the kitchen table to drink my tea.

Ivan shuffled up behind me, saying sheepishly, "You know, Lauren won't travel anywhere south of Sydney."

"You're going to Sydney to meet Lauren?"

He nodded, looking pleased and trying not to.

"You mean she's never been to Canberra?"

"It's a recent thing, this feeling the cold so much."

"I see," I said, wishing I did.

I finished my tea, and Ivan showed me to the door.

"It's just a weekend. Lauren wants to do the tourist thing, go to Taronga Park."

"Take care," I told him, holding out my hand and squeezing his, not jealous after all, suddenly wanting the best for him. "A zoo can be a tricky place for romance."

AT HOME, SITTING UP in bed alone, I tried to separate the clues on the screen from those in the air, the clues Ivan and I had begun teasing out together, from those whose presence insinuated itself into my nasal passages, my lungs. Ivan would never willingly let Lauren go, had not done

201

so. He'd follow her now if she gave him the slightest encouragement. Or if she gave him none.

I remembered him showing me her photograph. He hadn't volunteered to show me. It had fallen out of one of his computer manuals. I'd flicked the snap over. *Lauren Semyonov* and the date were written on the back.

It wasn't a good shot. That had been my immediate impression. The light meter hadn't been properly adjusted. The background was in shadow, and Lauren was wearing a dark dress. Her face shone palely out of a circle of black hair, and she wasn't smiling. She looked younger than I'd imagined her, and much more severe.

"Hates having her picture taken," Ivan had said softly.

"Did you take it?"

He'd nodded, tucking the photograph away.

Had I heard the fondness in his voice, or was my memory putting it there now? I had assumed that because Lauren's picture wasn't framed and sitting beside his bed, it didn't mean a lot to him.

Wishing I'd never set eyes on Lauren, or Ivan for that matter, wishing I'd gone to America with Peter, I puzzled over questions that were new, though they should not have been.

When I was growing up, there'd been just Mum and me. Mum had had her job, her friends, but family had been the two of us. There'd been no cousins, uncles, aunts, or grandparents. Why? What had my mother done, or suffered to be done, that had ended with her being so alone? And was I was somehow repeating a lesson I had learnt without wanting to, without even being aware that I was learning it?

There was a woman in my mother's life. Her name was Sylvia Billis. I'd scarcely taken any notice of her. To me, at thirteen, fourteen, she seemed already old. She was probably around forty at the time she and my mother became friends. Sylvia Billis hadn't cried at my mother's funeral. She'd stood there with her back as straight as Rae Evans's in the courtroom, her face the color of old chewing gum. People had stared at her. I know I had. I don't think she was aware of any of us.

A couple of months after Peter was born, I spent a Sunday going through my mother's things. I culled them savagely, throwing out nearly everything. I remember the day well. It was one of Peter's bad ones, and I parked him in another room and let him cry himself to sleep.

I recall finding a photograph of my mother and Sylvia Billis squinting into the sun, Sylvia standing behind my mother as though guarding her, a slim hand on her shoulder. I burnt it in a rage of grief and jealousy. Why hadn't I been curious about the parts of my mother's life that Sylvia had shared? Why had I refused to think about them for the last eight years?

Once memories started to return, they multiplied—Sylvia and my mother doing things together, sometimes with me in tow. They went shopping, and to meetings or a movie. Clearest, for some reason, were Sylvia's arrivals and departures, my mother getting ready for her friend with a look of trust and pleased anticipation on her face.

I didn't ask my mother any of the important questions before she died, nor did she ask them of me. Maybe I was too arrogant and self-cented. Or too frightened. Maybe she was too tired, in too much pain. Or confident that she knew me, knew who I was, and that I would not let her down.

THE NIGHT AFTER IVAN left for Sydney to meet Lauren, I wrote a long letter to Peter and gave Fred two extra dog biscuits and a cuddle while I watched the end of an old Cary Grant movie. Unable to settle to anything, not wanting to play tag with sleep, I got into my car and drove to Ivan's, telling myself I needed to check his log, make sure everything was going smoothly.

I used his spare key to get in. His workroom had the appearance of only having been left for a short time, but the rest of the house gave off a sour, abandoned smell. There was a coffee mug with a spoon standing in it on one end of the kitchen table. I picked it up and sniffed the weeks-old instant welded to the bottom.

His cat suit hung over the back of a swivel chair. To my wary eyes, it looked not so much hung as deliberately placed, glass eyes upraised, front paws eerily arranged. The skin didn't look empty, but as though there was a body inside. I wasn't going to poke it and find out.

Garfield seemed to be staring at me, crouched on top of the laser printer. I tried to lift him, and discovered that his feet had been stuck down. He couldn't move.

I shivered, and switched on Ivan's computer.

His plan to keep a detailed log of all dial-ins to the department had proved to be incredibly time-consuming. My gut feeling was that, with Rae's trial date set, our hackers were laughing down their modems for all they were worth. Ivan's hope that they'd return and trap themselves seemed a thin one to me, a hope with about as much meat on it as a skinny man turned side on.

After a few minutes, I stood up and began to walk around the room, scarcely seeing where I was going, stumbling over a pile of black cables. I flicked through CDs on a shelf, then moved to the cupboard where Ivan kept his manuals.

For ten seconds after I opened the door and saw them, I held my breath and couldn't move. Something that had been beating at the back of my head for so long was coming forward, and there was nothing I could do but wait for it to arrive and settle.

I bent down and began reading the printouts. Ivan had been spying on Rae Evans since before Gail's story in the *Canberra Times*. The date on the top sheet was more than a month before that. He'd highlighted sections dealing with Rae's budget for the previous financial year. There were some figures with double underlining.

My stomach contracted as though I'd been hit. My eyes blurred, and I wiped them angrily. I scanned through the cost breakdown for the outwork project, running a finger backwards and forward across the paper, as though underneath the ink there might be some sort of invisible writing that rubbing would miraculously bring to light.

The arrogance of it, tossing the printouts in a cupboard as if he

wanted me to find them, waiting for them to be found, the absurd clever-
ness of everything Ivan had done. He'd veiled himself in so many fantastic outfits, played so many parts at once, and with such enthusiasm.
Taking me to bed. The lonely wife. How he must have laughed.

Getting at me through Peter. That's what hurt the most. Their study
sessions, Peter's high, enthusiastic giggle, Ivan's many-legged word pictures. What I couldn't bear was that a part of me had always suspected
Ivan, had known without wanting to, without being able to face the
knowledge.

I toyed with the idea of taking the printouts home. Then it occurred
to me that if they were found at my house, there was nothing to prove that
they belonged to Ivan, not to me. I kept reading, looking for something
conclusive, something that would leave no room for doubt.

"Sandra!"

Ivan was standing in the doorway with his arms crossed. The light
from the corridor picked out his thick beard and high cheekbones. A single silver thread of light ran through his hair.

"I see you've found my stash."

The room was as quiet as a nocturnal animal in a hollow tree. Ivan
must have noticed my car in the driveway, the light in his room. He'd let
himself in without making a sound.

I clutched the wad of printout tightly, and began to back away.

Ivan threw back his head and laughed. "Oh Sandra, you're a sight for
sore eyes. You really are."

"You didn't go to Sydney, did you? That was a lie, too."

"Just let me explain one thing. After that, you can do whatever takes
your fancy."

My legs had a determination of their own, to fold and rest, no matter
what orders my brain was giving. I grabbed a chair and tried to make it
look as though I was sliding on to it with some residue of dignity.

"I've been taking apart Evans's hard disk line by line," Ivan said. "It
dawned on me after you left the other night. How could I have been so

stupid? What I needed was a record of the past from way back. The recent past's been fiddled with so often it's all tied in knots. I thought, if I went back before the viruses—"

"Why didn't you tell me?"

"I didn't want to get your hopes up, in case there was nothing there."

Ivan pulled his black swivel chair toward him, swung it round and straddled it. He smiled, waiting for me to catch up with his reasoning.

"Why the printouts?" I asked. It had been a mistake for me to sit down.

"I thought looking at paper might help for a change."

"What about those figures you underlined?"

"I've done a bit of cross-checking."

"And?"

"They're all correct so far."

"Why didn't you go to Sydney? Why walk in here and startle me? You must have seen my car."

"I did go." Ivan made a face. I couldn't tell whether it was disgust with himself, or disappointment, or possibly relief. "I decided to come back early."

"Lauren didn't show?"

Ivan leant across and switched off the light over his keyboard. In shadow, the lines on his face were deep and bold, his beard a tangled maze.

"Oh yes," he said, "she showed."

"How was Taronga Park?"

"Lauren fed the flamingos."

"And?"

"A zoo's a zoo. I don't want to talk about it."

His eyes went soft then, like an old man's in the sun. A funny wave of sadness washed over me, like the waves children make for themselves sometimes in the bath. I was left with a hollow feeling, like before, when I took the VR helmet off in that same room, dizzy and sick, anxious to escape something that was, and yet was not, meant for me.

*   *   *

DRIVING HOME, I TRIED to picture Ivan chasing Lauren from one hot city to another. Was he prepared to follow her till her desire for revenge grew thin, till she got tired, could no longer see the point? What was she punishing him for? Maybe Ivan had made up the whole business about meeting Lauren at Taronga Park. He'd made up the story about Rae's hard disk and the printouts, invented it on the spot when he'd surprised me reading them.

I wanted nothing more, just then, than to get on a plane and fly off to America, leave the sorry mess behind. The shock of seeing Ivan when I'd thought he was in Sydney had distorted my judgment, and I felt I could no longer be certain of identifying what was in front of my nose. A car was following me, twenty five or thirty meters back, but I was too tired to care.

I let Fred in, made sure all the windows and the doors were locked, then sat up in bed, knowing I would not be able to sleep.

I stared into the space ahead, feeling as though I was looking down at the bottom of a well and seeing, not water, but newly poured concrete, shining, silver-gray, giving the illusion of cool liquid and genuine reflection.

I was surprised that I should have come to this as an image of myself and what I faced, then it seemed to fit. An empty well, not just dry, but tantalizing me with wet cement. I had discovered very little that would help Rae when she came to trial. Instead, I was discovering all sorts of things that I would rather not. Maybe I should just give up. I was afraid to phone Rae, ask for another meeting, tell her what I'd found in Ivan's workroom. The suppression order was meant to make Rae invisible until her trial, and her trial would be conducted in a closed court, not open to the public, or the press. Whoever had framed her was also invisible. How could I possibly outwit them?

I reached for a pad and pen, drew two rough squares, and joined them by an arrow with two heads. I thought of flipping coins and always coming up with the same answer, or nonanswer. If I'd been Ivan, maybe I'd have drawn two horsemen, or women, facing one another, lances at the ready.

I flipped the pen over in my fingers. It was one of Peter's. I lifted it to my nose, wishing I could catch the faintest smell or hint of him. In the end, I left the two squares blank.

What did theft mean besides the obvious, stealing something of value that could be sold, or used? Nine hundred thousand dollars had gone missing, but no one had come forward to say, "Hey guys, here's a bill of sale!" There was the deposit in Rae's bank account, but apart from that, no fingerprints or paper trail to follow, only the whispering butterfly dust of computer files that kept their secrets well.

To Catch a Thief was one of my mother's favorite movies. She liked Cary Grant a lot. A truism, that thieves knew best how to set traps for other thieves—but was it also true that those who set themselves to catch thieves grew to resemble thieves in the process of doing so? And where did this end, if it ever did?

Memory is not abstract, yet, in trying to retrieve it, we force abstractions on ourselves. Memory is hunger for the taste and smell and heartbeat of a person, rage that they are not there with us now.

COFFEE IN
THE PARK

I VAN AND I FACED one another in the Glebe Park café, two business colleagues having morning tea. We were rehearsing for Friday, casing the joint. Was that the right phrase? It sounded too old-fashioned, trenchcoat pockets deep with guns. The warm day saw us both in shirt-sleeves, Ivan's rolled up to the elbows. He'd combed his hair and beard. I'd splashed out on a spring wardrobe that mimicked Rae's. I was still wearing my dark winter skirts, with a variety of white blouses.

Behind us, counters serving Indian potato pancakes, pizza, Malaysian and Lebanese, gave out their conflicting pre-lunch smells. Cooks were filling the warming trays with noodles, saffron rice, fish and chips—a smorgasbord that made my stomach turn.

I recalled meeting Allison Edgeware in the café, how Tony's friend Ateeq had shown up as well. Ivan and I had chosen a table with a clear view of an empty billiard table on a raised green dais. It looked like my kind of stage, the setting for a performance that never quite took place.

Someone had sent me another anonymous e-mail, not attached to a virus this time.

I know you fancy yourself as an investigator.

I'd decided on an equally flattering reply. Our correspondence hadn't ended there. Mr. or Ms. Anonymous had invited me for coffee in Glebe Park.

I licked froth from my cappuccino, and told Ivan, "Suppose you sit in here while I talk to him outside?"

"There you go again. The ubiquitous male pronoun. What if *she* recognizes me?"

I fidgeted, moving my cup and saucer around in a circle. The tables were white, with a squiggly pattern in yellow, red, and green.

I looked up at Ivan. "Suppose *she* spots you, knows who you are. Would that be so surprising? Would *she* expect me to have come alone?"

Ivan raised an eyebrow. I asked myself what he was really thinking, behind the banter that seemed to come so easily. The air hadn't been cleared between us since I'd stumbled on those printouts in his workroom. The more I thought about it, the more holes appeared in his explanation. Had Ivan been trying to disentangle himself from Lauren, and had sleeping with me been a part of that? Had he been using me, stringing me along? I'd kept plenty of secrets from him. He'd kept a major one from me.

I reached out my hand and brushed the back of his, missing his brown sweater and the feel of springy wool.

"What a pair we make," I said.

He smiled his shy smile, and I felt close to him. He squeezed my hand, but it seemed he didn't trust himself to answer my question, or say anything more.

We stood up to go. Two flat-faced statues guarded the café's sliding doors, a man and woman in simplified wooden dress. The man held a posy in one hand, his other arm bent across his chest. The woman stood with one arm stiffly by her side, the other neatly chopped off at the elbow.

Ivan walked beside me, reaching across to finger the leaves of a potted plant.

He gave me his Yogi Bear grin and winked. "Do you think I'm thin enough to hide behind a fern?"

* * *

I MUST FIND WORDS for what is essentially a picture story. Ivan's drawing of my cyclamen, which so startled me on my second day at work, my journey inside the Trojan Horse, the learning aids Ivan made for Peter, the viruses, our hacker's path—visual journeys these are, journeys of the eyes, other senses struggling to keep up.

My absent husband, Derek, has an unmistakable contempt for words. Most of all, he hates being made to discuss anything personal. Come to think of it, maybe it's Derek sitting on my shoulder, a censor crow or raven, that makes me doubt my ability to tell my story now. My guilt at not having told Derek the truth, and a kind of desperate misery that, even if I'd wanted to, I wouldn't have known what to say.

I needed Ivan. I needed his skills, his wayward, ready hands, his boy's enthusiasm, and his bitterness of a rejected husband. Another Ivan, one who'd been able to hang on to his Lauren, who'd stayed in Queensland, raised his own kids, would not have given me a second glance. And I needed the mindset that Ivan shared with Felix, their assumption that the lies computers tell will eventually be yielded to them, if they set up watching systems, kept complicated logs.

Ivan had tried to get me to tell Derek, had berated me for not having done so, but he hadn't mentioned Derek since we got back from Brisbane. His mood swings, from joking to serious and back again, were as hard to follow as they'd always been.

Fancy yourself as an investigator. I more than half-suspected that no one would turn up on the appointed day.

ALONE ON FRIDAY AFTER all, I chose an outside table with four white plastic chairs.

I counted thirty apple trees while I was waiting, arms upraised as if in a tree prayer. They were young, supple, molded, the nearest ones close enough for me to smell tight-fisted blossoms, tense and almost ready. In a few days they would all flower at once, become achingly white.

The park had its share of evergreens as well. A native pine plantation was reflected in a shallow pond, steps flushed with running water leading down to it. I'd hauled Peter out once, afraid of broken glass.

I didn't hear the man approach my table, and when I glanced around I caught my breath.

The sun was behind him. He was smiling, his one good eye engaging mine. His other eye was twisted far to the right, and cloudy, blind.

"G'day there." The man held out his hand for a businesslike shake, then pulled out a chair by its back. "You must be Sandra."

Curly blond hair touched his collar. His seeing eye was blue.

"That's right," I said. "And you're—?"

The man's lips curved in amusement.

"Suppose we exchange our bona fides, something of that kind," I went on, seeing he wasn't going to tell me his name. "Would you like to see my driver's license?"

He gave me a long look, curious, appraising, then said mildly, "Let me buy you a coffee instead."

When he came back with the drinks, I asked him, "Do you work for Compic?"

He laughed. Apparently everything I said amused him. He had the inward, but not withdrawn face of someone used to being stared at. "Drink up," he said, nodding at my cup. "The wind will make it cold."

"Someone framed Rae Evans," I said. "She's facing trial for computer theft and fraud."

The one-eyed man took a sip of coffee and leant back in his chair, enjoying upsetting me, making me wait. He wore only a thin jacket over a denim shirt, but the wind didn't seem to bother him.

"I'll tell you something about computer companies in this town. Mind if I smoke?" He pulled a packet of Alpines from his jacket pocket and bent over cupped hands to light one. "There's megabucks to be made from government contracts right now." He spoke with his head down, concentrating on his cigarette, which needed care and attention in the wind. "No secret that they're spending every cent of their budgets in expectation of leaner times after the elections. Even a small local outfit can turn over a few million a year, with a bit of luck and the right connections. That's why there's so many of us. We'd fry each other's balls in butter given half a chance."

His cigarette finally alight, he lifted his head and studied me thoughtfully.

"How well do you know Allison Edgeware?" I asked him.

"Who works for the lovely lady? That's a more interesting question. Ms. Edgeware subcontracts. Hires programmers for one job at a time. Doesn't rehire. And all of them are newcomers. She's never employed anyone from Canberra."

"Who does *she* work for?"

He laughed again. "I thought you might tell me that."

The wind was blowing menthol fumes my way. I waved my hand in front of my face, but he ignored it.

"Compic's quarantined their developmental programs," he said. "No wires in, no wires out. A shame, really. Like gagging a brilliant storyteller."

"Do you have a quarantined computer in your office, too?"

"I would, if I had anything to hide. My guess is that, whatever's on that quarantined computer, it isn't tatty graphics."

He seemed relaxed, and in no hurry. Had he already learnt what he wanted to about me?

"What does Compic produce?" he went on. "Graphics software. Not bad. Actually, some of it's quite cute. But nothing to shoot your granny over. The lovely Allison is perfectly capable of running the legitimate side of the business, as well as various bits of questionable marketing."

He looked across the thick, wet grass to a curve of flowerbeds. I followed his single line of sight and spotted Bambi in her red cloak, stooping to pick flowers. Bambi looked incredibly fragile, on the edge of some undreamt-of danger. Her face, as she bent over the soft bed, was mostly hidden by the cloak. I was gripped with fear in case a gardener or some security person reprimanded her, took her flowers away.

I turned back to the one-eyed man and said, "So you all spy on each other."

He was frowning. I sensed in him a certain apprehension where Bambi was concerned. Perhaps he regularly ate his lunch in the park, and knew her by sight, or otherwise.

"How can you expect me to give you information, when you won't tell me who you are?"

"But I thought you knew," he said. "I'm the competition."

He smiled as though being half-blind was deliberate, a conscious choice, like Bambi's cloak, her taste for stolen blooms.

Fancy yourself, I thought.

"You see, it's hard for small fry like us. As I said, Edgeware's perfectly capable of showcasing the business. She does that extremely well, catches the married men nicely."

"I'm not sure what you mean."

"It goes like this. Someone from your department rings up John Smith in Attorney-General's and happens to drop, in the course of conversation—'By the way, Compic's doing this fantastic job for us. Magic stuff. Give them a go, why don't you? And they've got this absolute babe heading them up.' John Smith has a coffee with our Allison, and the results are as you might expect."

"She sleeps with them," I said.

"Of course. After that, she's in a good position to persuade them to buy whatever it is she's selling above and beyond her considerable charms. John Smith has a drink with Bill Bloggs. Result, Bill Bloggs phones Allison and, would you believe it, he scores. See the pattern?"

I did. Now he'd said it, it seemed Allison's way of operating had been staring me in the face.

"You said, 'your department' just now. That means you think Allison is working with someone inside it."

"Don't you?"

When I didn't answer, he made a face, self-deprecating, still amused. "This is a such a wonderful city for gossip. And boy's clubs are the best source of gossip in the world."

"You mean if I was a man I'd have worked it out?"

"If you were male, and married, you would have been approached."

He waved his left hand toward the white curves of the casino in the distance. Next to it rose the huge rectangular block of the Industry Department.

"It's all very well to have rules about bidding for contracts. Which I must say, in my experience, most people follow most of the time. But the rules don't mean all that much if the decision is as good as made. People are talking about how Compic's landed a couple of good development contracts, and are about to land another one. A beautiful big fat Defense contract. If the rumor's true, it'll put them in the super-league. It's a crucial time for them, and they can't afford snoopers, even amateur ones like you."

"What's the Defense contract for?"

"That's where the rumor gets a bit vague. A fancy new way for presenting regulations on-line is what I heard. Novel way of interfacing with the public. The human face of government officials."

"Sounds familiar."

The one-eyed man nodded, then fished in his jacket pocket, pulled out several stapled sheets of paper, and handed them to me.

"I wrote to your crowd bitching about their tendering procedures. Got a 'we're looking into it' reply, and not a word since then. When it comes to bidding for these new contracts, it doesn't seem to matter what kind of a track record Compic has. Allison's promises are worth their weight in gold."

"Is that what made you decide to complain? Mr. Whitelaw, isn't it?"

"Thought it might be fun to stir the possum. I'd never heard of Rae Evans, but I'm not surprised by her subsequent misfortune. To tell you the truth, I was thoroughly pissed off. Compic haven't produced anything that my company couldn't produce as well, or better."

Having picked her fill of public blooms, Bambi was walking slowly toward the gates, holding her posy stiffly in front of her like a nervous bride.

I leant back, thinking hard. If the rumor about the Defense contract was true, it made Bernard Whitelaw's complaint significant. If word got around that there was a black mark against Compic, even a potential one, it might jeopardize their chances. I wondered how much the Defense contract was worth. Allison and her boss, or partner, would be sweating on getting it signed before a change of government.

"Have you told the police about your suspicions?"

"Yep. I gave them chapter and verse."

"And?"

"The detective I spoke to—big chap, lantern jaw—is convinced that Evans stole the money, or convinced he's got enough to make the charge stick. He gave me the distinct impression that he isn't interested in complications. And I've been watching Allison for a while now, but I've got no proof. Needless to say, none of the gentlemen who've compromised themselves are going to admit it."

Though Bernard Whitelaw had been acting like he had all morning to spend chatting to me, he checked his watch, and said he had to go. After a moment's hesitation, I gave him my phone number, and told him that, if he had any news to share, he could contact me directly from now on. He offered me his card, and said he'd be obliged if I'd return the favor.

GAIL TREMBATH RANG ME at home that evening.

"Sandra? Hi. Are you alone? This might be nothing. I saw that fat boy from your department."

"You mean Jim Wilcox?"

"The puddingy one. Yeah. I've just seen him. Tete-à-tete with Phil Theroux. In that parking lot off London Circuit."

Phillip Theroux was the Opposition spokesman for small business, and a wily politician.

"They might have met by accident," I said.

Gail snorted down the phone. "It struck me that you haven't been paying enough attention to the political angle in all of this. You haven't asked yourself the obvious question. Who's got the most to gain by discrediting you guys?"

"See if you can find out what their connections are," I told her. "And Felix Wenborn. If Wilcox is in this, I'm sure Felix is in it with him. But Gail? Do it discreetly. Oh, and one more thing, that office manager of yours, is he married?"

"Is he ever. Model family man," Gail said.

After I hung up, I recalled the one-eyed man's warning. *Not even amateur snoopers like you.*

I washed the dishes, tidied up a bit. While my hands were busy, I speculated about Allison's partner. Felix was so proper and correct in everything he did, or at least he tried to be. Could I see Felix lying, stealing, framing other people, ruining their careers? And for what? To build a successful company, fight off the opposition, make a lot of money all in secret, with a woman prepared to sell her body at the front.

FEAR

O N SATURDAY MORNING, I decided to do some exploring, and discovered that Compic had taken over part of an abandoned primary school for their office, sharing class-rooms with half-a-dozen other Canberra businesses, and trading the advantages of a central location for cheap rents.

Rows of pine trees lined the road on two sides of what had been a school oval. The slides and swings looked old, but still in working order. There were horses on springs and a roundabout. I walked slowly past them, keeping an eye on Fred, who was running from one rubbish bin to the next. Hardly any people were about. I passed a couple walking a corgi almost as wide as he was long.

When Peter had been starting school, the controversy over school clo-sures had been on the front page of the *Canberra Times* week after week. There'd been pickets at Lyons, I recalled, though I couldn't remember anything about the Downer school. I hadn't taken much notice of the de-bate at the time. Our local school had heaps of enrollments. Peter was go-ing. Between the hours of nine and three, I would be free of him.

The air was like new glass. The childless ovals and playground had a tranquil emptiness. I remembered how I'd taken Peter to the Downer playground sometimes, on days when Derek had left me the car. It was a change from the playground nearest us, and I'd itched for different scenery, no matter how slight and superficial the difference was.

Downer primary school was really very close to where I lived. It had taken me less than twenty minutes to walk there, and I hadn't hurried. It gave me an eerie feeling to realize that Compic had been so close all this time, practically in my neighborhood.

The school that was no longer a school had the same unreal serenity I'd felt everywhere in the suburbs, when I'd walked their length and breadth with Peter in his pram. I'd walked kilometer after kilometer once the fruit trees blossomed, in that secure warmth in the middle of the day, seldom speaking to, or even seeing anyone. I'd smiled at women in cars when they pulled up at the lights.

Sometimes I'd heard the whispering of a crowd of people, backstage, out of sight. Or else it was like walking about inside a painting, half-seeing, half-hearing an artistic crowd in front of me, with the itch, the butterflies in the stomach that warm weather brought. I'd never felt the imperious confidence of an Alice, or the ability to step right through a mirror. I'd had imaginary conversations with my mother, pretending I was telling her about Peter's new tooth; two steps, then five, my baby crossing a whole room upright on two stiff legs.

It was years since I'd seen that particular playground, those stands of trees, and if you'd asked me to describe them an hour before I'd looked up Compic's address in the phone book, and realized where it was, I would not have been able to.

Fred jumped on the roundabout, and managed to make it move. Did dogs get dizzy? I called him to me, and began to walk toward the school buildings. For a few moments, I was innocent of any ulterior motive, simply a lady in a floppy jacket, walking a brown dog for whom no amount of affection or reassurance was enough, who fell on each meal as though it was his last.

Strolling, in what I hoped was a casual way, around what had been classrooms, I spotted an upstairs window with the Compic logo. I checked the directory at the front of the building. It told me that the company occupied suite four, level one. Suite, I thought, is pushing it. Walking back, I noticed what I hoped was a broken catch on one of the windows.

THERE WAS A PHONE message from Ivan waiting for me at home, asking how I'd got on with Mr. Anonymous. I decided that I wouldn't ring him back just yet. I contemplated going round to Rae's, and decided against that, too. I did some more housework, made my plans, and waited for nightfall.

IN THE DARK, I could feel that Compic hadn't done anything to change the interior design of the classroom they'd taken over. I had a torch with me, but so far I hadn't used it. I was hoping that, when I found the right machine, the light from its screen would be enough. My hunch about the broken catch had proved correct. Compic might have well-protected computers, but their office had proved as easy to break into as any primary-school classroom.

I'd gone up the fire-escape stairs to the first floor, then edged along a narrow slatted veranda roof to the window with the broken catch. I'd managed that part surprisingly easily, and now I was inside. The section of the school that housed Compic's office faced a small quadrangle of asphalt and grass. No one could see it from the street. The quadrangle and the fire stairs were well lit, but I had to take my chance with that. There were lights in the corridors, but not in any of the classrooms. I'd checked that carefully before beginning my climb.

The venetian blinds were drawn. I'd slid underneath them with a small rattling sound. There was a faint lingering of the smells of dust and children, but no desks or chairs made to measure for small buttocks. I had a flash of Peter sitting in a room like this, then of Peter in America, waking up and eating breakfast with his father. In that raw-boned classroom, dark with the half-forgotten smells of childhood, I felt I could have found my way blindfold. The darkness was my friend, my ability to work with it, and within it, a common sense I shared with all intruders.

There were four computers, their monitors pale gray rectangles of eyes. I quickly worked out that two of them were connected to each other, but not to modems. They did not appear to have any links outside the office. If the one-eyed man was right, these two were the in-house machines that programmers needed to come into the office to use. They were what I was after.

I switched one on. It came to life with a small humming sound.

I took a folded sheet of paper from my jacket pocket. With shaking fingers, I typed in a password, one from a list the Trojan horse had saved. The night Ivan had fooled his way into Access Computing and installed the Trojan horse seemed long ago. I thought how far I'd come since then, how willing I was now to break the law. I also knew it was a gamble, and that very likely none of my passwords would work. It was clear that if none of them *did* work, it raised doubts about my theory linking Compic and Access Computing.

The fourth password got me in.

I began opening files, and found a list of Compic's sales to government departments. It seemed they'd sold software packages to every single one, as well as to numerous private companies and organizations, including the *Canberra Times*. Allison, as Compic's director, had successfully bid for development contracts with Finance, Health, and Education, as well as Labor Relations. The one-eyed man, Bernard Whitelaw, was correct so far.

One file contained Compic's accounts for the start of the new financial year. On July fifteenth there'd been a payment of just under $50,000 from Access Computing to Compic. I knew Compic had been using Access Computing's mailing list. Here was money going the other way.

I set off a search for Access Computing and came up with dozens of references. In a minute, I thought, I'll switch on the printer, and risk the noise it makes. I searched for Felix Wenborn by name. A file of Allison's notes came up. I skim-read as fast as I could. Allison had made a note of each time she'd met Felix, or spoken to him. There were at least ten times.

I was reading a comment on what she called Felix's "resistance," concentrating so hard that I hardly registered the noise, a soft sound, but metallic. Somebody was opening the door.

I swung round. A shadow passed through the doorway.

I was at the window before I'd taken breath, slipping under the venetians. I threw myself down, landing on all fours on the veranda roof outside, scurrying along it like a mouse escaping from a cat. Whoever it was would run down the main stairs and cut me off before I was halfway across the quadrangle. My only hope was to get to the trees before they figured out which way I'd gone. It flashed through my mind that there might be others waiting under the windows, at the bottom of the stairs.

I fell down the last few steps of the fire escape, grazing my hands and knees, then ran down the long side of the school, through an archway and across the oval, making for the pine trees on the side furthest from the driveway, where I'd parked my car.

I could hear footsteps behind me, but I couldn't tell if it was one person, or more than one. I'd driven my car to the edge of the trees bordering the playground, knowing it would be well hidden there. I prayed that I wouldn't fall and make a noise, that my pursuers hadn't seen my car, and that I'd beat them to it. The footsteps seemed to stop. Were they circling round to cut me off? I got to my car, opened it, jammed the key in the ignition.

A figure reached the car as I was lunging into first gear.

I swung the wheel hard to the left. Something heavy hit the side. I bumped and heaved along a gravel path, then found the road.

At home, I checked that all my doors and windows were securely fastened. My arms and legs felt as though all the hard bits had turned to mush, and I could no longer move them. I studied the cuts on my hands, then picked up the phone and dialed Derek's number, without thinking about the time difference. There was no answer.

*   *   *

MY EYES FIXED ON the black mandala of my steering wheel. It was eight-thirty the next morning. After a sleepless night, I was driving to Rae's flat.

At the corner of Wattle Street and Macarthur Avenue, I braked and nothing happened. I managed to steer around the corner, but the slope was downhill and the lights at the highway intersection coming fast. I jammed my foot on the brake as hard as I could. Nothing. It was as though the car didn't have a brake at all. The lights at the highway were mad red eyes, taunting me. My car refused to obey, though my foot, leg, whole right side pressed convulsively. I couldn't stop.

I heard a voice screaming and knew, with a sensation that was part hysteria, part shame, that it was mine. Then the light turned white. I felt a vaporising heat. The steering wheel became a skeletal black flower.

I LIFTED MY ARM a fraction, and smelt damp gauze, cooling plaster.

Ivan was leaning over me, his head refusing to be just one head. His beards made wavy patterns at the edges of my vision.

At the sound of Ivan's voice saying my name, I blinked and tried to speak. My voice cracked and would not obey me. I half-fell, half-propelled myself forward, and vomited into a green plastic bowl the size and shape of a small swimming pool.

"Don't worry, Sandy," Ivan said. "You'll be okay."

I raised my head. Multiple lips pursed above brown kelp waves of beard.

I tried to call the nurse, but all that came out of my throat was a rasp that an awkward person might make with a chisel against a piece of metal.

"How did you know I was here?" I whispered.

"I went round to your place. When your car wasn't there, and there was no answer, I was worried. You didn't phone me back. I hadn't heard from you all weekend, so I rang the police."

"Tell the nurse I have to phone Derek."

From the way Ivan leant forward, his strained expression, I suspected that he could scarcely hear me. "I know the number," I said. "Dial it for me."

"You'll soon be feeling better." Ivan's falsely soothing voice seemed to come from as far away as Philadelphia.

"It wasn't an accident," I managed to force out, before I flung myself over to be sick again.

Hacking could be printless, voiceless, sexless, yet at the same time carry the belly of black emotions—malice, hate, revenge. My enemies multiplied inside my head, a double, triple vision.

The nurse came in, and spoke softly to Ivan. I hoped she was telling him to go away. I slept, and when I woke again, the sun was slanting through the ward in long secure rays. It was a six-bed ward. A patient was asleep in the bed next to mine. The bed directly opposite had the curtain pulled right round. I heard low voices coming from inside. Ivan wasn't there.

I turned my head five centimeters in one direction, then another. So far so good. My throat felt dry and sore. I decided that in a few moments, if the room stayed put, I'd reach for the glass beside my bed and drink some water.

Making this small decision cheered me up a bit, but apart from that I felt too confused and sick to think. Someone had done something to my car. Who? The person who'd almost caught me at the primary-school.

I reached my hand out for the water glass, and grasped it firmly near its base. I lifted my head slowly, and managed to hoist myself up against the pillows. The water was cool and soothing. The low voices went on behind the curtain, but no one came to see how I was doing. I replaced my glass, and looked up through the window. A bloody sunset was throwing its red and purple cloak over Black Mountain.

I woke during the night to feel Ivan's beard surrounding me, ticklish and suffocating.

The nurse came as the nightmare faded. She gave me a drink, and helped me use the toilet.

I dozed again, still under the weight of painkillers and anaesthetic. This time, in the dream, Ivan was in the car with me. We rode along, so jolly oh, two codgers out for a Sunday spin. Then the white light of the crash, the black spokes of the steering wheel. And Peter's face above mine, Peter's wry mouth smiling from another world, the dignity of a small boy saying goodbye to his mother.

THE DETECTIVE SERGEANT RAN his hand loosely up and down his purple tie, and looked at me with something like embarrassment. I knew he was a detective sergeant because the nurse had told me. He wasn't wearing any kind of uniform. The early-morning sun filling the ward wasn't kind to him. His fingers were broad and stubby, his face pale, puffy, unhealthy-looking under a broad-brimmed Akubra hat. This hat was the most striking thing about him. It was gray, and much too big, and he wore it low on his forehead, as though he'd jammed it there out of spite, or irritation.

"They're letting you go home this afternoon," he said with a nod. He seemed to be confirming that everything was as it should be.

He glanced down at his fingernails as though checking them for dirt, then began to question me about my car. I told him exactly what had happened, and repeated what I'd said to Ivan, that it hadn't been an accident.

"Where was your car the night before the accident, Mrs. Mahoney?"

"In my carport at home. Was anybody else hurt?" I added, flushing with shame because I hadn't thought of this before.

"You hit a young chap. Bruises. Bit of whiplash. Apart from that, motorists managed to brake or steer away from you. Not many at that time on a Sunday morning."

Unsmiling, offering no words of comfort, the detective went back to his questions. Where did I park my car during the day? Did anybody drive it besides me? Had I seen any strangers in the vicinity of my car?

I told him I'd been out the night before, and that it had been dark when I got home. He made notes and spoke slowly, as though it was an effort. I tried to read the expression in his face. He was one of those men

225

whose age could be anywhere between thirty-five and fifty. Something—late shifts, personal difficulties perhaps—had deepened the lines around his mouth and eyes, and given his skin the quality of unbaked dough.

Finally, he stopped writing, brushed invisible dust off his suit lapels, and said it would be twenty-four hours before he got the report on my car from the police garage at Weston. There was a queue.

Something happened then that jogged my memory. If it hadn't been for the anaesthetic still making me feel woozy, I probably would have recognized the policeman straight away. He took a few steps toward the door and stumbled, righting himself almost immediately, with a shake of his shoulders suggesting intense irritation, and jamming his Akubra hat down hard with his left hand. A nurse, who'd been attending to a patient, was instantly beside him, helping him upright, speaking softly.

The detective shook her off, some color returning to his face. She smiled to reassure him. He left the ward without another glance in my direction. It was then that I remembered where I'd seen him.

HE PHONED ME AFTER lunch. I'd managed to eat a couple of sandwiches and keep them down. Detective Sergeant Brook. I mentally repeated the name to fix it in my mind.

"Seems someone did monkey with your car, Mrs. Mahoney."

"I thought you told me there was a queue."

"I jumped it," he said in a deadpan voice. "Looks as if they weakened one of the brake lines. Like to pop over to your place and ask you some more questions. Around sixish, if that's okay with you."

I started giving him my address, but he interrupted to tell me he already had it. He hung up, and I realized I'd been hunched over the phone, holding it awkwardly in my left hand, my broken right arm in its plaster heavy and useless and thick in front of me.

When Ivan arrived at the hospital at three o'clock, I was drinking a cup of tea and nibbling an Anzac biscuit. I dressed in my oily, torn clothes because they were all I had. Ivan didn't have a key to my house, so he hadn't been able to fetch clean ones. During the hours I'd spent lying in the ward, it had been one of my small comforts that I hadn't given anyone a key.

I signed the hospital discharge papers with my left hand, and shoved a pack of Panadeine Forte into my bag, every action, every breath an act of will. Ivan stood to one side, a hairy mountain in the wrong landscape, his face blotched and frowning, while I returned the nurse's curious glances with a fixed and narrow glare.

He got into the back of the taxi with me, taking no notice when I protested that I could manage perfectly well without him. He was tense beside me, uncharacteristically silent, hands between his knees.

I fumbled in my bag for money, and when the taxi pulled up in my driveway I shoved it at the driver, shouting, "Thanks! This man wants to go on into the city!" I'd been nursing my bag tightly all the way, grateful that I didn't have anything heavier to carry. Then I was out the taxi door, slamming it behind me.

"Sandra, for God's sake!"

I had my key in my good left hand, and it was working its magic on my front door, then I was falling through it, pushing it shut behind me.

SPRING HAD COME TO my street overnight.

Peter had been born in the spring. Derek had driven me to Royal Canberra Hospital when the prunus trees at the end of Goodwin Street were still gray and brown, quiescent. The three of us returned to a corridor of brides and bridesmaids, white, pink, white, pink, white, pink, all the way to my front door.

It had happened again. Until the pasty-faced policeman arrived, I was free to accustom myself to wedding trees dropping bits of bouquet over my back fence, new green of apple leaves, sprout of a neglected lawn. Back from the hospital with Peter, I'd walked haltingly around my yard, wincing at stitches that I had not wanted. Now I watched magpies scrape for bits of string and wool, and made a mental note that tomorrow, if I was feeling up to it, I'd give Fred a good brush and leave the hair for them. Fred welcomed me as though he'd been left alone for a month. I'd phoned a neighbor from the hospital, so at least he'd been fed.

It was Peter's first question when I rang him.

"Can you feed Fred, Mum? Should I come home and feed him?"

"I can manage. I'd like you to stay with Dad for a bit longer, love."

Peter chattered the way he did when he was happy. I pictured him and Derek eating American pizza, Derek washing up. When Derek came on the line, I had an overwhelming urge to tell him I was jumping on the first plane I could.

I took a deep breath and began to explain what had happened, pleased now that I hadn't insisted on doing so from the hospital. I had to make Derek understand that what was happening to me was serious.

Derek said very little—probably because Peter was breathing down his ear—but what he said was reassuring. I told him I'd write and send a copy of the police report on my car.

Next I rang a locksmith, and arranged for the locks on my doors to be changed, and for deadlocks to be fitted to all the windows.

A couple of hours later, I was staring at Detective Sergeant Brook standing splay-legged on my porch. He was wearing the same hat he'd on in the hospital, pulled low on his forehead, squashing his eyebrows too close to his eyes.

We sat in my living room. The air smelt musty. I went to a window and opened it clumsily.

"It's important that you tell me everything," the detective said. "Where were you the night before the accident?"

I took a deep breath, and began to tell him about breaking in to Compic's office. He stopped me after a few sentences, took out a tape recorder, switched it on, and pulled a notebook from his pocket. I continued with my story.

He stopped me again to say he supposed I realized that breaking and entering was a serious offense. I nodded. He asked question after question, and made copious notes. The tape finished, and he turned it over. I tried to make my answers logical and coherent, but I was aware how crazy much of the story sounded.

When I told him what I'd found on Compic's computer, he made me go back over the details three times. He asked me everything I knew about the one-eyed man, Bernard Whitelaw.

After what seemed like hours, I blurted out, "I suppose you wouldn't like a cup of tea? I need one."

The detective followed me into the kitchen, sat down on a wobbly chair, and lined up his notebook and pen on the table beside him. Now, I thought, now he'll take his hat off. But he didn't. He watched me boil water and open cupboards one-handed, with an expression of mild amusement, as though my difficulties, and his withholding of an offer to help, gave him some kind of pleasure.

"Might the case against Rae Evans be reopened?" I asked, with a small flicker of pride that I'd managed to make tea without breaking anything, or burning myself.

"Reopened?" He looked at me as though I was referring to a packet of stale biscuits. "It was never closed." He drank his tea without a word of thanks, and patted his lips with a large blue-and-white checked handkerchief.

My arm was beginning to hurt. I felt dizzy, and I longed for him to go so that I could pull the curtains in my room, and lie down underneath my doona.

"What will happen now?" I asked.

"I'll report back to the fraudies. See which way they play the ball." He paused and studied me. "The case against Ms. Evans is a strong one," he went on. "My colleagues in the fraud squad argue that it's strong enough for a conviction." He paused again, and I wondered if he felt I was owed some kind of explanation in return for my information, or whether it was his habit to set people straight, if and when he could.

"On the other hand, Mrs. Mahoney, your car was definitely interfered with. What you've told me needs examining, and there's half a dozen new people to be interviewed. I'll talk to the boss, make sure he's fully briefed."

The detective sighed. He looked exhausted. He raised his hat a little with two fingers, and I saw with a shock that he was completely bald.

After he'd left, I mulled over what he'd told me. By implication, though he hadn't said this outright, if he acted on my information, or persuaded his superior to do so, he'd be going against the detectives in the fraud squad who had handled the case against Rae. In particular, I guessed, he'd be going against Detective Sergeant Hall. Was he in a position to do this? Could he succeed? And what illness was he suffering from? What was wrong with him?

How easy it is to harm people. It hardly takes brains or planning. It had been no more than a few minutes work for someone to fix my car so the brakes were sure to fail.

Every one of Derek's letters and postcards had a return address. You're supposed to include the sender's address on the back of a letter, so of course Derek does. My postbox doesn't have a lock. It's never occurred to me that it should. And if I had bought one, it would only have been a simple padlock that any fool could break. Anyone watching me would know that Peter was staying with his father.

In my letter to Derek, which I typed with two fingers of my left hand, I told him the police were treating the case seriously, which I hoped was the truth. I begged him not to leave Peter alone, even for a few minutes. The closer Peter was to me, the closer he was to the trouble I was in. I repeated my request for him to stay in America for a while longer. I couldn't see that there was a better plan. My options were fewer, and clearer than before.

Ivan rang. I told him I was feeling scared and confused, and needed to be by myself for a while.

"Not the best Idea you've ever had, Sandy," Ivan said.

I wondered where I'd heard precisely that sentence before, but I was too tired and groggy to get my mind around it.

No one crept by my house that night to throw a brick through my window, and climb in with a knife between his teeth. No one jimmied open the back door, to strangle me where I half-sat, half-lay against my son's pillow, glad I hadn't washed his pillow case, sucking up his faint smell as I waited for the attack. No one burnt my house down, or shot me through the kitchen window while I made a cup of tea left-handed early in the morning. Or poured boiling oil down my chimney; or stalked me when I went outside with Fred, and brushed him, and left a pile of dog hair for the birds.

After this small excursion in the open air, I shut myself up in my house, while spring flounced along Goodwin Street. Every time I went into a room, I had to close the door behind me. My house was no longer open on the inside, but a box within another box, bordering on yet another. Not Chinese fashion, though I dreamed of this, of folding myself inside a small container that smelt of sandalwood, and then each time a smaller one, until, squashed antlike, I might at last be safe.

I rang America again. Listening to the dial tone, I broke out in an anxious sweat in case Derek shouted at me to stop being neurotic. He didn't, and for that I thank him now.

SOUTHWELL
PARK

O N DETECTIVE SERGEANT BROOK'S next visit, he and I
ended up walking further than we'd intended, along
Sullivan's Creek, under the bridge at Mouat Street, and
on through Southwell Park.

It was a spur-of-the-moment thing, my suggestion
of a walk, grabbing Fred's lead—a combination of sudden, choking
claustrophobia, and anxiety that needed movement, outside air. I doubted
that anybody would jump out at me from behind a bush when my companion was a policeman.

Detective Sergeant Brook was looking better, I noticed, his skin
firmer, less like unbaked dough.

"The Compic lady is being super-helpful," he told me. "Offered us
her books, any computer files we'd like to check."

"What did you find?" I asked.

"Everything seems to be in order. Those notes you told me about, referring to your IT director, there's no sign of them."

"They've been deleted," I said. "They would be. Allison and her partner couldn't know how much I'd found, or what I'd seen."

The detective stared at me, and didn't comment. I guessed policemen
all had their own ways of working out when somebody was lying. Watch
the body language, listen to the tone of voice.

We were approaching a line of young eucalypts. I lowered my head and pretended to fiddle with my sling. I knew I shouldn't be using one. The doctor had forbidden it. But the weight was punishing, and I cheated in the afternoons. I was supposed to go back to work in two days' time. I knew I had to, if there was to be any hope of getting the outwork report finished on schedule. I hated the thought of having to face any of them.

"Has anyone contacted the police to make a complaint about me breaking in to Compic's office?"

The detective shook his head. "I want you to go back over everything. Try and recall any details you might have left out."

We continued walking at Fred's pace while I talked, pausing as he sniffed at trees, and dug for crickets in the clumps of grass that bordered Sullivan's Creek. I remembered the silly episode with the disk in the first aid room, the even sillier one with me taped to a microphone trying to get Bambi to confess.

"Surely that's not her real name."

"Brenda, but she won't answer if you call her that."

"And she admitted to planting the disk? Who has it now?"

"Felix Wenborn," I said. "And no, unfortunately she didn't."

"Mr. Wenborn denies having had any improper contact with Ms. Edgeware. They corresponded on the telephone, discussing the contract her company bid for, that was all."

"I told you last time—I don't believe the company bid for the contract at all. Felix just gave it to them."

"Mr. Wenborn claims you're lying. He has an alibi for the night of your break-in, and for the next morning as well."

"Can I ask who he was with?"

"His wife."

The detective waited, watching me closely again.

"It's possible Dianne Trapani saw Felix and Allison in the bistro near the travel center," I said.

"I interviewed the girl myself. She saw someone with red hair. She thought it was a *Canberra Times* reporter."

I adjusted my sling again. "Speaking of the *Canberra Times*, their office manager bought heaps of Compic software. There's a pattern. Allison and her partner target certain married men."

The detective didn't comment on this theory. Instead he asked, "What else?"

We were heading toward a picnic table and chairs. I realized I hadn't said much about Di Trapani's brother Tony, and the mess he'd got himself into at the university. I said I'd asked Tony to introduce me to Allison, and that his friend Ateeq had been there as well.

Detective Sergeant Brook scratched his scalp underneath his hat. "What made you think you could help the kid?"

"I thought it might improve my relations with his sister. Tony's scared," I went on. "He's done some silly things. But he wouldn't booby-trap my car, I'm sure of it."

The detective gave me a quick, reproachful glance and said, "When I've got a few days to spare, remind me to tell you some stories about nineteen-year-old hackers."

Someone had lit a fire in a rubbish bin, and it had spread and blackened the whole picnic area. The smell of burning was strong, though the fire did not look recent.

He eyed the nearest bench. "Are you tired? Do you want to sit down for a minute?"

I nodded. I did feel tired, but I thought he'd asked because he wanted a rest. I noticed that when his energy ebbed below a certain level, his voice flattened out. If you represented it on paper, it would be a long flat line.

Fred ran down to the creek and began scratching for worms on the edge, where the soil was soft.

"Old habits die hard," I said.

The policeman didn't ask what I meant. He'd ignored Fred so far, and hadn't offered to help while I'd struggled one-handed to let him off the lead.

He lowered himself on to the bench, first brushing off some dirt and loose soot with his hand. As though deciding to repay my confidences with one of his own, he took off his hat and set it on the seat beside him. Pale, unbaked skin stretched across the bones of his skull, white and shining as my plaster when I woke in the middle of the night. He ran a hand lightly over his head, not touching the bald skin, his bloodless hand momentarily reflecting the milky water in the creek.

I bit my lip, and sat down on the opposite bench, trying to work out why he'd decided to remove his hat just then, what he expected me to say. "Are you ill?" was wrong. "What's the matter?" didn't sound right either. I was too embarrassed to ask, but my unspoken questions made the silence ring.

"Why did your colleague go through the rubbish bin when she searched Rae Evans's office?" I asked finally.

Brook looked surprised, then he smiled briefly and leant forward on his elbows.

"Let me tell you a story about trashing. This was back when I first joined the police, right? I knew how to direct the traffic and ride a motorbike." He shifted on the bench, making himself more comfortable. "I was on the city desk at ten o'clock one night. I remember that, because I had the 'flu, and I was already mentally at home in bed. An Inspector came in—this guy who thought he was the ants' pants, and I pretty much thought so, too, at the time. He handed me this floppy disk in a plastic bag and asked me to take a copy of it. Then he said he'd be back in half an hour and left. I photocopied the label on the damn thing—that's what I thought he meant by copy it. I got hung by the balls because the static on the photocopier erased all the data on the disk."

I laughed and said, "You must have felt terrible." After a moment I added, "You didn't answer my question."

Brook shook his shoulders. He crossed and re-crossed his legs, eyeing his hat on the table between us as a reformed alcoholic might a glass of whisky.

"I'm getting to it. This will give you an idea of my meteoric rise from the dork who thought copy meant *photo*copy. I might add that what I am about to tell you is my one and only venture into undercover work. A child porn case, right? Me and two other officers collect the rubbish at this house in Narrabundah for four months straight. Once a week, we're garbos. We turn up on the truck, empty the bin—a metal one, I might add. The residence is classy. Around the corner we peel off, drive to the station with our plastic bags, start going through the loot. After four months we hit pay dirt, no pun intended. Would you believe our suspect had tossed a *list* of his clients? Ripped into bits the size of snowflakes and covered with vanilla yogurt, but a list."

Everything he'd said up to that point might have been a speech that someone else had proofread, his natural way of speaking a creamy sun rising underneath his hat.

"Okay," I said. "So what did that policewoman find in Rae Evans's rubbish bin?"

Brook gave his head a small, sharp shake. "Nothing," he said. "Nix."

His gaze was fixed on his hat, and the sooty mess on the picnic table next to it. I wished he would raise his eyes, make contact, instead of leaving me to stare at a burnt table and a worn Akubra hat.

"Am I going to be charged with breaking in to Compic's office?"

"Someone has to accuse you first."

"Oh," I said, wondering if this meant what I hoped it did.

Two archers were practicing on the other side of the creek. Peter and I had sometimes stopped to watch the archery competitions on Saturday afternoons. Peter was fascinated by the bull's-eyes, white at the center, then red, blue, with an outer edge of darker blue. I had to hold tight to his hand to stop him running up to them. One afternoon, at a pause in the play, and after we'd asked permission, I'd held my son up so he could touch the white heart, the colors pricked by arrowheads.

Now two young men were practicing—I'd never thought of archery as a sport for young men. They'd set up a single bull's-eye and were sharing it, joined by their common purpose. Yet they didn't speak. There wasn't so much as a "good shot" or "hard luck" when one arrow missed the target altogether, sailing over the top of it into a stand of casuarinas.

"Shall we keep walking? The golf course is just along this way a bit."

I called Fred. He seemed more confident and relaxed than on any of our previous walks. The first time I'd taken him to Southwell Park, he'd crouched between my legs and hadn't moved.

Brook got to his feet, picking up his hat carefully in both hands, as though it was made of some precious substance that had mysteriously reached breaking point.

The sun had warmed a huge cement cylinder where Peter and I used to sit and watch the golfers. I'd never figured out exactly what the cylinder was for. It looked like part of an old-fashioned steamroller, the sort I'd watched pressing stones into new asphalt when I was a kid. I hadn't seen one on a road for years. But this cylinder had no holes in the sides. I couldn't see how it fitted to an engine. It had been there for as long as I knew, on the other side of the fence, where rubbish from the golf course tended to end up, part of an overgrown copse of self-seeded birch and she-oak. In summer, long grass hid bottles, newspapers, bricks, tangled bits of wire. Winter bared them again.

The cylinder's surface was weathered, roughened. Moss had colonized the shady side. Peter and I used to have favorite golfers that we barracked for. We liked to sit side by side, and watch them tee off from the rise directly opposite. We made bets about how many balls would land in the pond that ran the length of the fence a few feet from our seat.

I tried not to notice how uncomfortable the policeman looked with about an eighth of his bum resting against damp curved cement. I'd never found it an awkward place to sit before.

Pale new shoots were coming up through the long gray winter grass. Fred ran, fell over one shoulder, then rolled on his back. He stood up and ran again, into the tall grass a little way along. It covered him completely. He barked once. I wondered if he wanted me to come and find him. He'd never played like that before—not with me, at any rate.

"Did you bring a ball?" Brook asked.

"No, but you can throw a stick for him. Peter does. He likes it."

The game worked until Fred broke the stick in half and sat down to eat it.

Brook propped, out of breath, against the concrete block. This time he didn't try to sit on it.

"No one knew I was planning to go to Compic's office," I said. "Whoever booby-trapped my car must have followed me."

"Were you aware of being followed?"

"I thought I was being extra careful that night. But there were other times when I was sure a car was staying just behind me."

"Man, or woman?"

"The door opened. I saw a shadow, that's all. But they could run."

"Does Ivan Semyonov drive your car?"

"Ivan's got a license, but he doesn't drive. Not normally," I added, remembering the hire car in Queensland.

"Did he ever drive your car?"

"No," I said, recalling Ivan loping through the carport in the middle of a backyard game with Fred and Peter, banging his knee on the bumper bar, and swearing. I'd been washing up, looking out through the kitchen window, smiling at his fuss and bluster. Peter had laughed. My throat contracted at the domestic ordinariness and pleasure of it.

"You told me you were suspicious that Semyonov had been spying on Rae Evans."

My throat contracted again. "Yes."

Brook waited.

"It could have been Allison that night," I said. "Then there's the Trapanis. Claire and Guy Harmer. Claire was waiting outside the first aid room the day I found the disk. I heard her talking to a man, but he'd gone by the time I opened the door. I've crossed Bambi off my list because I just don't think she's up to it. Any of those people could have found out where I live. I don't have a lockable garage, just a carport. I didn't see any signs that someone had been messing with my car, but I wasn't looking for them. I didn't tell anyone I was planning to break into Compic's office. But that man with the one eye, Whitelaw, I think he'd been watching me, electronically at least."

Still Brook didn't comment. Fred was rolling over and over in the grass. I looked across at the pond. A shelduck skittered, sliding in to land feet first, water spraying up, her wake rippling out behind her.

"What do your colleagues in the fraud squad say?"

"Let me worry about that." With one swift movement, Brook pressed his hat low on his head. "I'm a fussy bastard when it comes to checking details for myself."

We would go back to the house, and this strange, sick policeman would get into his car and leave, and my fear would be there waiting for me.

He stared at me as I bent down to pick up Fred's lead. He hasn't let me off, I thought. He's mentally working himself through to a certain crossroads. I wonder if he'll tell me when he gets there.

I chose a different route for our return, one that was marginally shorter. About halfway to Mouat Street, we passed a mass of rotting old tree roots, where four years ago a top-heavy willow had fallen during a storm. Peter had spent a morning playing on it in the snow, the first and only snow I'd seen in Canberra.

He'd put out his tongue to catch snowflakes, and twirled with his arms out straight on either side, in a slow and graceful dance. Then, tired out with climbing on the tree, he'd giggled, crumpled to the ground, pretending to be dizzier than he was, while I'd pulled his too-small parka down to cover frozen skin.

Derek had said that night that he couldn't understand why I didn't dress Peter properly, when I had nothing to do all day but see to his needs.

I didn't know why myself. It was no more than a couple of hours' work to drive to Target, and buy my son new winter clothes. But I'd put it off. I didn't understand my lethargy, what Derek called being in a rut. At first it had to do with my mother's death. Gradually, a time of mourning had been replaced by—what?

I'd been looking for something, that day with the fallen tree and the snow. On all our outings. But I hadn't found it. I'd known that, whatever it was, it wasn't in the house.

I understood why Derek had been so angry when I refused to go to

America with him. He was offering me a chance to pull myself out of the rut. I'd become dull, lazy, and pig-headed. That was how he saw me. It took only a little effort for me to see myself the same way.

Those years at home alone with Peter. My two closest women friends had gone back to work after having children. I'd watched them stagger on through months and years of insufficient sleep, no time for themselves, or me. Friendship had shredded, becoming thin and light as an old gauze bandage.

When Derek had first told me about the invitation to Philadelphia, smiling in advance at the thought of my excitement, my congratulations, the plans we'd make, and I'd replied instead with, "Actually, I think I've got myself a job," it was the first time I'd ever seen him speechless. "Nonsense," he'd said when he recovered. "You're coming with me. We're going as a family. Don't be ridiculous." But he didn't sound convinced. He sounded different. As though he'd glimpsed something I thought only I could see.

And so it was easy to be stubborn, to present a stone wall to Derek's anger and his arguments. I was only proving what he said about me. I didn't have to exert myself for that.

The night that Peter had played on the fallen tree, I put him to bed with a sore throat, and Derek asked, "What were you thinking of?"

"I was thinking of the snow," I said.

Yet I knew that the night after, or the night after that, when Derek came home, and I felt like complaining because I'd been shut up inside all day with a sick child, I wouldn't be able to. The luxury of complaint would be locked inside a small square room with "I told you so" in bold red letters on the front.

I realized that Brook was still watching me carefully, and that his expression was interested, not unsympathetic.

"What are you thinking of?" he asked.

"Snow," I said. "And consequences. Cause and effect."

He didn't come back into the house. He shook my hand at the driver's door of his plain blue Toyota. I hesitated, wanting him gone, yet not wanting to be left alone. I'm sure he knew this. His brown eyes were shrewd, and he smiled at me from beneath his hat.

"HEARD ABOUT YOUR ACCIDENT."

It was the one-eyed man, Bernard Whitelaw, on the phone.

"Do you know who caused it?" I asked him.

"No idea. I really am sorry, Sandra. A broken arm's a nuisance." After a moment's pause, he added, "I get the feeling the police are still satisfied Evans is their lady. Do you agree?"

"I get feelings," I said, "but I don't know what any of them mean."

"YOU'RE SURE IT WAS Whitelaw?" Brook asked when I rang him a few minutes later.

"Positive."

"What did he want?"

"He rang to offer his condolences."

Brook had some more information about Allison. He wanted to know if it accorded with what I'd discovered. Her parents lived in Townsville. She had a younger brother in Brisbane, also working in computing. No sisters, apparently no relations in Canberra, and she lived alone, in a townhouse in Braddon.

Ashamed of the oversight, I said I hadn't found out where Allison lived. I didn't know anything about her personal life, apart from the fact that I believed she'd been dispensing her favors more than generously. I scrawled her address on the back of my shopping list. My left-handed writing looked as though Fred had dipped his claws in ink, and scraped them across the page.

"One more thing," Brook said, "Who told you about that chappy over at the *Canberra Times*?"

"Gail Trembath, the journalist who broke the story about Rae."

"Yeah, well," Brook said dryly. "Claims he never met Ms. Edgeware. Claims her company sent a demonstration CD, and he was so taken with it that he bought up big."

TO CATCH
A THIEF

MPTIED OF ITS TREASURES, Ivan's house had the look of a dark-eyed, abandoned woman.

Low clouds bringing rain made the interior dimmer than usual. I flicked a light switch. The phone rang. Brook picked it up and spoke in gruff monosyllables.

When Brook had rung to tell me Ivan's house had been burgled, I'd got in a taxi and gone straight there, without giving myself time to think.

Brook hung up the phone, and barked at Ivan. "Was your stuff marked? Have you got a list? How many people know about this set-up here?"

Ivan looked at him as though these questions were incomprehensible.

Brook flicked a chair around and straddled it, leaning both arms across the back. His hat was off. A brown shadow covered his head, the tiniest suggestion of hair. He ran his hand lightly, quickly, over the top of it.

Ivan said, "Bastard comes back, I'll grab him by the balls and lock him in the broom cupboard."

Unable to stand still watching the two men, I walked over to the wall and ran my finger down the place where the photograph of Alexander Graham Bell had been.

No one had switched on any lights at the back of the house. The glow along the corridor, no stronger than Peter's night-light, was like the chance illumination of a forgotten stage. A forensics van was outside, and voices echoed matter-of-factly through a wall, yet Ivan's house reminded me more than ever of a place of bad spells, cordoned off by magic rather than police tape, a place sealed up and silent for a hundred years.

I walked outside and began a circuit of the yard. The first few drops of rain hit the top of my head like dollar coins. I hunched my neck between my shoulders. Within minutes, it would be pelting down.

Outside the window of Ivan's workroom, spiky grevillea branches looked bitten into, as though there'd been a dog fight. I parted slippery spines, and saw the print.

I stared down at it, convinced that *it* was staring up at *me*, one round brown eye the color of neglected soil. Soon, any second now, it would fill with water.

"Who in their right mind would break into a house wearing stiletto heels?" I asked Brook, after I'd called him to come and look. He was kneeling beside me, head lowered, studying the shoeprint.

He grunted and stood up. "I don't think this little baby was made by anybody climbing in the window."

I put a hand to my head, realizing that the storm was holding off.

"The angle's wrong," Brook said. "Too straight, too flush with the wall. There's no high heel marks inside, no mud or dirt."

"Maybe she took them off?"

"It's just a little too convenient. This is how I think we got our lady's shoe mark."

Brook opened the window as wide as it would go. It screeched and protested. "Jesus," he said to Ivan, who was watching us silently from inside the room. "Your neighbors must be deaf."

Framed by the window in the semidarkness, Ivan looked like a misplaced illustration from the Old Testament.

"Just a minute," Brook said. He left me, and reappeared inside. Grunting again, he leant out and dug a stick into the soft earth beside the grevillea. It made a clear, almost perfectly round print.

"It's a *shoe*, not just the heel," I said, feeling ridiculous.

"Oh, I think whoever made the print had a shoe with them all right," Brook said. "They just weren't Cinderella."

Ivan had disappeared. I went around the back, and found him crouched on a dilapidated kitchen chair under the clothesline. Ordinary mayhem was erupting somewhere else. An ambulance siren sounded very loud, but it could have been a couple of miles away. I pictured Ivan in another rented house, in another city. Would he choose one with dark bushes all around it? Would he carry a photograph, or any souvenir of his time with me?

I wanted to touch him, make contact in some way, but I was scared to.

Brook appeared at the back door. "Semyonov!" he called out. "I need a list, a full statement of what's missing. Phone me when you've done it. Mrs. Mahoney. Would you like a lift?"

"Yes. Thank you."

The storm was in the sky's wings, waiting for its cue. Then the sun appeared beneath the clouds, and turned them gray and rose, a million parrots wing tip to wing tip.

"Take it as a compliment!" Brook directed a fist that was half a wave, half a punch in the air, toward Ivan, who hadn't moved. "They knew that if they crashed your system, you'd rewire, be up and running in twenty-four hours. Only way they could be sure to stop you was to pinch the lot!"

"Detective Sergeant Brook," I said, as we were backing out of the drive, and I was wondering if we shouldn't be looking for a nifty cross-dresser, "I love your hair."

IVAN RANG MY DOORBELL late that night. My porch light carved him in yellow. He smiled uncertainly, swaying from one side to the other. His skin was clammy, and the light picked out the gray wash of shock behind his eyes.

I moved forward instinctively to catch him, and we held each other, my thick, awkward arm for once not an encumbrance, but a fine buttress and a bridge.

"We'll get all your things back," I said.

I led Ivan in, through all my doors and locks, and those other barriers of the mind with which I'd kept him out. I made him a hot drink, and wiped his forehead, sticky as cement that wouldn't set, and offered him the most basic, the merest, I suppose, of comforts.

Ivan sipped his chocolate. "Know why I chose computer science?" he demanded. "My father was furious. A career for philistines, he called it. Something only an idiot would choose, when he could study history, philosophy, literature. You know, for a man who spent half his life committed to Marx and the other half denouncing him, my father misunderstood the basis of materialism."

He lifted his head and stared at me. "It was as far away from European politics as I could get."

I put out my hand and took his. "They could go on like this until the trial. It keeps them busy, but it keeps us busier, always on the back foot. We can't give in now."

Ivan's brown sweater was rucked up over his belly, his shirt loose, his long hair matted and untidy.

"I'll never be an inventor, Sandra. Did you know Babbage's plans for the analytical engine weren't rediscovered until 1937? And that was only because of Ada Lovelace?"

Most of Ivan's heroes I knew nothing about. But I'd heard of Ada Lovelace, daughter of Lord Byron, mathematician, friend, and colleague of Charles Babbage, who'd called her his Enchantress of Numbers.

"Ivan," I said, "come to bed."

He followed me into the bedroom, and watched while I plumped up my doona with one hand, then straightened the sheets.

My plaster throbbed in the near dark, grew swollen and then shrank, like the white, pulsating light outside the labor ward at Royal Canberra Hospital the night my son was born. I followed it with my eyes, my breath. There was the dark shape of a man, the smell, the hair, the beard. Naked, Ivan had the look of a bewildered calf.

In the middle of the night, he got up for a glass of water, and on the way back he walked into the end of the bed and cut his ankle and bled on the carpet.

"Don't you know?" he said, in answer to my question about Brook. "He's got leukemia. He's gone into remission."

I looked down at my breasts, and thought about how I continued to inhabit the same body, day in and day out. I kissed my fingertips, kissed the white skin of my plaster and found it tasted sweet.

Some people lose too young what they love best, while others anticipate, with every breath, the loss that has not yet crippled them, so that in the end they cannot tell the difference between being given something, and having it taken away.

Toward dawn, the phone rang and I ran to it, thinking only of Peter. It was Dianne Trapani. Tony had been in a car accident. He was in intensive care at Woden.

DRAGON LADIES

BANDAGES ACCENTED TONY'S THIN cheeks and dark coloring. He looked less Italian than French, a character made up for a part in a play about the Revolution.

Brook was standing in front of the window at the end of his bed.

"Where's the nurse?" I asked. "What's going on?"

Brook ignored my questions.

"Where's Dianne?" I demanded.

Brook turned as though registering my existence for the first time. He looked paler than Tony, in need of a nurse's attention himself.

"She went off with the doctor," he said. "She'll back in a few minutes."

I sat by Tony's bed and held his hand. His expression was unreadable. It could have been that he was trying not to cry. His parents were conspicuously absent.

On our way out of the ward ten minutes later, Brook and I stopped at the information desk to confirm what I was afraid of. Tony's parents hadn't come to the hospital, or left any message.

"I thought only kids could be that cruel," Brook said.

I glanced at him, wondering if he was thinking of his own.

We walked out of the hospital together, to get some fresh air and find a place to talk.

"Sorry for snapping back there," I said.

Brook accepted my apology indifferently.

Outside the hospital's main entrance, the air had the singing clarity of an early spring morning. White awnings stretched above automatic doors, and along a walkway to the road, giving the unlikely impression of a beach promenade at the height of summer.

We stopped in front of a low brick wall decorated with a mosaic of enamel and colored stone—a scene of grass, trees, a hill, a man with a watering can. All the man's internal organs were revealed—his heart, lungs, stomach, liver, thigh muscles, and brain. And they didn't look as though they would sustain life. They looked sick. A red-and-blue bird was flying past the man's left ear.

Brook leant against the mural, taking no notice of its subject matter.

"Let's sit over there," I said with a grimace, motioning him toward a bench underneath the awning.

"How did you find out about Tony's accident?"

"Policemen do talk to one another, Mrs. Mahoney."

"Did you tell him about my car?"

"What do you take me for, a ghoul?"

I smiled and said, "I don't know. You might be."

"Who'd link the kid with you?" he asked.

"Ateeq. Allison Edgeware. Professor Bailey. His sister, of course."

Brook rubbed his hand over hair which had grown a fraction longer.

"Anyone making the effort to monitor my computer would have seen the e-mails Tony sent me about Allison and Compic," I said. "Not that they contained any startling revelations."

It seemed that Brook was plotting the irregular steps he'd taken, surprised at the point they'd brought him to. Or maybe he was just tired.

A statue of a skinny heron standing over a fish looked skeletal and ugly. I stared at my thick wrist, turning it slowly toward the light and back.

Brook said, "I interviewed the boy and his mate. The Pakistani kid. Soon as you told me about them. Tony asked me not to say anything to his folks, so I didn't. At the time, there didn't seem to be a pressing need. But I did drop by Akewa Hi-Fi and have a chat with Ateeq's Mum. She told me they'd stopped paying his bills months ago. Cocky little bugger, boasting that his folks were loaded and didn't care how much he cost them. Mum had a different story."

"So where have they been getting the money from?"

"I reckon that crusty old Professor is spot-on. I went to see him, too. They were using his account. The university was footing the bill, no doubt about it."

Was Tony upstairs in that bed thinking that he could have died? Or that somebody might want him dead?

I got to my feet, saying, "I'm going back to the ward. I want to talk to Dianne."

Brook looked up. "You know, they've given me a deadline."

For a shocked moment, I thought he was referring to his cancer, to the doctors.

He stood up, too, in an oddly formal way, looking over my left shoulder, not meeting my eyes. "Boss reckons I'm barking up a gum tree. Fraudies have got their pinch. I should let justice take its course."

"And?"

"And I reckoned they owed it to me, you know, like instead of a gold watch."

"A deadline? You mean a date?"

"Yeah. I've got until October 1."

TONY SMILED WHEN HE saw me—at least I think he did.

The light was growing stronger, bleaching every corner of linoleum. In midsummer, heavy vertical blinds would make the ward a green-and-yellow upstairs cave, artificially cooled air flowing over every surface, creating the uniform temperature of a hole under the Nullarbor Desert.

Dianne wasn't back yet. I sat down again by Tony's bed.

"What happened? Can you tell me?"

Tony's bruised jaw opened just enough to make his words intelligible. "I was driving. Ran off road. Hit the—hit a tree."

"Has anyone from Compic phoned you?" I asked. "Or contacted you in any way at all?"

Tony shook his head. Dianne appeared before I could ask him any more questions, filling the swing doors with her ashen dress, her tangled hair and swollen eyes. She looked surprised to see me, as though she'd forgotten that she'd phoned. I said I'd like to talk to her, and that I didn't mind waiting in the cafeteria.

She nodded, too worried about her brother to take in much else. I squeezed Tony's hand and told him that that I'd call in to see him again soon.

On my way to the cafeteria, I took a wrong turn and ended up near the main entrance. I stopped to get my bearings next to a bridal-wear shop. Most of the window space was taken up with multiple white flounces and a veil. The shop was closed. It was hard to see how anyone would make the trip to Woden Valley Hospital to buy her wedding dress.

Some twenty minutes later, Dianne sighed and slid into the seat opposite me at a corner table. Dark brown patches crimped the skin under her eyes, deep lines curved from her nose to the corners of her mouth.

She spread her hands palms downward, fingers splayed and tense, then looked across at me and thanked me for coming.

"What did your parents say?"

Dianne felt for her cigarettes, then remembered she couldn't smoke them there.

"Tone was pissed, you see. I can't believe they're doing this to him."

"You don't think he deliberately—"

"He didn't think. He *doesn't*. That's his problem. He just had one too many."

We were on the third floor, level with the treetops. The cafeteria was practically empty. I realized that we were in the section reserved for staff. I'd misread the arrows at the entrance, which way was staff and which way public. But they couldn't be too particular about it, because no one came over and asked us to leave. A folded room divider was painted improbably cheerful colors—orange tree trunks, sky straight out of a tube.

I ordered two coffees. Dianne gulped hers down and reached for her cigarettes again.

"Do your parents know about the tribunal?"

"I told them last night. Only way to make them understand. The grog. That he was depressed. Got me bloody nowhere."

A sign on the noticeboard above our heads said WANTED: DRAGON LADIES. Women required to paddle a dragon boat. Training once a week. It could be a distraction. Of course, I'd have to wait for my arm to heal.

"What will Tony do when he's discharged?"

"He's not going back there. I won't let him, even if they will, which I doubt. He can stay with me."

I waited a few moments, then said, "Dianne? What happened between you and Rae Evans?"

She gave me a long look. I could see her thinking about brushing me off; how, under other circumstances, a brush-off would have risen quickly to her lips, followed by a dose of sarcasm large enough to shut me up. But she hesitated, and then it was too late.

"This coffee's shit," she said. "But I'm thirsty. Want another one?"

"No thanks."

Waiting for Dianne to come back, I remembered I was supposed to be at work. I looked around for a phone to tell them—tell who?—I'd be a little late.

When Di came back with her coffee, she looked at me levelly and said, "You're either with Evans or against her." She raised an eyebrow, testing my response, but I don't think she cared much what it was.

"Evans buys your allegiance, and then you have to sing her song."

"Which is?" I asked.

"You would have recognized the tune."

"Since it was interrupted, could you tell me? Spell it out?"

Listening to Dianne's story, told in her stop-go voice, more staccato than usual because of her fatigue and preoccupation with her brother, my throat went dry, and I found it hard to swallow.

"Let me get this straight," I said when she'd finished. "Rae wanted you to change some figures, to exaggerate the difference between out-workers' rates of pay and the award rates?"

"Not *change*. You've got to understand how these things are done. Evans made it clear to me that she wanted a particular interpretation."

"And you said no?"

"She didn't ask me directly, so I didn't have to, but I knew what I was supposed to do."

"What did you do?"

"I stalled. It wasn't that I objected outright to her interpretation. It was possible. Not the most likely, not the one I would have chosen, but possible. What I objected to was how she did it. Such a lady. So *superior*. I waited to see what she would do next."

"And?"

"She hired you."

"Who knew about this?"

"Apart from me and Evans? No one. I didn't tell a soul."

"There's one thing I don't get," I said. "I came on the scene—okay, I can understand that you were angry about that. But after Rae was forced to leave, and time went on, and you could see that the interpretation I was working toward was the same as yours—why didn't you say something, why were you still hostile to me?"

"I wasn't *hostile*, Sandra. I just didn't care any longer. The place gave—*gives* me the creeps. I can't stand it. I'm leaving."

"Where will you go?"

"Right out of the public service. I'd rather scrub floors than work in an atmosphere like that again."

* * *

I PHONED WORK AND spoke to Bambi. She told me there'd been no messages or memos concerning the outwork report. She sounded surprised, as though she'd forgotten its existence, and mine too.

A taxi dropped me in the city, where I needed to withdraw some money and do a bit of shopping.

Allison Edgeware appeared out of nowhere, in Garema Place. Had she seen me in the queue for the automatic teller machine?

I braced myself, heavy arm out to one side for balance, feet square on the concrete, while Allison walked toward me, holding out her hand and smiling. Her face clouded and she said, "Whatever happened to you, Sandra?"

"You're obviously a woman of many talents," I replied. "I should congratulate you."

"Congratulate me—what for?"

A posse of girls dressed in tiny denim skirts brushed past. Allison's brown eyes were locked on mine in an expression of concern.

"Let me buy you a cup of coffee or something, Sandra. You look as though you need it."

I stood flat-footed, lumpish in one spot, for a crazy second picturing my plastered arm as a weapon, thumping Allison with it, knocking her out cold.

"I've told the police everything I know," I said, "and now I'm staying out of it."

She smiled again, a picture of bewilderment and clear-eyed innocence. "Stay out of what? I'm sorry, but I've got absolutely no idea what you're talking about."

"Who is he?"

"What?"

"Your partner. Is it Felix Wenborn?"

Allison threw back her head and laughed.

"You crack me up, too," I said.

*   *   *

254

AT HOME, I CHECKED the locks on all my doors and windows, then sat on Peter's bed and hugged his pillow with my good arm. I thought how hacking blurred all boundaries, not just those it was convenient to blur. At certain times before, I'd had the feeling that I was closing in on Allison's partner—not in the sense that he or she was a stranger, and I was approaching from a distance. But accepting that whoever it was might turn out to be a stranger, but might, as credibly, be someone I saw every day— accepting both these possibilities—I now had the feeling that I was growing closer *inwardly*. I can think of no better word for it than that. I had mimicked my adversary's methods, and this had changed me more than I ever could have guessed.

BROOK PHONED TO ASK, "Do you like geraniums?"

He told me he'd finally prised the first-aid-room disk from Felix.

"What's on it?"

"Jokes," he said.

"*Jokes?*"

"Drawing of a great big terracotta pot with a red geranium, over water, but in the reflection there's no flower. I mean, the pot's completely empty."

"Jesus." I was thinking that whoever was listening to our call would have something to chew over at least. Brook hadn't found a bug on my phone, but I wasn't convinced.

"Detective Sergeant Brook? Be careful when you make a copy."

He chuckled, and hung up.

Unable to get to sleep that night, I began another detective novel. I crunched through them like chocolates with hard centers. I liked the moral ones best, Adam Dalgliesh and Inspector Thomas Lynley. Upright, sensitive, thinking men. Gorgeous.

I read until my eyes crossed, but as soon as I put out the light, settled into the pillows, I was wide awake again. I surfed TV channels, looking for a story as different from mine as I could imagine.

DRINKING
AT TILLEYS

I SEE YOU'VE TAKEN up drinking," I said to Ivan.

"Only when phoney coppers give me no choice." Ivan held up his glass. "Babe." He saluted me and winked, then looked embarrassed.

Brook ducked his head and grinned lopsidedly.

"Copper!" Ivan said. "Put your hat back on. You're indecent, man."

"What's the celebration?" I asked, looking from one man to the other, beginning to feel embarrassed myself.

Brook reached one arm round Ivan's shoulders, the other around mine, and brought our heads down close to his. "Know why I did those computer courses?" He chuckled in our ears. "I got sick of looking at dead people."

Real coppers, coppers with a future, he told us with the expression of a man giving away state secrets, were busy chasing real crooks who had beaten, knifed, or shot someone, or stolen something you could touch. Did he mean the fraud squad? Them, too. They were chasing money you could stuff inside your underpants. That's what they understood.

"I'll tell you about the case of the shoe factory." Brook made us lean further forward. His voice was a slurred hiss. "This was before my conversion. Called a factory, but in actual fact a whole lot of Vietnamese and Cambodian women cutting up leather in a shed at the back of a house.

You need sharp knives for that, and one day one of them took to the boss with hers. No doubt she was provoked. When we turned up, the women were sitting in the kitchen, drinking tea and working their way through the contents of the fridge. They were half-starved. The one who'd done it was cool as a cucumber. Offered me some spring rolls!"

Brook and Ivan laughed.

"What happened to her?" I asked.

"Her boss bled to death, unfortunately. She got manslaughter."

I leant back in my chair and stared at the stage, with its row of pretty cream lights winking round the edge. I liked Tilley's, but it seemed an inappropriate choice for my companions.

It used to be that men were only allowed at Tilley's if accompanied by a woman. The rule had been relaxed years ago, but it had given the bar an edge, a notoriety that it had never quite lost. I imagined myself up there behind the stage lights, and felt a stab of self-pity because I never would be. I couldn't sing, or play any kind of music. I'd taken myself to the bar a few times, when Peter was a baby and I'd persuaded Derek to stay home with him. I'd sat alone in the dark, fluid space, and soaked the voices, the guitars and keyboard through my skin.

I counted the lights—two large ones on the floor of the stage at either side, one at the back, and above, at ceiling height, nine more. Fans rolled above our heads. The carpet, walls, and ceiling were a deep burgundy shading into black. Photographs of famous artists filled two-thirds of a wall.

"As well as ger–geraniums," Brook said, "that disk of yours had a nice little present of a computer virus tucked away inside."

He inclined his head toward me. "Mr.–Mr. Wenborn is skeptical about your story."

I drew back. His tone of voice, the difficulty he was having with his words, upset me.

"If it hadn't happened," I said. "I'd be skeptical as well."

I glanced across at Ivan, whose head was bent over a glass of beer, and asked, "Why didn't Felix take the disk to the police before?"

Brook said with a bow, "Let's just say it's hard to refuse a sick man a legitimate request."

I did not know how to reply to this. "I thought it was Bambi who left it there," I said, though I'd already told Brook this. "I saw her go into the first aid room earlier that day. She could easily have tucked the disk up somewhere in her clothes."

Two young women were working behind the bar. Their shirts, under black waistcoats, glowed a luminous bluish white. Strongly angled lights made the cakes behind a glass display front twinkle and pulsate. The old feeling came to me of watching performers on a stage, and I was suspended, somehow, neither an actor, nor a legitimate member of the audience—ticket paid for, popcorn clasped in hand. I wasn't comfortable in either role. I had a giddy feeling that might have been stage fright, but was really closer to travel sickness, as though I was somewhere indeterminate, unfixed in space.

When Ivan went to get more drinks, I said to Brook, "I'm sure Allison has an accomplice. A partner. I bumped into her in Garema Place today. Yesterday, by now. I asked her if it was Felix. She laughed."

Brook seemed to be listening to me, yet his manner was distracted, and his eyes unfocused. He had one foot inside the shoe of his policeman's habits and responsibilities, but the other was way off somewhere, dancing to a different tune.

Ivan came back, and was handing me my glass, when he stumbled and spilt its contents over me.

"Sorry. Shit. Here." He pulled out his hanky and made a face of exaggerated apology.

I looked at the hanky and said, "No, thanks. There'll be a towel or something in the Ladies."

I dried my skirt as best I could with paper towels. My good hand was shaking. I knew I didn't want to stay there any longer. I hated seeing Brook drunk, and Ivan was behaving weirdly. I'd make my excuses and then leave.

I stopped in the doorway, and looked across at the two men. They were sitting shoulder to shoulder, with their backs to me. Brook's nail-brush head was bent. I noticed an odd thing. Brook in a sweatshirt, Ivan in his old brown sweater—their backs were the same shape, big and rounded. They looked to be comforting one another. They looked like twin thermos flasks that would warm your insides on a cold night.

IVAN TOLD ME LATER that Brook had had bad news from a blood test. He was starting chemotherapy again. He'd turned up on Ivan's doorstep, hat cradled in his arms like a precious bundle, called him a filthy Russian techno-head and said they were going out to get drunk together. He wouldn't take no for an answer.

"Why did you ask me to come?"

"I didn't know if I could manage on my own."

"You managed fine," I said.

Ivan had seen Brook into a taxi outside Tilley's, and then come on to my place.

We were both very tired, but too tense to sleep. We lay waiting for the dawn.

"Ivan," I said. "Do you think that we—that you and I might—"

"Might what, Sandy?" Ivan heaved himself up on the pillows, an action like a whale breaching, flumping a great volume of doona and sheet over me.

When I didn't finish my sentence, he said in a muffled voice, "You know, I've never been any good at it."

"At what?"

"The big picture, I guess."

"I haven't either. Do you know that dolphin mothers whose babies die will sometimes hold them on their backs up at the surface for days, or even weeks?"

"I suppose it's the smell of rotting flesh that finally gets through to them," Ivan said.

When the light turned blue under my curtains, he got up and called a taxi. I rolled over and finally fell asleep, telling myself I needed one more day.

In the afternoon, I brushed Fred and took him for a walk, planning what I would do when darkness fell again.

A BLACK
COTTON SLING

ELLO," I SAID, MOVING quickly in through Rae Evans's front door.

"Sandra! I don't know if anyone's—"

"I took care to see I wasn't being followed."

The adrenalin that had got me to Rae's flat was rushing out. I felt light-headed.

Rae stared at my arm. "What happened?"

"The brakes failed in my car."

"I'll take you out the back way." She was suddenly decisive. "Through the laundry. The back way's—"

"No," I said.

"What happened to you?" she repeated through cracked lips.

"I was in a car crash."

She put her arm around my shoulders and lifted my jacket aside, so that the sling I'd made out of black cotton, hoping to be less conspicuous, caught and drank the light.

"Does it hurt?"

"A bit."

Her hair looked dull and dry. Her clothes were creased, as though she'd been wearing the same sweater and tracksuit pants for days. Her face looked smaller, compacted and pressed down.

She let go of my arm, but stayed close to me, inclining her head, listening for a noise outside.

"Sit down. I'll get you something to drink."

"Thank you," I said. "Water will be fine."

She came back with the water, and I sipped it slowly while I told her about the accident, and breaking into Compic's office. She watched me apprehensively, and helplessly, too, as though I was a child she'd been asked to mind and did not know how to deal with. Yet, at the same time, it seemed to me that she couldn't be bothered any longer, that the hint about somebody watching her flat might be as much to get rid of me as anything, because all she wanted was to be left alone.

"There are two people behind all this," I said. "One is Allison Edgeware. The other is a man—I think it must be a man—in our department. It could be Felix. Is there anything about Felix that you haven't told me?"

Rae stood with both hands pressed down on the back of a chair.

"Felix *did* take an interest in those grants. He wanted to know all about Access Computing. But I didn't think there was anything odd about that. Felix always pokes his nose into everything. That's his way."

I drank more water. It cleared my head a bit.

"I found—on Compic's computer, before I was interrupted—I found a file with their sales to government departments. They've sold heaps of their trashy graphics. Plus they've successfully bid for development contracts—not just with us, with Health, Finance, and Education as well. I think they target married men, Allison and her partner. Allison gets them to sleep with her, and then she blackmails them. I found notes she'd made about Felix on the computer, too. They'd been deleted by the time the police got hold of it."

"The police?"

"There's a new detective. He came to see me in hospital. I wasn't going to tell him about breaking into Compic's office, but he got it out of me."

"You did that for my sake?"

"At the start—" I hesitated, not sure how to explain. "I thought it was for your sake. Now, I'm doing it for myself. If it's not Felix, my next bet is Jim Wilcox. What does *he* have against you?"

"I argued with Wilcox. It was stupid. I should have had more sense. It was about women's work, and women's rates of pay, as opposed to men's. He said it was right to pay men more, that society could never function the way I wanted it to. I called him a Neanderthal. Stupid," Rae repeated, with a short laugh like a strangled bark.

"Wilcox had the opportunity," I reminded her, "with his friend Charles Craven in Finance. I don't understand why the police didn't do more to follow that connection."

"Now there's a new detective?"

"I don't know what to make of him."

Rae said, "I don't know what to make of *you*."

I raised my arm a fraction, wondering if that's what she was referring to.

"It's not just that you've put yourself in danger, it's everything about you."

I'd been due for a change. I thought Rae knew that as well as I did.

"There's one more thing. Dianne told me—she said that when the two of you were looking at the early data for the report, you wanted a particular interpretation, one she disagreed with. Is that true?"

Rae said nothing for a while. When she spoke, her voice was soft and tired. "I've had a lot of time to think, over the last few weeks. I did put pressure on Dianne. It was wrong of me, I see that now. I was used to getting my own way."

"Would you have put the same pressure on me, if you hadn't had to leave?"

"Possibly. Probably. We'll never know that, will we?"

"My interpretation is the same as Dianne's."

"I guessed it would be."

"You didn't ask me about it. You didn't try and influence me."

"If you've changed, I've changed, too," Rae answered simply.

"Did you and my mother sleep together?"

Rae accepted the question unemotionally. "Once or twice. But it wasn't that. It was me, my job, my education, my ambitions. Somehow they came between us."

"How?"

Rae thought for a moment, then she said. "Your mother put out ideas of herself, ideas about all sorts of things, and then when it came to letting herself go with them, she wouldn't, or couldn't."

"You only saw one side of her," I said.

Rae looked different again, or maybe it was that I was looking at her with different eyes. Sadness seemed to fill her whole body, from her gray dome of hair to the toes of her sneakers. It occurred to me that she was dressed in the uniform of the '90s housewife, the uniform I'd lived in myself until a few months ago—tracksuit, running shoes, thick white cotton socks bought in packs of three—a uniform that announced itself as comfortable, serviceable, no need to look any further.

Rae held out her hand and said, "Come on. I'll show you out the back way. Someone, I don't know who, has been watching my flat."

We held each other briefly. "One more thing," I said. "Sack your lawyer. He's worse than useless. Get someone with a bit of fight."

I raised my broken arm in its white cast and black sling, a hopeful last salute.

Loyalty comes at you in such devious ways, I thought, as I made my way along the alley beside Rae's block of flats. Loyalty grips you by the scruff of the neck, and by the time you wake up and try to shake yourself loose, it's too late. You're caught. I should have known, from all those years of tagging along behind my mother, that the claims of loyalty were devious, with more legs than a centipede.

But it wasn't only that. As I'd said to Rae, my whole idea of myself, my pride in the new person I was intent on becoming, was bound up now with finding the right answer.

Keeping in the shadows, I walked to the main street and hailed a taxi. My mind played over images of Rae, and her changed appearance. I wondered if I was any closer to understanding the woman underneath than I had been that morning when I'd stood in her office clutching a potted plant. The taxi driver kept glancing at my arm, but he didn't ask me how I'd broken it. I paid him, and began walking up the path to my front steps, wishing I'd thought to leave a light on, knowing I'd have trouble with my key, left-handed, in the dark.

A figure moved in the shadow of my silver birch tree, no more than ten meters away. The streetlight caught a long black coat and fitted woolen hat, a pale, smooth, rounded face.

I froze, my fear honed suddenly to a single point, a shaft of fire on ice. Then I ran back down the street toward the city, pounding along the footpath, cursing my heavy arm. I closed my ears to the sound of footsteps running after me.

I could have gone to any of my neighbors, but I didn't think of that. I didn't stop running till I'd crossed the highway, close to the intersection where my car had crashed. I kept on until I reached the Dickson police station.

The young woman at the desk stared at me as though I must be mad. I couldn't blame her. I rang the number Detective Sergeant Brook had given me. A man answered, and told me Brook was on sick leave. I asked if he could transfer me to Detective Sergeant Hall. He would be on duty the following afternoon, I was told. I could speak to him then.

There was no one for me to tell my story to but the woman at the desk. She heard me out, though her expression said she cursed her luck for being landed with me. When I'd finished, she asked if there was someone I could stay with for the rest of the night.

No, I answered. Where could I go? Back to Rae's? To Ivan's burgled shell of a house? I didn't want to stay with either of them. I remembered Fred. What if whoever had been waiting for me had hurt, or even killed him?

I said I'd like to return to my own house, if a police officer could go with me.

The woman looked me up and down and said I'd have to wait until somebody was free. Then she repeated her question, adding, "You don't look as though you should be on your own."

I spent the time while I was waiting drinking strong black tea and trying not to think.

A tall uniformed policeman, who looked to be about the same age as the woman on the desk, came over to me and introduced himself. He glanced at my arm, without asking how it had been broken.

Back at my house, he circled it twice on foot, while I fetched Fred from his kennel and both of us waited beside the police car. He returned to tell me that everything seemed to be in order. I smiled grimly at this. My intruder could be waiting in the shadows. The young policeman knew that as well as I did. He gave Fred a pat, but didn't add what was obvious as well, that he was no sort of a guard dog.

He repeated what the desk officer had asked. Was there a friend I could spend the remainder of the night with?

I repeated my answer. "No."

He stood beside me while I unlocked the front door, and began turning lights on, then followed me from room to room. My living room, my bedroom and my kitchen, all my furniture and Peter's toys looked ordinary, undisturbed. At the same time, none of them seemed real.

"All okay?" he asked.

I told him it was.

He said he'd watch from his car for fifteen, twenty minutes, but then he'd have to get back to the station.

I thanked him, and said goodnight.

I sat up in Peter's bed with my arms around his dog, and waited once more for daylight to appear underneath the curtains. I was afraid of the hours of darkness still to pass, and the day ahead. I recalled the person I had been, or had pretended to be, just a few hours before, boasting to Rae about how I'd changed, patting myself on the back. Had the shadow under the tree followed me home, or had he been waiting there for me? I was sure the shadow had been a man, and that he was clean-shaven. A picture came to me, of myself staring down into a well, but now the well was shallow. Its bottom, covered with sticky cement, heaved upward. I jumped out of Peter's bed and ran into the bathroom to be sick.

Instead of returning to my son's room, I rang the number Brook had given me again, and was again told that he was on sick leave. I sat staring at the phone. I had no idea what the desk officer at Dickson would do with the form I had filled out, the statement I had made, the uniformed officer's report. Would they be passed on to Brook when he returned to work? When would that be?

I had to go back to the department. I'd been away too long. The report could easily be scrapped. Nobody would defend it. I did not want to break my promise to Rae, but it was more than that. The report was my achievement in a way I would not have dared to imagine before. It did not matter if the interpretations of the figures, the arguments and conclusions, were ones Di Trapani would have reached. Dianne had abdicated. I had moved in to fill, not her place, but my own. I wanted to claim this place, and to defend it. The shadow, whoever he was, stood between me and my ability to do this. He drew strength from my fear of him. I pictured again the flash of smooth cheek under the streetlight. If only he'd turned a little more, I might have identified him.

If I allowed myself to be beaten now, who would give me another job? How could I go on?

I showered and dressed, trying to ignore my scarecrow appearance, my pale, exhausted face.

I used the last of my cash to take a taxi to the Jolimont Center. I was paying the driver when I saw Felix coming out. It was not yet nine o'clock. Clearly, he was not on his way for a run. I recalled the first time I'd followed Felix, after Rae's committal hearing. How frivolous my tailing him that day seemed to me now, watching him examine ties, allowing myself to be irritated by how long he spent at the health food bar.

Felix was striding purposefully, head down. The wind rose. A plastic bag wrapped itself around my legs. Could the man in front of me be the same man who'd stood outside my house, waiting for me? What had he planned to do? Follow me inside? What then?

Abruptly, Felix turned a corner, without looking back or to the side. He passed the entrance to the mall, and quickened his pace. If he'd turned, he would have recognized me. My arm made me conspicuous. I didn't care. I wasn't hiding from him.

He stopped outside the pet shop window, and appeared to stare intently at a litter of Jack Russell puppies. I moved closer. The street and early morning shoppers faded from my field of vision, while one window, one person, came sharply into focus. Then there was no longer just one person, but two.

I held my breath, as Allison Edgeware stopped next to Felix, and began talking to him. Both of them stood with their backs to me. I moved again, to the opposite side of a tourist information kiosk. The woman at the counter looked at me inquiringly. I shook my head. I watched from that position until Allison moved away, then checked my watch. Their conversation had lasted scarcely seven minutes.

Felix turned around, gazing ahead with unseeing eyes. He moved unsteadily, like a much older man, to an outside table at the café next door to the pet shop.

I walked up to him. He stared at me, again having trouble focusing, and asked, "What are you doing here?"

I ignored this and sat down.

He glared at me. "You look terrible. What have you been doing?"

"Running, mostly. But that's over now. I told your friend I'd passed on everything I knew to the police. It's true. There's no need for anybody to come after me."

"What?" Felix asked. "What friend?"

"I saw you talking to her, right there, in front of the window." I nodded toward four Jack Russell pups tumbling over one another.

"Allison," I said, in case he should repeat his question. "Were you telling her about last night?"

"Last night? I was at home last night, with my wife and children."

"Your wife—it's Julie, isn't it?—must be getting used to providing alibis by now. You were at home with her the night my car was interfered with, too. I should think Julie would have had about enough."

Felix slumped forward with his elbows on the table. If I looked terrible, he wasn't doing much better himself.

"I saw Allison's notes about you," I said. "I read them in Compic's office. On her computer. You gave Compic a contract that they weren't entitled to. Allison blackmailed you."

"Blackmailed?"

"What's a better word for it?"

A waitress came to take our order. I shook my head. She hesitated, glancing at my arm, then backed away.

Felix stared after her. "That policeman kept on at me about those notes. What did you tell him? I'm not responsible for what some woman wrote about me. If she wrote anything. You're crazy, you know that? You need psychiatric help."

"A man was waiting outside my house when I got home last night. Was it you?"

"Last night? I was at home with Julie and my two children." Felix's voice rose, breaking on the last word.

"Did you booby-trap my car?"

"Of course not."

"But you *did* award Compic a contract that they weren't entitled to. And you *are* having a relationship with Allison."

Felix glared at me again.

"Allison is a very persuasive woman. What did she persuade you to do?"

Felix said nothing.

"Tell me about your relationship with Allison."

"There isn't one."

"Perhaps it would be a good idea if I paid Julie a visit."

"No! You saw me with Allison just now, you said? I told her it was over. I told her to get lost."

269

"Good for you. What kind of relationship *did* you have?"

Felix half stood up, shaking his head again.

"I will go to Julie," I said. "I can call a taxi now, this minute."

Felix swayed, then sat back down again. The waitress reappeared. I ordered two coffees, and two glasses of water.

He began with the first time he'd met Allison. She'd charmed him, as she charmed every male between the ages of eighteen and eighty. He'd bought some graphics packages from Compic, but Allison hadn't left it there. She'd phoned him, flattered him, bumped into him apparently by accident when he was out running. It seemed that she was everywhere. She'd talked to him about her plans for expanding the company, how she had the best software engineers in the business. He'd believed her. Who wouldn't grab the chance to be that close to a gorgeous woman on a daily basis?

I said, "The inevitable happened."

Felix ignored my sarcasm. Our coffees arrived. Felix took up his story as soon as the waitress was out of earshot.

"Allison had information she could only have learnt from someone inside my"—he corrected himself—"our department. She wasn't a good actress. But by then it didn't matter."

"Because you'd slept with her, and she threatened to tell your wife?"

"I was stupid. Don't think I don't know it. As I've said, she couldn't act. I thought I could call her bluff. But she knew exactly what we wanted with those on-line regulations. It was as though she'd read my e-mails, been there when I discussed the project, read the minutes of our meetings. A project like that was way outside Compic's area of expertise, I told her. That's when she"—Felix paused, licked his lips, and stared at his coffee without touching it—"suggested that she might pay a visit to Julie."

"Tell your wife yourself," I said.

"She'll leave me."

"Then tell me who Allison is working with. You must have some idea."

Felix said grimly, "When I asked her who was really running Compic, she got angry and accused me of sexism."

"Who *is* running Compic?"

"I don't know, I tell you. I don't know."

Felix stood up again. I asked him if he was going back to work, and he said he supposed he had to. I told him I'd phone him later that day. Maybe something would have happened to jog his memory by then.

I rang Brook from the pay phone in the travel center, and was told, for the third time in ten hours, that he was on sick leave. I called Rae, but for once she wasn't home, or wasn't answering her phone.

I took the lift to my floor, sat at my desk, and forced myself to concentrate. Bambi gave me curious, sympathetic glances. When I next checked the time, it was nearly midday. The office next door was empty. I realized I'd scarcely given Ivan a thought. I took a short lunch break, hunched over in a corner of the bistro with a cheese roll and a cappuccino, spying on Jim Wilcox buying a bagful of enormous chocolate muffins.

Bambi made a fuss of me that afternoon. She brought me a bunch of flowers, and I thanked her without wanting to reflect on where they'd come from. We sat down together and worked out how to steer the report through its final stage. Bambi was surprisingly sensible, and had one or two really good ideas. I felt my dull head clear, and though I suspected it was only a temporary reprieve, I let myself enjoy it.

Guy Harmer and Claire showed up, and Guy offered to help me any way he could. He wrote a get-well message on my arm. "Dear Sandra. Break a leg." He bent over my plaster in his Christian Dior shirtsleeves, while I savored the novelty of looking down on his blond head, with the slightest hint of thinning at the crown. The idea that Guy might go bald early made him seem more human, as vulnerable to aging as the rest of us.

When lines of print began to swim in front of my eyes, I phoned Felix's extension. I was put through to the switchboard, and told he wasn't expected to return to work that day. I rang his home number. A woman answered and asked in a suspicious voice who I was and what I wanted. I said I was a work colleague, and left my name and number, but no message.

THE TROJAN DOG

HAT NIGHT, IVAN USED Peter's computer to draw a desert flower.

Ivan was in mourning for the loss of his computers, which, as each day passed, looked less and less likely to be found. Peter's was a poor substitute, but better than none.

The flower's single leaf was brown, its pink petals thinner than the skin on water. A man stood hunched over the flower, watering it with his tears. The earth around it was bare and yellow, cracked. The man could have been Ivan, but he could as easily have been an older, sadder Tony Trapani.

A person could fall through the cracks in that landscape, a person grown skinny, weak from malnutrition, losing the battle to find water, or with that other, stick-like thinness that comes from losing hope. I wanted to climb in there, right into the screen, and add my tears to give the flower a better chance of life.

It was Ivan's gift to make me part of the story that he told in pictures. It was his gift, not to reproduce the likeness of a person or a thing, although he *could* do this—Felix and Rae on jousting horses, as clever a caricature as any political cartoonist's. But Ivan's greater skill was to make the viewer enter, and then become part of his subject. Computer animation, interactive graphics—these were like the technology of silent movies at the beginning of the century, creaking, unsubtle, relying on mechanical techniques. Ivan's horse was crude and obvious if you studied it second by second, took it apart and analyzed it. But when you put on the helmet, moved the joystick, you were there.

If this had been the first decade of the twentieth century instead of the last, fin de siècle dog days and all that went with that, Ivan might have become famous as an early director of silent movies. I doubted, though, whether he would have had the push, the charm, the entrepreneurial machismo.

You can have an enemy and pursue her, or him, and find them, and have it out with them. High Noon in Northbourne Avenue. Such confrontations are a staple of storytelling, nothing new about them. Or your enemy can be in your bed. You can discover him there. You can wake up, and there she is beside you.

But the enemies computers make are different, in quality and kind. They prolong discovery, and stretch and tease it out, and play their own games with disclosure. I found myself perversely wanting to go back to those moments at the school, wishing I'd stayed and confronted the shadow, body to body, flesh on flesh, and one of us had won.

I'd hidden from Ivan many of the paths and byways I'd been following, but that night I told him everything.

Ivan was practical, gathering into his large frame the energy that I no longer had. He said the first thing we had to do was contact Brook. Did I have a home number for him? I didn't. Ivan asked if I'd tried the hospital. I rang and found out that Brook was due to be admitted the next day. That was one problem solved, said Ivan. I didn't see how, but I didn't argue with him. I couldn't see how it helped to bring Brook up to date if he was too sick to continue with the case, but Ivan clearly believed there was still time, and that something might be done.

I rang the city station and asked to be put through to Detective Sergeant Hall. He was unavailable. I rang Dickson next. The young woman I'd spoken to the night before was back on duty, but had no news for me.

I considered ringing Felix again, but, in spite of my threats of the morning, I was reluctant to get him into trouble with his wife. It was up to him to tell her. I told Ivan that I believed Felix's story. His biggest crime was to have been duped by Allison. If Felix wasn't Allison's partner, who was? With Brook about to be admitted into hospital, and Rae's trial date approaching, I had run out of time.

Ivan and I sat drinking hot chocolate, raising then discarding options. Ivan jumped up, saying he had an idea.

He sat at Peter's screen once more, this time drafting a message to send to Allison. The message would say that Compic was going to be named in Parliament. Allison herself would be named, under parliamentary privilege, as having sold sexual favors in exchange for lucrative government contracts. To be thorough, Ivan prepared a question on notice from the leader of the Opposition. Too bad for Felix if it ever was asked in Parliament, but Ivan did not mean it to be. He meant to frighten Allison into blowing her partner's cover.

He went over his plan point by point. "Edgeware will get the message in the evening. Maybe even tomorrow. As soon as we can set it up. She'll either send an e-mail, or make a phone call. Her computer will be monitored. If she uses the phone, the call will be recorded."

"But how can Brook handle all that? There'll have to be a real question in the system."

"He'll handle it all right. It will give him something to think about."

We both knew that the plan was full of holes, but we could not think of a better one. The next step was to visit Brook in hospital, and put it to him. He would need to authorize the watch on Allison's computer, and the bug on her phone. But how much could a detective whose blood cells had betrayed him accomplish from a hospital bed?

"WHEN I PUKE," BROOK whispered hoarsely. "There isn't that much warning."

He stretched out his thin arm, with a drip attached, over a green cotton blanket. His hand was loose and open, and I was sure that if I cut it there'd be no blood at all. Yet his eyes shone, dark with life.

"So?" Ivan asked from behind my left shoulder. "You're up for it, you reckon?"

Brook hitched himself against his pillows, and said with an effort, "You're mad, the pair of you."

"Just a little bug," Ivan told him, grinning. "Nothing fancy, because we're in a hurry."

Brook let his arm fall back against the blanket. "I have a small problem with mobility."

"You're just going to have to overcome that, and do your duty as a policeman."

Brook tried to laugh, and coughed instead. "When are you planning this little celebration?"

"ASAP."

"Security in this place is tighter than a bloody jail."

I opened my mouth to speak, but Ivan was too quick for me. "No problem. Just tell me who to go and see."

"I think I've got a better idea." Brook called to the sister, "Nurse, I need a hat!"

The sister walked over and stood by his bed. "You're not going anywhere, mister," she said, obviously having heard this request before.

"I know that, sweetheart. Just need to be presentable for my official visitors."

When we said good-bye, I hung back to squeeze Brook's hand, thinking of Tony with his head covered in bandages. Tony had moved into his sister's flat, and was coming along fine.

WHEN I NEXT SAW Brook, he was sitting in state, propped against four pillows in a private room. The recording and computer equipment surrounding him gave the room the shiny solemnity of an operating theater.

A table held reel-to-reel-tapes and black and chrome boxes of different shapes and sizes, a red light flashing intermittently on the side of one.

It was dark outside. The curtains were open behind the bed. Lights seemed to climb along the building opposite in a carefree way, dancing and splashing down the Woden Valley. The detective talking to Brook in a low voice wasn't one I'd seen before. He was fair-haired, with the round, smooth face and neutral manner of a man used to being taken for younger than he was. He made it plain that he didn't want Ivan and me to be there.

Brook's white skin was drawn together in anticipation, his bare arms steady on the green blanket. He looked as though he was preparing for a test of physical endurance.

For some reason, Ivan appointed himself on guard outside the door. He sat on a chair and read the newspaper. I wondered if he was ashamed of his crude trick, now that the excitement of creating it had faded.

It was after ten when the red flashing light on one of the black boxes turned to green. We listened to Allison Edgeware pick up her phone and dial. Five double rings, then someone answered it. I strained after the voice on the other end, as though by willpower I could attach a head and body to whoever replied.

Allison said, "There's something really weird going on."

There was a pause, then she read Ivan's message straight off her computer screen. It gained a life of its own as she spoke. My heart gave a little leap and I thought, it's working.

"I'll see to it." A male voice. A familiar one.

"What the hell does it mean, all this?"

"Nothing. I said I'll deal with it."

"I'm frightened."

"Don't be," said the voice. I glanced at Ivan, and he nodded.

"It's nothing. A hoax. Don't touch it. Get yourself a glass of whisky. Go to—"

"But I'm *scared!*" A pause, then Allison asked, "What's the matter?"

"Nothing, a noise. I thought it might be Miranda. I'll talk to you in the morning."

"When?"

"As soon as I can manage."

Miranda? Miranda Harmer. Guy's long-forgotten wife.

Things happened quickly after that. In less than five minutes, Ivan and I had been hustled out of the ward. The youthful detective had played back the tape, then made several phone calls, while Brook said goodnight, winking and telling us he needed his beauty sleep. In spite of his pallor, he looked dignified and brave.

Ivan came back to my place. He sat on the sofa, leaning forward, elbows on his knees. We talked about Guy Harmer, and what would happen next. We hadn't questioned Brook about this, and now the whole thing was out of our hands. When I thought about Guy, two pictures came into my mind: his kindness to Peter the day Peter was sick and I'd had to bring him into work—and Guy with his head under the hood of my car, fixing it so the brakes would fall. I was worried that Ivan's trick had been enough to warn him, that in the time it would take to authorize a search warrant, Guy would get rid of anything that might incriminate him.

NEXT DAY TURNED OUT to be infuriatingly ordinary. I chose the colors for the cover of the outwork report, while I waited to hear that Guy and Allison had been arrested.

It wasn't until late in the afternoon that we got any news. The police had found a copy of the original leak to the *Canberra Times* on Guy's home computer, filed with his home-loan correspondence. They also found details of a bank account in the Cayman Islands, and a building society account in Brisbane under Guy's mother's name, over which he had a power of attorney. He'd withdrawn $150,000 from the building society on August 7, the Friday of the computer show. That evening, when Guy was wining and dining me, he'd had a reason to feel pleased. I remembered his barbed question about Rae visiting Brisbane to check on her investment. He'd been recouping the profits of his own.

Ivan's virtual reality helmet was stashed in a hat box at the back of Guy's garage. It was the kind of weirdo thing Ivan would have done. Ivan's laser printer had been hidden under an old carpet, still with a rather dusty Garfield stuck on top. The police had a warrant, and Guy hadn't been able to stop them. But, according to Brook, he'd barred his door and tried to fight them off.

Two days later, I walked across to the magistrate's court for Guy's and Allison's committal hearing. Their lawyers were joined by one representing Isobel Merewether. The reading out of the charges, and the responses of guilty, took about ten minutes. Isobel Merewether's barrister surprised everyone by pleading guilty to the charge of misuse of confidential information. Then the magistrate announced that the more serious charges against Isobel—conspiracy to defraud, and conspiracy to steal from a Commonwealth department—had been dropped. There could only be one reason for this. She had decided to give evidence against Allison and Guy.

After the hearing was over, I caught the bus out to the hospital to visit Brook.

Sitting up in his room, propped against fat pillows, looking tired but pleased with himself, Brook told me how Isobel had confessed with very little prompting.

She'd described how Access Computing had been Guy's idea. He'd taken care to have her establish a genuine membership, run an information service, and do everything Access Computing claimed to do in their prospectus.

"Did she know why?" I asked.

"Oh yes."

"What about the money?"

"Merewether had never heard of Rae Evans until she filed that grant application."

"Now she's getting off practically scot-free," I said.

"We needed the girl's cooperation." Brook didn't sound a bit apologetic.

"What about Claire Disraeli?"

"Claims she had nothing to do with any of it."

"Do the others back that up?"

He nodded.

"What about Felix?"

"Poor Felix," Brook said. "There's at least half a dozen like him."

"Including Graham Arnold, the *Canberra Times's* office manager. Poor Felix," I echoed. "I was sure he was Allison's partner."

"Only in one sense," Brook said dryly. "But going after him the way you did—well, you and that hairy pal of yours got there in the end."

I blushed. I thought it was the only praise I was likely to get from Brook, but it meant a lot to me. I'd received an official letter from his superintendent, thanking me for the information I'd provided, and my part—"no small part" the letter said—in bringing the case to a successful conclusion. I was proud of the letter, especially since I read between its lines a rap over the knuckles for Detective Sergeant Hall. It thanked me for uncovering Compic's and Access Computing's illegal operations. I wondered if the superintendent knew that some of the methods I'd used were illegal, too.

Brook was watching me shrewdly, as though he could tell what I was thinking. We shared a grin of mutual self-congratulation.

"I hope they're giving you a gold watch for your part," I said.

Brook laughed. "A wig, perhaps?"

As far as Compic was concerned, the police were confident they had the paperwork sorted out. It was remarkable how much information you could gather in a short time when you put the resources of a few healthy officers into it, Brook said. Allison and Guy had been partners, and Allison's share of the profits was considerable, though most of the plans and decisions had been Guy's. Guy had used his privileged position inside the public service to target certain men, and Allison had persuaded them to break the rules. Guy had been very thorough in the way he'd spied on IT directors, read their e-mail, accessed the minutes of their meetings.

He'd changed the figure on Kerry Arnold's payment disk, after Kerry had signed for a hundred thousand dollars. Most of the missing money had been traced. Twenty thousand had gone into Rae's bank account. Isobel Merewether had been paid in cash for her part in the scheme. Some had been used by Allison to pay programmers, and the rest had found its way into Guy's private accounts.

"Was Access Computing just Isobel?" I asked. "No one else?"

"They needed another signature for the grant application," Brook said, "so they invented Angela Carlishaw."

"That was a mistake."

"A bad move. Harmer got too smart for his own good."

"Did they set up Access Computing just to frame Rae Evans?"

"Harmer could never be sure they'd get the grant. That was a gamble. He started Access Computing because he saw a way to make a few extra bucks. Then, when that complaint about Compic turned up, he dreamed up a way to knock Evans out of the game. Harmer likes to gamble, and my guess is the more strings he's pulling at any one time, the more he likes it."

"Until they came unstuck," I said. "And Bernard Whitelaw?"

"Exactly who he said he was, one of Compic's rivals who finally got jack of them."

"Was it Guy who called Gail offering to sell her more lies about Rae?"

"It was."

Gail must have been mistaken about the New Zealand accent, I thought. Or perhaps Guy had put it on.

I pressed my lips together. I'd been saving the question that mattered most to me. "Was he the one who booby-trapped my car?"

Brook said again, simply, "Yes."

"Why on earth did he keep all of Ivan's things in his garage?"

Brook shrugged. "He'd got away with so much by then, maybe he thought he was invincible."

I recalled Isobel Merewether, how she'd looked when she'd opened the door to that office in Brisbane, high and light as an air balloon, how she and Claire Disraeli could have been sisters.

The answer had been there, that afternoon, if only I'd been able to see it. Isobel and Claire were the same type—Guy's. Claire was Guy's girlfriend. I bet Isobel and Allison had been, too. For all I knew, they still were. One man at the center of a female wheel.

"How did they meet, Allison and Guy?" I asked.

"In Brisbane. She's a Queenslander."

Like Lauren, I thought, but didn't say.

"So is Harmer," Brook told me. "Before he transferred down here, he worked for the Queensland government."

"Was he ripping them off, too?"

"I hadn't actually thought of that. He and Edgeware met at a seminar he ran for new graduates wanting to join the public service."

"And had an affair?"

"A brief one. Soon after that, Harmer and his wife moved to Canberra."

"Miranda Harmer knew about Allison?"

"I'm not sure."

"Allison followed him?"

"He invited her to head up Compic. He thought it would be a novel idea to start a local software company run by a single, independent, beautiful young woman. According to him, she jumped at the idea."

"Did she know what he expected her to do?"

"I believe so, yes."

"What about that Defense contract? How much was it worth?"

"A quarter of a million. They were planning to call it quits after that."

"And the money would have been divided between them, Guy's share into his account in the Cayman Islands, or his mother's building society account in Brisbane? We keep coming back to the sunshine capital, don't we?"

Brook made a wry face. "Harmer was intending to move back there, with his wife and kids. Start a new business with the money he'd stolen. Quietly let Compic fade away."

"But what about the contracts?"

"Oh, Edgeware would have hired programmers to do the work. Or attempt to do it."

"He was leaving Allison?"

"That's what he says."

"How did she feel about that?"

"I don't think he'd actually discussed that part of the plan with her. She seemed surprised when it was suggested."

"Angry?"

"Very angry."

"Do you think she would have let him go?"

"She's had plenty of experience when it comes to married men. I can't see her letting Harmer get away without a fight. Can you?"

"No," I said, recalling Felix once again. "I'm surprised they confessed to so much."

"Harmer talked a lot more than the girl. It's a funny thing about Harmer—it's almost as though he still believes he can talk his way out of it. If he goes on long enough, he'll convince us that he's really a good bloke underneath, just got carried away a bit, that's all."

"Allison never would have let him get away. I *hope* she wouldn't."

I blushed. Brook laughed.

"I know, I know," I said. "She's far from innocent. But still."

Brook's eyelids drooped, and he looked as though he'd had enough talking for one day. I squeezed his hand and told him I'd call in again to see him soon.

A LAST MEETING
WITH CLAIRE

NCE THE OUTWORK REPORT was at the printers, Bambi and Dianne took leave, Di to take care of Tony, whose tribunal hearing was coming up in a few days. I was told my contract wouldn't be renewed, and I suspected that they had both been told the same.

I missed Bambi's flit of nervous color, the after-smell of Dianne's cigarettes. Next door, Ivan was on his own, as well. Claire had not shown up for work since Guy Harmer's arrest. With Felix on leave, too, the building seemed emptier, and quieter.

"You know, I finished the horse for our constabulary friend," Ivan told me, propping in the doorway. "I think he'll like it."

"If he gets to see it."

"Of course he'll see it. I'll set it up in that ward if I have to."

I spent an hour or so packing up my things, then walked over to the mall to buy Peter a coming home present.

I ran into Claire just outside the entrance. To my surprise, she didn't brush past, ignoring me. She seemed to want to talk.

She asked me how I was, and if my arm was better, studying me from under her thick blonde eyelashes. I was struck by the falseness of her self-control, and reminded myself that I'd only ever seen the surface of this woman, and not very much of that. What Claire really thought about Guy and Allison would remain forever unknown to me, hidden behind the veneer of a woman so well-groomed that it was difficult to imagine her sleeping without makeup.

"It was you who left that disk in the first aid room, wasn't it?" I asked her. "You left it there by mistake. That's why you were waiting outside the door. You'd gone to get it back."

Claire's bottom lip shook, and she clamped it down.

"You were taking the disk to Rae Evans's office," I persisted. "Guy asked you to. He told you to leave it in her office. He was going to ring the police, or maybe the *Canberra Times*, and tell them about our viruses, and where they came from."

I saw by Claire's expression that my guess was at least partly right.

"Did Guy bother to tell you what was on the disk? Did you bother to ask?"

Claire blinked as if her eyes were hurting.

"I was feeling so rotten that day," she said. "I wasn't thinking straight. My period was two weeks late. I thought if I just lay down with my eyes shut for ten minutes, then I'd be okay. It was dark in there, and private. No one would know where I was. But I stayed too long, and then I left that stupid folder sitting on the bench."

I pictured Claire, ill and wretched, trying to explain to Guy that I'd got hold of the disk and taken it to Felix. I could imagine Guy's reaction. Had she been pregnant? Had she had an abortion? I couldn't ask.

Claire had never looked coerced, or as though Guy was pressuring her. She'd looked as though she was living well and enjoying every minute of it. She'd hidden her misery well. But then, for someone who fancied herself as an investigator, perhaps I hadn't been very observant where Claire was concerned. I bet Guy had talked to her about Allison, tortured her every now and again with images of Allison's beauty. Further than that, Claire hadn't wanted to look, and so she hadn't.

Claire said, "He had a one-night stand with that Edgeware woman.

That's all it was—one night. It didn't mean anything. He told me all about it. Their physical relationship was over by the time he met me, well and truly over."

"Forget him," I told her. "He's not worth another minute of your time."

Claire looked at me as though I was advising her to jump over the moon.

I said good-bye, and turned around to leave. But I felt her staring at my back, and stopped after taking a few steps. What was keeping her there? Was it something simple, something it had never occurred to me to wonder about before? Did Claire suspect Guy of having slept with me in Brisbane? Had Guy, in order to demonstrate his irresistibility, hinted that he had?

I turned again to face her. She shook her head and murmured "bye," in a voice almost too soft to hear.

And I was left there in Alinga Street, knowing I should get a move on, but unable to put one foot in front of the other, struck by a feeling of incompleteness, of incomprehensible regret. No more stumbling over pronouns, speculating about ladies' high-heeled shoes. My invisible hacker had been so much more protean and various than Guy Harmer with his perfect suits and mistresses to match. It occurred to me that greed, when you got down to it, was a pretty boring motive.

I opened my newly painted car door and prepared to back out of the parking lot. I'd had my plaster off for five days, and the day before I'd picked my car up from the smash repairers. My wrist felt strong and good. I was exercising it carefully, following instructions. I'd asked about driving, half-hoping to be told to leave that for a while. But my doctor had smiled and said, "Why not?" He was a cheerful man. "Get right back on the horse."

"I could always try a bicycle," I'd told him. "If someone wrecks the brakes, I can just throw myself on the footpath and knock down a pedestrian."

"Sounds fine to me," he'd chuckled, knowing I was dependent on my car.

I braced myself, head over left shoulder, hands and wrists rigid with tension.

But once safely out on Northbourne Avenue, the straight run home ahead, my mind returned to Guy and Allison. I wondered what had made Guy greedy in the first place. Had the good life become more than his public servant's salary could handle? Satisfying his various lovers and ex-lovers, placating his family, his lawful wife? It seemed his business plans had come first, and he'd selected his women with these plans in mind. I wondered again how much Miranda Harmer knew, and whether she, like Claire, had chosen *not* to see.

Guy hadn't allowed a single letter of complaint to set back his plans for Compic. He must have been confident that he could make the charge against Rae stick, while keeping the relationship between Access Computing and Compic a secret. He'd been willing to sacrifice Isobel Merewether, feed her to the press. Isobel was getting her own back now.

Perhaps part of Guy's confidence, or overconfidence, had been that he knew his people: Rae. Felix. Wilcox. Claire, Isobel, and Allison. Even Ivan. But he hadn't known me. I thought of Guy sweating over how close that Defense contract was to being signed, knowing that to be safe it had to go through before the elections, knowing the importance of gossip, and having to hope that nothing about the complaint would get passed on, that no one at Defense would get to hear of it. As Brook saw it, Guy had planned to resign from our department, kiss our cold capital goodbye, as soon as he had his hands on the Defense money. He'd planned to jump, and all of us left behind would have watched, enviously, as he landed on his feet.

AN END AND
A BEGINNING

HE *CHAP* AND *QUAT* of basketballs forms a steady backbeat to my thoughts. I sit at the dining room table in front of the window, watching a high school teacher show some students how to throw a javelin. The teacher wears a wide-brimmed straw hat, a khaki shirt, and shorts. He steps back on one foot in a strained, balletic pose, half-sport, half-sculpture, then moves his arm forward in a wide, slow-motion arc. The group of watching students—and me through my window—see a golden spear shoot forward and fly. After what seems like an age has passed, it falls into the well-washed turf.

Kids go on shooting for goals on the high school court way after it gets dark. If practice can make them Michael Jordans, then each one will be for sure. I see them as Peter in a few years' time, but the picture no longer carries with it the anxiety it once did. I feel more confident about facing the challenges of raising a son, and Peter has conquered his reading problem, thanks to Ivan's help and the practice Derek kept up in America. Ivan and Peter get on even better than they did before Peter went away, now there is no secret hanging over Ivan's continued presence in my house, and in my life.

Peter's over at Derek's while I'm finishing this, my account of the events of the past winter—mine as opposed to Gail Trembath's, or anybody else's. I gave Gail an exclusive on how we set a trap and caught Guy Harmer, and made her the happiest reporter in the southern hemisphere, for a while at least.

I'm in the Lyneham house, and Derek's doing what he said he always wanted—building from his own design, from the dirt up, on a block out along the Murrumbidgee. Meanwhile he's renting a flat in Braddon, where Peter has his own bedroom, but can't take Fred.

The story of the end of my marriage to Derek both is and isn't part of this account. I feel a bit guilty for not saying more about it, and Derek, when he reads this, will hate it, and say I've misjudged him.

Derek looked at me when he got off the plane, looked at me over the top of Peter's head, and we both knew our marriage was over. His face was blank with the need to tell me what he'd put off for so long. He'd met someone in America. She was flying out within a month to join him. He wanted a divorce.

Derek and I had more in common that morning at the airport than we'd had in years. Peter has accepted the separation, with the quality in him that makes him, at times, seem much older than he is. He likes Valerie, and is happy spending time with her and Derek. Valerie was there when I phoned after the accident. Peter never said a word about her. I asked him why, and he told me, "Mum. You were stressed out enough."

I've spent a fair amount of time thinking about adultery, how I was guilty of it, how Ivan tried to make me face that and I refused. I've thought about the part adultery played in the scheme Guy and Allison almost got away with. The paths I followed had quite a lot in common with the paths *they* chose. I haven't got to the bottom of that yet. I was lucky, that morning at the airport. Derek and I forgave each other. Valerie and Ivan made forgiveness easier than it would otherwise have been.

I like to take Fred for a walk when it's beginning to get dark. We cross the road to the school oval, listening to the steadiness and urgency of the traffic on the highway. I stare at the poplars that grab and hold the last light as it disappears behind O'Connor Ridge. We move toward the belt of trees where the high school students eat their lunch, Fred scavenging, me with my head up. Fred always hopes for the bonanza of a whole discarded sandwich, or a piece of cake. He misses his master. Sometimes, when I'm turning for home, he disappears and won't come when I call.

The lights over the path, and the shadows all around them, give rise to memories, full-throated memories that take not only human forms, but those of clever machines as well. I've learnt to face my recollections of my mother, and I do so with a steady heart.

Who haven't I accounted for? Tony's tribunal hearing turned out much better than it might have done. Perhaps his car accident had something to do with it, but the university was kind to him. He has a year's probation, and a hundred hours of community service to complete, but no criminal charges have been laid. A lot of bad blood found its way out at the hearing, Dianne told me, criticisms of Professor Bailey from those whose word counted for something.

Bambi's doing dressmaking at home. Between seams, she's reading the job ads and hoping to strike it lucky for an interview, as I am. I visited her one afternoon, and we drank Red Zinger tea and chatted. I wondered how I could ever have believed Bambi capable of framing Rae Evans, and wrecking my car. I realized I shared with her the impulse to carry color around with me, to be captured by bright petals and the hungry opacity of leaves.

There was a postcard from Rae waiting for me in the letterbox when I got home from Bambi's.

"Hello Sandra," Rae wrote, in her small, backsloping hand. "I don't think about many of my ex-colleagues, but I do about you. So let me know how you're keeping."

I flicked the card over, and studied the photograph of a North Queensland rainforest, imagining the light of the tropics glancing off Rae's indoor skin. A feeling of escape rose from it like perfumed oil.

Ex-colleague? Was that how she thought about me? Was that all?

I remembered Rae as she'd been when I first met her, and then by the lake that evening. I recalled the passivity and weakness that had puzzled me, combined with a disdain for people who refused to see things her way. I thought of how I'd liked her, and felt I owed her something, of how frustrated she had made me. And then of what might have happened if she hadn't left Canberra the day after the charges against her were dropped.

I don't think Rae will ever willingly come back to Canberra to live. I stared at her address in tiny letters at the bottom of the card, as though she'd added it as an afterthought. She'd already said thank-you, and congratulated me on the report—on the bookshelves at last, between maroon and pale blue covers.

Rae had said I'd changed, but I wondered if she grasped just how deep and difficult some of those changes had been, and her own part in initiating them. The irony was, even if she did understand this, I don't think she cared.

I doubt whether the department will have Rae back, even if she wants to return, if the department still exists after the elections. The elections have been so long in coming that, now they're only a few days away, I feel strangely calm about the result.

I received a surprise phone call the day after Rae's postcard. A security guy at another department had walked into a problem with a hacker, and wondered if I'd consider a little low-key investigating.

"Why me?" I asked.

Well, he said, he'd heard about me. His "problem"—the way he said the word made me feel as though he was asking me to walk across a roomful of eggs without breaking them—required an indirect approach.

I put down the phone, thinking that I couldn't possibly say yes. I'd make a hash of it, succeed only in humiliating myself. But, then, I thought again. I'd already had a fair amount of practice. I could follow clues and not be defeated by the maze they led me into. I could watch and listen for the unexpected, as Felix had once advised me to do. I realized I was proud of the methods I'd developed, awkwardly and so often reluctantly. They seemed durable to me, and hardy. If they drew me back into an ethical shadow-land, well, I wasn't afraid of that place any longer. I wanted to return.

Before I made a decision, there was one question I needed to ask.

I phoned Ivan, who'd just come back from a job interview, and was not in the best of moods.

"Don't worry about that," I told him. "Listen."

When I'd finished speaking, Ivan laughed.

I was stung. "If you don't think—" I began.

He laughed again. "You don't know what you're capable of, Sandy. You frighten me, if you want to know the truth."

"This is no time for teasing," I said. "Are you game? Do you think we can make it work?"

"Of course we can," said Ivan.

I rang the security guy and told him I'd like to have a go, but that I'd be working with a partner. Ivan Semyonov. He'd have to hire the two of us together.

Computer Security Consultants. Does that sound grand? With a bit of luck and good connections—with one thing leading to another, with Ivan to plot the technical side of things, and teach me about it as we go along—who knows, even *I* might find a way to get along in cyberspace.

IVAN GAVE BROOK THE completed horse as a coming-home-from-hospital present. Brook is learning to program. He still has to go in for chemo once a week, and he's on extended leave.

I was there when he tried the horse out for the first time.

He pirouetted slowly, his face and head invisible beneath the helmet. Because I couldn't see his eyes, I didn't know how he felt, how he was reacting; but his movements reminded me of ballet steps: slow, untutored, with an uncommon grace. He held the joystick at arm's length for balance, moving it slowly forward, then back toward his body with a calm precision.

He stopped his slow circling, and for a few more moments swayed from side to side. Ivan went to him and grasped him by the shoulders, taking the helmet off as gently as if he was removing a bonnet from a newborn baby.

Brook's face was washed clean of expression, and his bald head shone with the movement and exhilaration of the dance.

Curious, I climbed up on the platform. There was nothing to frighten me now, in the dull hiss of illicit spears against a horse's wooden sides.

I thought it would be the old VR, with perhaps the battle added on. I expected to move inside a burning city, buildings collapsing inward, the sounds of screaming, heavy timber falling.

Instead, there was blackness, slowly taking the shape of a horse that was both mythical and lifelike, a creature made for destruction, yet somehow surviving.

I was inside it, as before. But this time I felt its heart beat next to mine, its life, its vital organs warm between my breasts. Then I was riding the horse, over a dry land, eucalypt forests, a river, toward a crystal coastline and the sea. I wept when it was over, somehow too spent to lift the helmet off. My tears wet the blue padded leather, and I balanced unsteadily, one hand on either side of the corral.